Easton gl ⬙ **S0-AGT-279** jaze
snapped back on the road.

The moment had been fleeting, but she'd caught something in that eye contact—something deep and warm.

"So you had a crush," she said, trying to sound normal. She still sounded breathy to her own ears. Bobbie started to whimper in the back seat, and Nora reached over to pop her pacifier back into her mouth.

"It was a weird thing to bond over," Easton admitted. "But I was the one guy who thought you were just as amazing as your dad did."

"I kind of knew you had a crush," she admitted.

"It was more."

Nora's heart sped up. She cast about for something to say but couldn't come up with anything. More than a crush... What was that? Love?

The Cowboy's Baby Bonanza

PATRICIA JOHNS
&
TRISH MILBURN

Previously published as *The Triplets' Cowboy Daddy* and *Twins for the Rancher*

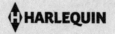

 **HARLEQUIN**®

ISBN-13: 978-1-335-17998-2

Recycling programs for this product may not exist in your area.

The Cowboy's Baby Bonanza
Copyright © 2020 by Harlequin Books S.A.

The Triplets' Cowboy Daddy
First published in 2017. This edition published in 2020.
Copyright © 2017 by Patty Froese Ntihemuka

Twins for the Rancher
First published in 2018. This edition published in 2020.
Copyright © 2018 by Trish Milburn

This edition published by arrangement with Harlequin Books S.A.

For questions and comments about the quality of this book, please contact us at CustomerService@Harlequin.com.

Harlequin Enterprises ULC
22 Adelaide St. West, 40th Floor
Toronto, Ontario M5H 4E3, Canada
www.Harlequin.com

Printed in U.S.A.

CONTENTS

Patricia Johns writes from Alberta, Canada. She has her Hon. BA in English literature and currently writes for Harlequin's Heartwarming and Love Inspired lines. You can find her at patriciajohnsromance.com.

Books by Patricia Johns

Harlequin Heartwarming

Home to Eagle's Rest

Her Lawman Protector
Falling for the Cowboy Dad
The Lawman's Baby

A Baxter's Redemption
The Runaway Bride
A Boy's Christmas Wish

Love Inspired

Montana Twins

Her Cowboy's Twin Blessings
Her Twins' Cowboy Dad
A Rancher to Remember

Comfort Creek Lawmen

Deputy Daddy
The Lawman's Runaway Bride
The Deputy's Unexpected Family

Visit the Author Profile page at
Harlequin.com for more titles.

The Triplets' Cowboy Daddy

PATRICIA JOHNS

To my husband and our son. You are the best choices I ever made. I love you!

Chapter 1

Nora Carpenter could have cared for one baby easily enough. She could somehow have juggled two. But three—she'd never imagined that accepting the role of godmother to her half sister's babies would actually put her into the position of raising those babies on her own. She was still in shock.

Nora stood in her mother's brilliantly clean farmhouse kitchen, more overwhelmed than she had ever felt in her life. The three infants were still in their car seats, eyes scrunched shut and mouths open in hiccoughing wails. She stood over them, her jeans already stained from spilled formula and her tank top stretched from…she wasn't even sure what. She unbuckled the first infant—Rosie—and scooped her up. Rosie's cries subsided as she wriggled up against Nora's neck, but anxiety still made Nora's heart race as she fumbled with Riley's buckle. She'd come back to Hope, Montana, that afternoon so that her mother could help her out, but even that was more complicated than anyone guessed. These babies weren't just orphans in need of care; they were three tiny reminders that Nora's father hadn't been the man they all believed him to be.

Everything had changed—everything but this kitchen. The counters were crumb-free, as they always were, and the room smelled comfortingly, and very faintly, of bleach. Hand-embroidered kitchen towels hung from the stove handle—two of them, one with Monday sewn across the bottom, and one with Thursday. Today was Friday. Unless Dina Carpenter was making jam or doing canning, this was the natural state—immaculate, with no care for properly labeled towels. The babies' cries echoed through the house.

Rosie, Riley and Roberta had finished their bottles just before Nora's mother had left for a quick trip to the store for some baby supplies.

"I'll be fine!" Nora had said. Famous last words. The minute the door shut, the cries had begun, and no amount of cooing or rocking of car seats made a bit of difference.

There was a knock on the back door, and Nora shouted, "Come in!" as she scooped up Riley in her other arm and cuddled both babies close. Riley's cries stopped almost immediately, too, and that left Roberta—Bobbie, as Nora had nicknamed her—still crying in her car seat, hands balled up into tiny fists.

Nora had no idea who was at the door, and she didn't care. Whoever walked through that door was about to be put to work. Served them right for dropping by.

"Need a hand?" The voice behind her was deep—

and familiar. Nora turned to see Easton Ross, the family's ranch manager, standing in the open door. He wore jeans and cowboy boots, his shirt pushed up his forearms to reveal ropy muscle. He'd changed a lot since their school days. Back then he'd been a skinny kid, perpetually shorter than she was. Not anymore. He was most definitely a grown man...and she was no longer the one with all the power. When her father died a few months ago, he'd left Easton a piece of property.

"Easton." She smiled tiredly. "Would you mind picking up Bobbie there? She needs a cuddle."

Her personal grudge against the man would have to wait.

"Yeah...okay..." He didn't sound certain, but he crossed the room and squatted in front of the car seat.

"You know how to pick up babies, don't you?" she asked.

"Uh...sort of." His face had hardened, his jawline now strong and masculine. He used to have acne as a teenager, but there was no sign of it now. Looking at him squatting there, she realized that she'd missed him more than she'd realized—and that wasn't just the fact that she didn't have enough hands right now. And yet, while she'd been away in the city, he'd been here with her dad, building a relationship that her father would reward him with her great-grandparents' homestead. Bile rose every time she thought about it.

"Support the head and the bottom," she instructed. "The rest will take care of itself."

Easton undid the buckle then cautiously scooped up the baby in his broad, calloused hands. Bobbie settled instantly as Easton pulled her against his chest. He looked down at the baby and then up at Nora.

"There," he said. "That worked."

"Thanks…" Nora heaved a sigh. The quiet was more than welcome.

"Bobbie?" he asked. The babies were all in pink sleepers.

"Her full name is Roberta. But she's my little Bobbie. It suits her."

Nora had only had the babies in her charge for a few days of her twelve-week parental leave from work, but she was already attached. They were so sweet, and so different from each other. Rosie was the quietest of the three, and Riley couldn't abide a wet diaper. Bobbie seemed to have the strongest personality, though, and Nora could already imagine their sisterly dynamic as they grew.

"Yeah, I guess so," he said. "Hi."

"Hi." She gave him a tight smile. "Nice to see you again."

Last time she saw him was at the reading of the will. She pushed back the unpleasant memory. Regardless, Easton was a fixture around here. They used to be good friends when they were younger, and they'd spent hours riding together, or just sitting on a fence and talking. When times were tough, Easton always seemed to materialize, and his solid presence made a difference. Apparently, her father had had equally warm memories.

Easton met her gaze, dark eyes softened by a smile. "You look good."

"Babies suit me, do they?" she joked.

"So the word around town—it's true, then?" he asked.

There it was—the beginning of the town's questions.

There would be a lot of them, and the answers were complicated.

"What did you hear?" she asked warily. "How much do people know?"

"That you came back to town with triplets," he said. "That your dad had an affair, and you had a half sister…" He winced. "It that part true? I find it hard to believe of him. I knew your dad better than most—"

She chafed at that reminder. The homestead was an old farmhouse her great-grandparents had built with their own hands. Over the years, the Carpenters had maintained it and Nora's parents had used it as a guesthouse. It mattered, that old house. It was Nora's connection to her family's past and she'd loved that old place. For her father to have left it to someone else… that had stung. She only found out that he'd changed his will when he died. Her mother had been surprised because she said they'd talked about doing something for Easton, but hadn't landed on what exactly. Normally Cliff and Dina talked through everything. But it looked like even Easton had been in the dark about her father's biggest secret.

"Yes, it's true." Easton wouldn't be the only one to be disappointed in this town. "My half sister, Mia, introduced herself a couple of months ago. Her mom—the other woman—" those words tasted bitter "—passed away a few years ago, and Mia was looking for her dad's side of the family. When I met her, she was already pregnant. There was no dad—she'd gone to a sperm bank. She really wanted kids and hadn't met the right guy yet."

Mia had had no idea about the affair and she never got a chance to meet Cliff. She had introduced herself after he died. It had been an awkward meeting, but Nora and Mia had recognized something in each other. Maybe they felt the genetic link. They'd both been raised only children, and to find a sibling was like a childhood daydream come true. Except this was real life, and they'd both had to come to terms with their father's infidelity.

"And you're godmother," Easton concluded.

"Yes. When she asked me to be godmother, I swear, I thought it was just a kind gesture. I never imagined this..."

Mia had died from childbirth complications—triplets being a high risk pregnancy to begin with—and Nora had grieved more deeply than she thought possible for a sister she'd only known a couple of months, whose existence rocked her own world. Nora was certain they'd have been close.

"Wow." Easton cleared his throat. "So your mom... I mean, these babies..."

"Yes, these babies are my father's illegitimate grandchildren." Nora sighed. "And Mom isn't taking it well."

That was an understatement. Nora hadn't told her mother, Dina, about Mia for a few weeks, afraid of causing her mother more grief than she was already shouldering since her husband's death. So Dina Carpenter hadn't had long to adjust to this new information before Nora and the babies arrived on her doorstep.

And Dina *hadn't* adjusted. She was still coming to terms with her late husband's infidelity and learning to run the ranch on her own. The babies only seemed to fuel more heartbreak.

"So what are you going to do?" Easton asked.

Footsteps sounded on the wooden staircase outside;

then the door opened and Dina came inside, dropping some shopping bags on the floor. She was plump, with graying blond hair pulled back into a ponytail. She shut the door behind her then looked up.

"You're back," Nora said.

"I got some baby clothes, diapers, formula, soothers, three bouncy chairs—they might help with…" Dina's voice trailed off. "Hi, Easton."

Nora recognized the trepidation in her mother's voice. The secret was out. She'd been holding this one close to her chest, and Nora knew how much her mother dreaded the whole town knowing the ugly truth about her husband's affair. So did Nora, for that matter. It was worse somehow that her father wasn't here to answer any questions, or take the brunt of this for them. He deserved to feel ashamed; they didn't. Nora and her mother hadn't been the ones to betray trust; he had. But he was dead, and they were left with the fallout of Cliff Carpenter's poor choices.

"Hi, Mrs. Carpenter." Easton stood awkwardly, the baby nestled against his chest, and seemed almost afraid to move. "Just lending a hand. I came by to tell you that we're rotating pastures for fence maintenance, and that will require a bit of overtime from the ranch hands."

"More overtime?" Dina sighed. "No, no, do it. The southwest fences, right? We put them off last year, so…" She sighed. "Is that all?"

"Yeah." Easton nodded. "I can get going." He looked down at the baby in his arms then at Dina as if he didn't know what to do.

If the homestead was still in the family, Nora would have moved in there with the babies to give her mother some space, but that was no longer an option. Nora and Dina would just have to deal with this together.

"I guess we'll have to get the babies settled in your old bedroom," Dina said. She paused, put a hand over her eyes. "I still can't believe it's come to this."

"Mom, you know I can't take care of them alone—"

"And why did you agree to be godmother?" Her mother heaved a sigh. "I swear, your generation doesn't think!" She pressed her lips together. "I'm sorry, Nora. What's done is done."

Dina grabbed the bags and headed down the hallway toward Nora's old bedroom. Nora and Easton exchanged a look.

"She's not taking this well," Nora said, feeling like she had to explain somehow.

"I can see that." Easton glanced in the direction his boss had disappeared. "You going to be okay here?"

"Do I have a choice?" Nora failed to keep the chill from her tone. The guesthouse would have been the perfect solution, but Easton owned it now. That wouldn't be lost on him. No matter how big the ranch house, the five of them would be cramped. Her mother was right—she hadn't thought this through. If she'd imagined that she'd ever have to step in and raise these girls, she would have found a polite way to decline the honor. Mia must have had some close friends…maybe some relative on her mother's side that she could have named as godparent.

Dina came back into the kitchen, her eyes redder than before. Had her mother been crying in the other room?

"Okay, let's figure this out," Dina said, her voice wooden. "Where are they going to sleep?"

* * *

Nora was staring blankly, and she looked like she wanted to cry. Two of the babies were snuggled in her arms. It was a stupid time for Easton to be noticing, but she was just as gorgeous as she'd always been, with her honey-blond hair and long, slim legs. He'd been halfway in love with her since the sixth grade. She'd never returned his feelings—ever.

Bobbie took a deep breath in her sleep then scrunched her face. He felt a surge of panic and patted the little rump as if soothing the baby would fix all of this. He glanced toward the car seat then at Bobbie. He wanted out of here—to get some space of his own to think this through. Except Nora and Dina looked like they were ready to collapse into tears, and here he stood, the legal owner of the obvious solution.

Easton was a private man. He liked quiet and solitude, and he had that with his new home—Cliff had known exactly how much it would mean to him. But Cliff hadn't known that he'd have three granddaughters landing on his doorstep after his death…

Dina obviously needed some time to process all this, and Nora needed help—he could feel her desperation emanating from her like waves…

Guilt crept up inside him—a nagging certainty that he stood between Nora and her solution. He didn't want to go back to the way things were when they were teens, and he certainly didn't want to give up that house and land that his boss had given him, but he couldn't just stand here and watch them scramble for some sort of arrangement as if it didn't affect him, either. He felt responsible.

The words were coming out of his mouth before he

had a chance to think better of them. "You can stay with me, Nora. It's not a problem."

Nora and Dina turned toward him, relief mingled with guilt written all over both faces. There had always been tension between mother and daughter, and the current situation hadn't improved things.

"You sure?" Nora asked.

"You bet. It'll be fine. There's lots of room. Just for a few days, until you and your mom figure this out." He was making this sound like a weekend away, not a complete invasion of his privacy, but he was already entangled in this family and had been for years. This was for old time's sake—for the friendship that used to mean so much to him. And maybe this was also a guilt offering for having inherited that house to begin with.

The next few minutes were spent gathering up baby supplies and getting the car seats back into Nora's four-door pickup truck. As Nora got into the driver's seat, Dina visibly deflated from where she stood at the side door. She'd been holding herself together for her daughter's sake, it seemed, and she suddenly looked small and older.

Cliff may have been many things, but he had been a good man at heart, and no one would convince Easton otherwise. A good husband? Perhaps not, given the recent revelation. But a man could be good at heart and lousy with relationships. At least Easton hoped so, because he seemed to fall into that category himself. If it weren't for Cliff, Easton's life would have turned out a whole lot differently. Loyalty might be in short supply, but Easton knew where his lay.

He got into his own rusted-out Ford and followed Nora down the familiar drive toward his little house.

His house. Should he feel so territorial about the old place? He'd fixed it up a fair amount since taking ownership, and the work had brought him a lot of comfort. He'd grown up in a drafty old house in town filled with his dad's beer bottles and piles of dishes that never got washed. So when he found out that Cliff had left him the house and the land, something inside him had grown— like roots sinking down, giving more security than he'd ever had. He'd stared at that deed, awash in gratefulness. He'd never been a guy who let his feelings show, but he had no shame in the tears that misted his eyes when he shook the lawyer's hand.

I shouldn't have gotten attached. And that was the story of his life, learning not to get attached, because nothing really lasted.

The farmhouse was a small, two-story house with white wooden siding and a broad, covered front porch. He hadn't been expecting company when he'd headed out for his morning chores, and he hoped that he'd left it decently clean. But this was his home, and while the situation was emotionally complicated, the legalities wouldn't change. Mr. Carpenter had left it to him. The deed was in a safety deposit box at the bank.

After they'd parked, Easton hopped out of his truck and angled around to her vehicle, where she was already unbuckling car seats.

"Thanks," Nora said as she passed him the first baby in her seat. "I don't know how to balance three of them yet. I should probably call up Mackenzie Granger and see if she has any ideas. She's got the twins, after all."

He held the front door open for her with the heel of his boot and waited while she stepped inside. The sun was lowering in the sky, illuminating the simple interior. Nora paused as she looked around.

"It's different than I left it."

"Yeah..." He wasn't sure how apologetic he should be here. "I got rid of the old furniture. It was pretty musty."

Easton hadn't put anything on the walls yet. He had a few pictures of his mother, but they didn't belong on the wall. She'd run off when he was eight—left a letter stuck to the fridge saying she couldn't handle it anymore, and that Easton was now his father's problem. He'd never seen her again. Considering the only family pictures he had were a few snapshots of his mom, the walls had stayed bare.

"Why did my dad leave this house to you?" Nora turned to face him. "I can't figure that part out. Why would he do that?"

Easton hadn't been the one to hurt her, but he was the one standing in front of her, regardless, and he felt an irrational wave of guilt. He was caught up in her pain, whether he meant to be or not.

"I don't know..." It had been a kind gesture—more than kind—and he'd wondered ever since if there were hidden strings. "A while ago, he said that he needed someone to take care of it, put some new life into it. I'd assumed that he wanted to rent it out or something. I didn't expect this."

"But this is my great-grandparents' home," she said. "I loved this place..."

She had... He remembered helping the family paint the old house one year when he was a teenager, and Nora had put fresh curtains in the windows in the kitchen—she'd sewn them in home economics class.

She did love this old house, but then she'd gone to college and gotten a city job, and he'd just figured she'd moved on.

"You had your own life in the city. Maybe your dad thought—"

"That doesn't mean I don't have roots here in Hope!" she shot back. "This house is mine. It should have been mine... My father should *never* have done this." She had to point her anger at someone, and it was hard to tell off the dead.

"What he should have done is debatable," Easton said. "But he made a choice."

She didn't answer him, and he didn't expect her to. She hated this, but he couldn't change facts, and he wasn't about to be pushed around, either. They'd just have to try to sort out a truce over the next few days.

"I'm making some tea," he added. "You want some?"

They'd been friends back in the day, but a lot had changed. Easton grew up and filled out. Nora had gone to college and moved to the city. He was now legal owner of a house she was still attached to, and an old friendship wasn't going to be cushion enough for all of this.

"Yes, tea would be nice." Her tone was tight.

"Nora." He turned on the rattling faucet to fill up the kettle. "I don't know what you think I did, but I never asked for this house. And I never angled for it."

"You didn't turn it down, either."

No, he hadn't. He could have refused the inheritance, but it had been an answer to midnight prayers, a way to step out from under his past. Mr. Carpenter's gift had made him feel more like family and less like the messed-up kid who needed a job. Mr. Carpenter had seen him differently, but he suspected Nora still saw him the same way she always had—a skinny kid who would do pretty much anything she asked to make her happy.

And as dumb as it was, he also saw her the same way he always had—the beautiful girl whom he wished could see past his flaws and down to his core. He was a man now—not a boy, and most certainly not a charity case. Nora was a reminder of a time he didn't want to revisit—when he'd been in love with a girl who took what he had to offer and never once saw him as more than a buddy. It hadn't been only her…he'd been an isolated kid looking for acceptance anywhere he could get it, and he didn't like those memories. They were marinated in loneliness.

That wasn't who he was anymore. Everything had changed around here. Including him.

Chapter 2

Easton heard the soft beep of an alarm go off through a fog of sleep, and he blinked his eyes open, glancing at the clock beside him. It was 3 a.m., and it wasn't his alarm. The sound filtered through the wall from the bedroom next door. He had another hour before he had to be up for chores, and he was about to roll over when he heard the sound of footsteps going down the staircase.

Nora was up—though the babies were silent. It was strange to have her back…to have her here. She'd stayed away, made a life in the city where she had an office job of some sort. She would come back for a weekend home every now and then, but she'd spent her time with friends, cousins, aunts and uncles. Easton didn't fit into any category—not anymore. He was an employee. He'd worked his shifts, managed the ranch hands and if he got so much as a passing wave from her, he'd be lucky.

Now she was in his home. Her presence seemed to be a constant reminder of his status around here—employee. Even this house—legally his—felt less like his own. There was something about Nora Carpenter that put him right back into his place. For a while he'd been able to forget about his status around here, believe he could be more, but with her back—

He wasn't going to be able to sleep listening to the soft sounds of a woman moving around the house anyway. He swung his legs over the side of his bed, yawning. The footsteps came back up the narrow staircase again, and he rose to his feet, stretching as he did. He was in a white T-shirt and pajama bottoms, decent enough to see her. He crossed his bedroom and opened the door.

Nora stood in the hallway, three bottles of milk in her hands, and she froze at the sight of him. Her blond hair tumbled over her shoulders, and she stood there in a pair of pajamas—a tank top and pink, pin-striped cotton shorts.

She's cute.

She always had been, and no matter how distant or uninterested she got, he'd never stopped noticing.

"Sorry," she whispered. "I was trying to be quiet."

He hadn't actually been prepared to see her like this—her milky skin glowing in the dim light from her open bedroom door, her luminous eyes fixed on him apologetically. She was stunning, just as she'd always been, but she was more womanly now—rounder, softer, more sure of herself. They should both be sleeping right now, oblivious to each other. That was safer by far.

"The babies aren't crying," he pointed out.

"I'm following the advice of the social worker who

gave me the lowdown on caring for triplets. She said to feed them on a schedule. If I wait for them to wake up, we'll have three crying babies."

It made sense, actually. He'd never given infant care—let alone infant care for triplets—much thought before. He should leave her to it, go back to bed…maybe go downstairs and start breakfast if he really couldn't sleep.

"Need a hand?" he asked.

Where had that come from? Childcare wasn't his domain, and frankly, neither was Nora. He'd been through this before with her—he knew how it went. She batted her eyes in his general direction, he got attached, she waltzed off once her problems were solved, and he was left behind, wrung out. Letting her stay here was help enough. As was picking up the crib for the babies after he brought her to the house. He couldn't be accused of callous indifference, but he also couldn't go down that path again.

She smiled at his offer of help. "I wouldn't turn it down."

Well, that took care of that. He trailed after her into the bedroom. The crib sat on one side of the room, Nora's rumpled bed on the other side. A window, cracked open, was between the two, and a cool night breeze curled through the room. The babies lay side by side along the mattress of the crib. Rosie and Riley looked pretty similar to his untrained eye, but he could pick out Bobbie. She was considerably bigger than the other two. But "big" was relative; they were all pretty tiny.

"I was hoping my mom would be able to help me with this stuff," Nora said as she picked up the first baby and passed her to him along with a bottle. "That's Rosie," she added.

She proceeded to pick up the other two and brought them to her unmade bed, where she propped them both up against her pillow. She wiggled the bottle nipples between their lips.

"Time to eat," she murmured.

The babies started to suck without any further prompting, and Easton looked down at the infant in his arms. He followed Nora's lead, teasing the bottle into Rosie's tiny mouth, and she immediately began to drink. It felt oddly satisfying.

"So this is how it's done," he said with a soft laugh.

"Apparently," Nora replied.

They were both silent for a few moments, the only sound babies slurping. He leaned an elbow against the crib, watching the tiny bubbles move up the bottle and turn into froth at the top of the milk. He'd done this with calves on a regular basis, but never with a baby.

"I don't blame your mom," Easton said.

"Me, neither," she replied quietly. "I just didn't know where else to go. When you feel lost, you find your mom."

Easton had never had that pleasure. His mom had abandoned them, and his dad…well, his dad could barely keep his own life together, let alone help Easton.

"Sorry…" She winced. "I forgot."

Yeah, yeah, his pathetic excuse for a family. Poor Easton. He was tired of that—the pity, the charitable thoughts. *Be thankful for what you have, because someone else thinks you're lucky.* It was a deep thought for the privileged as they considered how bad they could truly have it, before they breathed a sigh of relief that they still retained their good fortune.

"So why didn't you come back more often?" Easton asked, changing the subject.

"I was busy." She shot him a sidelong look. "Why?"

"It just seems to me that two weekends a year isn't much time with your family."

"We talked on the phone. What's it to you?"

He'd struck a nerve there, but she had a point. Who was he to lecture her about family bonds? He didn't have any of his own that counted for much. Besides, his complaint wasn't really about how much time she spent with her family. He'd missed her, too. His life kept going in Hope, Montana, and hers had moved on in the wider world. He resented her for that—for forgetting him.

"Mom and I—" Nora sighed. "We locked horns a lot."

"Yeah…" He hadn't expected her to open up. "I noticed it, but I never knew what it was about."

"Everything." She shook her head. "Politics, religion, current events…you name it, we land on opposite sides of it. When I left for college, it gave me a whole new freedom to be me, without arguing with Mom about it. So I stayed away a lot."

"Is that why you didn't tell her about your half sister?" he asked.

He was watching her as she sat on her bed facing the babies, one leg tucked under herself. Bobbie finished her bottle first, and Nora put it down, still feeding Riley with the other hand. She was oddly coordinated as she bottle-fed two infants. Maybe it came from bottle-feeding orphaned farm animals. If you could wrangle a lamb or a calf into taking a bottle, maybe it was a skill like riding a bike.

"I needed to sort it all out in my own head before I told her about it," Nora said, oblivious to his scrutiny. "It was like anything else. I thought I could have a sister—some semblance of a relationship with her—but I was pretty sure Mom would see that as a betrayal."

"I get it."

In fact, he understood both sides of it. It had to be hard for Dina to see her one and only daughter bonding with her late husband's love child. Yet he could understand Nora's desire to know her sister. The whole situation was a painful one—the sort of thing that made him mildly grateful for his lack of family coziness. At least he couldn't be let down any more than he already had been. Rock bottom was safe—there was no farther to fall.

Rosie was almost finished with her bottle, but she'd stopped drinking. He pulled it out of her mouth, leaving a little trail of milk dribbling down her chin.

"Is she done?" Nora asked.

"She stopped drinking." He held up the bottle.

"Okay. Just burp her, then."

Burp the baby. Of course. He knew the concept here—he wasn't a Neanderthal. He lifted Rosie to his shoulder, and she squirmed in her sleep, letting out a soft cry. Great, now he'd done it.

"Just pat her back," Nora said.

Easton gently tapped Rosie's back and she burped almost immediately, leaving a warm, wet sensation on his shoulder, dripping down toward his chest. He cranked his head to the side and could just make out the mess.

Nora chuckled. "Sorry."

Riley had finished her bottle, and Nora reached for Bobbie. It was an odd sort of assembly line as she burped them and he laid them back in the crib. He pulled the white T-shirt off over his head, getting the wet material away from his skin. He wadded up the shirt and gave his shoulder an extra scrub. It was then that he realized he was standing in front of Nora shirtless. Her gaze flickered over his muscular chest, and color rose in her cheeks.

"I'll just—" He pointed toward the door. He needed to get out of there. He'd fed and burped a baby—mission accomplished. He wasn't supposed to be hanging out with her, and he definitely wasn't supposed to be this casual with her, either.

"Okay. Sure—"

Nora's gaze moved over his torso once more, then she looked away quickly. She was uncomfortable, too. Soiled T-shirt in hand, he headed out of the room. That hadn't been the plan at all, and he felt stupid for not thinking ahead. Who knew what she thought now— that he was hitting on her, maybe? That couldn't be further from the truth.

Blast it, he was up now. He might as well go down and make some breakfast. An early start was better than a late one.

Nora hadn't ever seen Easton Ross looking quite so grown-up. And she hadn't imagined that under that shirt were defined muscles and a deep tan. He had a six-pack—that had been hard to miss—and it left her a little embarrassed, too. A good-looking man might be easy enough to appreciate in a picture or on TV, but when he stood in your bedroom in the moonlight...

She laid Bobbie next to Riley and Rosie in the crib and looked down at them for a moment, watching the soft rise and fall of their tiny chests.

It wasn't because she'd never seen a man without a shirt before. She'd always had a pretty healthy romantic life. But this was Easton—an old buddy, a quiet guy in the background. If he'd looked a little less impressive, she wouldn't have felt so flustered, but my goodness... When exactly had skinny, shy Easton turned into *that*?

She was awake now—she'd have to get used to going back to bed after the 3 a.m. feeding, but she could hear the soft clink of dishes downstairs, and she had a feeling that she and Easton needed to clear the air.

Grabbing a robe, Nora pulled it around herself and padded softly down the narrow, steep staircase. She paused at the bottom on a landing that separated the kitchen from the living room. Looking into the kitchen, she could see Easton at the stove, his back to her. He was in jeans and a fresh T-shirt now, his feet bare. The smell of percolating coffee filtered through the kitchen.

"Easton?" She stepped into the kitchen, tugging her robe a little tighter.

He turned, surprised. "Aren't you going to try to sleep some more?"

"I'm not used to the up and down thing yet. When I get tired enough, I'm sure I will."

He nodded and turned back to the pan. "You want breakfast?"

"Kind of early," she said with a small smile.

"Suit yourself." He dropped several strips of bacon into the pan.

"Look," she said, pulling out a kitchen chair with a scrape and sitting down. "I think I'm in the way here."

"Since when?"

"Since I woke you up at 3 a.m."

"I'll be fine." His tone was gruff and not exactly comforting. Was he doing this because she was the boss's daughter? It had to factor in somewhere.

"This is your home, Easton."

"You noticed." He cast her a wry smile then turned around fully, folding his arms across his chest. Yes, she had noticed. She didn't have to like it, but she was capable of facing facts.

"I should take the babies back to the house with my mom," she said. "I'm sorry. I hate that my dad left this place to you, but he did. So…"

She was sad about that—angry, even—but it wasn't Easton's fault. He could have turned it down, but who would turn down a house? She wouldn't have, either.

"You don't need to leave," he said.

"Oh." She'd thought he'd jump at any excuse to get her out of his home. If this night had proven anything, it was that this space was very much Easton's, and that felt awkward. This kitchen, where she remembered making cookies with her great-grandmother, was *his* kitchen now. She'd imagined she'd find peace here, but she'd been wrong. She shouldn't be surprised. A lot of her "perfect" memories hadn't been what she thought.

"You don't seem comfortable with me here, though," she countered. "And if I'm bound to make someone feel uncomfortable, it should be my own mother, don't you think?"

"I don't have a problem with you staying here," he replied, turning back to the pan. He flipped the bacon strips with a fork, his voice carrying over the sizzle.

"Do you realize that I've worked on this land since I was fourteen?"

"Yeah. It's been a while."

"That's sixteen years. And over those years, you and I became friends."

"I know."

"Real friends." He turned back, his dark gaze drilling into hers. "Do you remember when you broke up with Kevin Price? We talked for hours about that. I was there for you. I was there for you for Nathan Anderson, Brian Neville... I was there to listen, to offer advice. I mean, my advice was always the same—pick a better guy—but I was there."

Easton *had* been there for her, and she felt a blush rise at the memories. One rainy, soggy autumn day, they'd sat in the hayloft together, talking about a guy who wasn't treating her right. They'd sat for hours, just talking and talking, and she'd opened up more in that evening than she had with any guy she'd dated. But then her father had found them, ordered Easton back to work and told Nora to get inside. She could still remember the stormy look on her father's face. He hadn't liked it—probably assumed more was happening in the hayloft than a conversation.

Nora had talked too much back then. It had just felt so nice to have someone who listened like he did, but she might have led him on a little bit. She was a teenage girl, and her emotional world was vast and deep—in her own opinion, at least. She was mildly embarrassed about that now, but she wasn't any different than other girls. Easton was just a part-time ranch hand, and a guy. He hadn't been quite so in touch with his own "vast and deep" emotional life, and maybe he'd been a little in awe of her…maybe he'd nursed a mild crush. But she hadn't ever considered him as more than a buddy.

"I was an idiot," she said with a short laugh.

"And then you picked up and left for college, and that was it."

Well, that sure skipped a lot—like all the college applications, the arguments with her mother about living on campus or off and all the rest of the drama that came with starting a new phase of life. And since when was college a problem?

She frowned. "I went to college. You knew I was going."

"Thing is," he said, "you walked away, and life went on. For sixteen years I worked this land, drove the cattle, worked my way up. I'm ranch manager now because I know every job on this ranch and could do it myself if I had to. No one can get one over on me."

"You're good at what you do," she confirmed. "Dad always said so."

"And when you did come back to visit, you'd wave at me across the yard. That was it."

Admittedly, their relationship changed over the years. But having him here—that was the awkward part. If they'd just been school friends, then a change in the closeness they shared would have been natural—like the ebb and flow of any relationship. But he'd worked with her father, so unlike her school friends—where some of those old friendships could die a quiet death— she still saw Easton on a regular basis. From a distance, at least. He couldn't just slide into the past. When she did come home, she only had a few days, and she had to see a lot of people in that time.

"I was busy," she replied. "Friends and family—"

She heard it as it came out of her mouth. Friends—and she hadn't meant him. She'd meant people like Kaitlyn Mason, who she'd been close with since kindergarten. She winced. There was no recovering from that one, but it didn't make it any less true. Easton hadn't been high enough on her list of priorities when she'd come back.

"Yeah," he said with a sad smile. "Anyway, I was the worker, you were the daughter. Well, your dad saw fit to give me a little patch of land. I *worked* for this. I know that your great-grandparents built this house, and I know it means a whole lot to you, but I'm not about to sell it or tear it down. I actually think I might take your dad's advice."

"Which was?" she asked.

"To get married, have a few kids."

That had been her father's advice to him? Her father's advice to her had always been "Wait a while. No rush. Get your education and see the world." The double standard there irritated her, but she couldn't put her finger on why. Whoever Easton decided to marry and whatever kids they'd have, they'd be no kin of the people who built this house with their own hands. Her family—the Carpenters—had been born here, had died here... Easton might have worked for her father, but he didn't *deserve* this house.

"Anyone special in mind?" she asked, trying to force a smile.

"Nope."

There was no use arguing. The house was his. She couldn't change it or fight it. Maybe one day she could convince him to sell to her, but that was about as much as she could do.

"If you ever want to sell this house," she said, "come to me first."

He nodded. "Deal."

Easton turned back to the stove and lifted the bacon from the pan with his tongs, letting it drip for a moment in sizzling drops before he transferred it to a plate. She had to admit—it smelled amazing. He grabbed a couple of eggs and cracked them into the pan. Was that it? Was that all she could ask from him—to sell to her if he ever felt like it? Probably, and he didn't look like he was about to back down, either.

He'd had a point, though. He'd spent more time with her dad than she had…he'd know things.

"Did you know about the other woman?" Nora asked.

He grabbed a couple thick slices of bread, dumped the bacon onto one of them, added the eggs sunny side up, and slapped the second piece on top. He turned toward her slowly and met her eyes.

"I get that you're mad at him," he said. "And you've got every right to be. But he wasn't my father, and what he did inside of marriage or outside of it wasn't my business."

Nora stared at him, shocked. Was that the kind of man Easton was? He was just talking about a marriage and family of his own. She'd thought he'd have a few more scruples than that.

"But did you know?" she demanded.

"I'm saying he was my boss," Easton retorted, fire flashing in his eyes. "His personal life wasn't my business. I had no idea about the other woman—how could I know? We were working cattle, not cozying up to women. I'm not going to bad-mouth him, even if that would make you feel better for a little while. He was good to me. He was honest and fair with me. He taught me everything I know and set me up with this house. If you're looking for someone to complain about him and pick him apart with, you'd better keep looking. I'm not that guy."

He dropped his plate on the table and squashed the sandwich down with the palm of his hand. Then he grabbed a few pieces of paper towel and wrapped it up.

"You're nothing if not loyal, Easton," she said bitterly. Loyal to the man who'd given him land. He should have been loyal to a few basic principles.

Easton tossed the wrapped sandwich into a plastic bread bag then headed to the mudroom.

"I'm sorry for what he did to you," he said, not raising his head as he plunged his feet into his boots. "I get that it was a betrayal. But I'm staff, and you're family. I know the line."

The line? What line? Was he mad that they'd grown apart over the years, that she'd moved away to Billings for a degree in accounting? What line was so precious that he couldn't stand up for the women who had been wronged?

"What does that mean?" she demanded. "Do you want me to go? Have I crossed a line with you?"

He grabbed his hat and dropped it on his head.

"No," he said quietly. "Stay."

He didn't look like he was going to expand upon that, and he pulled open the door, letting in a cool morning draft.

"You forgot your coffee," she said.

"I leave it on the stove to let it cool down a bit," he said. "I'll have it in an hour when I get back."

With that, he stepped outside into the predawn grayness. Then the door banged shut after him, leaving her alone with a freshly percolated pot of coffee and three sleeping babies.

Easton had made himself clear—his loyalty belonged to her dad. Well, her father had lost hers. Ironic, wasn't it, that the one person to stand by Cliff Carpenter's memory was the hired hand?

Chapter 3

Around midmorning, Nora heard a truck rumble to a stop outside the house. She looked out the window to see her mother hop out of the cab. She was wearing a pair of fitted jeans and boots, and when she saw Nora in the window, she waved. Nora hadn't realized how much she'd missed her mom until she saw her, then she felt a wave of relief. It reminded her of waiting to be picked up at Hope Elementary School. All the other kids got on the bus, and Nora had to sit on the curb, alone. Her heart would speed up with a strange joy when she finally saw her mom in the family truck. She felt that joy on that school curb for the same reason: sometimes a girl—no matter the age—just needed her mom's support.

The babies were all sleeping in their bouncy chairs, diapers changed and tummies full. Nora's ridiculously early morning was already feeling like a mistake. She was exhausted. Back in the city, she'd been working in the accounting office for a company that produced equestrian gear. She'd worked hard, put in overtime, but she'd never felt weariness quite like this. A work friend had told her that her twelve weeks of parental leave would be more work than the office, but she hadn't believed it until now.

Nora pulled open the side door and ambled out into the warm August sunshine.

"Morning," she called.

"Mackenzie Granger dropped this by," her mother said, pulling a collapsed stroller out of the bed of the truck. "She said she got the triplet stroller for the boys and the new baby, but hasn't used it as much as she thought she would."

Nora couldn't help the smile that came to her face. She'd been wondering how she'd ever leave the house again with three infants, but thank God for neighbors with twin toddlers and new babies.

"I'll have to call her and thank her," Nora said. "And thank you for bringing it by."

Her mother carried the stroller over and together they unfolded it and snapped it into its open position. It was an umbrella stroller with three seats lined up side by side. It was perfect. Not too big, not too heavy, and she could transport all three babies at once.

"I had an idea." Dina shot Nora a smile. "Let's load the babies into this and you can come pick the last of the strawberries with me."

They used to pick strawberries together every summer when Nora was young. They'd eat as they picked, and even with all the eating, they'd fill bucket after bucket. Dina would make jam with some of them, freeze

a bunch more and then there would be fresh strawberries for everything from waffles to ice cream. Nora
used to love strawberry-picking. Then she became a
teenager, and she and her mother stopped getting along
quite so well.

Nora met her mother's gaze, and she saw hope in
Dina's eyes—the flimsy, vulnerable kind of hope that
wavered, ready to evaporate. Maybe her mother was
thinking of those sweet days, too, when they used to
laugh together and Dina would let Nora whip up some
cream for the berries.

"Yeah, okay," Nora said.

They transferred the babies to the stroller quickly
enough, and the stroller rattled and jerked as Nora
pushed it down the gravel road—the babies undis-
turbed. Maybe this was why Mack hadn't used it much.
The wheels were quite small, so every rock could be felt
underneath them. But Nora had gotten them all outside,
and that was a feat in itself.

"So what are you going to do about the babies?" her
mother asked as they walked.

"Would it be crazy to raise them?" Nora asked.

"Three infants on your own?" her mother asked.

"Three infants, you and me."

Her mother didn't answer right away, and sadness
welled up inside Nora. It *was* crazy. And it was too
much to ask of her mom right now. Maybe ever. Her
mother reached over and put a hand on top of Nora's
on the stroller handle.

"I've missed you," Dina said quietly. "It's nice to
have you home."

It wasn't an answer—not directly, at least—but it
was clear enough. They were still on opposite sides,

it seemed, even with the babies. But Nora had always been stubborn, and she wasn't willing to let this go gracefully.

"I came home because I thought you'd help me," Nora pressed.

"And I will. As much as I can."

They all had limits to what they could give, and Nora had taken on more than she could possibly handle on her own. The problem was that she was already falling in love with these little girls. With every bottle, every diaper change, every snuggle and coo and cry, her heart was becoming more and more entwined with theirs. But was keeping them the right choice?

The strawberry patch was on the far side of the main house, and Nora parked the stroller in the shade of an apple tree then moved into the sunshine where Dina had the buckets waiting. Dina came back over to the stroller and squatted down in front of it. Sadness welled in her eyes as she looked at the sleeping infants.

"I get it," Dina said, glancing up at her daughter. "When I first held you, I fell in love, too. It couldn't be helped."

"They're sweet," Nora said, a catch in her voice.

"Adorable." Her mother rose to her feet again and sighed. "Your dad would have—" Dina's chin quivered and she turned away.

"Dad would probably have hidden them," Nora said bitterly. Mia had told her enough to be clear that Cliff had known about her existence, even if they'd never met. "He hid his daughter, why should his granddaughters be any different?"

That secrecy—the whole other family—stabbed at a tender place in Nora's heart. How was it possible for a man to have secrets that large and never let on? Didn't he feel guilty about it? Didn't something inside him jab just a little bit when he sat in church on Sunday? He had a reputation in this town, and this didn't line up with the way people saw him. She hoped that he did feel guilt—the kind to keep him up at night—because this wasn't just his private mistake; this had affected them all.

"Let's pick berries," her mother said.

But hidden or not, Nora's father would have fallen in love with these baby girls, too. He'd probably cherished a secret love for the daughter he'd never met. And hidden that love. So many lies by omission...

"Mom, if Dad had lived," Nora said, grabbing an ice cream pail and squatting at the start of a row, "what would you have done? I mean if Mia had suddenly dropped on our doorstep and announced herself, what then?"

"I'd have divorced him." There was steel in Dina's voice, and she grabbed a pail and crouched down next to Nora. They spread the leaves apart and began picking plump, red berries. "I had no idea he had someone else..."

"Mia said he wasn't in her life at all, though," Nora said. "Maybe the affair wasn't long-term."

Her mother shook her head. "I don't care how long it was. When your husband sleeps with someone else, there is nothing casual about it. It's no accident, either. He chose to do the one thing that would tear my heart in two. He chose it."

"Do you hate him now?"

Her mother's voice was quiet. "I do this morning."

The berries were plentiful, and they picked in silence for a few minutes. Nora's mind was moving over her plans. If she kept these babies, she'd need help. She'd taken her twelve weeks of parental leave from her bookkeeping job, but when she went back to work again, she'd be paying for three children in day care. She couldn't afford that...not on her middling salary, and certainly not as a single mom. Staying in Hope to raise the girls would be the smart choice, but she hadn't taken her mother's emotional state into the equation. She didn't have her mother's support in keeping the babies, and she didn't have that little homestead where she could have set up house. She didn't have a job here, either, besides the family ranch. So she'd come home, unsure what the next step should be, but certain that this was the place where she could make her decisions.

They were halfway down the second row, six buckets filled with ripe, plump berries, when a neighbor's truck pulled into the drive.

"It's Jennifer," Dina said, glancing up. Then she added with a dry tone, "Great."

The neighbor woman hopped out of her truck and waved, then headed across the lawn toward them. She wore a pair of jeans and a loose tank top, a pair of gardening gloves shoved into her back pocket. She was also Dina's second cousin twice removed or something to that effect.

"Morning!" Jennifer called. She was in her early fifties, and her hair was iron gray, pulled back with a couple of barrettes.

"Morning." Dina looked less enthusiastic, but she met Jennifer's gaze evenly. "What brings you by?"

"Curiosity." Jennifer peered behind them at the stroller. "I heard about the triplets."

Nora watched as her mother pushed herself to her

feet. It was already out there—their deepest pain being bandied about by the local gossips.

"Well…" Dina seemed at a loss for words.

"They're sleeping right now," Nora said, and she led Jennifer toward the stroller.

The older woman looked down at them then glanced at Dina.

"I had no idea Cliff was that kind of man. To live with a man for what—thirty-five years?—and you'd think you knew him."

"You'd think," Dina replied drily.

"So what happened?" Jennifer asked, plucking a berry from one of the filled buckets and tugging off the stem. "Did you see the signs?" She popped the strawberry into her mouth.

"Of my husband fathering another child?" Dina asked, anger sparking under the sadness. "What would that look like exactly, Jen?"

Jennifer's ex-husband was a known philanderer, while Nora's parents had always appeared to be the most devoted couple. Nora had never seen her parents fight—not once. Her father was a tough, unbending man, but somehow he and Dina could look at each other and come to a decision without saying a word. People commented on the strength of that marriage. Jennifer and Paul, however—everyone knew what Paul did on the side. And Jennifer and Paul had very public arguments about it on a regular basis.

"Paul was obvious," Jennifer retorted. "Cliff wasn't. I can normally point out a cheating man a mile away— I mean, I'm kind enough not to tell the wife, but I can spot it. Cliff didn't seem like the type."

Jennifer was enjoying this—there was a glimmer of

gaiety under the external show of concern, the cheeriness of not being the one in the crosshairs for a change. But this was Nora's father being torn apart...and Nora couldn't help feeling a strange combination of anger at her dad and protectiveness toward him at the same time. He deserved to be raked across the coals—by Dina and Nora, not the town. He was *theirs* to resent, to hate, to love, to be furious with. The town of Hope, for all its good intentions, could bloody well back off.

"I don't want to talk about it," Dina replied shortly.

"Oh, I get it, I get it..." Jennifer hunched down next to a row of strawberry plants and beckoned toward the pile of empty buckets. "Pass me one, would you? I'll give you a hand."

They wouldn't get rid of her easily, it seemed, and Nora exchanged a look with her mother. This wasn't just her mother's shame, it was Nora's, too. Cliff had left them in this strange position of being pitied, watched, gossiped over. And in spite of it all, he was still her dad. Besides, she couldn't help but feel a little bit responsible for bringing this gossip down onto her mother's head, because she'd been the one to bring the babies here. Without the babies, no one would have been the wiser.

"It's scary," Jennifer prattled on, accepting a bucket and starting to pick. "I mean, will it affect the will? Do you remember the exact wording? Because if the wording is about 'children' in general, it includes any children he's had outside of wedlock, too. But if he names Nora specifically..."

There wasn't much choice but to keep picking, and Nora realized with a rush that keeping these babies in the family wouldn't be as simple as winning her mother over. Dina wasn't the only one who would be thinking about Cliff's infidelity when she looked at those girls—the entire town would.

Those babies represented a man's fall from grace, a besmirched reputation and hearts mangled in collateral damage. It wasn't that this town was cruel, it was that a sordid scandal was interesting, and people couldn't help but enjoy it a little. Gossip fueled Hope, Montana, and these three innocent babies had just brought enough fuel to last for years.

"You know what, Jennifer?" Nora rose to her feet and wiped the dirt off her knees. "I think Mom and I have it from here. Thanks, though."

The older woman looked startled then mildly embarrassed.

"Oh…yes, of course."

Jennifer wiped her own knees off and took some long steps over the rows of strawberry plants until she was on the grass again. They had an awkward goodbye, and then Jennifer headed back toward her vehicle. The gossip would be less congenial now, but it would have spiraled down into something nastier sooner or later anyway.

"Let's go eat some strawberries, Mom," Nora said, turning toward her mother. "And I want to sit with you on the step and dip our strawberries in whipped cream. Like we used to."

She wanted that whipped cream so badly that she ached. She wanted to rewind those angst-filled teenage years and bring back the sunny, breezy days where she'd been oblivious to heartbreak—when both of them had been. She wanted her mom—that calming influence, the woman who always had an answer for everything, even if that answer was "Some things we don't need to know."

"Okay." Dina nodded, and tears came to her eyes.

Everything had changed on them, spun and tipped. But they could drag some of it back, like whipped cream and strawberries on a warm August day.

That afternoon Easton came back to the house, his body aching from a day of hard work. He'd ridden Scarlet over to the southwest pasture to check up on the fence that was being rebuilt. Scarlet was his favorite horse; he'd bought her from the Mason ranch five years ago, and he and that horse had a bond stronger than most people shared. Scarlet was a good listener—recently, Easton had started talking. Not to people, but letting the thoughts form words and then spill out of him was cathartic. He could see why Nora had relied on him to just listen for all those years.

Out at the southwest corner, one of the ranch hands had broken a finger, so Easton sent him back, called the medic and took his place for the afternoon with the pole driver. He'd have to fill out a pile of paperwork for the injury, but the fence was complete and all in all it had been a good day.

Now, as he ambled up the drive toward the house, he was ready for a quiet evening. But he had to admit, he'd been thinking of Nora all day. He'd gotten used to her hurried trips back to the ranch, that wave across the yard. He'd made his peace with the fact that their friendship was something from long ago when she needed someone to listen to her problems. It had never been a terribly reciprocal friendship. He'd been quiet by nature, and she'd never asked too many questions. Maybe she'd assumed all was fine in his world because he didn't feel the need to vent.

As he came closer to the house he could hear the chorus of baby wails. Wow—it sounded like all three of them were crying. He picked up his pace, concerned that something might be wrong, and when he emerged from the mudroom, he was met by Nora's frantic face.

She stood in the middle of the kitchen—two babies crying from their little reclined bouncy chairs on the floor, and Bobbie in Nora's arms, also wailing.

"Everything okay?" Easton asked, dropping his hat onto a hook.

"No!" Nora looked ready to cry herself. "They've been like this for an hour…more? What time is it?"

"Almost five," he said.

"I'm so tired…" She patted Bobbie's diapered bottom and looked helplessly at the other two.

He couldn't very well leave them like that, and seeing those little squished faces all wet with tears, tiny tongues quivering with the intensity of their sobs, made him want to do something. He didn't know how to soothe an infant, but he could pick one up. He bent and scooped up the baby closest—Riley, he thought. But he could be wrong. He tipped her forward onto his chest and patted her back.

"Hey, there…" he murmured, looking down at her. She didn't look any happier, and he followed Nora's example and bounced himself up and down a couple of times to see if that improved the situation.

Nada.

He hadn't meant to start singing, but a tune came into his head in the same rhythm of his movement— a song he hadn't heard in a long, long time. Brahms's

"Lullaby." He hummed it at first, and Riley stopped her hiccoughy sobs and listened, so he started to sing softly.

"Lullaby and good-night, hush my darling is sleeping.

On his sheets, white as cream, and his head full of dreams.

Lullaby and good-night..."

The baby lay her face against his chest and heaved in some shaky breaths. It was working—she liked the song...

He looked up to see Nora staring at him, an odd look on her face. She looked almost soothed, herself.

"I have an idea," she said, pointing to the couch in the living room. "Go sit there."

He did as she asked and sank into the couch. She deposited Bobbie next to her sister on his chest, and Bobbie had a similar reaction as Riley had, calming, blinking, listening as he sang. It was unexpectedly comfortable—the weight off his feet, two babies on his chest. Rosie still wailed from the kitchen, but when Nora scooped her up, she calmed down a little, and when Nora sank onto the cushion next to him, Rosie seemed to be lulled into quiet, too.

He sang the only verse he knew of that song a few times and the babies' eyes drooped heavier and heavier until they fell asleep, exhausted from their crying.

"I didn't know you could sing," Nora said softly.

"You never asked." He shot her a smile. "You know that cowboys sing. It soothes the herd."

"But they don't all sing well," she countered.

He chuckled softly. "I break it out when absolutely necessary."

There was an awful lot she didn't know about him.

He knew more about her—she'd opened up with him. He knew that she hated sappy songs but loved sappy books, that her first horse had been her best friend and that her dad had been her hero. She'd talked and talked… But as he sat here with her, the babies breathing in a gentle rhythm, he wished he'd said more back then. She'd taken more than she'd given, but that hadn't been her fault. He'd given and given, and never asked for anything in return. Ever. Maybe he should have asked.

"I heard that song on TV years ago," he said. "I was maybe ten or eleven. I thought it was so beautiful that I nearly cried. So I tried to remember the words to it but could only remember the one verse. I imagined that one day my mother would come back and sing that song to me."

"Did you ever hear from her?" Nora asked quietly.

He shook his head. "Nope."

His mother left when he was eight, and he didn't have a solid memory of her. He knew what she looked like from the pictures, a woman with curly hair and glasses, one crooked tooth in the front that made her smile look impish. Those photos replaced his memories of her somehow—maybe because he'd spent more time with the pictures than the woman herself. His father had destroyed the other photos. "She left us," he used to say. "Don't even bother trying to remember her. She sure isn't thinking about us."

Easton couldn't trust his memories of her. He'd made up so many stories about her, so many situations that had never really happened, that he almost believed them. In his imagination, she was gentle and soft, and she stroked his hair away from his face. In his imagination, she loved him so devoutly that she'd never leave. When he lay in his bed at night, his dad drinking in front of the TV, he used to close his eyes and pretend that his mother was sitting on the edge of his bed, asking about his day. He'd imagined that well into his teen years...longer than he should have needed it.

"Do you know why she left?" Nora asked.

"She and Dad both drank a lot. They fought pretty viciously. I don't know. She left a note that just said that she'd had enough. She was leaving, and we shouldn't try to find her."

"But she didn't take you with her," Nora pointed out.

Easton had questioned that over the years. If life was such hell here in Hope, why wouldn't she take her little boy along? Why would she leave him like that? She'd walked out, and he'd been left with an alcoholic father who could barely function. It was selfish. If she hadn't loved Dad, he could understand that. But why hadn't she loved *him*?

"Yeah..." He didn't have anything else to say to that. It was a fact—she'd left him behind.

"Do you remember her?" she asked.

"Not much," he admitted. "My dad dumped her stuff out into a pile and burned it. I guess that was cathartic for him. I managed to sneak off with one of her shirts— some discarded thing she didn't feel like bringing with her, I guess. I kept it under my mattress. It smelled like her cigarettes. I have that still."

"Why didn't I know about this?" Nora murmured.

A better question was, why had he told her now? Nora came from a loving home with parents who both adored her. Her family ran the ranch very successfully, and she'd had a bright future. He'd had none of those things, and yet he was still willing to be there for her, give her whatever support she needed. Why? Because he'd been in love with her, and maybe deep down he was afraid that if she knew the mess inside him, it would turn her off him.

"That's not how we worked, you and I," he said after a moment.

"Meaning I was self-involved." She winced. "I'm sorry. I must have been."

He shook his head. "I don't know. You were used to happier days than I was. You were more easily disappointed."

"I wish I'd been a better friend," she said.

But it wasn't friendship that would have soothed his teenage soul. If she'd been a more attentive friend, it might have made it harder. He might have actually held out hope that she'd see more in him. But being six inches shorter with a face full of acne had taken care of that.

"It's okay," he said. "It was a long time ago."

Easton needed to be careful, though, because not much had changed. She was still the heir to the ranch he worked, she was still the much loved daughter of the owner and she still needed his emotional support right now…except he wasn't so naive this time around. He knew how this ended. Nora would pull things together and she'd step out into that bright future of hers, leaving him right where he'd always been—on the ranch. She'd walk away again, and she wouldn't think to look back.

"You have the magic touch with the babies," she said, easing herself forward to stand up. "Thank you."

"No problem." What else was he supposed to do

when three tiny girls had taken over his home? She walked toward the stairs with Bobbie in her arms.

"Why didn't you call your mom when the babies wouldn't stop crying?" he asked, and she looked back.

"Because she isn't really on board with this. Getting my mom's help isn't as great a solution as I thought. If I'm going to raise these girls, I'll have to figure out a way to do it on my own."

He'd suspected as much. While she'd probably pitch in, it was a bit much to expect Dina to joyfully embrace raising her late husband's other family.

"I'll get them back up to the crib," she said. "I'll be back."

And she disappeared from the room. He wasn't a long-term solution, either. He never had been, not in her eyes, and he wasn't about to make the same mistake he'd made as a teen. He didn't cross oceans for someone who wouldn't jump a puddle for him. Not anymore.

Chapter 4

That night Nora had managed to feed the babies without waking Easton, and when she got up again for their 6 a.m. feeding, Easton was gone, leaving behind percolated coffee cooling on the stove while he did his chores. She'd gone back to bed—her theory had been right and exhaustion made sleep possible—and when she opened her eyes at eight and got dressed, she'd found another pot of coffee freshly percolated on the stove. He'd been back, it seemed. And he'd be back for this pot, too, but she took a cup of coffee anyway—she desperately needed the caffeine kick.

The house felt more familiar without Easton around, and she stood in the kitchen, soaking in the rays of sunlight that slanted through the kitchen window, warming her toes. She sipped the coffee from a mug that said Save a Cow, Eat a Vegetarian. That was a sample of

Easton's humor, apparently. She let her gaze flow over the details of this kitchen that she'd always loved…like the curtains that she'd sewn as a kid with the flying bluebird-patterned fabric. She'd made them in home ec, and she'd been so proud of them, despite the wandering hemline and the fact that one side was shorter than the other.

He kept those.

It was strange, because Easton hadn't kept much else of the original decor—not that she could blame him. The furniture and kitchenware had all been cast-offs from the main house. Anything of value—sentimental or otherwise—had been distributed amongst the extended family when Great-Granny passed away. Easton's furniture was all new, and the kitchen had gleaming pots and pans. The dishes in the cupboard were a simple set of four of each dish, but they had obviously been recently purchased except for a few well-worn mugs like the one she was using now. There had been some renovations, too—fresh paint, some added built-in benches in the mudroom. He'd taken pride in this place.

And yet the floor was the same—patches worn in the linoleum by the fridge and stove. Though freshly painted, the windowsills still had that worn dip in the centers from decades of elbows and scrubbing. Nora used to stand by those windows while her elderly great-grandmother baked in the sweltering kitchen. She used to scoot past the fridge, wondering if Granny would catch her if she snagged another creamsicle. This old place held so many childhood memories, so many family stories that started with "When Great-Granny and Great-Grandpa lived in the old house…"

It felt strangely right to come back to this place, or it would have if Easton didn't live here. If her father had just done the normal thing and left everything to his wife, then she would be settling in here on her own—her future much easier to handle because of this family touchstone. But it wasn't hers—it wasn't *theirs*. Instead she felt like an interloper. She still felt like she needed permission to open the fridge.

It was after eight in the morning now. She'd fed the babies and changed their diapers, and now she was antsy to get outside into the sunshine. She'd thought she wanted space and quiet, but the silence was getting heavy. Solitude wasn't going to cut it. She needed a plan for her future, how she'd take care of these girls by herself, and that didn't seem to be formulating on its own.

The day was hot, and Nora had dressed the triplets in matching yellow sundresses—clothes that Mia had lovingly purchased and set aside for her daughters. The babies squirmed a little as Nora transferred them into the stroller outside the door, but once in the stroller, they settled back into deep slumber, tiny legs curled up around their diapers. She brushed a wisp of chocolate-brown hair away from Bobbie's forehead, love welling up inside her. It was dangerous to be falling in love with these girls, but she was.

Nora shut the door behind her and pushed the stroller over the dusty path that led from the house to the dirt road. The morning was still cool, the sun bright and cheerful in a cloudless sky. Dew still clung to the grass in the shady patches of lawn that Easton seemed to keep mowed around the little house. Thatches of rosebushes grew unfettered beside the sagging fence that encircled it. She paused at one and fingered a lush, white bloom.

Her father had been wrong in giving this house away. More than wrong—cruel. And what he'd been thinking, she had no idea. Easton was treating the house well, but no amount of appreciation or hard work would make him family, and this house belonged with family.

Had Dad been angry that she'd created a life for herself in the city? Maybe there was unspoken resentment she'd never known about. Nora pushed the stroller on, bumping onto the dusty road. The ditch beside the road was filled with long grass and weeds, but beyond that ditch, and beyond the rusty barbed wire fence, green pasture rolled out. The old barn stood a hundred yards off, grass growing up around it. Every year it bowed a little lower, hunching closer to the ground that longed to swallow it up. Her father had never been able to bring himself to tear the structure down. Cliff was a practical man in every sense, but when it came to that old barn, he used to say, "Leave it. It makes a pretty picture."

And yet he'd given away the house. Blast it—why couldn't his sentimental streak have stretched long enough to keep the house in the family? If he'd willed it to a cousin, she'd still be upset, but at least the person living there would have a personal connection to the family history.

The road led around to the main barn—a large, modern building—and as she walked, her nerves seemed to untangle. There was something about the open country that soothed her right down to the soul. There had been countless times in the city when she'd considered coming back, but things were complicated here in Hope. She and her mother had always been at odds, and Nora loved having her own space. She'd never been able to spread her wings under her parents' roof, in the same tiny town that would always see her as a kid.

As she crested a low hill, she spotted Easton a stone's throw down the road. A rusted pickup truck was parked at the side of the road, and the cattle were nearby the fence, a steer trying to push through a sagging stretch to reach the lush weeds beyond. Easton shouted something at the steer and waved his arms.

He had toughened into a tall, muscular man over the years. How had she failed to notice? His shirt was rolled up to expose his forearms, and he moved with the ease of a man accustomed to physical labor. But under the muscular physique was the same old Easton she'd always known—an uncomfortable combination of hardened muscle and old friend. It almost made her feel shy watching him work, and she'd never felt that way around Easton before. She'd always been the one in control, the one with all the power. Somehow the years had tipped that balance.

Nora picked up her pace—that was a two-person job by the look of that steer, but she had the babies with her, too. There was no way she could leave him alone with this.

"Easton!" she called.

He turned and spotted her. He pushed his hat back on his head and gave her a wave, then returned his attention to the fence. If he could get the steer to back up, she could staple up the barbed wire and the problem would be solved. She put the brakes on the stroller, making sure it was well off the road, then jumped the ditch.

"Give me the staple gun," she said.

He passed it to her then took off his hat and swatted the steer with it. "Come on," he grunted. "Get going!"

The animal bawled out a moo of frustration and took a few steps in reverse. Nora grabbed the barbed wire, pulled it taut and stapled it in one deft movement. She could feel the tongs of the wire pressing into her hand, but she didn't have time to complain. Then she grabbed the next wire down, being more careful this time where she touched it, and stapled again.

"Done," she said, stepping back.

"Thanks." Easton took the staple gun back and shot her a grin. "You're handier than you look."

"Accounting is tougher than you'd think," she joked.

Easton bent down and eased through the space between the wires, emerging on her side of the fence. He was closer than she'd anticipated, close enough for her to smell his musky scent. Her breath caught in her throat as she looked up at him. He was tall and broad. While those eyes hadn't changed, the rest of him certainly had.

"Is it?" he asked teasingly. "All those numbers and cushy office chairs?"

"I fixed the fence," she shot back. "And I have the blood to prove it." She held up her palm where the scratch had started to bleed.

"You okay?" Was that sympathy she saw in his eyes?

"It's a scratch, Easton. I'll survive it. Give me a hand over, would you?"

He jumped the ditch first then took her hand as she jumped across. He followed and she bent over the stroller, checking on the babies, who were all still asleep.

"Let's see that hand," he said, and she straightened, holding it out.

His touch was gentle and warm. "You'll need some antiseptic on that."

Nora turned the stroller around. "Yeah, I'll take care of it. Where's the first-aid kit in the house?"

"Never mind," he said. "I'll come along. I'm ready for my coffee anyway."

"What about the truck?"

He shrugged. "Not going anywhere."

It was nice to have his company, and if she didn't look over at the new, taller, stronger Easton, it almost felt like old times. Except that it wasn't.

"I'm sorry about when we were teenagers," she said after a moment. "When I was only focused on my own issues, I mean. I feel bad about that."

"It's okay," he said. "It was a long time ago. We've both come a long way since then."

"Maybe not as long as you think," she said wryly. "I also had a cup of your coffee."

He glanced over at her, dark gaze drilling into her for a beat longer than was comfortable.

"Okay, that's it," he deadpanned. "That's where I draw the line." He paused. "You did leave me at least one mug, right?"

"Of course." She grinned.

Rosie woke up and squirmed, letting out a little whimper. Bobbie slept on, but Riley pushed out one tiny fist.

"Good morning, sleepyheads," Nora said.

The warm, low sunshine, these tiny girls, the sweet scent of grass carrying on the breeze, this good-looking cowboy walking next to her—it felt impossibly perfect, and the contentedness that rose up inside her was bittersweet. Staying in the old house—raising the girls here as would have been the plan if it weren't for her father's surprise will—wasn't an option. And having it so close, but just past her fingertips, made her ache for everything she couldn't keep.

She wanted to raise these girls, but she had to be realistic. She was an accountant, after all, and she knew how to look at a bottom line. And raising these girls alone didn't look possible.

Thanks a lot, Dad, she thought bitterly.

Back at the house, Easton rummaged up the first-aid kit from under the sink and pulled out some iodine and some bandages, tossing them onto the counter. His coffee sat on the stove, the smell warming the room. He'd get himself a mug in a minute.

He'd been impressed by her quick thinking out there with the steer at the fence. She'd been around the heavy work on the ranch, of course, but when the men were working, Cliff made sure she kept a more supervisory position—out of the way. She was family, not a hired hand, and there had always been a line there. After her time in Billings, and now with her focus on the babies, he hadn't expected her to be on her game when it came to ranch work.

"I can do it," she said, taking the bottle from him. She winced as the brown drops hit the torn skin.

Nora had always been that rare combination of vulnerable and stubbornly independent. She needed people, but she wouldn't stick around for long. She was like a wild deer, leaping to her feet and dashing off the moment she'd regained enough strength. But while she sat next to him, close enough to touch, opening up about her internal world, it was possible to forget that the leap for freedom was in her nature.

Easton peeled the backing off the bandage and put

it over the scrape. She smiled her thanks, ran her fingers over the bandage then moved toward the fridge.

Coffee. That was what he needed—his practical routine. He liked his coffee lukewarm—an oddity, he knew. But he liked what he liked, and his way of doing things provided for it. It had started when he was a young teenager, working part-time and trying to keep up with his schoolwork. He hated the taste of coffee back then, but it buzzed him enough that he could get everything done. And if he put enough cream in coffee, it ended up lukewarm. He preferred more coffee to cream now, but the lukewarm part remained oddly comforting.

And having Nora here was oddly comforting, too, as much as he hated to admit it.

"I'll get breakfast," Nora said, taking a mesh basket of eggs from the fridge. She paused to look down at the babies in their little bouncy chairs then glanced at her watch. "They'll need their bottles in an hour."

"I've already eaten." He put down his coffee on the counter and reached up for the slow cooker from the top of the cupboards. "But I'll start dinner."

Dinner was going to consist of pulled pork on some crusty rolls. The beauty of a slow cooker meant that the cooking could happen while he was out working. Single men had to suss up their dinner somehow, and he'd had a lot of practice in fending for himself. He had a whole lot less practice in providing for a family, though, even if they weren't his. He could have steeled himself to Nora again, but the babies complicated things. Or that was what he told himself. It was impossible to look down at a baby and refuse to feel something, and once he let in one feeling, the rest all tumbled in after it.

"You have Great-Granny's iron skillet!" Nora exclaimed, and he glanced over his shoulder.

"Your dad said I could have it if I wanted, and those iron skillets can go forever if you care for them right."

She looked like she was trying to hold back something between tears and anger, and he cleared his throat. Was that wrong to keep the skillet? He felt like he'd messed up somehow.

"Look, if you want it, take it," he said. "I can buy another one in town easy enough. It just seemed like a waste not to use it, that's all."

"I do want it," she said quickly.

"It's yours."

"Thank you."

Nora pulled a loaf of bread out of the bread box. She moved comfortably in this space—like she owned the place. But that didn't offend him this morning; it made him imagine doing this every day for the foreseeable future…her footsteps in the house, the scent of her perfume wafting through the place, navigating around her in the kitchen come breakfast time.

"Is that why you kept the curtains?" she asked as she cracked eggs into a bowl.

He glanced toward the window and shrugged. "I kept them for memory's sake. You told me how you'd made them to fit that exact window, and I—"

How to explain… He hadn't been able to take them down. They'd been something made by Nora, and she'd meant something to him. So he'd kept the curtains as a part of his own history—a piece of her.

"I guess I just thought they belonged. You can take them, too, if you want."

"No, that's okay." She kept her head down as she

whipped the eggs. "They belong there. I'm glad they made the cut, that's all."

She tossed some butter into the pan and it sizzled over the heat. It looked like she was having French toast.

Easton grabbed the pork roast from the fridge and deposited it into the crock pot. An upended bottle of barbecue sauce was as complicated as it got. They worked in silence for a few minutes, the sound of frying filling the kitchen in a comforting way. He hated how good this felt—a quiet domestic scene. He wished that having another person in his space were more irritating, because he didn't want to miss her when she was gone. It would be easier if he'd be relieved to see her go.

Cliff had suggested that he find "some nice girl" and get married, but "some nice girl" wasn't going to be enough to wash out his feelings for Nora. He suspected Cliff was trying to be helpful. He'd never told the older man how he felt about Nora, but Cliff wasn't stupid, and Easton wasn't that great of an actor. But it wasn't going to be quite as easy as hooking up with a "nice girl," nor would it be fair to the woman who ended up with him.

"My great-grandparents had seven kids in this house," Nora said, breaking the silence.

Easton glanced at the ceiling, toward the two bedrooms upstairs. There was another room that could have been used for a bedroom off the living room downstairs, though he used it for storage.

"That would have been cozy," he said wryly.

"Well, there was a bit of a gap between the eldest two and the youngest five. So by the time the youngest baby came along, the eldest were getting married and leaving home."

"And your dad—" Easton had never heard too many

details from Cliff. This was family land, accumulated over generations—he knew that much. Cliff had never expanded upon the story, though.

"My grandfather was the eldest, so he inherited the farm, and in turn left it to his eldest son, my dad," she said.

"And you'll inherit it next," he concluded.

"Yes." She pulled some French toast out of the pan and began soaking the next batch of bread.

"So why did you leave?" he asked.

Nora shot him an irritated look. "Did my dad complain about that?"

"No, I'm just curious," he replied. "You're next in line to run this place, and you take off for the city and get a degree in accounting. It doesn't make sense."

She was quiet for a moment then heaved a sigh. "Accounting is important for ranching these days. You need to know where the money is going and where it's coming from. If you don't have a handle on the numbers, it doesn't much matter how good you are with the cattle."

"Except that you didn't come back."

"Because I didn't want to," she snapped.

Easton was silent. She was ticked off now, and he wasn't quite sure which button he'd pushed. She was the one with all this family pride.

She sighed, and her expression softened. "I'm not living for a funeral," she said after a moment. "I've seen cousins doing that—constantly planning for the day they inherit, but my parents had me young. My mom is fifty-two. What am I going to do, spend the next twenty or thirty years living at home, trying to wrest the reins away from her? I could work with Dad really well, but you know exactly how well my mom and I get along. I had a choice—stay close to home and keep my thumb in the pie, or put some distance between us and have a life of my own. I chose to make my own life. I could always come back when they needed me, but coming back before then—"

She didn't have to finish the thought—he knew about the tensions between Nora and Dina. Nora had only ever visited for a few days at a time, and he knew that her stay in Hope would wear thin sooner or later. There had been a reason why she'd stayed away, and these babies didn't change the underlying problem.

"You won't be here for long, will you?" he asked.

"Probably not," she admitted. "I only have twelve weeks parental leave and I'll have to go back to my life in the city sooner or later."

"Okay." He wished his voice sounded more casual than it did, but he could hear the tension in it. He cleared his throat.

"Easton, I'm a grown woman."

"I know." He was painfully aware of that fact. "I just wanted to know what to expect. Thanks for telling me."

It suddenly occurred to him: she'd probably been counting on this house for when she did come back to stay. That would explain why she was so upset—her dad gave away her safety net. He didn't know how she planned to make this work with the babies, with the ranch, with her mom…but the old homestead would have been a convenient answer. Except he now owned the solution to her complicated situation, and he couldn't help but feel mildly guilty about that.

"I don't have a whole lot of options here in Hope," she said.

Her self-pity was irritating, though. She had actually

expected to waltz back into a life here at the ranch—at *her* convenience, not anyone else's.

"Not a lot of options?" He shot her an incredulous look. "You're the sole heir of six hundred acres. You have a university degree. Seriously, Nora. You're spoiled. You have every privilege and you don't even see it."

She blinked. "Did you just call me spoiled?"

Yeah, he had. If he was a little better rested, he might have rethought that one, but it was the truth. She always had been—her dad had mollycoddled her from the start. Nothing was too good for his little girl.

"Figure out what you're going to do," Easton said. "And for the record, I'm not pushing you out. I'm just not feeling as sorry for you as you'd like."

This was the thing—life was hard for everyone, not just Nora. In fact, life was arguably harder for pretty much everyone else. He could appreciate the position she was in, but she wasn't as stuck as she seemed to think.

"I didn't ask for your pity," she snapped. "And I *will* figure it out, but I'm not in any position to make promises about how long I'll be here."

Well, Easton wasn't in a position to make promises, either, and he had his own complications to sort out, without the benefit of a massive inheritance to come or a university degree to bolster him up. Cliff had left him this house for a reason, but the older man wasn't much of a talker. He'd told him that having someone living in the place full-time, someone with a stake in it, would take a load off his shoulders. Easton had even been considering renting the place from his boss, and then Cliff had passed away.

If he'd been a renter, would it still have been this awkward? Easton needed a few answers of his own if he was going to be able to go on living here, making a life out of this once-in-a-lifetime gift. He needed to know why Cliff Carpenter had given him this small patch of land, and ease his nagging conscience.

Chapter 5

The days here on the ranch were bleeding into each other. Maybe it was the lack of sleep or the constant feedings and diapers, but Nora was getting to the point where she wasn't even sure what day it was anymore. She'd had to check the date on her cell phone to be sure—it had been a full week now since she'd arrived. She had a doctor's appointment for the babies that she couldn't miss. She wasn't used to the blur of motherhood. It was exhausting in a whole different way than she was used to—no breaks, no turning off. At least in her bookkeeping job she could leave the office and turn off her phone. She could have silence, a bubble bath, let her mind wander. But with the babies, she was on constant alert, listening for cries or thinking ahead to feedings…

The last few days, she and Easton had been on egg

shells. He'd been out a lot, checking fences and cattle—more than was necessary, it seemed to her. And she'd been trying to stay as polite as possible, to keep her intrusion to a minimum. This wasn't going to last, and one of these days, she had a feeling one of them was going to snap again.

Today Nora could use another nap—the only way she seemed to get sleep these days—and she was about to try to lie down for ten minutes when her cell phone rang. She seriously considered ignoring it, but when she saw the name on her screen, she relented. It was Kaitlyn Mason, her oldest friend.

"Why didn't you let me know you were in town?" Kaitlyn asked when she picked up.

"It's complicated…" Nora confessed.

"Yeah, so I heard. Even more reason for a friend, right? You need coffee. I'm sure of it. And you need to vent."

"And you need to tell me about married life," Nora added. "I haven't seen you since the wedding. It's been like two years. Wow."

"See?" Nora could hear the smile in Kaitlyn's voice. "It's an absolute necessity. Now, do I come to you, or do we meet up in town?"

It would be nice to get out alone, if that was possible. Was it? Or was that selfish, like Easton has accused her of? Just then Riley started to whimper—very likely a wet diaper. She poked a finger into the top and felt dampness. Yep, wet diaper. Was it wrong to want some time to herself this badly? And was it normal to feel guilty about it?

"I'm going to call my mom and see if she can watch

the babies," Nora said. "I'd love to get out to see you for a couple of hours—alone. I'll call you back, okay?"

So Nora changed Riley's diaper, and then Bobbie's and Rosie's, too. Then she dialed her mother. Dina agreed to look after the girls for a couple of hours, and Nora felt a weight lift off her shoulders. Still, she felt that same nagging guilt—not only because she was getting some time off, but also because her mother was going to be looking after Mia's babies. Doing this alone was hard...really hard. And this was what grandmothers were for, right? Grandmas were on a whole different level than babysitters. If these weren't Mia's babies, but Nora's own, she wouldn't feel any guilt at all about having her mother babysit. Her own grandmother had watched her on a regular basis when she was young, and she'd treasured that relationship. Her grandma had played with her, told her stories and after a few hours together would look down into her face and say, "You are such a special girl, Nora." The triplets deserved to have a grandma who thought they were special girls, too.

When Nora arrived at the main house a few minutes later, her mother helped her to unload the babies from their car seats and get them settled inside. They were awake by then, and three pairs of brown eyes stared up solemnly from their bouncy chairs. Dina squatted next to the babies, her expression melancholy.

"They've all been fed and changed," Nora said. "Their next bottle is due at 2:30, but I find it helps to start about fifteen minutes early. I feed Rosie or Riley first and feed Bobbie last. She's able to wait a little more patiently than the other two. Riley can't stand a wet diaper, so if she cries, you can be pretty positive it's that. If you change Riley, it's a good idea to change the other two at the same time, otherwise it gets really overwhelming. Rosie is a snuggler, and she'd stay in your arms the whole time if you let her. I don't like Bobbie to be neglected, though, just because she's a little stronger—"

"Sweetheart." Dina stood up and put a hand on Nora's arm. "We'll be okay."

Would they? It wasn't really the babies she was worried about; it was her mother. This couldn't be an easy task for her. Dina regarded her with misty eyes. Suddenly, the strong, resilient woman who had strode through Nora's life with an answer for everything looked fragile.

"Mom, are you all right?"

Dina wiped an errant tear from her cheek.

"It's not what you think."

"Do they remind you—"

"No, no." Dina shook her head. "I mean, of course they do, but it's not that. It's just that I remember knowing you that well, once upon a time. You liked being on my hip every waking hour, and you'd toddle around in a wet diaper for hours. You hated being changed."

"I grew up," Nora said with a small smile. "It happens to the best of us."

"I know, but I could make anything better for you back then. I can't anymore." Dina sighed. "And while you grew up, I never stopped being your mom."

There had been a time when her mother had been able to predict every passing mood that Nora had, but that was in the days of strawberry-picking and whipped cream. If she raised these girls, would they drift away one day, too? Would she lose this ability to make things right for them?

Nora was tired, overwhelmed. She hadn't slept properly since the babies arrived almost two weeks ago, and every waking moment was taken up with diapers and bottles, crying and soothing…all times three.

"Mom, you doing this—taking care of the babies for a couple of hours—this is just what I need right now. And I really appreciate it."

And she meant that with every fiber of her being.

"Well." Dina cast her daughter a smile. "I'm glad."

Nora adjusted her purse on her shoulder and looked down at the babies. "I've been thinking about it lately… And I'm not sure that I'll be able to, but I want to keep these girls. And if I would be Mom to them, that will make you their grandmother…sort of. Right?"

Dina winced and swallowed hard. "I'm not their grandmother. Angela Hampton is their grandmother."

"Angela's dead," Nora replied. "And so is Mia."

"We're the *other* family." Dina's eyes glittered with tears. "It's not the same. I know you love them, sweetheart, but it's not the same at all."

If they were looking for *the same*, they could stop searching. Nothing would be the same again—Nora's father was gone, and his memory was tarnished. The security she'd had in her parents' marriage had been whipped out from under her. That was the thing—she was just recognizing it now: her father's affair had taken away her ability to trust. If she couldn't trust her own father, how could she trust anyone? Even an old friend like Easton suddenly became suspect.

"No, it's not the same as if I were the natural mother, but we're all the babies have," Nora countered.

"You're not the one who was cheated on," her mother replied. "It's easier for you. These girls are the grandchildren of the woman who slept with my husband behind my back. They belong to your idiot father and that woman—together. And I'm left out of that."

Did her mother think that Nora was unaffected by her father's infidelity? She'd been affected—very deeply—but she also had three innocent babies looking to her for love and comfort. She'd been thrown into the deep end of motherhood, and she didn't get the luxury of sifting through her feelings.

"This *isn't* easy for me," she retorted. "My dad cheated on my mom. That's not pretty. That's not pleasant. I had a half sister I never knew—a half sister I shouldn't have had. My role model for what to look for in a husband of my own turned out to be the wrong kind of man."

"I'm just suggesting that you think it through," her mother said, her tone tense. "Because I'm not Grandma. I can't be."

That felt like a rejection to Nora—of the babies, but also of her. "You actually could," Nora replied, emotion catching her throat. "If you chose to be. You're *my* mother."

"I can't…" Her mother shook her head, sorrow shining through her eyes.

Nora could see the truth in her mother's words. This wasn't about what should be or what could be…this was about what her mother could give and what she couldn't. She'd had her heart broken twice—first by her husband's death, and then by the revelation that he hadn't been faithful. Dina couldn't be the grandmother Nora needed her to be. She couldn't look down into these girls' faces and tell them how special they were …

"I'll cancel with Kaitlyn," Nora said.

"For crying out loud, Nora, I'm not a monster." Her mother tugged a hand through her hair in exasperation. "I can babysit."

Nora met her mother's misty gaze. Right now all Nora wanted was for her mother to become that strong, resilient font of all answers again. She wanted to hear her mother say that everything would be all right, and that they'd figure this out together. But that wasn't going to happen, because everything would not be all right. Everything was broken.

"Thanks, Mom," Nora said past the lump in her throat. "I won't be more than a couple of hours."

Nora shut the door and headed out to her truck. She'd come home because she couldn't imagine doing this alone, but it didn't look like she'd have much option. If she kept these babies, she'd be a single mom in every way.

That afternoon when Easton came back to the house for a coffee, he found a note on the fridge from Nora saying that she'd gone out for a few hours. It was strange, because coming back to the empty house had been all he'd wanted lately—to get back to normal— but it felt lonely, too. He'd started getting used to having her around, was almost tempted to call out "I'm home!" when he got back from working in the fields.

When he'd gotten back to the house after their argument, they'd both apologized for being too harsh and agreed that being both overtired and under the same roof was stressful for the both of them. So he'd been trying to be a more gracious host. He wasn't sure if it was working or not, because Nora was almost too nice to him lately, too—like someone who didn't know him well enough to be straight with him. And they had enough history to make that flat-out wrong. Regardless, there had been no more fights.

That afternoon he'd ridden out to the north field to check on the bulls, and on the way, he'd talked to Scarlet about the whole situation. Except that talking to Scarlet only made him realize all the things he wanted to say to Nora—if they weren't in the middle of this politeness standoff, that is.

Cliff had advised him to find a nice girl, and maybe he should do that. This time with Nora could be used to get her out of his system, and then he should look around next time he was at church and start thinking more seriously about filling up this house with a family of his own. Playing house wasn't going to suffice.

Easton had an hour or so before he needed to head out to the barn and check up on a sick cow, and without Nora here, he had a chance to do something he'd put off for too long. He gulped back some coffee then headed up the narrow staircase to the top floor. He paused, looking up at the attic door in the ceiling above.

Easton had seen a couple of boxes in the attic when he'd moved in. When he'd peeked inside, they looked like Cliff's things so he'd let them be. Maybe it was grief, or he'd simply been too tired to deal with the boxes then, but now that Nora had made him question why Cliff had left him the house, he'd been thinking about those boxes again. Maybe there'd be a few answers. And maybe not. Cliff had left these boxes in the homestead for a reason, and Easton suspected it was because he hadn't wanted his wife and daughter to know about them.

He pulled on the cord, and the attic stairs swung slowly down. He unfolded them and they hit the wooden floor with a solid thunk. He climbed the narrow steps and ducked as he emerged into the A-frame room above. A single bulb hung nearby, and he clicked it on.

The attic was dusty but otherwise clean. An old single-width metal bed frame leaned against one side, half-rusted. A couple of cardboard liquor boxes were stacked next to it, and beside them some rat traps which were, thankfully, empty. There wasn't much else up here— probably cleaned out when the original owners died. He loved the feel of the attic—the warped panes of glass in the two square windows at either end of the room, the knot holes in the floorboards and the sense of lives lived for decade upon decade in this old house.

Easton had to duck to keep from hitting his head on the slanted roof, and he pulled the first box toward him and squatted next to it. He opened the flaps and peered inside. He found a worn denim jacket, a pair of old cowboy boots, a chipped coffee mug—nothing that looked terribly precious. Underneath the boots was nestled an old manila envelope. He took it out.

The envelope hadn't been sealed. Inside were what appeared to be a few old letters and a handful of photos. Easton sorted through the photos first. One was of a newborn, all bundled up, the date September 12, 1988 written on the bottom next to Mia's full name: *Mia Alexandra Sophia Hampton.* Angela hadn't used the Carpenter name for their daughter. There were a few pictures of a blonde toddler with her brown-haired mother. Angela was rounded, with a full bust and ample hips. She was attractive enough, and Easton paused, looking at the photo, trying to imagine Cliff Carpenter with this woman. Angela wore a little too much makeup for Easton's taste, but he could see her love for the little girl in her arms, and that was what mattered. A few years of photos seemed to be missing, and then a school picture of Mia as a blonde little girl with braces and freckles, and then as a teenager without braces. Mia had been quite lovely. Next was a snapshot of her as a young woman in front of a Route 66 sign, squinting into the sunlight. She had her mother's full bust and ample hips, but her face looked more like the Carpenters. There was something in her sparkling blue eyes that reminded him of Nora.

Easton sighed, putting the photos aside. Mia had grown up, and Cliff had known about his daughter, apparently. He looked at the address on the envelopes—a PO box in town. Cliff had gone out of his way to keep this hidden. There were about a dozen letters, and he picked one at random.

These probably weren't his business. Cliff hadn't meant them to be anyone's business. Still, Easton would take a look and see what was here. If it was damning enough, he would burn the lot and let Cliff keep some posthumous privacy. But there was the chance that this might give Nora and her mother a few answers.

The first letter he opened was dated May, 1998.

Dear Cliff,
Mia is doing well. She's getting As and Bs in school, and the money you sent will go for her summer camp. Her best friend is going and she's been pleading to be allowed to go for months now, so your money couldn't have arrived at a better time. She still wants to play the violin, but I can't afford the lessons, or the instrument. I've looked into it, but it's just too much. Maybe you

could consider helping her with that if her interest doesn't change.

Thank you for your support. You should know that she's been asking more and more questions about why she doesn't have a dad. The other kids have dads, even if they aren't in their lives. It would mean a lot to her to know your name, at least. She wouldn't have to contact you. I know you have your family and we wouldn't interfere. Please reconsider letting me tell her.
Angela.

The next letter was dated December, 2008.

Dear Cliff,
Thank you for the recent money. Mia is working two jobs to pay for her college tuition, and she's exhausted. She's switched majors, and now she's taking Education. She wants to teach elementary school. The money you sent will help to buy books next semester, and she's very grateful. She asked me to thank you.

I have some bad news. I've had back pain for a few months, and finally went to a doctor about it. It's cancer—stage 3. It's in my spine—quite treatable—and in my liver. There's hope, and I'll fight it, but my insurance will only go so far. I have no intention of dying yet—our daughter still needs me. I haven't told Mia yet, though. She needs to focus on her studies.

If the worst should happen, don't forget about your daughter.
Angela.

It looked like Angela had told Mia about her father at some point. Easton knew from Nora that Angela had passed away, and he could only assume it was from the cancer.

He opened another envelope, and this one was different than the others—written in a child's hand. His breath caught in his throat as he scanned the printed words:

Dear Dad,
I only call you Dad because I don't know your name, because if I knew your name, I'd call you that. But Mom—Mom was underlined three times—*says she'll mail this to you, and I can say anything I want to you. So here goes.*

I hate you. I think you're awful. You don't even know me, and you don't want me. I'm a nice person. My friends say that I'm too good for a deadbeat dad like you. I don't care that you send money, because I don't want any of it. You can keep it and spend it on whatever stupid stuff you buy yourself.

My mom loves me and we do just fine on our own. We don't need you, and we don't need your money. So if you don't want to know me, and I'm a super-good person, you know, then you can get lost.

But if you wanted to know me, you'd find out that I'm pretty smart, and I'm nice to people, and I love animals, and my favorite color isn't purple like every girl in my class, it's green. And I'm going to be a marine biologist when I grow up. That's what you'd find out, and you'd probably

*like me, too. But you don't get to find out how nice
I am, because even if you wanted to meet me, I'd
say, "Sorry, I'm too busy being super-nice and
super-fun."*
Without any love at all,
Mia Hampton.

There was a PS tagged at the end in Angela's handwriting: *I'm sorry about Mia. She's really angry right now, but I promised I'd send this letter no matter what. We do need the money. One day she'll understand how much you provided. I promise you that.—A*

The poor kid. Her loneliness, her anger, her desperation to be wanted by her dad—it all just shone through that letter, and Easton couldn't help but wonder how Cliff had dealt with all of that. Obviously, he had never told his wife and daughter about the other little girl out there who hated him because she wanted to be loved so badly.

Had Cliff ever written his daughter back? Or had that letter gone unanswered? Easton wished he knew, but everyone concerned had passed away.

Nothing else was in the box, and the one underneath it held only an incomplete set of old encyclopedias.

This child hadn't been a secret from Cliff, obviously, but it also didn't look like the affair was long-lived. Angela had never seemed to be pleading for anything, and Easton wondered if that would be a relief to Nora on some level. Maybe it was a one-time mistake and not some lifetime of philandering.

This was an odd relief to Easton, he had to admit. He'd always looked up to Cliff, and his fall from grace had hit Easton, too. He knew what it was like to have a disappointing father. He'd grown up with a father who embarrassed him constantly and hadn't been able to provide for him. But Cliff had been different—principled, successful, solid. Cliff had been the kind of man Easton would have wanted in a father, and he'd become a sort of father figure to him over the years. So finding out that Cliff had another child out there—that had hurt his sense of decency, even if Easton didn't have a right to feel it.

"You weren't my dad," he muttered.

But even with this mess, Nora was lucky. She still had more than she thought she did because while her father had been flawed, Cliff had at least been there for her. He'd raised her, provided for her, taught her what he could. Easton probably had more in common with Mia—standing on the outside of something they'd never have. So while Cliff's fall from grace was disappointing, it wasn't a betrayal to Easton. At least it wasn't supposed to be.

It hung heavy around his neck, but mostly he felt sorry for Cliff... In life, the man had been respected, admired, trusted. If Cliff had lived to see this, he'd have been crushed.

Maybe it was too late to offer, but this was one thing Easton could give his late boss: absolution, from him, at least. Because Cliff owed him nothing.

Chapter 6

Nora arrived at The Vanilla Bean coffee shop and parked in the angled parking out front. She could feel the pressure leaking out of her. She needed a break, and she still wasn't sure if that made her a bad mother. All she knew was that she felt lighter already for having driven by herself without three infants in the back of her truck.

"Kaitlyn!" Nora wrapped her arms around her friend and gave her a squeeze. "It's so good to see you!"

The Vanilla Bean hadn't changed a bit over the years. It still sported the same framed photos from decades past—Main Street before the murals had been painted, the old grain elevator in use, a grinning bull rider having won a ribbon in the 1957 county fair. There was also a bookshelf with a sign above that read "Lending Library—take a book, leave a book." Nora had read her first romance novel from that shelf—a scandalous secret that she hid from her parents and read out by the barn. This place held the town's history as well as their own, and no matter how long she stayed away, there was a part of her that counted on places like the Vanilla Bean to stay exactly the same.

Kaitlyn had put on a little weight since Nora had seen her last, but it suited her—adding some roundness to her figure. And she wore her hair in a bob now. Kaitlyn's eyes crinkled as she smiled. She motioned toward the table by the window where two coffees were already waiting. "I hope you aren't dieting, because I got you a mochaccino—for old time's sake."

They felt oh so grown up when they'd come here as teens. The last time they'd been here was just before Kaitlyn's Christmas wedding a couple of years earlier. Nora slid into the seat and pried the lid off the cup. This felt good to be out, away from it all for a little while. She watched as two pickup trucks going in opposite directions down the street stopped so that the drivers could talk through open windows.

"It's perfect," Nora said. "So how are you?"

"I'm good." She sipped her drink and licked her lips. "I'm not pregnant—that's what everyone asks. I swear, you gain a pound and everyone wants to be the first one to call it."

"They don't." Nora grimaced.

"They do." Kaitlyn nodded. "But it's okay. I survive it. Everyone is doing it to Nina, too, so I feel better."

"How is Nina?" Nora asked. Kaitlyn's sister had a bit of a scandalous past, having cheated on her fiancée who was fighting in Afghanistan and marrying his best friend while he was away.

"Their son is two now—smart as a whip, that kid. He already knows his alphabet. She's exhausted, but happy...but exhausted. So Brody and I wanted some time alone before we threw ourselves into that."

"I don't blame you," Nora agreed. Kaitlyn's husband came back to Hope when he was wounded in the war, and he was still recovering emotionally. "I'm exhausted, too, and it's only been a few days with the babies. It's harder than I thought."

"So what's going on?" Kaitlyn asked. "I heard a few rumors, but..."

Nora gave as brief an explanation as possible, and as the words came out, she felt relief. She'd been taking this one step at a time from discovering her half sister's existence to becoming the mother of three newborns overnight, and Kaitlyn's expression of sympathy and disbelief was comforting. Her life had turned upside down in a matter of weeks, and some sympathy helped.

"How are you and your mom dealing with all this?" Kaitlyn asked.

"We're—" Nora paused. Were they even dealing with it? They were stumbling through it, not exactly handling anything besides putting one foot in front of the other. "We're in shock still, I think," she concluded. "Thank God Mackenzie thought of us and sent a triplet stroller. I didn't even know where to start."

"Mackenzie is great," Kaitlyn agreed.

"The funny thing is, I keep seeing married couples having babies everywhere I go," Nora confessed. "Mack and Chet have three now, right? And here I am with three babies and no husband...or boyfriend. And the explanation is just so freaking complicated."

"Look, you'll feel like you have to explain yourself

no matter what. I'm married, and everyone is anxious for me to have a baby. If you're not married, everyone is anxious to find you someone. There's no point in worrying about public opinion, because you'll always be lacking in something. Those babies are lucky to have you."

"Are they?" Nora sighed. "The truth is, I can't afford them. Not alone. That's why I came home. I was hoping that I could sort something out with my mom so we could take care of them together. I could quit my job in the city and come back to Hope and find something part time in bookkeeping and put the rest of my time into the girls. But that's not really an option."

"And there's no help?" Kaitlyn asked.

"I'm a bookkeeper, Kate." Nora shook her head. "I work hard. I have a one-bedroom apartment in Billings. I can't afford day care, a bigger place in a decent part of town, clothes, formula, diapers... It's overwhelming. And if I can't sort something out—"

She didn't want to finish the thought out loud, because she hadn't actually admitted it to herself until now. She'd have to give the babies up to another family that could give them the life she couldn't provide herself.

The thought caught her heart in a stranglehold, and for a moment, she felt like she couldn't inhale. Give them up. That was the obvious solution that she'd been avoiding looking at all this time. She'd been hoping that something would present itself—some solution that would make it all come together.

"*Would* you give them up?" Kaitlyn asked quietly.

Nora shook her head. "I really don't want to, but I have to wonder what's best for them. My mom can't be a grandmother to them...they remind her of what my dad did to her. How do you explain that to your kids—this is my mother, but don't call her Grandma. It's not right. The girls would be the ones to suffer."

"I can understand that, though," Kaitlyn said. "If I found out that Brody had cheated on me—even that many years ago—and I was supposed to just accept his child by another woman, or his grandchild… That's a lot to ask."

"I know." It all felt so impossible. "I don't know what to do. Eventually, I'll have to figure something out."

"Maybe give it time?" Kaitlyn suggested.

Did time make it better or worse? That depended on whether her mom changed her mind about this. If she didn't, then Nora would have taken even more time to fall in love with the babies before she had to let them go.

"I'm not sure," she confessed. "But that's okay. I was hoping to hear all the news today, not wallow in my own self-pity. How are Dakota and Andy?"

Dakota had married Andy Granger just before Kaitlyn and Brody got married. Andy sold his half of the ranch he and his brother inherited and then left town. Everyone hated him at that point, because he'd sold out to some big city yahoos. But then he came back to help run a cattle drive for his brother, and Dakota had been hired onto the team. She'd hated him, but something happened on that drive that changed it all, because when they got back, they got engaged.

Tears misted Kaitlyn's eyes, and Nora felt a flash of alarm. What had she said? She reached out and took her hand. Kaitlyn swallowed a couple of times and blinked back tears. Something was wrong. Here she'd been so focused on her own life that she'd completely missed that something was deeply wrong in her friend's.

"What's going on, Kate?" Nora asked, leaning forward.

"Dakota's pregnant. Andy is over the moon—you've never seen a happier guy. He keeps trying to do things for her, and Dakota is all hormonal and wants to kill him." Kaitlyn forced a smile, although it didn't reach her eyes. "It's cute. If he survives this pregnancy, they'll make great parents."

"And yet you're crying," Nora said. Those hadn't been sympathetically happy tears.

Kaitlyn was silent for a moment, then she licked her lips. "I can't seem to get pregnant. Everyone else around me is either pregnant or a new mom... You aren't the only one noticing it. We've been trying since the honeymoon. I told you that we're just taking some time to be a couple, but that's not even true."

"Oh, Kate..."

"I was never the baby fever type. I just assumed that since we were...doing all the things it takes to make a baby...that it would just happen. Like with Nina. Like with Dakota. Like with every woman I seem to come across! This is supposed to be natural."

"It'll happen..." Nora said, but she knew she couldn't promise that any more than Kaitlyn could assure her that she'd find the man of her dreams. Sometimes life didn't pan out the way you wanted it to. Sometimes deeply devoted couples remained childless. Sometimes good women didn't find their guy.

"It'll happen when it happens," Kaitlyn agreed. "We're doing all the right things—on a daily basis."

A smile flickered across her face. "I shouldn't complain, should I?"

Nora laughed softly. Considering that Kaitlyn had a gorgeous husband to "do all the right things" with on a *daily* basis... She felt some heat in her cheeks. "They say the trying is the fun part, don't they?"

"They do say that." Kaitlyn smiled and wiped her eyes. "Sorry, I honestly didn't want to talk about this. I was supposed to be *your* supportive friend. So where are you staying? With your mom?"

"No, in the old farmhouse," Nora said. "With Easton, actually."

Kaitlyn's eyebrows rose, and she paused in the wiping of her eyes. "With Easton? How is that?"

"You know my father left him the homestead in his will, right?"

"I'd heard." Kaitlyn winced. "I'm sorry about that."

"Well, he has a guest bedroom so I'm using that with the babies. My mom can't deal with three newborns right now, and it's all so complicated, so this is a way to give her some breathing space. There isn't a huge amount of room in the homestead, but we're squeezing in."

"I'm not asking about sleeping arrangements," Kaitlyn replied with a quirky smile. "Unless I should be?"

"No!" Nora leaned back in her chair. "I haven't changed that much."

"But how is it with Easton?" Kaitlyn pressed. "I remember how crazy he was about you."

That was an exaggeration. Kaitlyn had always thought that Easton was in love with her, but Nora never believed it. They were friends, that was all. They talked about her boyfriends and sometimes went riding together. Easton had a bit of a crush for a while, but they'd moved past that.

"It wasn't as exciting as you think," Nora replied.

"You're wrong there." Her friend finished wiping her eyes. "What he felt for you was significantly more than friendship."

Had Easton really felt more for Nora? She'd thought that Easton got a lot from their friendship…like friendship. But maybe she'd been the naive one.

"I didn't think it was anything more than me hitting puberty first," she admitted.

"Do you remember that one birthday—I think you turned fifteen—when the girls snubbed you, and I was the only one to show up at your party?" Kaitlyn asked. "I think Easton had just started working at your place, and he brought you those wildflowers from the far pasture."

"That was sweet," Nora agreed. Easton had always been thoughtful that way, and she'd often thought that whatever girl he settled down with would be lucky to have him. He'd be a good boyfriend—to someone else. She just hadn't been attracted to him. And it wasn't because of his acne—that wasn't his fault, and she wasn't that shallow. He was a good friend, but she couldn't make the leap to something more.

"And when you broke up with whatever guy you were dating, who was there to talk you through it?"

"I get it, I get it." Nora shrugged weakly. "He was a decent guy—more than decent. I just wasn't interested back then."

"And now?" Kaitlyn asked.

"Now?" Nora shook head. "*He* isn't interested anymore, either. That's all in the past."

"Oh. That's too bad, because he most certainly grew up." She shot Nora a meaningful look.

Nora wasn't oblivious to how ruggedly good-looking Easton had turned out to be, but she chuckled. "He's not the same guy willing to do anything to make me happy anymore. So you can rest easy on that. He's willing to tell me what he really thinks of me now, and frankly... it's better this way."

Spoiled. That had been his descriptor. She'd been rather shocked to have Easton talk to her like that, but it was better than leading him on. The last thing she needed was to be pussyfooting around Easton's feelings. She had enough to worry about with the babies, with her mom...

"That *would* be better," Kaitlyn agreed. "For him, at least."

"Besides," Nora said. "He came out on top. He's walked away with three acres and my family's history."

"Did he know your father was changing his will?" Kaitlyn took a sip of her latte. "He was getting a lot of job offers at bigger ranches. He's good, you know. Your dad must have kept him around by putting him into the will."

That would actually make sense. Maybe her father hadn't signed it over because of tender feelings—it was possible he'd been negotiating with his ranch manager. That would make everything different...including her view of Easton. Her father had kept secrets—why not one more? Could it really come down to something as common as holding on to a skilled employee?

If that were the case, then Easton would be a whole lot less innocent than he appeared. Could he have actually been angling for that land? He'd said he wasn't, but he wouldn't be the first man to lie to her, either.

"You might be onto something," Nora said. "I've been going over this in my head repeatedly, trying to figure out why my dad would do that… It's like I never knew him."

"You know as well as I do that a good ranch manager is worth his weight in gold," Kaitlyn replied. "Easton is honest. He works like a horse. He's smart, too. My dad has said more than once that if he could afford Easton, he'd try to lure him over to our ranch."

"He wouldn't." Nora frowned.

"My dad?" Kaitlyn shrugged. "Maybe."

Mr. Harp was a jovial guy—but he was also a shrewd rancher. There was a strange balance with the Hope ranches—they were neighbors who supported each other and helped each other out, but they were also in competition for the best employees. The ranch would one day be hers, and it affected the way she'd looked at their land—including the three acres her father had left to Easton.

Easton could take another job if he wanted to. But another possibility made her stomach sink: maybe Easton was less of a nice guy than she'd always assumed. Just because he'd had a rough childhood didn't make him some kind of saint. Easton had some negotiation room, and he may have taken advantage of that.

"Who was trying to get Easton?" she asked.

"Not us," Kaitlyn said with a shake of her head. "But rumor around town was that some larger ranches out of state were putting their feelers out for experienced managers. A lot of people were mad. It's not nice to poach someone's manager after they've spent years grooming him."

Nora had no idea. Was it possible that she'd been duped by more than just her father?

Easton sat in the easy chair in the living room, listening to the sounds of Nora putting the babies to bed. Her voice was soft, the gentle tones carrying through the floorboards, but the words were muffled. It didn't matter what she was saying, of course. It was the comforting lilt that the babies would respond to.

His mom had never been that way—not that he could remember, and certainly not according to the stories his father had told him.

The stairs creaked as Nora made her way down and Easton looked away. He liked having her here, but he was getting increasingly aware of her presence. She was his guest and in his home, yet he still felt like he shouldn't be listening to the soft rustle of her moving around his home—like that was overstepping somehow. He certainly shouldn't be enjoying it.

"They're almost asleep," Nora said, emerging into the living room. She tapped her watch. "Three hours and counting."

She'd been distant all evening—polite, but closed off.

"You tired?" he asked.

"Always." She smiled wryly.

He'd been debating how much he should tell Nora, if anything, all afternoon. Was it his place? What would Cliff have wanted? And how could he possibly know? He shouldn't be in the middle of all this family drama—but maybe he should have seen complications coming.

"I went through the attic today," he said.

Nora sank into the recliner kitty corner to the couch and stifled a yawn. "Was there anything up there?"

He couldn't shoulder Cliff's secrets alone. He wasn't even sure it was fair of him to keep the letters to himself. Cliff wasn't his father, and Nora was the one who would live with a lifetime of questions.

"Your dad had put a box of personal effects up there," Easton said. "I saw it when I moved in but then forgot about it. I remembered it today, and I thought I'd take a look through it."

"My dad did?" She shot him a sharp look. "Why would he do that?"

Easton pushed himself to his feet and retrieved the box from the other side of the sofa. The contents would answer her questions better than he could.

"I don't know, exactly," he said. "But he did."

"That isn't true, though, is it?" She put a hand on top of the box but didn't look at it. Her gaze was fixed icily on him.

"What do you want from me?" he demanded. "Nora, this is awkward. I'm not supposed to be in the middle of your family issues. I found a box with your dad's things in it, and I'm handing it over."

"I had coffee with Kaitlyn Mason today."

That was supposed to mean something to him? Kaitlyn and Nora had been friends since school days. "Great. Glad you got out."

He was frustrated. He was a private man who had been sharing his personal space for a week now with a woman he used to love, and having her here with him, sleeping in the next room and sharing his living space… He was liable to start feeling things he shouldn't all over again if he let down his guard.

"She told me that you had job offers from bigger ranches," Nora went on. "And she suspected that you negotiated for this land in exchange for staying."

Easton blinked. She made it sound sordid, somehow, but it wasn't. "Why is it so surprising that I'd be in demand?" he asked. "I run a tight ship. I had offers, that's true. But I didn't strong-arm your dad into changing his will in exchange for sticking around."

"It didn't factor in at all?" Her tone made it clear she wasn't buying that.

"I was offered a position in Idaho for almost twice what I was making here," he said. "I mentioned it to your dad, but I hadn't even decided if the extra money would be worth it. But that had nothing to do with this house. He said that the house should be lived in, not just sitting there like a relic to days gone by."

"A relic. This is my great-grandparents' house!"

"I wasn't supposed to own it," he retorted. "He wanted me to live in it. I wasn't sure how I felt about that."

"And he decided to just leave it to you in the will?" She shook her head. "These three acres are more precious than the other five hundred ninety-seven. This is where it all started."

And this was the problem—family versus staff. She felt a connection to this land through blood, but for some reason that didn't evolve into actually doing anything. He was an employee here, and he could stay as long as he did his job. Family belonged in a whole different way, but ranches didn't run on sentimental feelings or rightful inheritances—they ran on hard work.

"If you cared about it so much, why didn't you tell him?" Easton retorted. "It isn't my fault you weren't helping out around here. If you showed the least bit of interest in your family's land—and this house—your dad might have done something differently."

"And you're just some innocent bystander who accidentally got some land." Her sarcasm was thick, and his patience was spent.

"All of a sudden I'm some thug, waiting to rob your family of three acres?" he demanded. "I'm the same guy I always was, Nora! You *knew* me! Have I ever been the kind of guy who would manipulate and lie? Cut me some slack!"

"I thought I knew my dad, too!" Her voice quivered and she shook her head, looking away. So that was it—she didn't know what to trust anymore, who was telling her truth. And he couldn't help her. Those were personal issues she'd have to sort out on her own.

"That's the box," he said instead. "I'm not hiding things from you, Nora."

A kind gesture from his boss had turned ugly fast. Her guess was as good as his when it came to why Cliff had done what he did, but he wasn't accepting the blame.

Nora sighed and pulled at the flaps. The boots were on top, and she put them on the floor.

"My mom kept trying to throw these out. They were worn through, and they had no more ankle support…"

She looked at the jacket and put it aside then pulled out the envelope. He knew this was the difficult part. She removed the letters one by one, fanned out the pictures on the floor in front of her. She opened the first letter, read it through, then the second. Easton just watched her.

"He knew about Mia," she said, looking up at Easton.

"Yeah." He wasn't sure what to say to that. This version of his boss—the secretive cheater—didn't sit right with him.

"It doesn't look like Dad and Angela were involved for long."

"That's good news, isn't it?"

"I think so." She pulled a hand through her hair. "I'm taking what I can get at this point. This is not the dad I remember."

"You'd know better than I would," he replied. He might have worked with Cliff, but the man had doted on his daughter. If anyone would have known that softer side of him, it would be Nora.

"He lied to me, too," she said woodenly.

He understood her anger at being lied to, but she didn't understand what utter honesty could get you. His mother had walked out and never once tried to contact him again—that had been honest. His dad had drunk himself into a stupor—that had been a pretty honest reaction, too. He'd have settled for some insincere security from his own parents any day, if it had meant that they'd actually stuck around and been there for him.

"Whatever the fallout," Easton said, "he made his choice—and you won."

Nora was silent for a couple of beats, then she sighed and began to gather the letters and photos back together into one stack.

"You're going to be okay," he said after a moment.

"Do you know that you're the first person to tell me that?" Her expression didn't look convinced. How could anyone comfort Nora in this? She'd lost her dad twice over, and nothing anyone said could make it better.

"And you can't forgive him?" Easton asked.

"I *believed* in him, Easton."

That seemed to be the part that cut her the deepest—she'd been fooled. And now she thought Easton had fooled her, too. But Easton knew he was the one man who hadn't been lying to her. He never had.

Nora pushed herself to her feet and stood there in the lamplight, her eyes clouded with sadness. He wished he could do something, say something, hold her, even, and make this hurt less. He could have been the teenage Easton again, looking at the girl he longed to comfort, knowing that she didn't really want what he had to offer. She wouldn't accept platitudes: *You deserve better.*

And she did deserve better—she always had. She deserved more than a sullied memory of the father she'd adored. She deserved more than the broken, scarred, albeit loyal heart of a man whose own mother hadn't wanted him.

"I'm going to go up to bed," she said after a moment of silence. "I have a doctor's appointment for the babies in the morning, so I'd better get some rest."

"Okay, sure."

She turned and left the room, and he watched her go. The scent of her perfume still hung in the air, as subtle as a memory. The creak of the stairs dissipated overhead. He had some evening chores to check up on, and he was grateful for the excuse to get out, plunge into the fresh air and get away from all of this for a little while. Work—it was cheaper than therapy.

Chapter 7

The next morning Nora sat in the driver's seat of her truck. The babies were all in their car seats behind her, diapers changed, tummies full. She felt like she'd achieved something, just getting this far. There had been two spit-ups just before leaving, one leaked diaper, Rosie had wanted nothing more than to be cuddled and Bobbie decided that she hated her car seat and didn't want to be strapped in. By the time Nora got them all into the truck, her nerves were frazzled. Now it felt good to just sit in relative silence—the soft sucking of pacifiers soothing her.

Nora had been angry the night before, and that hadn't exactly changed. He said he hadn't used his job offers as any kind of leverage with her dad…was she stupid to believe that? Apparently, she'd lived a lifetime of being altogether too trusting. And when she returned to Hope she'd trusted that Easton would be the same…to never be someone who would hurt her. Someone harmless.

He'd always been quiet, eager to please, willing to step aside for her. Now that she was an adult, she knew she didn't want him constantly giving in to her, but it was possible that she'd still expected it of him. But Easton had grown into a man—strong, resilient, with his own goals and objectives, and he was certainly not harmless anymore. She'd been comfortable feeling a little sorry for him, but she didn't like this new power he seemed to wield around here. And yet, mixed in with all that resentment, she missed him…or what they used to have…the guy who used to sit with her in haylofts and lean against fences as they talked.

Nora turned the key, and the engine moaned and coughed, but didn't turn over. She stopped, frowned then tried again. Nothing.

"Great!" she muttered. This was exactly what she needed. This doctor's appointment was important, and if she couldn't even manage this… She leaned her head against the headrest then heaved a sigh and tried to start the truck again. It ground for a few seconds but didn't start.

The rumble of an engine pulled up behind her, and she looked in the rearview mirror to see Easton. He must be done with his morning work and was back for some coffee. She'd been hoping to be gone by the time he returned. She unrolled her window as he hopped out of his truck and came up beside her.

"Morning," he said. "Everything all right?"

"Not really," she admitted. "I can't start the truck."

"Want me to take a look?"

Even if he got the truck to start, would she make the

appointment? She glanced at her watch. "I guess I'll call the doctor's office and say we can't make it."

It was like everything was against her succeeding in one small parenting task this morning. This was the goal for the entire day—go to an appointment. There was nothing else scheduled. Why did it have to be so hard? Was it like this for every mom, or just the wildly inexperienced ones?

Easton crossed his arms and looked away for a moment then nodded toward his vehicle. "Would you rather have a ride into town?"

Right now she didn't really feel like spending any extra time with Easton, but his offer would solve her problem.

"You probably need to eat, and I don't really have time, and if I'm not going to be late, we'd have to leave now," she rambled.

"Let me just clear out the backseat of my cab, and then we can get the car seats moved over," he said.

A kind offer wasn't going to make her trust him again. Regardless, she needed this favor, and she wasn't about to turn it down. Not this morning. If anything, he owed her after whatever he'd done to secure that land—this and so much more.

Ten minutes later they were bumping down the gravel road, past the barn and toward the main drive.

"Thank you," she said as they turned onto the highway. "I appreciate this."

"Sure," he said.

They fell into silence, the only sound the soft sucking of pacifiers from the backseat. It was a forty-minute drive into town, and Nora leaned her head back, watching the looping telephone wires zipping past outside the window.

"Remember that time we rode out past the fields and along the edge of the forest?" Easton asked.

Nora glanced at him. She did. It had been early spring, and she'd asked Easton to go with her. He hadn't wanted to at first because he still had work to do, but then she'd threatened to go alone, and he'd caved in.

"It was fun," she said. "Dad was furious when we got back."

"You were a terrible influence," he said with a teasing smile.

"Oh, I kept your life fun," she countered, chuckling. She'd always known she could convince Easton to do pretty much anything she wanted. All it took was a bat of her lashes. She felt bad about that now.

"You did." The teasing had evaporated from his tone. "Work kept me distracted from home, and you kept me distracted from work. You kept me sane. I ride out to check on fences and cattle, but I don't ride on my days off anymore."

"You should," she said.

"It's different without the company."

He didn't take his eyes off the road. Did he miss her, too? She could remember Easton with those sad eyes. He used to pause in the middle of a chore and look out into space, and she'd always been struck by the depth of sadness in his dark eyes. That had been part of why she liked to drag him away from his duties, because with her he'd laugh. She'd felt like she was rescuing him, saving him from whatever it was that was breaking his heart when he thought no one was looking...

"I was pretty mad last night," Nora said.

"Yeah, I got that."

She glanced over to catch a wry smile on his lips.

"You still mad?" he asked.

"Yes," she said. "I am, but not exclusively at you."

"That's something." He slowed as they came up behind a tractor, signaled and passed it.

"Here's what I want to know," she said. "And honestly. What was there between you and my dad that was so special? And don't say it was nothing, because obviously you were special to him."

Easton was silent for a few beats, then he said, "I didn't take him for granted."

"And I did?" She couldn't hide the irritation that rose at that.

Easton glanced at her and then back to the road. "Of course. He was your dad, and it was perfectly normal to take all that for granted. That's what kids do—they get used to a certain way of living, and they don't stop to think about all that goes into achieving it. That isn't a terrible thing, you know."

"But you were saintly and appreciative," she said, sarcasm edging her tone.

"I wasn't his kid," he retorted. "You're going to inherit all of that land, and I certainly won't. Cliff loved you heart and soul and always would. He was generally fond of me because I'd been around so long and I worked my tail off. There was a massive difference. I wasn't nosing in on your turf."

"That's ironic, because you ended up with my turf."

Easton smiled slightly. "Land isn't love, Nora. It was years of knowing my place. I wanted to learn from your dad, and he liked to teach me stuff. I would do anything extra he asked of me in order to learn. He made me into the professional I am today, and I never took that time with him for granted. Because he *wasn't* my dad."

"And that's why he liked you so much," she clarified.

"I think so," he said. "That and—" He stopped and color crept into his face. For a moment she could see the teenage boy in him again.

"And what?" she pressed.

"It's a little embarrassing," he said, "but he knew how I felt about you." He glanced at her, dark eyes meeting hers, then his gaze snapped back on the road. The moment had been fleeting, but she'd caught something in that eye contact—something deep and warm.

"So you had a crush," she said, trying to sound normal, but she still sounded breathy in her own ears. Bobbie started to whimper, and Nora reached behind her to pop her pacifier back into her mouth.

"It was a weird thing to bond over," Easton admitted. "But I was the one guy who thought you were just as amazing as your dad did."

"I always thought my dad hated the idea of us together," she said. "Anytime he caught us alone, like in the hayloft, he'd blow his top."

"That was then," he said. "After you left, he seemed to change his mind. He never liked the guys you dated, you know."

"They weren't so bad," she countered.

Easton chuckled but didn't answer. She'd known that her dad hated the guys she went out with in Billings. They were the kinds of guys whose boots had never seen mud.

"I kind of knew you had a crush," she admitted. "Kaitlyn thought it was more than that, but I told her it wasn't. You might have to reassure her."

"It was more."

Nora's heart sped up, and she cast about for something to say but couldn't come up with anything. More than a crush...what was that? Love?

"Anyway, after you left, your dad used to joke around that if he had to choose between one of those city slickers and me then he'd take me," Easton said.

"He never told me that." Not directly, at least. Her father had pointed out Easton's work ethic to her more than once. "He's the first one up, and the last one in," her dad had said. "He reminds me of myself when I was his age. You could do worse than finding a man who knows how to work hard, Nora." Was giving Easton the house her father's way of "handpicking" her husband? That wasn't really Cliff's style.

"Look, it was nice to have your dad's respect," Easton said. "But I wasn't the kind of guy who could be led to water, either. Regardless of how I felt about you. I respected your dad, and I appreciated all he did for me, but I make my own life choices."

"So you didn't really want anything more with me—" She didn't know what she was fishing for here—absolution, maybe?

"I didn't want to be the guy always chasing at your heels," he replied. "What I felt for you was considerably more than a crush, but I didn't want to chase you down and try to convince you I was worth your time. If you didn't know it yet, then that ship had sailed. I put my energy into getting over you instead."

"Pragmatic..." She swallowed.

"Always." He laughed softly, and her heart squeezed at the sound of it. He was every inch a man now, and it was a whole lot harder to ignore. But he'd made the right choice in getting over her.

"So you think Dad wanted us to get together," she clarified.

"I don't really think it matters what he wanted now," Easton said frankly. "He's gone."

Gone with her father were the days when Easton could be talked into horseback riding, and that was probably for the best.

"You're right," she admitted. "I might be able to pick that bone with him if he were still alive, but he's not."

Easton glanced toward her again, and she could see the warmth in his gaze—something that smoldered deeper. It wasn't the same shy look from years ago when he'd had a crush. This was the steady gaze of a man—unwavering, direct, knowledgeable.

He didn't say anything, though, and neither did she.

Easton parked in front of the two-story building that housed the doctor's office. It took a few minutes to get the babies out of the truck, and then Nora carried two car seats and he carried Rosie's into the waiting room. While Nora went to tell the receptionist that they'd arrived, Easton glanced around at the people seated in the chairs that edged the room. He nodded to two men he knew, and a couple of older ladies looked from the car seats to Nora and then up at Easton, their expressions filled with questions and dirty laundry, no doubt.

Easton glanced at his watch, wondering how long this appointment would take. They were getting low on calf formula. He could let Nora call him on his cell when she was done, and he could head down to the ranch and feed shop... Rosie started to fuss, and Nora glanced back at him. She looked overwhelmed by all of this, and he felt a tickle of sympathy.

"Do you mind?" she asked hopefully.

Easton unbuckled Rosie from her car seat and picked her up. That settled the infant immediately, and she snuggled into his arms, big brown eyes blinking up at him. Rosie definitely liked to be held. Bobbie and Riley were asleep in their seats, and Nora was rooting through her purse for something. He wasn't getting out of here anytime soon, was he?

"They're very cute," one of the older ladies said, putting down her copy of *Reader's Digest*. She had short, permed hair that was dyed something close to black. It made her face look pale and older than she probably was.

Easton used his boot to move the car seat toward a line of free chairs then sat down in one of them. The woman scooted over, peering into Rosie's tiny face.

"These are...the ones..." She looked at Easton meaningfully. Had gossip really gone around town so fast that people he didn't even recognize were asking about the situation? He decided to play dumb and hope she took the hint.

"They're cute all right," he said.

"But these are Cliff Carpenter's grandchildren, right?" she plowed on. "These are the babies with that poor, poor mother..."

He closed his eyes for a moment, looking for calm. "It's private," he said, trying to sound more polite than he felt right now.

"I never imagined," she went on. "My husband did some mechanic work for him on the tractors—you know, when it got beyond what they could handle on site—so I knew Cliff pretty well. And he just seemed so devoted to Dina. So devoted. Just..." She shook her head, searching for words.

"Devoted," Easton said drily. Why was he encouraging this?

"Yes!" she exclaimed. "He really was. He talked about her all the time, and he only ever mentioned his daughter—I mean the *local* daughter. He never, ever mentioned anyone *else*, if you know what I mean. If he had, I might have said something, but he never did. I wouldn't have guessed if those babies hadn't arrived."

She straightened, looking up guiltily as Nora came in their direction, a car seat in each hand. Nora sank into the chair next to Easton and nodded to the woman.

"Hi, Ethel," Nora said.

"Morning," Ethel murmured, but her gaze moved over the babies, her mouth drawn together in a little pucker of judgment.

"I never knew," Ethel said, leaning forward again. "Just so you know, Nora, I never knew."

Nora cast Ethel a withering look—apparently she was past polite at this point, and Easton had to choke back a smile.

"If I had, I would have said something, too," Ethel went on, not to be dissuaded. "I side with the women. How many times have we been tilled under by a man with a wandering eye? So I wouldn't have kept a secret like that. I'd have spoken up, and let him face the music. That's what I'd have done."

"It's a sensitive topic, ma'am," Easton said quietly.

"I'd say it is!" she retorted. "My sister married a

man who couldn't keep it in his pants, so I know exactly how sensitive these things can be. It is amazing what some men do with their free time. My sister's husband didn't even try to be faithful. He slept with everyone within reach, and she knew it, but she wasn't about to give him his walking papers, either. It's all well and good to tell her that she should kick him out, but it was her life, and her marriage, and I couldn't interfere now, could I?"

"Hardly," Easton said wryly, but she didn't seem to read his tone, because she kept talking.

"Everyone in her town knew that her husband had fathered two other children. In fact, I attended the wedding of one of those girls. My sister's husband wasn't there, of course, because he was still pretending that he wasn't her daddy, but I was a friend of a friend, so I went to that wedding. I wasn't invited to the reception, but—"

"Ethel," Nora said, shooting a dangerously sweet smile in the older woman's direction. "Shut up."

Ethel blinked, color rising in her cheeks, and she opened her mouth to say something then shut it with a click.

"Ethel Carmichael," the receptionist called. "The doctor is ready for you now."

Ethel rose to her feet and stalked toward the hallway in time for Easton to overhear the nurse say something about taking her blood pressure. They might want to wait on that to get a normal reading, he thought, and when he glanced over at Nora, she sent him a scathing look.

"What?" he asked.

She rolled her eyes and looked away. This one wasn't his fault. Ethel was the storyteller. Women like Ethel had memories like elephants for juicy gossip, but looking down into Rosie's tiny face, the humor in the situation bled away.

This baby girl—and her sisters—would experience the kind of sympathetic tut-tutting that he had for most of his growing-up years. Easton had enough scandal surrounding his own parentage, and he knew what it felt like to have every woman in town look at him with sympathy because his mother had walked out on him. That kind of stigma clung like a skunk's spray.

When Easton was in the fifth grade, they were supposed to make key chains for their mothers for Mother's Day. Easton had dutifully made that key chain, braiding leather strips as they were instructed. All he'd wanted was to blend in with the class, but that never happened. The other kids whispered about him—he didn't have a mom to give the gift to—and the teacher was extra nice to him, which he'd pay for at recess time. So he'd finished his key chain and in the place where they were supposed to write "I love you, Mom," he'd written something profoundly dirty instead. He wanted to change that look of pity he saw into something else—anger, preferably.

It worked, and every Mother's Day afterward, he pulled the same trick, because things like Mother's Day couldn't be avoided. These girls would have the same problem, except for them it would be at the mention of grandparents, and everyone would clam up and look at them with high-handed sympathy. And they'd hate it—he could guarantee that. With any luck, they would find something better than profanity as a distraction.

Hang in there, kiddo, he thought as he looked down into Rosie's wide-eyed face. She flailed a small arm then yawned. He couldn't say it would get better, because it wouldn't. But she'd get used to it.

Chapter 8

That evening Easton stood over the open hood of Nora's truck where it had stalled out in front of his house. It needed a part—one he could swap out of another Chevy that was parked in a shed. The truck would be up and running in no time. He'd get the part tomorrow during his workday and fix her vehicle the next evening. Lickety-split.

The sun was sinking in the west, shadows lengthening and birds twittering their evening songs. He liked this time of day; after his work was done he had the satisfaction of having accomplished something. That was what he loved about this job—yeah, there was always more to do the next day, but a day's work meant something. He'd been thinking about that trip to the doctor's office with the babies earlier that afternoon, and he couldn't quite sort out his feelings. Truth was, he felt protective of those little tykes, but that didn't sit right with him. He wasn't supposed to be getting attached.

Their ride home from town had been quiet. He'd wanted to say something—he knew Nora was upset about Ethel Carmichael's attempt at conversation, but she'd probably be in for a whole lot more of that. People had known Cliff, loved him, which meant he'd left more than just Dina and Nora stunned by the truth. And in spite of it all, Easton still felt like he owed his late boss something more—a defense, maybe. He just didn't know how.

A cool breeze felt good against his face and arms. The bugs were out—he slapped a mosquito on his wrist. Easton wiped his hands on a rag then flicked off the light that hung from the hood of Nora's truck, unhooked it and banged the hood shut. Above him, a window scraped open and he looked up.

Nora stood, framed between billowing white curtains, and she lifted her hand in a silent wave. She looked so sweet up there, her skin bathed in golden sunlight, her sun-streaked hair tumbling down around her shoulders. Her nose and cheeks looked a little burned, and squinting up at her like that, he couldn't help but notice just how gorgeous she was.

"Hey," he said.

"I just got the babies to sleep," she said. "Are you fixing my truck?"

"Yup." He turned his attention to rubbing the last of the grease out of the lines in his palm. "But I won't be done until tomorrow."

"Thank you." She brushed her hair out of her face and leaned her elbows onto the windowsill. "You don't have to do that, you know."

"Yeah?" he retorted. "You gonna do it?"

It was a challenge. She'd never been one to tinker with an engine, and he'd fixed her ride more than once when they were teenagers.

"I'd call a garage."

A garage. Yeah, right. A garage was for quitters. Any cowboy with a lick of self-respect knew how to fix his truck, and only when it was halfway flattened did he lower himself to calling in a mechanic.

"You're going to be my boss one day," he said. "I might as well make nice now."

She rolled her eyes. "We'll be in our sixties by then."

She had a point. It'd likely be years before her mother grew too feeble to actually run this place. And she'd told him before that she wasn't living for a funeral. But if she settled down with her mom at the main house, he'd be fixing her truck for a long time to come as her employee. Did he mind that?

"You should stick around," he said, shooting her a grin. "You'd enjoy fighting with me more often."

"I thought you said you'd make nice," she countered.

"Yeah, how long can that last?" he asked with a low laugh. "I'm not sixteen anymore, Nora."

She raised an eyebrow. "Me, neither."

Then she disappeared from the window. He stood there, looking up at the billowing curtains for a moment before he smiled to himself and scrubbed his hand once more with the rag. Some things didn't change, like the way Nora could fix him to the spot with a single look... but she was no teen angel anymore. She was a grown woman, with a woman's body and a woman's direct gaze. He wasn't a kid anymore, either, and he wasn't at her beck and call. This had been about his job—a truck on this ranch that needed work. That was it.

The drive into town—okay that had been more than official duties around here, but he and Nora had some history. She'd always be special to him. Didn't they say that a first love was never fully erased? Something like that. She'd been part of his formative years.

Easton's cell phone rang, and he glanced at the number before picking it up.

"Dad?"

"Hi." His dad's voice sounded tight, and sober for a change. "What are you up to?"

"Working."

"Well...take a break. You need to come over."

"Why?" Easton looked at his watch. "It's not a good time, Dad. I have to get up early. You know that."

"You'll want to come by, son," his father said. "There's someone you'll want to see."

"Yeah?" He wasn't convinced. "Who?"

"Your mom."

Easton froze, the rag falling from his hand and landing in the gravel. He tried to swallow but couldn't. A cold sweat erupted on his forehead, and the breeze suddenly felt chilly.

"Ha," he said, forcing the word out. "Not funny. Actually, kind of mean."

"I'm not joking," his father said. "I'm looking at her right now. If you wanted to see her, now's the time."

"Okay," he said, his heart banging in his chest. "I'll be there in fifteen minutes."

Hanging up the phone, he fished his keys out of his pocket and headed for his own vehicle. Mom was back? Was Dad hallucinating? Maybe he'd widened his addictive repertoire to include some drug use. Easton scrubbed a hand through his hair and hauled open the door. He had to stop and suck in a few deep breaths because his hands were trembling. There was something in his dad's voice that told him this was no joke.

After twenty years' absence, what could she possibly want? After missing his childhood…after letting him grow up with a drunk of a father and a hole in his heart the size of Wisconsin, what brought her back to Hope?

Nora looked out the window in time to see Easton's truck back out of the drive then take off down the gravel road, leaving a billow of dust behind him.

That's weird, she thought. Where was he off to in such a hurry?

Maybe an evening to herself was better anyway. Flirting with Easton hadn't really been part of the plan, yet she kept finding herself doing it. Was it habit? A throwback from her teenage years? Or maybe she missed all the control she used to have—a boy following after her who'd do anything she asked.

"I'm not that shallow," she muttered to herself.

Her day had been tiring. The doctor's appointment itself had been routine. The babies had been weighed, measured and declared to be healthy. It was that encounter with Ethel Carmichael that had gotten to her. It was only an old woman's gossipy streak, she told herself. Nora shouldn't worry about it…but she did.

She sighed and rubbed her hands over her face. Hope, Montana, was a nice town—friendly, helpful, attractive—but it was also a town where not too much happened. Everybody knew everybody else, or just about, and half the town was related to each other by marriage. People remembered each other's stories because they were a part of each other's lives. And when people saw the girls in Beauty's Ice Cream Shop or saw them in church, they'd think of Cliff and the scandal around the triplets' arrival. These things didn't just go away.

Nora could handle some gossip. But these three little girls deserved a happy life. What options did Nora have? She could stay in Hope where the girls would have a distanced grandmother they weren't allowed to call "Grandma," and where the story of their grandfather's infidelity would follow them everywhere they went. That was assuming that Nora could make a life here—get a job, find a place that didn't cost too much... maybe with enough family about, she'd be able to pull together a decent life for the girls, financially, at least.

Or she could go back to Billings where she'd have to drop them off at day care every day...and maybe get a second job doing some contract bookkeeping to be able to afford that. They'd have a tired, overworked mom who did her best to keep up with everything. They wouldn't have many new clothes or the toys they wanted. There wouldn't be summer vacations, unless you counted coming back to Hope where everyone would look at them sideways and the girls still couldn't call their grandmother "Grandma."

Or—and this was the option that brought a lump to her throat—she could accept that she couldn't provide the kind of life that these babies deserved. She couldn't give them a comfortable home with a bedroom for each of them, or summer vacations, or new clothes. She couldn't even provide a stable family life to make up for those other things. She wasn't married. There would be no dad to give them that important male influence in their lives. There wouldn't even be a doting grandma to cuddle them and tell them stories about their family. And she'd never make this town look past the scandal the triplets' grandfather created...

Nora sank onto the side of her bed, her heart sodden with anxiety. That was what the visit to the doctor's office had shown her—she could provide the basics, but she couldn't shield them from the rest. And if there was a family out there that would adopt these girls together, love them and celebrate them, provide birthday parties and new shoes... If there were adoptive grandparents who would make cookies with them and read them stories, look them in the eye and tell them how loved and wanted they were... Could she really deny these little girls that kind of life?

Nora looked through the bars of the crib at the sleeping babies. Their lashes brushed their plump cheeks; their hair swirled across their heads in damp curls. Bobbie was making phantom sucking noises, her little tongue poked out of her mouth, and Riley let out a soft sigh in her sleep. Nora put a finger in Rosie's tiny hand, and she clamped down on it.

"I love you," she whispered.

It was true—she'd fallen in love with her girls, and if money didn't matter or if she could wave a magic wand and make everyone forget the pain associated with these children, she'd raise them herself and be their mom. But money did matter, and so did scandal. They were brand-new to this world, and already they were steeped in it. She was the one Mia had designated as their provider, and she had to do what was best for the babies.

A tear slipped down Nora's cheek, and she wiped it away with her free hand. She gently stroked Rosie's soft fingers, inhaling the delicate smell of sleeping infants. She'd remember this, cherish it always. She wasn't their mother—Mia was. Nora was an in-between person who had to give them her heart in order to take care of them. But she couldn't keep them, no matter how much her heart broke at the thought of letting go.

When she'd taken the babies from the hospital, they'd given her some business cards from social workers and adoption agencies. She'd shoved them into her wallet and forgotten about them, but she knew what she'd have to do.

Tomorrow. Not tonight. Tonight she had to let herself feel this pain and have a good cry. Then in the morning she'd call an adoption agency and see what kinds of options the girls might have.

Chapter 9

Easton's father, Mike Ross, lived at the end of Hunter Street. There were no shade trees, just brown lawns and old houses—several of which were empty. The Ross house was at the end of the road before asphalt simply evaporated into scrub grass. A couple of cars were on blocks in the front yard, and a chain and a massive dog bowl sat abandoned by the front door. The dog had died years ago, but the reminder of his presence seemed to help keep thieves and religious proselytizers at bay. Which was good when it came to thieves, but in Easton's humble opinion, a little religion wouldn't hurt his old man.

When Easton pulled into the driveway behind a red SUV, all those old feelings of anger and resentment settled back onto his shoulders, too. This was why he never came home—it reminded him of things he'd rather leave in the past. Like constantly feeling like a failure no matter what he did, and acting rough and angry to get away from the pity.

Except he'd longed for his mom every day since she'd left, imagined ways she might return, set scenes in his mind when she'd see him as a grown man and her heart would fill with pride. Those had been fantasies, because her actually coming back would solidify the fact that she'd been able to return all along and had chosen not to.

He sat in his truck for a couple of minutes, his hands on the steering wheel in a white-knuckled grip. That was probably her SUV, all new and shiny. So she had enough money for that. Maybe she'd stayed away for the same reasons he did now—because she didn't like to remember. He undid his seat belt and got out of the truck.

The front door was never used; in fact, his dad had a bunch of junk piled in front of it from the inside. Easton angled around to the side door. He didn't bother knocking, just opened it. The kitchen was smoky from his father's cigarettes, so Easton left the door open to let it clear a bit.

"Hello?" he called.

A woman emerged from the living room—slim, made up, wearing a pair of jeans and a light blouse. Her hair was dyed brown now, cut short but stylish. Her face was the same face he remembered, though. Even that one crooked tooth when she smiled hesitantly.

"Easton?" she whispered.

"Mom." Tears welled up in his eyes, and he stood there looking at her awkwardly.

"Oh, sweetheart—" She came forward as if to hug him, but he didn't move into it, so she ended up patting his arm a few times. She looked up into his face, and he could see that she'd aged. She was no longer the woman in her early twenties matching his dad drink for drink—she would be forty-seven this year. He'd done the math.

"So—" He cleared his throat. "Where've you been?"

"Can I hug you?" she asked softly.

"Not right now." If he let her hug him, the tears he'd been holding back for years would start, and he couldn't let that happen. He could cry later, alone, but not in front of her. He needed answers.

His father came into the room and scraped back a kitchen chair. He was thin and tall, lined and slightly yellowed from nicotine.

"Should we sit?" she asked cautiously. "Just come sit with me, son."

He followed her to the flier-strewn table and sat opposite her. She looked him over then reached out and put her hand on top of his.

"You look good," she said. "Really good."

"Thanks." He pulled his hand back as the tears started to rise inside his chest. "You look like you're not doing too badly for yourself. What took so long to come see how I was doing?"

"I wanted to—" She looked toward his father. "I talked to your dad on the phone a few times, and he said you were doing really well. He said if I came around I'd ruin things for you."

"What?" Easton darted a disgusted look at his old man. "And you believed that lying sack of—" He bit off the last word and sucked in a shaky breath. Profanity was a bit of a habit when he felt cornered. *"You left me."*

And suddenly, he was nothing more than an eight-year-old boy again, staring at the mom who was supposed to be better at this. In that note she'd left on the fridge, she hadn't said anything loving. Her last words had been "He's your problem now." She'd ditched him, left town, and while he'd squirmed his way around those words over the years, trying to apply different meaning to them that would still allow her to return for him, looking at his mother now brought the words back like a punch in the gut.

"I know…" She blinked a few times then licked her lips. "I was young when I had you—seventeen, if you remember. I didn't know how to deal with everything. I was so overwhelmed…"

"Except you weren't seventeen when you left. You were twenty-five. That's a solid adult."

"Yes." She didn't offer any excuses.

"And the note—"

"I wasn't in a good place when I scratched that out," she interrupted. "I don't remember exactly what I said."

"I do." Easton glanced at his old man. His dad would remember that note, too. "You said you were sick of this life and I was Dad's problem from then on."

She winced. "I didn't mean—"

"Sure you did. Or you would have come back."

She swallowed, glanced at his father. What was she looking for, some kind of united front?

"So you figured you'd leave me with him." Easton jutted a thumb toward his father. "He was a more suitable parent?"

"He had the house," she said. "I just drove away one day. I wasn't thinking about the future—just about getting some space." She was quiet for a moment. "And I knew I wasn't much of a mom."

Yeah, that was evident. With her sitting in front of

him, he was able to separate the fantasies of the gentle mother stroking his hair from the reality of the emotionally distant mother who'd spent hours a day smoking in this very kitchen.

"I tried to see you," she added.

"When?" he demanded. He found that hard to believe.

"The summer you were fourteen. I was in the area and I called your dad. He said he got you a job at a local ranch and you were doing really well. He said you were happy, and you didn't remember me."

"*You* said that?" Easton glared at his father across the table. "I was happy, was I? I didn't need her?"

His father shrugged. "We did okay. She's the one who left."

That had been his father's mantra over the years— she was the one who left, as if all their problems had been caused by the one who walked away instead of the parents who hadn't done their job to begin with.

Easton turned back to his mother. "I was doing okay because Cliff Carpenter hired me and took over where Dad left off. I wasn't happy. I was making do. And Dad didn't get me anything. I waited outside the ranch and feed store and asked every single rancher that came and left if he'd hire me. Cliff was the only one to say yes. Dad didn't do squat for me. He drank every day, ran this house into the ground and smacked me around if I was within reach."

"Hey—" his father started.

"Shut up, Dad." Easton wasn't in any mood to argue about facts with his old man, and his father seemed to sense that, because he subsided back into a brooding silence.

"I—" His mother swallowed hard and dropped her gaze. "I didn't know all that."

"I'm a ranch manager now," he added. "I own my own home. I have a life, and I steer clear of this dump."

"Maybe I could—"

"No!" He knew what she was about to ask—to see the life he'd built for himself. And while he'd dreamed of that opportunity since he was eight years old, he realized that he didn't actually want it now. She didn't deserve to feel better about how he'd turned out. He wanted to hurt her back—make her feel the rejection he'd felt his entire life. "You aren't welcome in my home."

They fell into silence for a few beats. He could take all his pain and anguish out on her, or he could get some of those answers at last.

"So what have you been doing all these years?" Easton asked. "You're dressed pretty well."

"I'm—" She looked down at her hands splayed on the tabletop, and his eye followed hers to the wedding ring. "I'm married again. His name is Tom. He's very sweet. I'm a recovering alcoholic, so I don't drink. It took a few years of hard work, but I got there."

"So where'd you find… Tom…then?" The name tasted sour on his tongue.

"Church," she replied. "We've been married sixteen years now. He's a good man."

Sixteen years of marriage, and she'd stayed away from him. There had been a home she could have brought him to, a cupboard full of food… He did the mental math, and he'd been twelve when she'd gotten married—plenty of time to have given him some sort of childhood.

"What does Tom do?"

"He's an electrician."

Blast it—so normal and balanced. His mom walked away and got to marry some utterly normal Tom, afford new clothes—something he'd never had growing up— and drive a new SUV... And he'd been left in addiction-induced poverty, dreaming of some fantasy mother.

"Where do you live?" he asked.

"Billings."

"Three hours away?" he asked incredulously. "I was here missing you, longing for my mom to come back for me, and all that time you were a mere three hours from here?"

Easton rubbed his hands over his face. He'd dreamed of a chance to see his mother again, to try to mend this jagged hole in his heart that she'd left behind. Some days he wanted answers, and other days he wanted comfort. Today he had the chance to hug her and he couldn't bring himself to do it. He was finally face-to-face with his mom again, and he felt something he'd never expected—he hated her.

"I'm so sorry—" Her voice shook and she wiped a tear from her cheek. "I thought you were doing well, that if I came back I'd ruin things for you. I was so ashamed of the woman I used to be. I was mean, drunk most of the time and just a shell of a person..." She shook her head. "I thought you'd remember all of that."

"Not really," he admitted. "A bit, I mean. But I was young. I think Dad remembered that more. I...uh... I kept your Led Zeppelin T-shirt under my mattress. I remembered the smell of your cigarettes in the morning, and the sound of your laughter."

"My T-shirt—" The look on her face was like he'd punched her with those words.

"It helped me sleep sometimes." Why was he telling her this? Blast it, his complaints made him sound like a whimpering puppy! He wasn't meaning to open up, but he'd been holding all of this in for so long…

"I wasn't sure you'd *want* me back."

"Not sure I do now, either," he snapped. That was half of a lie. He did want her back, but he also wanted her to pay for her absence. He wanted her to feel some of what she'd done to him. "So why now?"

"I don't know," she said quietly. "I got into my vehicle and started driving. I called Tom from the road and said I was coming to see my son. I need to go back tonight, but I had to see you again. I missed you so much."

"Not enough to drive the three hours before this," he pointed out.

"I wanted to…" She swallowed hard. "I couldn't shake the guilt of having left you like I did. Then Brandon had his eighth birthday…"

"Brandon?" he asked slowly. "Who's that?"

"My son—your half brother…" She grabbed her purse from the back of her chair and rummaged through it. She pulled out a school photo and pushed it across the table toward him. Easton didn't touch it, but he looked at the smiling face of a kid with dirty-blond hair and a lopsided grin. *Her son.*

Easton's stomach dropped as the reality of this moment settled into his gut. She'd gotten married, had another little boy and she'd been the mom she should have been to Easton to this other kid.

"So…" Easton's voice shook. "I have a half brother."

"Yes." She nodded, a tentative smile coming to her lips. "And he's a sweet boy. I know you'd like him. He's got such a big heart."

"And you've been there for him," Easton clarified, his voice firming up as rage coursed through him. "You've taken him to soccer practice and given him birthday parties…hell, even birthday presents?"

"He likes chess, actually, but—" She stopped, sensing where he was going with this. "I was older. I was wiser. There's enough money now—"

Easton let out a string of expletives and rose to his feet, the chair underneath him clattering to the floor.

"You were my *mother*!" he roared.

She sat in stunned silence, and his father shuffled his feet against the crumb-laden floor. Easton stared down at the parents who'd brought him into this world and then failed to provide for him. He couldn't stop the tears anymore—he was blinded by them. His shoulders shook and he turned away, trying to get some sort of control over himself, but now that it had started, he couldn't seem to dam it up. He slammed a hand against the wall then leaned there as he sobbed.

He felt his mother's arms wrap around him from behind, and she shook with tears, too.

"Damn it, Mom, I hate you," he wept.

"I know," she whispered. "I know…"

Then he turned around, and for the first time since he was eight years old, he wrapped his arms around his mom and hugged her. He hugged her tighter than was probably comfortable, but she didn't complain, and he didn't dare let go.

She'd learned how to be a mother after all, but she'd

learned with somebody else. And that didn't do a thing for Easton. He'd already grown up, and he'd done it without a mom.

Nora stood in the kitchen mixing baby formula at the counter. She shook up the third bottle, watching the bubbles form. She was getting used to this hour, and she woke up before her cell phone alarm now. It was midnight, and she was in her white cotton nightgown, the cool night air winding around her bare legs. It was strange, but this house, which had always been so firmly *hers* in her heart, felt empty without Easton in it. He'd driven off that evening, and he hadn't come back.

Earlier that evening, her mother had asked if she'd come for lunch at the house. She was having Nora's aunt and uncle come over, and she needed some moral support. This was Cliff's sister and her husband—both of whom had been close with Cliff.

"They'll want to meet the babies, too, I'm sure," her mother had said. "They're Cliff's grandkids, after all."

There weren't going to be any easy explanations, no simple family relationships for these girls. And they needed family—the supportive, loving kind, not the backbiting, gossiping kind. Nora needed to know now if that was even a possibility after what her father had done. She was willing to look into adoptive options for the girls, but she hadn't fully committed to it—not yet. Other single mothers managed it—pulled it all together on their own—but *how*?

Normally at this time of year, the Carpenters hosted a corn roast and barbecue for family and friends, also as a way to thank the staff for their hard work over the summer. She'd asked her mother if she wanted to go ahead with it this year, but with Cliff's death and the subsequent drama, it hardly seemed like a priority.

Standing in the kitchen at midnight, Nora put down the last bottle of formula. She'd considered calling Easton's cell phone a couple of times, but hadn't. This was her problem to untangle on her own, and while a listening ear might be comforting, no one else could give her the answer. Besides, it wasn't Easton's job to listen to her go on about her problems. He had problems of his own. But would it be too much to ask of a friend?

As she gathered up the bottles, a truck's engine rumbled up the drive. She felt a wave of relief. Why she should feel this way, she didn't know, but perhaps it was just old habits dying hard—tough times nudging her toward Easton. She really wanted to talk to him about the girls—but more than that, she wanted to hear what he had to say about them. It would help her hammer out her own feelings out loud with another person who wouldn't judge her, because Heaven knew she was judging herself pretty harshly right now.

The back door opened and Easton stepped inside. His shoulders were slumped, and his face looked puffy and haggard. If she didn't know him better, she'd think he'd been crying. He didn't look up at her as he kicked off his boots and hung his hat on the peg.

"Easton? Oh my goodness, are you all right?"

He scrubbed a hand through his hair. "Yeah, I'm fine."

"No, you're not!" She crossed the kitchen and caught his arm on his way past. "Look at me."

He turned toward her and she could see the red rims

of his eyes, the same old sadness welling up in his dark gaze. "My mom came back."

Nora stared at him. A slew of questions cascaded through her mind, but they swept past as she saw the pain etched in Easton's features.

"She was at my dad's place."

Nora's breath came out in a rush and she looked from Easton to the bottles and then back at her friend again. His mom—she knew what this meant...or at the very least she knew how heavily this would have hit him.

"I need to feed the babies," she said quietly. "You want to help? We could talk…"

He was silent for a beat, and she half expected him to say no, that he was fine, and to go up and lock himself into his bedroom.

"Sure," he said.

She picked up the bottles from the counter and they moved together toward the stairs.

"What happened, exactly?" she asked as they climbed the narrow staircase. "Is she still here?"

"She's left already—for Billings. She's been there this whole time. She's remarried with another kid."

His voice was low and wooden as he went over what had happened tonight. Nora picked up Riley and passed her to Easton. He was more practiced now in handling babies, and he took the infant easily. His expression softened as he looked down into the sleeping face.

"They're so little," he said quietly. He teased the bottle's nipple between her lips. Nora scooped up Rosie and let Bobbie sleep for another few minutes. "Can you imagine anyone just walking away?"

Tears misted her eyes. Wasn't that exactly what she was considering with the triplets? Was she just as bad as Easton's mother? Or had Easton's mother done the best that she could under the circumstances? Maybe she just wanted to excuse Easton's mom because it would make her look infinitely better by comparison.

"How do you feel now that you've seen her again?" Nora asked quietly.

"Conflicted," he admitted. "I've wanted this for years—a chance to see her, to hug her again—and now that I have it, I'm filled with rage."

"You're probably in shock," she said.

"I spent years loving her in spite of her faults." He heaved a sigh. "But she figured out how to be a decent parent when she had her second child—Brandon. I saw a picture. Cute kid. And all I could feel was anger. That's awful, isn't it? He's just some kid. Do I really want him to suffer like I did?"

She didn't respond, and the only sound in the room was that of the babies drinking their bottles.

"She wants me to meet him," Easton said after a moment.

"Do you want to?" Nora asked.

"I don't know. Not really. Yes." He shook his head. "You know what I want? I want to go back in time and have her be there for me, too. She takes Brandon to chess club three times a week, and she drives him to birthday parties. She's a stay-at-home mom." He muttered an oath then looked sheepishly at Nora. "Riley'll never remember that."

Nora smiled. "She'll be fine."

Easton jiggled the bottle to get Riley drinking again and adjusted her position, then he continued, "My mom said she wanted to be home for Brandon, because her husband works long hours, and he needs someone to talk about his school day with. Talk about his school day! What I would've given for my mom to just sit and listen to me for a few minutes."

"Will you see her again?" she asked.

"She'll come back again on Saturday afternoon. She'll text me the details."

Nora tipped Rosie up against her shoulder and patted her back. Easton did the same with Riley. From the crib, Bobbie was starting to squirm in her sleep, probably feeling hungry. Riley burped, and Easton wiped her mouth with a cloth, then laid her back down in the crib. He picked up Bobbie next. When had he gotten so good at this?

"Should I feed her?" he asked.

Rosie hadn't burped yet, and Nora nodded. Easton grabbed the third bottle and Bobbie immediately started slurping it back.

"It's funny—I have her cell number. I could call her if I wanted to… I could text my mom. How many times have I wished I could contact her—say something to her? Now I could…with a text." A smile creased his tired face. "That's something, isn't it?"

And in those shining eyes, she saw the boy she used to know, who would sit next to her in the hayloft, listening to her go on about her small and insignificant problems. He hadn't mentioned his mother often back then, but she could remember one time when he'd said, "When my mom comes back, I'm going to buy her a house."

"A house?" she'd asked. "How will you do that? Houses cost more than you've got."

"In three years I'll be eighteen. I'll drop out of school and work full-time," he'd replied. "And then we'll live in that house together, and my dad can rot by himself. I'll take care of her."

He'd always planned for his mother's return. Somehow he'd been convinced that she'd come back, and he'd been right. Except when they were kids, he'd been certain that she'd need him.

They resettled the babies into the crib, but they stayed there in the darkness, standing close enough together that she could feel the warmth of his body radiating against hers.

"The one thing she didn't tell me—" His voice broke. "She never said why she left me behind."

She couldn't see him well enough in the dim light, but she could hear that rasp of deep emotion against his iron reserve. That was a wound that wouldn't heal.

"Easton…"

She wrapped her arms around his waist and leaned her cheek against his broad chest. He slipped his muscular arms around her and she could feel his cheek rest on the top of her head. He smelled good—musky, with a hint of hay. His body was roped with muscle, and he leaned into her, his body warming her in a way that felt intimate and pleading.

Neither of them spoke, and he leaned down farther, wrapping his arms around her a little more closely, tugging her against him more firmly. She could feel the thud of his heartbeat against her chest, and she closed her eyes, breathing in his manly scent. Somehow all either of them seemed to want was to be closer, to absorb all of each other's pain into their bodies and share it.

Easton pulled back and she found her face inches from his, and his dark eyes moved over her face. She could see the faint freckles across his cheekbones, the soft shadow of his stubble veiling a few acne scars. He was the same old Easton, all grown up, and while she could still see the sweet boy in those dark eyes, she could also see the rugged man—the survivor, the cowboy— and the intensity of that gaze also reminded her that he was very capable of being so much more than that...

"I missed you," he whispered.

"Me, too." And standing there in his arms, his muscular thighs pressed against hers, she still missed him. Pushed up against each other wasn't close enough to touch the longing for whatever it was that they'd lost over the years.

His dark gaze met hers and her breath caught in her throat. She couldn't have looked away if she'd wanted to. His mouth hovered close to hers, a whisper of breath tickling her lips. He hesitated, and before she could think better of it, Nora closed the distance between them, standing on her tiptoes so that her lips met his. He took it from there, dipping his head down and sliding a hand through her hair. His other hand pressed against the small of her back, nudging her closer, closer against his muscular body, her bare legs against his jeans, her hands clutching the sides of his shirt. His lips moved over hers, confident and hungry, and when he finally pulled back, she was left weak-kneed and breathless.

"Been wanting to do that for a while," he said, running the pad of his thumb over her plumped lips.

She laughed softly. "Oh..."

"Don't worry," he said, his voice a husky growl. "We

can chalk that up to an emotional evening, and tomorrow you won't have to think about it again."

Easton's gaze moved down to her lips again, then he smiled roguishly and took a step back, cool air rushing over her body. She didn't know what she thought, or what she wanted, but he wasn't asking for anything. He moved to the doorway and looked back.

"Good night," he said and then disappeared into the dark hallway.

Nora stood there, her fingers lightly touching her lips. He'd *kissed* her just now, and she realized that the attraction he felt for her was very, very mutual.

Nora went to close her bedroom door, and she paused, looking out into the hallway. All was quiet, except for the soft rustle of movement coming from the room next door. He was probably getting ready for bed, and she pulled her mind firmly away from that precipice.

If only she'd seen deeper into Easton's heart when they were younger…she might have been a bigger comfort to him, a better listener. If she'd realized then the man he'd mature into in a few years—but all of that was too late. If there was one thing the discovery of her father's unfaithfulness had taught her, it was that a man could be as loving and doting as her father had been, and he could still cheat, lie and hide his tracks. Nora needed to be able to count on a man for better or for worse, or those vows were pointless. She'd been lonely for what she and Easton had experienced together in that innocent adolescent friendship, but she'd been hungry for something more just now—something that hadn't existed before. She'd wanted security—she'd wanted kisses in the moonlight that didn't have to end, that could be hers and only hers...

Nora shut the door and slid back into her bed. Two and a half more hours until the girls needed another bottle. She'd best get some sleep.

Chapter 10

The next afternoon Easton wrapped the starter in a clean rag then used another one to wipe the grease off his hands. He'd have Nora's truck up and running tonight as promised.

He'd left early that morning, not wanting to run into her after the kiss last night. He still carried that image of her in a knee-length nightgown—totally chaste by all accounts, but still… What was it about Nora that could make a granny nightgown alluring? If he hadn't left when he did, he wouldn't have stopped at holding her close, and he wouldn't have stopped at the kiss, either. Her bed had been right there—yeah, he'd noticed—and if he'd been listening to the thrum of the impulses surging through him, he would have nudged her over to those rumpled sheets and pulled her as close as two bodies could get.

Except he wasn't just a horny teenager; he was a grown man, and for the most part he didn't do stupid things he'd regret the next morning. He knew where this led—the same place it had led when they were teenagers. She was vulnerable right now, her life was upside down and she needed someone to lean on. His shoulders were broad enough for the weight of her burdens, and that was all she really wanted deep down—he was convinced of it. She'd been there for him, too, and he was grateful for that. But a moment of mutual comfort wouldn't turn into anything that would last. He knew better. He could try to convince himself that she was interested in a real relationship with him, but had she been, she'd have shown that interest long before now. When things got tough for Nora, she came to him. Then she left again. It was their pattern.

Easton didn't have the emotional strength right now to deal with yet another rejection from the one girl he'd always pined for. Pining didn't do a thing—even as a boy, longing for his mom to come home. Now she had, but it wasn't what he'd imagined. It hadn't smoothed things over—and it certainly wouldn't fix the past. He was a grown man now, and he wasn't willing to set himself up for more heartbreak. So he'd kissed Nora, and while he didn't regret it, he wasn't about to do it again. He'd been serious when he said he was chalking it up to an emotional night. He was letting them both off the hook.

He heard the scrape of boots on the cement floor, and Easton turned to see Dale Young, Cliff's brother-in-law. He was an older guy, skinny and tall with a prominent nose and gray brush of a mustache.

"Hey, Dale," Easton said. "What brings you here?"

He crossed the garage and shook the other man's hand.

"Just checking up on things," Dale said. "I told Dina I'd come say howdy. One of your ranch hands told me where I could find you."

"Just getting a part for Nora's truck." Easton held it up. "So how've you been?"

"Not bad…" Dale winced. "The gossip around this place has been something fierce. My wife has been taking it personal."

Easton shrugged his assent to that. Nora and Dina were taking it hard, too.

"Did you know about the other woman?" Dale asked.

"Before my time," Easton said. "And from what I gather, it wasn't a lengthy affair. Just a mistake."

"Hmm." Dale grunted.

"I don't like how people are talking," Easton admitted. "Cliff was a good man—a solid neighbor, a helping hand. How many times did he help with a cattle drive or with hay baling when someone was sick?"

"Preaching to the choir," Dale replied. "I know you two were close. He was good to you, too."

The two men walked out of the garage into the sunlight, and Easton adjusted his hat to shade his eyes. Cliff had been good to him, and it wasn't just about the three acres and the old house. That land came complicated, and it had been rubbing at his conscience ever since Nora's return.

"Dale, I was wondering about that," Easton said, pausing. "The land he gave me, that is."

"Yeah?"

"It's your wife's grandparents' house," Easton said.

"Does that rankle her at all, me having it? I'm not family."

Dale sucked in a deep breath then let it out slowly and shrugged. "A little, truthfully."

Easton expected as much.

"She'd never say nothing about it," Dale went on. "Cliff owned that house, and could do what he wanted with it. None of us expected that he'd just give it away like that, though."

"And you?" Easton pressed. "Do you have an issue with me living there?"

"Nah." Dale smoothed his fingers over his mustache. "It's a house, and Cliff wasn't a man to do something like that lightly. He gave it to you for a reason. He wanted you to have it."

A reason—that was what Easton needed to nail down. Why had Cliff done that—written over a piece of his family history?

"Before he died, he wanted me to move into that house and live there. He said he wanted someone to take care of the place for him. Thing is, I can't rest easy knowing that I'm sitting on land that means this much to the Carpenters. I mean, it's a godsend for me, but that's because I come from a hard place. I was just a cowboy who respected his boss. Nothing more and nothing less. Was I really worth that kind of gift? If I knew what made him do it, it might make it easier to carry on as he intended."

Because if Cliff had only been trying to keep him as an employee, he'd feel really bad about that. He didn't need to be bought off, especially with something that meant so much to the rest of the family. Now that Cliff was gone, Dina might be okay with replacing him eventually.

Dale nodded slowly. "I think Cliff had a big heart."

Was that it? Was this emotional?

"What do you mean by that?" Easton pressed.

"Meaning you weren't just an employee to him. He cared for you—and while you think you weren't family to him, there's three acres of land that begs to differ." Dale shrugged. "You mattered to him, and he made sure you were taken care of. God knows your own dad wasn't going to leave you nothing. People are gonna talk—and that's not gonna change. They'll talk about Cliff's affair, and about your land… It's what people do. If you really can't rest easy there, then sell it to Nora. You'd have some money to start fresh somewhere else, and she'd have that precious house back."

Nora's problem seemed to be that she had nowhere to call home in Hope anymore—nowhere truly hers. If she had that house back, the seat of her family's memories, then maybe she could have what she wanted most. And a fresh start for him…it gave him a little hopeful rush to even consider it right now.

"It's a good idea," Easton said with a nod. "Thanks."

"Not a problem." Dale eyed Easton for a moment. "Or marry her. That could take care of the family issue pretty quick."

Easton smiled wryly. "I've known Nora for a long time, Dale. I've been friend-zoned since we were fourteen."

Dale barked out a laugh and shook his head. "Those Carpenter women are a handful."

And Dale would know—he'd been married to Cliff Carpenter's sister for the last thirty-five years. But he had a point. Selling the house to Nora would take care of things right quick. She'd get the house she loved; he'd get a new start somewhere else. And if his mom could have a fresh start—all clean and respectable— then why not him? She'd left him behind in that hole with his father, but that didn't mean he had to stay here in Hope. What was holding him here now, after all? Cliff had passed on, his father had never had much right to Easton's loyalty and his mother was raising another son with her electrician husband, *Tom.*

This was a big country—heck even the state of Montana was pretty large. He'd had some job offers before; he'd be able to find another position without too much trouble—a new life where no one knew the skeletons in his closet. Everyone had issues—that wasn't the problem. It was having everyone know you well enough to be able to point out your issues plain as day. That was the aggravating part. But a chance at a life where no one else knew the things that stabbed him deepest? Well, that was a whole new kind of freedom that he longed to taste.

But still—that took walking away, and just leaving Nora and the babies. While it would solve everything, it would be hard. He wasn't a part of that family—wasn't that what he'd been acknowledging all along, that he wasn't really family? But still, while he may want a fresh start, a small and stupid part of him stayed the hopeful teenager, and saw Nora by his side.

His phone blipped and he looked down to see a text from his mom.

Hi Easton—how about Saturday at 11 at Beauty's Ice Cream? Brandon wants to meet you.

He stood, frozen for a moment, his mind spinning. She'd done it. She'd gotten that fresh start, and the thing he hated most about it was how blasted happy she looked now. A husband, another kid, a comfortable life... If his mom could do it, then why not him?

He texted back:

Sure. See you then.

Nora, Dina and Aunt Audrey sat around the kitchen table in the main house, mugs of coffee in front of them. Dale had left after lunch to go take a look at the ranch. With Cliff gone, Dale had taken it upon himself to make sure things didn't slump while Dina grappled with her grief. People could get taken advantage of during times of tragedy, and it took a family pulling together to make sure that didn't happen.

Lunch dishes were piled on the countertop, mugs of coffee replaced them on the scratched table and the women sat together, sipping their coffee, waiting for Dale to get back. Audrey bore a striking resemblance to her late brother. She had his mix of blond and white hair, the same stalky build, the same short fingers.

Audrey held sleeping Bobbie in her arms. Nora was snuggling Riley, and Rosie lay in her car seat. Dina's arms were empty. She leaned her elbows on the table, a half-finished mug of coffee in front of her.

"They look like Carpenters," Audrey said. "I can see it in the shape of their faces. All the Carpenter babies have these little chins."

Dina glanced at Audrey, her expression blank.

"They're here now," Audrey said pointedly. "You might want to accept it, Dina."

"And if Dale had another family somewhere?" Dina retorted. "You'd just open your arms to all of his grand-children?"

Audrey smoothed a hand over Bobbie's downy head. "Dale isn't the type—"

"And Cliff was?" Dina demanded. "You're telling me you saw that coming?"

"I told myself I wouldn't mention it, but is it possible that you were a tad too controlling with Cliff?" Audrey's voice stayed quiet, but her tone hardened. "He had to come home and ask you before he did *anything*. Maybe he had a small revolt—an inappropriate one, obviously, but—" She paused and put her attention back into the baby.

Dina's eyes flashed, but her chin quivered with repressed tears. She pushed her mug away and stood up, turning her back on them and stalking toward the kitchen window.

"What do you know about my parents' marriage?" Nora snapped.

"He was my brother," Audrey replied. "I knew *him*."

"Dad wasn't whipped," Nora retorted. "He respected her opinion. And what did he come home and discuss with her—lending you and Dale money? Has it ever occurred to you that he wanted to say no to giving you more cash, and needed some distance to do it?"

The room hummed with tension, and Nora looked at her mother's rigid back. This was what Dina was facing now—judgment from women who didn't want to believe it could just as easily have happened to them. Dina would be the one to blame, because if it was her fault, then the others could avoid her fate. Heaven knew no one would want to cheat on a woman like Audrey—

always so virtuous and right all the time. Nora suppressed the urge to roll her eyes.

"All I'm trying to say," Audrey said at last, "is that these children are here, and they are my relatives, too. If you can't be a granny to them, Dina, then I'll step in."

Was that a solution? Audrey was a blood relative to these baby girls, and if she'd be "Grandma," then perhaps it would let her own mother off the hook. Audrey lovingly stroked Bobbie's hand with one finger, but Nora caught the look of stricken grief on her mother's face as she turned back to face them.

Dina would be pushed out. Nora could see how this would unfold. The girls would be loved and spoiled by Audrey and Dale, but that wouldn't stop gossip about their grandfather, and it would only put Dina, the loving wife of their grandfather, on the sidelines where she would still be blamed for her husband's cheating. Because if there was one thing about Audrey, it was her utter conviction that she was right.

Nora didn't want Dina to be Grandma because of her relationship to Cliff; she'd wanted Dina because of her relationship to *her*. Audrey's offer wasn't a solution so much as a threat—step up as grandparent, or live forever in the shadows.

Dale's boots echoed on the side steps, and the door opened. He took off his hat as he came in.

"Howdy," he said, then he stopped short. "Everything okay in here?"

"Just snuggling babies," Audrey said, a shade too chipper. "Why don't you come hold this little angel, Dale?"

Dale's gaze moved to Dina then back to his wife. He seemed to do the math pretty quickly, because his mustache twitched a couple of times, then he said, "We'd better get back, Aud."

"Seriously, Dale, come and see these little treasures..." Audrey leaned down and breathed in next to Bobbie's head. "They smell so good."

"Aud." He didn't say anything else—his tone was enough, and he stared at his wife flatly until she sighed, rose to her feet and brought Bobbie over to Nora.

"You remember what I said, Nora," she said quietly. "There's more than one way to be family."

Dale waited by the door until Audrey had collected her purse and said her goodbyes. Before shutting the door, Dale cast Nora an apologetic look.

"Take care now, Nora," he said with that usual flat tone of his. "And take care of your mom, too, okay?"

"Bye, Uncle Dale." She smiled, but she wasn't sure she pulled it off.

Then they were gone.

Nora sat with her mother in silence. The two babies slept on in Nora's arms and she looked at their peaceful faces. The clock ticked audibly from the wall, and Nora felt like her heart was filled with water. This was a mess. Audrey would make her mother miserable for the rest of her life if she was given the chance. Dina and Audrey had respected each other, but there had always been a little bit of a chilly distance there—history that Nora didn't know about, no doubt.

"Was I controlling?" Dina asked hollowly.

"Not with Dad," Nora said. "You were the toughie with me, though."

"I was the toughie because your dad wouldn't discipline you," Dina said with a sigh. "He wanted to be the good guy all the time, so he'd leave getting you back into line for me. Do you know how badly I wanted to be the good guy every once in a while?"

"Really?" Perhaps their marriage had been more complicated than Nora realized. She blinked back sudden tears. Her dad had been the quiet strength in her life, the one who would nod slowly and say, "Your mother isn't as wrong as you think..." But still, someone had to draw lines and give lectures. Just not Cliff.

"Dad just did things differently." That was probably an understatement. They were only finding out now how differently he'd been doing things.

"Yeah." Dina rubbed a hand over her eyes.

Nora hadn't told her mother about the letters Easton had found yet—she hadn't been sure it was a good idea, but now she reconsidered. Audrey would love nothing more than to pass around that Cliff had been keeping up a long-term romance with Angela, but that wasn't the case.

"Easton found some letters that Angela wrote to Dad," Nora said. "They didn't seem to have any kind of ongoing affair. But she kept Dad up-to-date on Mia, it seems."

Dina frowned. "What—did he have a secret post office box or something?"

"Yes."

Dina shook her head but didn't say anything. Another betrayal. Another secret. How many would they unearth before this was over?

"Mia really hated him as a kid," Nora said. "She wrote him a letter telling him how much she hated him for not being a part of her life."

"I hate him right now, too," Dina said, and a tear escaped and trickled down her cheek. She wiped it away then sucked in a breath, visibly rallying herself again. "It's just as well we've canceled the corn roast."

"Is that what you really want?" Nora asked.

"What I want is to have my husband back," Dina retorted. "And for his sister to go jump in a lake."

"Yeah, she's not my favorite, either."

Nora looked out the kitchen window, her mind going back over all those other Carpenter corn roasts—the fun times, the laughter... Her dad had always been the center of it all, barbecuing up burgers for everyone. They could abandon the tradition, or they could face it.

"Will it help to skip it?" Nora asked after a moment. "I mean—they'll talk anyway, but if we call off the corn roast and keep to ourselves, will they talk more?"

"That corn roast turned into tradition over the years," Dina said thoughtfully. "What if... I mean, it might be our last one, but I think you're right. Let them come and see us in our complicated mess. The less they see of us, the more they'll talk. And with any luck at all, Audrey will get food poisoning."

Nora barked out a laugh. "Okay. Sure. In Dad's honor."

Rosie started to fuss from her car seat, squirming and letting out a whine. She hated being out of arms, that little girl, but Nora had both Riley and Bobbie in her arms and she couldn't pick up a third. Nora glanced pleadingly at her mother. "Help me?"

Dina slowly undid the buckles and lifted Rosie into her arms. She stood there, looking down into the baby's tiny face, her expression softening.

"They do look like Carpenters," she said. "Your idiot father would have been so proud..."

Nora felt laughter bubbling up inside her. "Are you

going to call him my idiot father for the rest of your life?"

"Yes." Dina smiled wryly. "I think I will. He's certainly earned it."

Rosie immediately settled now that she was in Dina's arms, letting out a soft sigh of contentment. It was impossible not to fall for these babies, and Nora could see that reality in her mother's face as she gently patted the diapered rump.

"You were this small once," Dina said. "And it was easier then. So much less complicated."

"Are you saying it'll only get worse—this mess, I mean—as the girls get older?"

Dina nodded slowly. "I'm afraid that's the case, but I can't make those calls for you, Nora. You're a grown woman now, and these are your choices."

They were her choices, but some choices had very little wiggle room.

"I've been looking into adoption for the girls," Nora said. "Another family, I mean. It's all so messed up here, and I can't do this without you. I'm certainly not doing it with Audrey as my go-to support, either."

Her mother met her gaze sadly. "You'd give them up?"

"I don't think this situation is good for them," Nora said. "We could hope that things would get easier, but what if they don't?"

Dina didn't answer. Nora knew that her mother couldn't help her to make this choice. She was the only one who could decide what she could live with. Easton's mother had left him, and he resented her so much because she hadn't been thinking about Easton and what was best for him—she'd only been thinking of her own escape. Nora didn't want to make that mistake. She needed to do what was best for the girls, regardless of what it did to her.

"I emailed an adoption agent," Nora went on. "We went back and forth a little bit, and she'll come by and see us next week, give us some more information."

She tried to blink back the tears that welled up in her eyes, but they slipped down her cheeks. She hated this—she loved these girls so much that she was willing to give them up. But it hurt so much more than she'd thought it would. Dina came over to Nora, and Nora leaned her face into her mother's side. She could feel her mother's fingers smoothing over the top of her head, just like when she was little.

"I'm so sorry, baby," Dina whispered. "I'm so, so sorry…"

They both were—everyone was. It seemed that pain was the price paid for having loved.

Chapter 11

Saturday morning Easton pulled up in front of Beauty's Ice Cream. His mom had brought him here once that he could recall—after some massive fight she and Dad had had, and she'd bought him an ice cream cone and stared at him morosely while he ate it. Treats didn't come often, so he'd scarfed it down, but he could still remember offering her a bite. She'd said no. Funny the things that stuck.

He parked next to the red SUV—she was here already, apparently. Glancing in her window, he saw a kid's hoodie in the backseat, next to an empty chip bag. This was it. He was about to meet his brother for the first time, and he honestly couldn't say he was looking forward to it.

Beauty's Ice Cream was a quaint little shop with a red and white awning. Windows lined the front, and he could see the back of a woman's head in a booth. Was that Mom? He assumed so. Most guys could pinpoint the backs of their own mothers' heads easily, but his mom had changed a lot over the last twenty years.

Mom… He still felt a well of emotion at the thought of her, and he hated that. It would be easier to just be angry, or to resent her, but his true feelings were more complicated—so much more difficult to separate.

He opened the front door and entered the air-conditioned interior. Trent, the owner, stood behind the counter. He wore a heavy metal shirt, partially covered by a white apron, and he gave Easton a nod.

"Morning," Trent said. "What can I get for you?"

"Uh—" Easton glanced toward his mom, his gaze landing on the sandy-haired boy. He had a sundae in front of him, chocolate sauce in the corners of his mouth, and Easton found all of his thoughts suddenly drain from his head. "Nothing right now," he said, then angled over to the booth.

"Easton." His mother smiled up at him then scooted over. "Come sit."

Brandon stared at Easton wide-eyed then took a bite of ice cream as if on autopilot. Easton scooted into the semicircular booth so that his mom sat at the bottom of the curve between both sons.

"Brandon, this is your brother," she said.

"Hey," Easton said. "Nice to meet you."

"He's a *man*," Brandon whispered, eyeing his mother questioningly.

"Yes. He's grown-up."

Brandon's clothes looked new, and he had an iPad on the table next to him, a set of headphones draped around his neck. The kid had stuff to entertain him, that was for sure. Easton had never had a Game Boy or decent headphones. His headphones had always been taped together where they broke so that they wouldn't fit right.

They were silent for a few beats, and Easton searched his mind for something to say.

"Easton is a ranch manager," his mother said at last. "He runs someone's ranch for them—he's very good."

"Oh." Brandon frowned slightly. "I'm in grade three."

"Yeah…" Could this get any more awkward? This kid didn't care about meeting his mom's adult son. If anything, Easton's existence was confusing.

"Brandon loves horses," his mother tried again. "He draws them all the time."

"Not anymore," Brandon replied. "I draw monster trucks now."

Easton wondered if this had been a mistake. What had his mother been expecting from this little get-together—warmth and coziness? She hadn't provided that when she'd been in his life, and it wasn't going to suddenly materialize because they all shared some DNA.

"Mom brought me here once when I was your age," Easton said.

Brandon looked around. "Here?"

"Yeah. She used to live in this town with me and my dad."

"She lives in Billings now," Brandon said, and Easton caught the flicker of fear in the boy's eyes. He was eight years old, and he was scared of losing his mom. That was something Easton could sympathize with. Eight was too young to worry about those things, and this kid had all the security that Easton had lacked growing up. He had the clothes, the toys, the stay-at-home mom who drove him to chess practice.

"I know," Easton said quietly. "I'm grown-up, so I don't need our mom to take care of me anymore. She belongs with you. So don't worry about me trying to keep her here."

His mother's eyes filled with tears, and she put a hand out, tentatively touching Easton's arm. What, did she suddenly want to be needed in his life?

"Dad was right about me being okay," Easton said, turning to his mom.

"I'm glad," she said. "I'd hoped so… I made mistakes, son. I wasn't sure if I'd want to do this in front of Brandon, but I think it's better for him to see his mother acknowledge her mistakes than to wonder about them for the rest of his life."

"Were you a little kid when Mom left?" Brandon asked.

"Yeah." The same age as Brandon, but he wouldn't torment the boy with that. "I was. I had my dad, but he drank a lot, so…" He sucked in a breath. He didn't exactly want to horrify the boy. "You know, I got a job, and my boss was a really decent guy. He helped me figure things out, and he taught me how to work a ranch. So I was okay, actually."

"Didn't you miss her?" The kid was connecting the dots here. He was thinking about what it would be like to face his young existence without his mom by his side.

"I did," Easton nodded, a lump rising in his throat. "I missed her a whole lot."

Mom reached out and brushed Brandon's hair off his forehead, and Easton saw it—his fantasy of a loving mother being played out in the life of his half brother. He'd longed for a hand to brush his hair off his forehead just like that…

Easton cleared his throat. "So tell me about your dad."

"Dad works a lot," Brandon said. "But when he's home, he plays LEGO with me. I've got the whole cops and robbers setup, and I play cops and Dad plays robbers. Have you seen the new prison?"

Brandon scooped up his iPad and turned it on. "I'll find it for you—Mom, is there Wi-Fi here?"

For the next few minutes they talked about Brandon's love of LEGO, they discovered that Beauty's Ice Cream did not, in fact, have Wi-Fi and Easton ordered himself a chocolate cone. Brandon was a sweet kid—an untarnished version of himself at that age. Easton had grown up with substance abuse, poverty, neglect, and he'd raised himself. He'd been tougher than other kids his age, and while he used to think of himself as resilient, he wondered now if he'd merely been damaged.

Brandon was smart, intuitive, passionate about his interests. But he wasn't tough—his emotions swam over his face and he didn't hide behind a mask of indifference. Easton was willing to bet that this kid didn't know half the curse words he did at that age. Maybe this was what he'd have been like if he'd been raised in a safer environment.

"Do you have a girlfriend?" Brandon asked him.

"No—" Easton paused and looked into the face of this boy who was finally relaxing a little bit. His little brother. Whatever happened all those years ago, this kid was related to him, and he'd probably want to be in his life somewhat as the years went on. He could close off and keep this impersonal, or he could share something. He decided on the latter.

"There's a woman I care about a lot," Easton said.

"Who is she?" Brandon asked.

"Her name is Nora, and I've had a crush on her since I was a bit older than you. Do you like girls yet?"

Brandon shook his head. "But they like me. Isabel T. said that Olivia liked me last year. I think she did. She was really annoying."

So it began. Easton shot his mother a rueful smile.

"Does Nora like you back?" Brandon asked. "Because if she likes you back, then she's your girlfriend."

"It's a little more complicated when you get older," Easton said.

Life was pretty simple if you were a kid—especially a protected kid like Brandon. But life had a way of getting difficult when you least expected it; of kicking your expectations out from under you. Easton needed a woman who would face the hard times with him, be the shoulder he needed once in a while. Love wasn't enough to make a relationship last, and Easton had been let down in life too many times to take a risk when it came to a life partner. And Nora was a risk. A beautiful, passionate, intoxicating risk. She could be there for him when he needed some emotional support—like that kiss in her bedroom in the moonlight—but Nora also had a pattern of taking off again once her own problems were solved. Had she changed now that she had the babies to care for? Or was he just hoping?

An image rose in his mind of that morning he'd woken up to find his mother gone. His father was drinking already at the kitchen table, and he'd pointed to the note on the fridge.

"Your mom took off," his father said, words slightly slurred.

"What?" Easton hadn't believed it. She wouldn't just

leave *him*. He was her kid, and moms didn't walk out on their kids. He'd searched around, looking for the things that cemented her in their home—her nightgown, her jewelry, the hairbrush that always had hair stuck in it like a small animal. They were gone. Her clothes—the nicer ones—were gone, too. There was an empty space in his parents' closet. Her purse—that sagging bag he was forbidden to touch—was gone from its place on the back of a kitchen chair.

He could still remember what it felt like as the truth dawned on him—Mom was gone. He'd headed up to his room and sobbed his heart out. He wasn't safe alone with Dad—he knew that well enough. He'd have to fend for himself now, because his father sure wouldn't be doing his laundry or cooking him meals. Dad didn't make school lunches.

And when he crawled into his bed that night, the house silent except for the sound of the TV downstairs, he'd closed his eyes and imagined that his mother was stroking his hair away from his face...

"Will you come visit us?" Brandon asked, and Easton pushed the memories back.

His mother looked at him, her brow furrowed, and she clutched at the handle of a new purse—something expensive by the look of it.

"We would really like that," his mom said. "Tom wants to meet you, too. You'll like him, I think."

Had she ever wondered how he went to sleep at night without her there to say good-night? Or if he was eating properly, or if he was embarrassed at school because his dad had drunk away the money for bigger clothes? Did she ever wonder if she'd broken his heart beyond repair?

"Okay. Sure. One of these days."

His mom was back. As weird as this felt. She looked so successful now, so put together. Her hair was nicely done, her makeup making her look a little younger. And he was glad that she was doing it right with her second-born. That was something, wasn't it?

Even if it had all started with an escape...from him.

That evening Nora sat on the front steps of the homestead, her arms wrapped around her knees. She'd found an old framed photo up in the bedroom closet, and she sat outside in the lowering light, looking at it. She hadn't seen this one before. There were a certain number of photos that everyone had a copy of—her great-grandparents' wedding portrait, a picture at some family member's funeral with all the extended family present, grouped around the coffin. There were a few others of her great-grandparents and their children seated on kitchen chairs stuck out in the yard—their equivalent of a family portrait. But this photo was different than the others.

The photo was a small rectangle, not even filling up the entire frame. It depicted her great-grandparents standing alone, likely in their first years of marriage because there were no children about. They were in front of a large tractor—the kind that would be in a museum these days. Her great-grandmother was wearing a pair of overalls, her light hair swept back by the wind, and she leaned against a tractor tire. Her great-grandfather was in a pair of patched jeans, looking at his young wife with adoration. His shirt was open a few buttons, and his sleeves were rolled up to reveal tanned forearms. It was such a perfect moment, and Nora could understand why someone had framed it.

Tomorrow they'd have the corn roast, and somehow she thought her great-grandmother might have made the same choice she and Dina had, to face it head-on. There was something brave and almost defiant in her eyes, and when Nora looked closer at the photo, she noticed something she hadn't seen before in the other, more formal pictures.

Mia looked an awful lot like their great-grandmother. Wow. Funny how DNA worked. Nora didn't take after their great-grandmother physically. She looked more like her mother's side of the family, but she'd still felt a great connection to the Carpenter lineage. Yet Mia, who was the accidental love child conceived during some tryst, was the spitting image of their ancestor. Genetics certainly didn't take legitimacy into account. Mia would have liked to know this, Nora realized sadly. She might have even taken some pride in knowing where her looks came from.

Easton's rusty truck rumbled up the drive, and she watched as he parked and got out. He slammed the door behind him and came toward her. He paused before he reached her then took off his hat.

"Hey," he said. "Care for some company?"

"Sure." She moved over and he sat down next to her, tossing his hat onto the step beside them. His hair was disheveled, an errant piece of hay stuck into one of his flattered curls. He was dusty, and he smelled like hard work and sunshine.

"How was your day?" she asked.

"Not bad." He nodded slowly. "I met my half brother."

"Really?" She shot him a look of surprise. "What's he like?"

"A nice kid," he said. "He's got the whole package—parents who love each other, financial security, all the attention that he needs."

"That's a good thing," she said. "Right?"

"Yup." He smiled wanly. "At least Mom figured it all out eventually."

"Will you see them again?" she asked.

"Probably," he said. "But I'm not ready to hammer out Christmas plans or anything. I'm taking it slow."

That was fair. Still, she could see how much this had hurt him. Sometimes when a person's deepest longing was fulfilled, it hurt as much as it healed. Mia might have discovered the same thing if she'd ever met their father. To Nora, her dad was a superhero. To Mia, he was the selfish jerk who missed her childhood. It might have hurt a lot to see the parenting he was capable of.

Easton nodded toward the photo in her hands. "What's that?"

"My great-grandparents," she said. "I found it up in the closet in your guest bedroom."

He leaned closer to look, slipping a hand behind her as he did so, but it didn't seem intentional. Without really thinking about it, she leaned back against his arm. He looked startled, then he nodded back to the photo.

"He loves her," Easton said, his voice low and next to her ear.

"They were the great Carpenter love story," she said. Easton straightened, pulled away. She swallowed, trying not to let her discomfiture show. "She came from a moderately wealthy family in the city. She and my great-grandpa met at a dance, I think. I don't know how that worked out exactly, but she ended up eloping with him. It took years for her family to forgive her. Even then, she never got a penny from them."

Easton smiled then shrugged. "I'd say she made the right choice."

"They ended up having seven children together," Nora said. "But that picture—I've never seen it before."

"No?"

He leaned forward, his elbows on his knees, and she found herself so tempted to slip her arm through the gap and take his hand. Why was her mind constantly going there with him?

"It makes you wonder," she said quietly, "if he was faithful."

"Why wouldn't he be?" Easton asked. "He had a beautiful wife."

"So did my father."

That was the problem all along—there had been no good reason for her father's cheating. Not that there ever was when someone did that kind of thing. Had he loved Angela? Had it been meaningless sex, or had he fallen for her on some level? And if it was love, how could he claim to love his wife at the same time? She'd believed that her father was above that kind of ugliness, but she'd seen that he wasn't.

"I saw my aunt today," she said after a moment of silence. "She blamed Mom for Dad's affair."

"What?" Easton straightened and shot her an incredulous look. "How'd she figure?"

"She said Mom was too bossy and she implied that it was understandable that Dad would use cheating as a way to gain a bit of freedom from her."

"That's BS."

"Yeah, well… I always thought my parents had a

marriage of steel. My dad would come and talk to my mom before he made any decision. I mean, *any* decision. He wouldn't buy a cow without her input, and it wasn't because she demanded it. He just really wanted to know what she thought first. But Audrey said that Mom was too controlling. Was I wrong about it? Did I see a strong marriage, where really my father was suffocating?"

Easton was silent—probably the smart choice, she realized wryly. He wouldn't know any more about their marriage than she did.

"Because I'm just like my mom in a lot of ways, Easton."

That was what scared her. She and her mother were both strong personalities with their own way of doing things. So if Dina wasn't woman enough to deserve fidelity…if Nora's mother was too controlling or too opinionated…if there was something innately unworthy about Dina that made Cliff feel like cheating was an option for him…what about Nora?

"Your dad talked about your mom a lot," Easton said. "He said he was lucky to have her. He said he wouldn't have been half as successful without her, so his advice to me was to find a good woman with a head on her shoulders and get married. He said two were better than one. I saw your mom consulting with your dad just as often. They relied on each other. He loved her… I don't know what happened when he cheated, but I do know that he loved her."

"And yet, he did cheat." She'd never make her peace with this. How could someone claim to love a woman and then step out on her? How could he see how much she added to his life and then betray her?

"Maybe he lived to regret it," Easton said. "Sometimes that's all you've got to hang your hat on—that the person who wronged you regretted it."

"Did your mom regret leaving you like she did?" Nora asked.

"I think so," he said.

"And is that enough for you?" She arched an eyebrow and caught his gaze.

"No," he admitted. "But it's a start."

"They were no better than we are…just the generation before us. So what makes us so different? We have their DNA, we come from the same genetic line and our formative years were under their care."

Easton reached over and moved a hair out of her eyes. His fingers lingered against her cheek, and those dark eyes met hers tenderly. He didn't seem to have an answer for her, but he leaned in and kissed her lips gently. He pulled back then moved in again, sliding an arm around her and slipping a hand across her thigh as his warm lips met hers.

From the open window above, a baby's cry filtered down to them. Nora pulled back, heat rising in her cheeks. Why did she keep falling into kissing this man? She swallowed hard and rose to her feet. She was supposed to know better, and the minute her pulse slowed down, she'd remember why.

"I'd better go see what the trouble is," she said and headed into the house.

Chapter 12

The next morning was Sunday, the day of the corn roast, and Nora's cell phone rang while she was feeding Bobbie. She fumbled with the phone and picked it up, pinching the handset between her shoulder and ear. Bobbie's big brown eyes were fixed on Nora's face as she drank.

"Hello?"

"Hi, is this Nora Carpenter?"

"Speaking." A dribble of milk dripped down Bobbie's chin, disappearing into the cloth Nora had waiting on the baby's chest. She was getting better at this—anticipating burps and dribbles like a pro.

"This is Tina Finlayson from the adoption agency. Do you have time to talk?"

After a few brief pleasantries, Tina got down to business. "I've just had a home visit with some new clients this morning, and I have a feeling this is something that would interest you."

Nora looked at the clock on the wall. It was nine in the morning on a weekend. "That's early."

"They have a toddler who is an early riser. In my line of work, I make a point of being flexible."

She felt a wave of regret. Emails were one thing, but a phone call made all of this feel a lot more real. Was she absolutely certain about this?

"I haven't made my decision yet about whether I'll be finding another home for them," Nora qualified. "I know we've been emailing—"

"I don't mean for this to pressure you, but it might help to have some concrete information to work with. Are you interested in knowing a bit about them?"

Nora adjusted Bobbie in her arms, and the infant stretched out a leg. This wasn't a decision—it was only getting some facts. Right? That was what she'd been telling herself all along.

"All right," she agreed.

"These are people in a suburb of Billings," Tina went on. "He's a children's psychologist and she's a stay-at-home mom. They live in a large home, are financially secure and they're looking to expand their family. They have one adopted son who is three right now, and they are looking to adopt siblings. They'd love newborns, but they know that isn't always possible."

Nora realized she'd been holding her breath and she released it. They sounded perfect, actually.

"Would they be able to deal with triplets?" she asked.

"The mother has two sisters living in the same neighborhood," Tina went on. "And his parents live on a nearby acreage where they have horses and a hobby farm. So they'd have plenty of support in baby care."

A family that could offer the girls everything from cousins and grandparents to horseback riding on weekends. A father who was trained in child psychology would be an excellent support as they grew up, and a mom at home with them, too. They'd even have an older brother to grow up with.

What could Nora offer? She had a job in Billings—so she couldn't stay home with them. There would be day care, a single mom struggling to make ends meet and little extended family if Nora wanted to protect the girls from all the talk. But they would be loved. The most valuable thing she could offer was her heart, and right now that hardly seemed enough.

"Do they know about the girls?" Nora asked.

"I told them only the basics," Tina said. "That you weren't positive about what you wanted to do yet, but there was the possibility of three newborns becoming available. They were very eager to hear about them."

Of course. For another family, these three babies would be an answered prayer, a dream come true. Didn't the girls deserve to be wanted that desperately?

"Maybe I could meet them," Nora said.

"That would be wonderful," Tina agreed. "Don't feel pressured, but we could set up a little meeting where you could see them in person, get a feel for the type of family they are and you could see where you stand then. They might even be willing to have an open adoption where you could receive updates on how the girls are doing and perhaps be included in some major life events."

Not a complete goodbye…that might be something.

Nora's parental leave wouldn't last forever, and right now she was getting a fraction of her normal pay. Maybe it was better to meet this family before she got so attached to the triplets that she couldn't possibly change her mind.

"Are they free today?" she asked.

"Let me call them and see if we can set something up. I'm sure they'd be very happy to meet with you."

As it turned out, the family was more than happy to meet with her that day. Dina agreed to watch the babies, and Nora drove the three hours into Billings. Her GPS led her down the wide streets of a new subdivision, large houses on either side of the road. It was picturesque, idyllic city life. This was the kind of neighborhood that Nora couldn't hope to afford.

She found the house, and when she parked in the driveway, the front door opened and the dad came out, a toddler in his arms.

"Hi," he said, holding out his hand to shake hers as she slammed the driver's side door shut behind her. "I'm Mike. This here is Bryce."

Nora shook his hand then smiled at the toddler. He was clean with blond curls and new clothes.

"Nice to meet you both," she said. "I didn't bring the girls—my mom is watching them right now." Why did she feel the need to explain to these people?

"Totally understandable," Mike said and as she came around the truck she saw his wife, Sarah. She was pretty—brunette waves framing her face, big eyes and plump lips. She looked like she'd give good hugs. Blast it—why did she have to be so perfect?

But this wasn't a competition. This was about a situation beyond her control, and what would be better for the girls. Yet somehow, Nora didn't much like this motherly looking woman. They shook hands, too.

Tina had arrived before Nora had, so they had some professional guidance for their meeting. And over the course of the next hour, Nora toured their home, which had two extra bedrooms that weren't being used, a hot tub out back and a large vegetable garden that Sarah apparently had time to keep up. The kitchen was covered in little drawings that Bryce had done—scratching on paper with a fisted crayon, by the looks of it.

The house was clean, and the couple was affectionate and seemed to be in a secure and happy marriage. They even showed her some family photo albums from their wedding onward. They seemed to travel a lot.

"What are you looking for in a family for the girls?" Sarah asked once they were all seated in the living room. Nora had an untouched iced tea in front of her. Tina was smiling encouragingly at all of them.

"I don't know exactly," Nora said. Was there anything this family was missing? "A loving home, enough money to raise them well, a supportive extended family..."

Sarah and Mike exchanged a hopeful smile.

"Do you have any questions for us?" Mike asked.

"Have you considered an open adoption?" Nora asked. "It's going to be so hard to let go of them, and..." She didn't even know how to finish that.

"I had mentioned that it was a possibility," Tina said, her tone professional.

"We'd be willing to talk about that," Mike said with a nod. "They used to think that just closing all those doors was best for the children, but not anymore. It's good for kids to know that it was hard for their families to give them up. And if they can have contact with their birth family—limited, of course, without drama and stress—it's thought to be better for the kids overall."

"And we're interested in what's best for the children," Sarah added. "Children aren't owned, they're lent to us by God. And that's not an honor we take lightly."

"How much contact with the girls would you want?" Mike asked, and Nora didn't miss the caution that entered his tone.

"I don't even know." Nora swallowed then heaved a sigh. She felt like she was failing here—sitting in the living room of a "better" family, interviewing a couple that would be a stronger support to the babies she adored.

"Do you have any pictures of them?" Sarah asked.

Nora shook her head, and she suddenly felt protective. She didn't want to share photos of the girls. She didn't want to get this couple's hopes up, either. Knowing that a couple was interested in adopting the babies was one thing, but seeing that interest shining in their eyes hit Nora in a whole new place. This was real—too real. But she was here to see who they were—what they had to offer.

"They're two weeks old now," Nora said. "Their names are Riley, Rosie and Roberta."

"My grandmother's name was Rosie," Sarah said with an encouraging smile.

Would they even get to keep their names? Or would Bobbie turn into a Tiffany or an Elsa? All things that Nora hadn't thought about until this moment. And she'd have no control over that. This couple could rename them, and who would Nora be to complain? This room was suddenly feeling very small, and Nora glanced toward the door.

"To be honest," Nora said, "I haven't made up my mind. I'm pretty sure Tina told you that."

"Yes, it was clear," Mike said. "We aren't trying to pressure you."

Of course not. They were trying to impress her, show her the beautiful home they could give to the girls, if only Nora could find it in her to walk away from them.

"I love these girls." Tears misted Nora's eyes. "If I could provide for them, I'd keep them in a heartbeat. I don't want to do this. At all. I hate this, as a matter of fact."

"We understand." Sarah leaned forward. "It can't be easy."

Why did this woman have to be sympathetic, too? Couldn't she just show a crack already? Reveal some imperfection?

Bryce sidled up to his mother and she scooped him into her arms. He settled into his mother's lap, and she smoothed his hair with one porcelain hand. One day in the not-too-distant future, the girls would be toddlers like Bryce, and they'd be coming for hugs and attention—reminders that they mattered. Did Nora want to give that up? Or did she want to be the one who got to scoop them into her lap and cuddle them close? Could she really let another woman do that?

This wasn't about what she wanted…this was about her financial and emotional reality. If she'd given birth to them herself, she might feel better about dragging them through hard times in her wake, but she wasn't their biological mother. And they deserved better than what she could offer.

She looked at her watch. It was only one-thirty, but it was a three-hour drive back, and they still had the corn roast today. She'd seen enough of this couple to know what they could offer, and it wasn't Mike and Sarah who were the problem.

"Thank you for meeting with me." Nora stood up abruptly. "I have a lot to think over."

Everyone else stood, too, and Nora looked around herself for a moment. She held all the power right now, and they were all being incredibly nice about it... What was the polite way to get out of here?

"If you'd like to talk further, Mike and Sarah, you can give me a call and I'll contact Nora on your behalf. And the same goes for you, Nora." Tina was handing out business cards. "Sometimes after everyone has had a chance to think things through, choices are a little easier. This has been a very good start."

Tina made it all sound so normal, but nothing about this felt normal. Mike and Sarah were a lovely couple, and she hoped they managed to adopt a whole heap of kids, because they had a lot to offer. But *her* girls...

Nora said her goodbyes—shook hands, thanked people for their time—and then escaped to her truck. She needed to call her mom and see how the babies were doing, and then she needed to get back. This was the longest she'd been away from the girls since their birth, and instead of a welcome break the way coffee with Kaitlyn had been, this felt like guilt-ridden abandonment.

Was it possible that she'd already passed the point of no return—that she was selfish enough to put her needs before what was best for the girls?

Easton looked forward to the corn roast every year—light duties, good food and a chance to relax. This year was the first one without Cliff. In a way, today would be goodbye to the boss they'd all loved.

The day started out like any other with general ranching duties, but when those were complete, he and some other ranch hands started the fire pits that would be used to boil corn and bake potatoes. Several barbecues would cook up everything from sausages to steaks. Then they'd indulge in a veritable feast.

"Tony, carry that tub of ice over to the table," Easton said, and the ranch hand in question gave a nod and headed in that direction.

Trucks were arriving in a steady flow now—family giving hugs and waving to each other. Dale and Audrey arrived, and Dale spotted him across the yard and tapped his hat in a salute. Audrey made straight for the babies, but there were already a few ladies who'd beat her there.

He found himself watching the hubbub around the babies more closely than he needed to. Nora was there—she had it well in hand. He had no reason to supervise, but he made note of where the girls were. Audrey had Rosie, Nora held Bobbie and another aunt held Riley, but then there was a trade off and someone else had Bobbie—why on earth was he bothering about this?

Easton pulled his attention away and noticed Dina coming in his direction.

"Easton!" she called. "We need to bring one more table out to where the barbecues are—do you mind?"

"Yes, ma'am," he replied, touching the rim of his hat.

Easton gestured for another ranch hand to help him, and they headed around the side of the barn to the shed where folding tables and chairs were stored. They returned a few minutes later, carrying the large table between them, and that was when he spotted it...

Tony was moving a box of unshucked corn, and as he turned, he swung the box past a woman who had Riley in her arms. The box came within a breath of the baby. Easton's temper snapped and he dropped his end of the table and marched in Tony's direction.

"What was that?" he bellowed.

"What?" Tony looked around.

"Did you see her?" Easton demanded. "You came within an inch of the baby!"

"There was lots of space," Tony retorted. "It's fine."

"It's not fine," Easton said. "Get over here!"

Tony complied, and Easton couldn't quite explain this level of rage. He normally operated on a "no harm, no foul" philosophy, but there was something about those babies that sparked a protective instinct in him.

"The corner of a box connecting with a baby's head would be fatal," Easton said, keeping his voice low and his glowering gaze firmly on the ranch hand in front of him. "There are three newborns and numerous kids around. You walk carefully and look where you're going."

Tony seemed annoyed, but he nodded anyway, and Easton let him get on with his work. Another ranch hand helped get the table over to the barbecues, and Easton looked around. It was all running smoothly. One of the large cauldrons of water had already come to a boil and two uncles were feeding corn into it. A couple of ranch hands were checking the temperature of the barbecues. The food was starting, the setup was virtually complete and now they'd all cook and eat. Mission accomplished. He still felt irritable and unsettled. What was his problem?

Nora stood with a group of family. Kaitlyn was there, too—and across the yard her husband, Brody, was chatting with some other men. But it wasn't Kaitlyn who drew his eye—it never had been. Nora's hair shone golden in the smattering of sunlight, and his heart sped up a little at the sight of her. His irritation wasn't rational. Nora was being friendly, but there was still a gulf between them—family and staff were in different ranks around here. And he wanted more. Blast it, that was the problem—he'd been happy enough over on this side of things when Cliff was around. He'd been grateful for the opportunity to work here, grateful for a boss who was willing to help him mature as a rancher. But now it wasn't that he wasn't grateful…he wasn't satisfied.

Easton was respected, liked, trusted by the family… He was relied upon, irreplaceable in their eyes, but he was still hired help, and looking across the ranch yard at Nora, he realized what he wanted—to be next to her. Not as a friend. Not as the ranch manager. Not as a secret, either. He wanted to be with her, the man by her side.

There was work to be done, and he was the manager around here, so he turned away to check on the barbecues. Cliff wasn't here anymore to keep everything running smoothly. That responsibility was Easton's now.

From across the yard, he heard Rosie's soft cry. Strange that he should be able to pick out which baby was crying, but he could. The last little while with the girls in his house had attuned him to their schedules and the sound of their whimpers and wails. He glanced over to see Audrey trying to shush the little thing. Nora was feeding Bobbie her bottle, and Riley was with a younger cousin who looked absolutely thrilled to be holding a baby. Kaitlyn took Rosie from Audrey's arms, but Rosie wouldn't be soothed, and she wouldn't take the bottle, either.

"Everything okay, boss?" Tony asked, following the direction of Easton's gaze.

"Yeah, of course."

Easton turned away. This wasn't his job, and he tried to ignore that plaintive cry. She was in good hands— most of the women there had raised babies of their own. But he couldn't cut himself off from Rosie's wail. It wasn't just "some baby," it was Rosie, who normally was happy as long as she was being cuddled.

Why couldn't he just tune this out? It was like Rosie's cry was tugging at him.

Tony had the barbecues under control. He turned and strode across the yard.

Rosie's face was red with the effort of her cries. Her tiny fists pumped the air, and while all logic said that he shouldn't have any more success than Audrey did, he had a feeling that he might.

"Howdy," he said, giving Audrey a disarming smile. "Let me try."

"What?" Audrey looked surprised to be spoken to, let alone that Easton would offer to take the baby from her. "No, I'm fine. Thank you." She turned bodily away from him as if he was some stranger instead of the man who'd been helping to care for these babies for the last couple of weeks.

"Audrey, let him," Nora said from a few paces away.

The older woman reluctantly passed the infant over, and Easton gathered her up in his arms, flipped her onto her back and patted her diapered rump with a few firm pats. Rosie's wails stopped, and she opened her eyes, looking up at him in mild surprise.

"Hey, there," he said quietly. "Miss me?"

Rosie blinked a couple of times and opened her mouth in a tiny yawn.

"Well, I'll be—" Audrey said, her tone chilly. "I don't think he's washed his hands, Nora."

"He's fine," Nora replied. "Rosie likes him."

And she didn't like Audrey—that much was clear. It was a strange relief to have this little girl in his arms again, and to know that she wasn't crying her heart out anymore, either. That irritating tug at his heartstrings had relaxed, and he heaved a sigh.

"That did the trick," Nora said, coming up beside him. "Thanks."

"Yeah, sure." He smiled slightly then put Rosie up on his shoulder. She snuggled into his neck. "Not sure how I'm going to do anything else around here, though."

"Supervise." Nora shot him a grin. "I'm sure Rosie would love the walk around."

So he'd be a cowboy trotting around with a baby in his arms. Somehow that didn't seem so bad. He might not be family, but he was the answer to Rosie's cries, and that resonated deep inside him in a way that he knew would only hurt all the more when this was over.

And his time here at the Carpenter ranch was coming to an end. He'd known that Cliff's death had changed things, but Nora's return home had solidified that in his mind. Easton reached out and tucked a tendril of hair behind Nora's ear. He'd miss her—oh, how he'd miss her. He'd miss these girls, too. But any more time spent at the Carpenter ranch, and he'd never be able to disentangle his heart.

Sometimes a man had to put his future first.

Nora let one of her cousins take Bobbie from her arms, and she glanced back toward Easton. He was walking Rosie around the fence and appeared to be pointing out horses to her. She had foggy memories of being held in her own father's strong arms, her dad sitting her on the top rail of the fence and pointing out the horses. She'd have been three or four at the time, but the similarity still made her heart ache.

Why was it that a man could make an excellent father, and still not be capable of fidelity? What was it her dad had said about Easton? "He's a younger version of myself, Nora. You could do worse."

Daddy, you ruined him for me...

Her father had ruined a lot of things for her, now that his secret was out. He'd broken a part of her foundation.

"He loves the babies," Kaitlyn said, coming up next to her.

"Yeah..." Nora nodded. "They took to him."

She shouldn't have agreed to stay with Easton. She'd been thinking of giving her mother space, but instead she'd gotten herself into an impossible situation—playing house, almost. They weren't a couple, but sharing a bathroom and a kitchen made imagining herself as part of a couple that much easier...

Kaitlyn looked pale and she slid a hand over her stomach.

"You okay?" Nora asked.

"I think the corn's not sitting right."

Was the corn off? That wouldn't be good. But Nora

could see several other people munching on butter-drenched corn on the cob, and no one else looked sick.

"Do you want a drink?" Nora asked. "There are cans of ginger ale on the table."

Kaitlyn nodded. "Yeah, I think I'll get one."

Her husband, Brody, was already at the drink table, and Nora watched as her friend tipped her head against Brody's shoulder. He slid an arm around her waist, and Nora couldn't help but feel a stab of envy. Brody handed his wife a can of ginger ale, and Nora didn't miss the way he looked at her. Kaitlyn had it all—the doting husband, the supportive extended family, a home that was ready for kids.

Like the adoptive family in Billings who were anxiously awaiting her decision, she realized bitterly. They were ready for more children. They had it all, too—the home, the marriage, the money, the career... Everything that Nora lacked, that family could give. And family most definitely mattered.

Nora turned back toward her own milling family and ranch hands, who were starting to line up for freshly barbecued sausages and burgers. A family was more than support, it was a library of personal histories. Family never forgot the details, even if you'd rather they did. Rewriting history wasn't possible with a family this size—there was no avoiding the truth.

It was one thing to embrace who you were, but it was that very history that would plague these girls for the rest of their lives in this town. Did she want to raise them and have them move away from her as quickly as possible to get away from the dysfunctional family tensions?

Rosie seemed to have fallen asleep on Easton's shoulder, and he patted her back idly, chatting with one of the ranch hands.

Babies were simple—diapers, bottles, hugs. It was raising the older versions of these triplets that truly intimidated her. And she couldn't do it alone. Sometimes true love meant hanging on through thick and thin, and other times it meant backing off to allow happiness to come from someone else. As much as she hated to consider it, giving the girls up might be the best choice.

Chapter 13

Rosie slept for a while propped up on Easton's shoulder. The other ranch hands showed him an odd amount of respect with a baby in his arms, and when a couple of guys were getting too noisy, one look from him silenced them.

Clouds had been gathering again after a clear afternoon, and the wind had cooled noticeably. People were gathered around various tables of food, some sitting in lawn chairs and others lounging on blankets. A few ranch hands were sitting on upended firewood as they ate their burgers. The day might stay fair yet, though a smudge of cloud could be seen a few miles west.

"Looks like rain," Tony said, biting into a burger and talking past his food.

"Yeah, maybe," Easton agreed, although for the sake of the corn roast, he hoped not. Rosie pulled her knees

up and wriggled. A smell mingled with the scent of barbecued meat. Was that what he thought it was?

Tony looked at the baby in Easton's arms and made
a face. "Baby's leaking," he announced.

Easton pulled Rosie away from his chest and gave
her a once-over. The ranch hand was right. A smear had
formed by the edge of her diaper, corresponding with
that suspicious smell.

"Wow, Rosie," Easton said, and Rosie opened her
eyes enough to blink at him before shutting them again.
"I'd better bring her back to Nora."

"Good call," Tony agreed.

Easton headed back through the yard where Nora
had been earlier, but she was nowhere to be seen now.
Neither were the other two babies.

"Nora's inside," Kaitlyn called. She was sipping from
a can of pop. He smiled his thanks and headed in the
direction of the side door.

He stepped inside and the screen door banged shut
behind him. The house was silent, everyone outside
with the food, and he paused in the entryway to the
kitchen, unsure of what to do.

"Nora?" he called.

Nora looked around the doorway to the living room,
and he stopped short when he saw her face. Her eyes
were red, and she wiped at her cheek with one hand.
She'd been crying.

"You okay?" he asked.

His boots thunked across the kitchen floor, and he
emerged into the living room. She wiped at her face
again as if trying to hide the evidence.

"Fine," she said quickly. "Just working on diapers."

She wasn't fine—he wasn't blind. Nora had the babies laid out on towels on the floor. She added a third towel when she saw Rosie, and he laid the baby next to her sisters.

"Hey," he said softly. "Nora—"

"I'm fine!" Her voice rose, and he could tell she was fighting back tears. Something had happened—had someone said something? Was there more flack about her dad? Protectiveness simmered deep inside him— he'd deal personally with whoever had caused this. But she didn't say anything else.

Nora unsnapped Riley's onesie and peeled back the tabs on the diaper. He could stand there, or he could help. Easton knelt next to her and started with Rosie's diaper. If nothing else, he could do this. He'd seen Nora do enough diapers that he knew the drill—theoretically, at least.

"Wipes," he said, and she passed them over.

They worked silently for a couple of minutes, and Nora passed him a new sleeper for Rosie.

"I need help with this one," he said. He had Rosie diapered, but the sleeper was going to be tricky. Nora smiled feebly, and gave him a hand with tiny arms and legs that just kept curling back as if she were inside an egg. When the babies were all changed and dressed, Easton and Nora sat on the floor and leaned against the couch. The babies were snuggled up together in front of them. They looked so peaceful—Riley's little fist resting on Bobbie's face, and Rosie making sucking noises as she dozed. These girls had the life right now—anything could be fixed with a diaper change and a nap.

"So what's going on?" Easton asked.

Nora looked toward him for a moment then sighed. "I visited a family that wants to adopt the babies."

The information took a moment to sink in, and when it did, Easton's stomach sank. "You did? When?"

She shrugged weakly. "This morning. They live in Billings—the father is a child psychologist…" She licked her lips. "They can give the girls so much. Financial security, love, good schools, a stay-at-home mom—" Tears misted her eyes again. "More than I can." The last words came out in a whisper.

The thought of these babies going to another family felt wrong—like a betrayal, although he had no right to feel that way. He knew it—this wasn't about him.

"And you're really considering this?" he asked.

"I can't do it alone, Easton. Mom is so hurt by Dad's affair that she can't face doing this with me, and I don't even blame her. You know people are talking about it. It's one thing to deal with what he did, and quite another to face the questions and pitying looks that she'd get constantly with the girls living with her…"

Easton understood, but was that really the end of it? Was there no other way for Nora to keep the girls with her? He knew firsthand how much she loved these babies, and he knew exactly what it would do to her to give them to another family. If he left Hope, at least he'd hold on to the mental image of Nora and these triplets together. Separating them…

"The homestead," he said. "If your father hadn't left it to me, you'd have been able to stay there."

Was he the one standing between her and keeping these girls?

"What if you bought me out?" Easton asked. "Dale suggested that. You could have that house again. It belongs with family anyway. I know your dad was trying to do something nice for me, but if he knew what it would do to you and his granddaughters, he wouldn't have willed it to me. I know that for a fact."

"I can't buy you out." Her voice was tight and she swallowed hard. "If I stay here, I won't be working right away. I can't get into a mortgage."

"Then stay with me." The words surprised him, but this was a solution. He didn't have to leave Hope, did he? They were already staying together quite successfully. He could continue helping out with the girls, and she wouldn't have to worry about rent or anything like that. He could rethink that escape he'd been planning—if she needed him.

"How would that work?" she asked, shaking her head.

"Like it has been." He turned to face her and slipped his arm behind her. "We've been working it so far. I could get used to this. Couldn't you?"

"No." There was a tremor in her voice.

Did she mean that? Was she already finished taking what she needed from him?

"Why not?" he asked, irritated. They'd better just get this out into the open. If she was done with his help, he needed to hear it, because that was the only way he was going to accept this—if she told him straight.

"Because it doesn't solve *us*!" Nora's voice shook and she blinked back tears. "What are we going to do, keep cuddling on the couch, kissing on the porch and live together like a couple? That's *not* a solution, Easton. That's a shortcut to heartbreak, and I'm not doing it. You're a lot like my dad, you know." She swallowed hard. "He said it over and over again—that you're just like he was when he was young. You know what that means to me. It's so hard to trust—"

Yeah, he understood all of that, but in spite of it all, they'd been taking care of those girls together. He wished she could trust him, see deep inside him and recognize the man in there—but apparently some things would never change between them.

Easton leaned closer as her words trailed off, and she met his gaze, her breath catching as he took her lips with his. Her eyes drifted closed and she leaned into his kiss. She was warm and soft, and he moved closer, tugging her into his arms. Why couldn't this work? He'd had reasons of his own up until this moment, but he couldn't seem to think straight when he was with her, and certainly not with his lips moving over hers.

She pulled back and shook her head, her fingers fluttering up to her lips. "We've got to stop that," she breathed.

"Do we?" he asked, catching her gaze and holding it. "Really?"

Because he sure didn't want to. She looked ready to reconsider, and given a chance he'd move in for another kiss, but she moved back.

"Easton, stop it."

That was clear enough. He pulled his hand back.

"I'm not starting something I can't finish." She whispered. "Love you or not—"

And maybe he should appreciate that she wouldn't start up with him if she could foresee herself walking away…but she'd mentioned love and his heart skipped a hopeful beat.

"*Do* you love me?" His voice dropped and he swallowed.

Tears rose in her eyes. "Against my better judgment."

He felt the smile tug at his lips. How long had he

waited to hear that confession? How many years had he dreamed of her finally seeing the man he was at heart?

"Because I've loved you for years." He remembered all those years of loving her from afar, being there for her in her tough times and watching her walk away when she pulled it all together again. He could push those memories aside and ignore it in a heated moment when he was so focused on getting closer to her...but what about after the conquest? What about after he had her, and they settled into a routine? She'd never wanted what he could offer before—not for the long-term. His own mother hadn't wanted him, either. He knew better than to start expecting things.

She was vulnerable. He was pushing this, and pressure wouldn't change the end result.

"But I know what you mean," he said gruffly. "I want to short-cut this so badly, but you're right. We should stop."

Tears glistened in her eyes, and he leaned forward and pressed his lips against her forehead. How he longed to kiss those lips again, to forget all the logic and clear thinking, and just melt into her arms. But she was right. Trust was the problem here—she was afraid he'd turn out just like her dad, and he was afraid that she'd walk away when things got tough. There was no point in starting something that would end in him staring at an empty spot in the closet...again. There were only so many times a man could have his heart torn apart in one lifetime, and he was pretty sure he'd already reached his limit.

"So I'm right." Nora swallowed hard. This would be a first—a man admitting that he would likely be unfaithful. But what was she wanting him to do—try to change her mind? She wasn't that easily swayed.

"Not about me cheating," he said, "but I understand why you're scared. I doubt I could convince you that I'm any different. That's an argument I can't win."

Nora's chest felt tight. "It shouldn't be an argument, should it?"

"Probably not." He rubbed a hand over his face, and the gesture brought back memories of the teenage Easton in a flood. He was no kid anymore, and he'd proven that over the last two weeks. This was a man in front of her—a man just like her father.

"Thing is, Nora, I can't offer you the world. I don't have it to give. You're used to a better life than I am, and I'm pretty sure I can't match what you're used to. You're afraid of me turning out like your dad, and you couldn't face that kind of heartbreak. Well, I can't face being walked out on by another woman I love."

Another woman like his mom? For years Nora had watched that sadness swirl inside Easton, and only recently did she discover what had caused it. Now, she blamed his mother, resented her, even. Easton deserved better…and he thought she'd be no different? That hurt.

"Do you really worry about that?"

"Life gets hard," he said quietly. "Really hard. I don't think my mom imagined herself leaving, either, until she did it." He scrubbed a hand through his hair. "And maybe I'm a little bit like her, too. She got out of this town—started fresh where no one knew her past. I get why she'd want that so badly. I've been thinking seriously about doing the same thing."

Easton's words hit her like a blow to the stomach. He would leave? Somehow that hadn't occurred to her as even a possibility, even though she knew other ranchers had been trying to woo him. Easton had been a constant around here. The ranch ran like clockwork because of his professional skills. But he was more than an employee at the ranch—her dad had made sure of that. It was impossible to imagine this place without him. It would be empty here—lonely.

"But you *live* here." It sounded so trite, but she couldn't articulate the depth of her feelings about this. This was his home—over the years he'd become an integral part of *her* home, and she'd taken his presence here entirely for granted. Could he really just walk away?

She rose to her feet, walked toward the window then turned back. He stood up, too, and they stared at each other for a few beats. Easton nodded a few times as if coming to a conclusion.

"I wanted to sell you the house—it would give me money for a new start—but I'm used to roughing it. I'll sign the house back over to you. I'll give your mom my written notice tomorrow."

Anger writhed against the wall of sadness, and she strode back over and punched him solidly in the chest. "You're seriously just going to leave?" she demanded. "Just like that?"

"I can't do this!" His voice raised and he stopped, shutting his eyes for a moment. Then he moderated his tone. "Nora, I'm *not* doing this anymore. I'm not sitting here, loving you, and not having anything more. We both know why it can't work, and you're right—playing house isn't going to take the place of a real, honest commitment. I don't want to just see what happens—I want a family that I can claim as mine. Call that old-fashioned if you want, but it's what I want. And I know myself—I'm not going to get over you that easily. You don't love a girl for over a decade and just bounce back." He swallowed hard. "I never have."

He was right—just like when they were teens, she wanted too much. She wanted him to be there, her support, her confidant. If the last couple of weeks had taught her anything, it was that skirting that line between friendship and more was harder than she'd imagined. He wasn't the only one who sailed past "just friends" in a vulnerable moment. It wasn't fair to expect him to keep trying to toe the line, and she knew that, but the thought of losing him completely...well, that tore at her heart. Their balance wasn't a long-term solution.

He deserved a full life. He deserved a family of his own. Who was she to stand between him and his happiness?

"I'm going to miss you." Her chin trembled, and she struggled to maintain control.

"Me, too. But at least I'll have made it possible for you to keep the girls. I think it's what your dad would have wanted."

Outside, lightning flashed and there was a boom overhead. Rain spattered against the living room window. Easton put his hat on just as the kitchen door opened and people came pouring inside. He held her gaze for a moment, those dark eyes swimming with regret. Then he turned and walked away as the first wave of aunts and cousins flooded, laughing, into the living room.

He'd sign the house back over to her. All would be balanced again, and she'd have a home to raise the girls. She'd have the homestead in her name—her family's history back where it belonged. It wouldn't solve everything, but it was a good start. Yet despite all she would gain, she was losing the man she'd loved against all her better judgment. Pain was the cost of having loved, but the price of saying goodbye to Easton was almost more than her heart could bear.

Chapter 14

Easton stood in his kitchen, the coffeepot percolating on the stove next to him. He felt gutted, scraped out. His throat felt as raw as if he'd cried, although he hadn't shed any tears. He'd been trying to avoid this kind of pain by not starting up with her, but that hadn't exactly worked, had it? He was alone—Nora had stayed at her mother's house to weather out the storm, but he didn't get that luxury. He still had a job to do, and it only got harder during inclement weather.

Even with Nora gone, there were reminders of her, from the baby chairs lined up across the kitchen table, to the soft feminine scent that lingered. What was that— soap, shampoo, just her? He couldn't tell, but he liked it. He'd never had a woman living with him before. Not since his mother, at least, and he wished he didn't know how soothing a voice filtering through the floorboards could be, or how nice a hallway could smell while the steam from a shower seeped through the crack under the door.

Easton had been serious when he said he'd sign the house over to her. He couldn't keep this land and still like himself. He could let Nora live in this house and keep it in his name, but even that felt wrong. It should be hers—completely hers.

The bird-patterned curtains billowed in the wind that whistled through the open window, and he heaved it shut. From the very beginning he'd known that she belonged here, and that was why he'd never been able to take down those curtains. The house had a soul, and it was time for him to stop making another family his own, and start fresh.

The coffee was done percolating, and he flicked off the stove. He'd let his brew sit until he got back. He needed to double-check that all the horses were inside the barn, check the locks for the night and then he could call it a day. Tomorrow he'd give his notice. It was prob-ably better to do this as quickly as possible.

Thunder crashed outside, and it shook the house hard enough for some silverware to rattle in the sink. He headed to the mudroom and grabbed his hat and an oil slicker.

He'd miss this house, this family and its connection to the only woman he'd ever loved. Until he left, how-ever, he had a job to do, and they could count on him to be professional. It was all he had left.

Nora stood by the window, watching the rain come down in sheets. The storm had raged for hours now without any respite—the savagery of the weather matching her mood. Wind whipped through the trees, tearing at the leaves and whistling ominously. A crack, a boom and then a flash of lightning lit up the sky. She glanced back to the couch where the babies lay in their usual row, sound asleep and oblivious to nature's tantrum. Dina sat in a rocking chair next to the couch, and when the lightning flashed, she'd instinctively put a hand out toward them.

"Why don't you look happier, Nora?" her mother asked quietly.

Nora came back to the couch and bent down to push a soother back into Bobbie's mouth.

"I told you—he's leaving."

"But you said that he's signing the house back over to you," her mother said. "You can raise the girls. You wanted that…"

"I'm still wondering if that's the right choice." Nora ran a finger down Bobbie's silken cheek. "I want it, but with all of the gossip here…" She pulled her hand back and straightened. "I came home for you, Mom. Not for Aunt Audrey, or Uncle Dale, or anyone else. I came for *you*."

"I know. And that was the right thing to do—"

"Except in this—" Nora bit back the rest. It was wrong to push this—to plead for more. But when she came home, it was because it was the only way she could handle all of this. She needed her mother's support, and if raising the girls meant she'd be isolated in that little house, trying to explain away people's attitudes to little girls with tender hearts, then keeping them would still be a mistake.

"It's all been a shock to me," Dina said quietly. "The love of my life cheated on me, and I didn't even get the chance to scream at him." Tears misted her eyes, and she sighed. "That's the thing that I'm angriest about—he didn't give me the chance. I needed to deal with this whole mess with him, not *after* him." She reached out and touched Rosie's tiny, bare foot. "I just needed some time, sweetheart."

"Has anything changed?" Nora asked cautiously.

"I suppose," her mother said. "You have no idea how much I appreciate you giving me space in my own house, Nora. I did some crying and screaming into my pillow. I've had my time to argue with your dad in my head, play out on all the different scenarios, but at the end of it all, I come to one thing—I love him. Not past tense. I still do. I always will. I just don't think I can be Grandma."

Anything less than Grandma wasn't good enough—it was too distant to be any use. They were back to where they'd been all along—

"I think I'd be Nana," Dina said. "I've always thought I'd be a good Nana."

Nora blinked, her heart speeding up. "Nana?"

"Does it suit me?" her mother asked uncertainly. "Or is that too old-sounding?"

Nora wrapped her arms around her mom and swallowed against the emotion in her throat.

"It's perfect, Mom."

Dina squeezed Nora's hand and looked up into her daughter's face. "If your dad had been brave enough to tell me the truth, I'd have been angry—that's true. I'd have screamed and cried and stomped out for as long as I needed to. But after we worked through all of that, I'd have stood by him." Her chin trembled with emotion. "I'd have been a stepmom to Mia. He didn't give me the chance."

And how different Nora's childhood would have been! She'd have had a sister—but whether or not they'd have been able to like each other at that stage was up for debate. She'd have known the worst, and that would have been easier in some ways. But it wouldn't change the fact that she'd never quite trust that a man could stay faithful.

"I don't think I'd be that noble myself," Nora said. "When Dad cheated on you, he broke more than your trust, he broke *mine*. I thought he was the world, Mom. I really did. I thought if I could find a man like my dad, I'd be happy ever after. But that's no guarantee, is it? Because even Dad couldn't stay faithful."

"And you're afraid that Easton wouldn't be faithful, either," her mother concluded.

Nora was silent, and her mother shot her a rueful smile.

"I still know you better than you think. You love him."

Nora tried to swallow the lump in her throat. "It's so stupid…"

"No, it isn't," her mother replied. "He's loved you for years. In the last few years your dad hoped that you'd—"

"My dad doesn't get a vote!" Nora snapped.

Her mother rose to her feet and went to the sideboard. She picked up the small framed photo that Nora had brought from the old farmhouse. She looked at the photo for a few moments then handed it over to Nora.

"Did you ever hear the story about that tractor?" Dina asked.

"No, I don't think so."

"This picture reminded me of it because it probably happened at about this point in their marriage, before the kids. This picture is in the summer, but the winters could be really harsh. One winter, your great-grandfather had gone out to check on the cows. Their breath could freeze over their noses, even in the barn. So he went out in a blizzard to do his check. Anyway, he didn't come back, and your great-grandmother waited and waited. She got worried—her husband had his routines and she knew something had gone wrong. So she bundled up and went after him. She found him in the barn, but he was knocked out cold underneath the tractor. No one knows what happened exactly, but he must have slipped on some ice, the tractor had rolled and he was pinned. You see the size of her in that photo—"

Nora looked down at the slim, light-haired woman, leaning up against the wheel of that tractor.

"The story goes," her mother went on, "that she picked up that tractor herself, hoisted it off her husband and carried him from the barn back to the house. She saved his life that day."

"Is it true?" Nora asked. She hardly looked big enough for those kinds of heroics.

Her mother shrugged. "It's family lore. You can decide if you believe it. But the point I'm trying to make is that when you choose a man, you're not trusting in his strength alone. You bring strength to the table, too. Your great-grandfather couldn't have run that dairy without her, and he'd surely have died that night if she hadn't gone after him. So yes, men can make mistakes. They can let you down. They can break your heart. Heck, they can even die on you. But you aren't passive in all

of this, and you aren't putting your faith in him alone."
Her mother fiddled with the wedding ring on her finger. "You're strong, Nora. And you're smart. You're a force to be reckoned with. You aren't trusting in a fallible man, you're trusting in what the two of you are together. Don't underestimate what you bring to the relationship."

Nora turned back to the window, her heart hammering in her chest. She had no control over the future, and she had no guarantee against heartbreak. But she knew what she felt for Easton, and she knew what he felt for her. She'd felt the strength of his feelings when he held her in his arms, and if she was only trusting emotion alone…

Easton had told her that he wasn't sure she could handle a life with him—the ups and downs, the uncertainties. But she knew in the depth of her heart that she could. She could weather any storm with Easton, if she knew that they were weathering it together. She could be his strength, just as much as he could be hers.

But he was leaving—and that realization shook her to the core.

"Mom, I need to talk to him," Nora said, turning to face her mother. She looked toward the babies then back out at the storm.

"I'll stay with the girls," her mother said. "Go."

Nora went through the kitchen to the mudroom, grabbed a hat from a peg and snatched up her mother's oil slicker. She needed to talk to him…there was more to say. He might still leave, but at least she'd have said it all before he did.

Chapter 15

Nora slammed the door to the old homestead behind her and shook off her rain slicker. She'd barely been able to make out the road through the deluge on her windshield, and she'd nearly gone off the road a few times, but she'd made it all right. There were lights on in the kitchen.

"Easton?" she called.

Silence. She glanced around the kitchen and saw nothing amiss. She went over to the stove and lifted the lid of the coffeepot—it was completely full, but only barely warm. She knew his routine. He percolated his coffee then left it to cool a little while he did his last rounds, checking locks and whatnot. If the coffee was nearly cold, then he'd been gone a long time.

Thunder rumbled again, a pause then a mighty crack as the room lit up in a momentary blinding display. She looked out the window as the realization dawned on her. Easton was out there somewhere, and if there wasn't a problem, he'd have been back long ago. The other ranch hands were supposed to have done the last of the work, and he was only doing the last check. Even in a winter storm, it shouldn't take this long.

Nora pulled her cell phone out of her pocket and dialed his number. It rang, but there was no reply. Obviously not—he'd be crazy to pick up a call in that downpour, if he even heard it. Should she stay a little longer and wait? Accidents happened in storms, and a mental image of that tractor in the black-and-white photo rose in her mind. It was silly, maybe, but she'd feel better if she found him.

She slipped back into the rain slicker and pushed her hat back onto her head. She opened the door and had to shoulder it to beat back the wind. Rain swamped her as she pushed through the blinding torrent. It took twice as long to get to her truck, and when she was finally creeping down the road toward the barn, she could barely see a thing past her swishing wipers. She knew his circuit ended with the barn, so she'd try there.

The wind changed direction momentarily, and she could see movement in the horse corral. Horses couldn't possibly still be outside, could they? She pulled up next to the barn and tried to see through the downpour, but couldn't make anything out. She'd have to check in person. She pulled her coat up around her neck—it wasn't going to do much good, but it was something—then hopped back out into the driving rain.

"He's fine," she muttered to herself, preparing to come across him dry and safe in the barn, but through the howl of the wind, she caught the terrified whinny of a horse.

Had she heard that right? Her boots slipped in the mud as she made her way around the side of the barn, rain pounding against her so that she had to keep her eyes shut until she made it to the gate to the corral. She shielded her eyes, and in a flash of lightning, she saw him. He was holding a lead rope, and Scarlet had reared up on her hind legs, pawing the air in fright. As the mare came down, she didn't see the point of contact, but Easton crumpled.

Nora fumbled with the latch, but soon she was through. She slipped and slid through the mud, and grabbed the lead rope again, pulling Scarlet closer.

"Easton!" she gasped.

He crawled farther away, one arm tucked around his side. He'd need medical attention tonight after that kick, but first the horse had to be calmed. She fumbled with the buttons of her coat, and as she tried to take it off, Scarlet reared again. Nora jumped back and tore the coat from her body at the same time. A blast of cold rain hit her, but she was too focused to shiver. She caught the lead rope again, and when the horse came down, she whipped the coat over the mare's head. The horse whinnied in fear, but didn't rear again. Without the lightning to spook her, she'd be able to find her calm again.

Nora gulped in deep breaths of humid air and murmured softly as she led Scarlet toward the barn door. Easton pushed himself to his feet and followed. His face was ashen as he came into the light of the barn, and he hunched forward with a grimace.

"You okay?" she asked.

"Sure." That was a lie, because he leaned back against the wall, wincing. "Just let me rest a second."

Every breath lanced through Easton's side, and he breathed as shallowly as possible as he watched Nora get Scarlet settled in her stall. He'd been impressed—she'd known exactly what to do. If she hadn't shown up when she did, Scarlet might have been seriously hurt. Let alone him…

Nora locked the stall and headed in his direction. He tried to straighten a little more, look slightly less pathetic, but he wasn't sure it worked. She hauled a stool over to him and helped him sink down onto it. That made things easier, but he still didn't like being the winded one.

"Let me see." She eased his slicker off his shoulders and he grimaced as he straightened. Then her fingers deftly undid the front buttons of his shirt and she pulled it aside to reveal purple and red welts across his side. She ran cool fingers over his skin and when she reached his ribs, he let out a grunt of pain.

"Broken," she confirmed.

"Why were you out here?" he breathed.

"Your coffee was cold," she said irritably. "You never let your coffee get cold."

She knew him better than he thought, and he was grateful that she'd come after him. She wasn't calming down, though. Her eyes snapped fire and she took a step back.

"You know as well as I do that you're not supposed to be working with spooked animals alone. That's a safety issue! You could have been killed, you know! A good kick to the head, and it could have been over for you!"

"Had to make a choice," he said, pushing himself up against the pain. He caught her hand as she went to touch the spot again. "Nora, I'm fine."

"You are *not* fine!" Tears welled up in her eyes, and the blood drained from her face. He squeezed her hand and felt her trembling.

"Stop." He tugged her against his other side, but the pain was nearly unbearable.

"I'm hurting you." She pulled back.

"Just a bit." But yeah, maybe less squeezing. He attempted to adjust his position. She was watching him, and it was more than sympathy in those cloudy eyes. "What?" he asked.

She pushed a wet strand of hair out of her face. "I had to ask you to stay."

This only made it harder. They'd been over this already.

"Nora, I can't just be your—"

She moved in closer, her mouth a breath away from his, and the words evaporated on his tongue. Then she closed the distance. His body immediately responded to her, but when he leaned into the kiss, he was stopped by that slice of pain.

"Nora, you gotta stop doing that to me," he said with a low laugh. "A guy's liable to get the wrong idea."

"Please stay," she whispered.

"I thought we talked about this." Did they have to rehash this again to convince themselves that this was folly? It wasn't a matter of not wanting her—he wanted her so much it would probably scandalize her. But if he let himself go, really let himself love her with all the passion that he kept sealed away inside him, he wouldn't be able to turn it off when she couldn't face the hard stuff. That would be a heartbreak that would never heal. What man walked into that willingly?

"My mom told me something tonight that made a whole lot of sense. She said that when you choose a man, you aren't just putting your faith in his strength and his character, you're choosing what the two of you are together. I'm scared, I'll admit that, but I'm no wallflower, either. Together, you and I are pretty tough, Easton. It isn't just you—it's who you are when you're with me. And who I am when I'm with you. And I think—" She blushed slightly then looked down. "I think we're something special when we're together."

He reached out and caught her hand, easing her closer until he could put his arm around her waist. He held her there, his mind spinning. She'd just braved the worst storm in a decade because his coffee was cold. Obviously, he'd misjudged how tough she was. She'd come after him and hauled a spooked horse away from him, to boot.

"I'm not staying here for friendship," he clarified. "I'll lay it out for you. If I stay, I want to get married and raise those girls together. I want the whole package, Nora. Three kids. Mr. and Mrs. Maybe-More-Kids-Later-On."

Her gaze flicked up to meet his—steady, constant.

"And I can't offer much money. Heck, I work for your mom. I might move on to another ranch—depends on the future. If you take me, you take me in the good times and the bad. But I'll work my hardest to keep those times good…" His voice caught. Would she accept him when she really thought it through? He was putting it all on the line—everything he had to offer. He wasn't holding anything up his sleeve.

"You want to raise the girls with me?" she asked. "You really do? Because there is no halfway with three kids, Easton."

"I'm not offering halfway," he said, running his work-roughened hands over her smooth ones. "I know what it's like to grow up under a shadow. My family has a stigma around here, so I get it. I don't ever want those girls to feel like they were less than wanted. I want to raise them together, love them like crazy and teach them how to let stupid comments roll off their backs. I love you, Nora. I want to marry you, and I want to be the only daddy those girls ever know. So if you're serious about this—if you're willing to be something with me, then I want to be married. What do you say?"

"I say yes." Her eyes sparkled with unshed tears and she nodded.

It took him a moment to register her words, but when he did, he pulled her into a kiss until he couldn't take the pain anymore. He let out a soft moan and she eased out of his arms.

"Let's go," she said, helping him to stand. "You need a doctor."

"I'll be fine," he muttered.

"Are you going to try to fight me?" she asked incredulously. "Because if you can stand up straight, I'll let you be."

He smiled ruefully. "Never mind." He allowed her to guide him to the door. The wind had died down and it was just rain now, thunder rumbling in the distance.

"I want to marry you just as soon as you can find a dress you like," he said with a low laugh. "I hope you shop fast."

After all these years of holding himself back, he was

never going to get tired of pulling that beautiful woman into his arms. She was right—they were better together, they were tougher together and they were just what those girls needed around here. The triplets might have been born Hamptons, but they'd be the Ross kids, and no one would ever make them feel less than the beautiful gifts that they were. Their dad would make sure of it.

Epilogue

On a chilly autumn morning, as rain pattered down on the little church in downtown Hope, Nora stood in front of a full-length mirror willing her heartbeat to calm. The veil blurred her vision as she regarded her reflection. She wore a dress of clinging satin cream that spread into a rippling train behind her. The veil was simple, attached to a jeweled tiara that sat on her golden waves. She spread her hands over her fluttering stomach, the engagement ring glittering in the low light.

She was getting married this morning… She'd become Mrs. Nora Ross.

The door opened and Kaitlyn slipped inside the room. She wore an empire waist bridesmaid dress of mint green, and Nora was glad she'd chosen such a forgiving cut now that Kaitlyn's belly had started to grow. After the nausea at the corn roast, Kaitlyn had disbelievingly taken another pregnancy test… She was five months along now and glowing with the new life she carried.

"Are the girls okay?" Nora asked.

"They're all asleep," Kaitlyn reassured her. "And the bottles are ready. They'll be fine. Are you ready?"

"I think so." Nora shot her friend a nervous smile.

"Easton told me to give you this—" Kaitlyn handed her a black velvet box, and Nora looked down at it in surprise.

"Was I supposed to buy him something?" she whispered.

"Oh, stop," Kaitlyn laughed. "Just open it."

Nora pried open the clamshell. Inside was a white gold charm bracelet. She lifted it out of the box, running her fingers over the delicate charms. There were three pink crystal pairs of booties, and on either side of them were two silver halves of a heart. A lump rose in her throat.

"It's us…" she whispered.

At the clasp there was a tiny silver horseshoe—luck. But she didn't need luck. Today they'd confirm their promises in front of friends and family, but these were words Easton had already murmured to her that morning.

I'm going to love you every day, Nora. I'm going to tell you the truth always. I'm going to stand by your side whatever comes at us. I'm yours.

Kaitlyn helped her to put the bracelet on, and as she looked down at the sparkle on her wrist, the old organ's music swelled from the sanctuary where everyone was waiting. Easton was at the front of that church, and imagining him up there, all her nervous jitters melted away.

I'm going to love you every day, Easton. I'm going to tell you the truth always...

These weren't hard promises to keep—they were simply putting into words what was already there. Today she was marrying her best friend.

"Okay," Nora said, gathering up her train. "I'm ready."

* * * * *

Trish Milburn writes contemporary romance for the Harlequin Western Romance line. She's a two-time Golden Heart® Award winner, a fan of walks in the woods and road trips, and a big geek girl, including being a dedicated Whovian and Browncoat. And from her earliest memories, she's been a fan of Westerns, be they historical or contemporary. There's nothing quite like a cowboy hero.

Books by Trish Milburn

Harlequin Western Romance

Blue Falls, Texas

Her Perfect Cowboy
Having the Cowboy's Baby
Marrying the Cowboy
The Doctor's Cowboy
Her Cowboy Groom
The Heart of a Cowboy
Home on the Ranch
A Rancher to Love
The Cowboy Takes a Wife
In the Rancher's Arms
The Rancher's Surprise Baby
Her Texas Rodeo Cowboy

Visit the Author Profile page at Harlequin.com for more titles.

Twins for
the Rancher

TRISH MILBURN

Thanks to Beth Pattillo for helping me brainstorm Lauren's character and for being a friend from back when I was taking my first fledgling steps into the world of romance writing.

Chapter 1

The floorboards creaked as Lauren Shayne took her first steps into the building that she'd become the owner of only minutes before. Her hands shook from the enormity of what she'd done. The mortgage on what had been a German restaurant called Otto's years ago wasn't small, but neither was her dream for the place.

A dream that she would have never guessed would take her so far from home.

Despite her initial "this is perfect" reaction to seeing the inside, the fact it was four hours from her home in North Texas gave her significant pause. Taking the leap had required a week of denial, then pondering and number-crunching after every adult member of her family had told her to go for it. She'd finally reasoned she could get the place opened and leave the day-to-day running to a manager who lived in Blue Falls or nearby.

If it did well enough for her to expand in the future, then maybe she could finally find a space closer to home.

But she couldn't let her imagination run wild. Not when there was still a lot of work and a ton of luck standing between her and making even one restaurant a success. Loyal watchers of *The Brazos Baker* cooking show, or fans of her cookbooks and magazine alone, weren't going to be enough to keep the place afloat. And she needed to get the bulk of the work done before her TV show resumed production after the current hiatus—that would require her to be back in her kitchen on a regular basis.

She attempted a deep breath, but it was a bit shaky. She hoped she hadn't just gambled her daughters' future security away with a bad business decision.

As her steps echoed in the rafters, where forgotten cloth banners decorated with German coats of arms hung, Lauren saw beyond the dust and detritus to a restaurant filled with people enjoying her grandfather's prize-winning barbecue, and baked goods made with her recipes, while they took in an unbeatable view of Blue Falls Lake.

She smiled as she imagined the look on Papa Ed's face when she finally revealed the finished product to match the images that had been in her head for a couple of years. At times, those images and the support of her family had been the only things that got her through one of the toughest periods of her life.

"Now, that looks like the smile of a woman about to do great things."

Lauren startled at the sound of a guy's voice and grabbed the back of a dust-covered chair at the sight of a tall man standing between her and the front door. He held up his hands, palms out.

"Sorry, I didn't mean to scare you."

"Can I help you?" Miraculously, her voice didn't reveal the runaway beating of her heart.

"Actually, I'm hoping I can help you." He didn't advance any closer, giving Lauren a few moments to take in his appearance, looking for clues to his meaning. Dressed in dark slacks, pressed white shirt and pale blue tie, he didn't come across as a laborer looking for a job. She guessed he stood a bit over six feet, had sandy brown hair and was attractive in that clean-cut "businessman who used to be the high-school quarterback" sort of way.

"Tim Wainwright with Carrington Beef. We provide top-quality beef products to restaurants all over Texas. And it's an educated guess that a barbecue restaurant is going to need a lot of ribs and brisket."

Lauren tilted her head slightly. "How could you possibly know I'd be here or that I planned to open a restaurant? I literally signed the papers fifteen minutes ago."

Tim smiled. "I'm just that good."

Lauren made a sound of disbelief. This guy was full of himself.

Tim motioned, as if waving off his previous words. "It's my job to know when potential new customers come on the scene. I heard from a friend on the local city council about your plans and that you were closing on the property this morning. Took a chance we'd cross paths."

"You must really need the business if you're here now." She indicated their surroundings, covered with enough dust they could probably make dust castles. "As you can see, I'm a long way from opening my doors for business."

"It's never too early to make a good decision."

She lifted an eyebrow. Did he brainstorm these business pickup lines? Her thoughts must have shown on her face because the teasing look on his disappeared. He reached into his pocket and retrieved a business card, which he extended as he walked closer.

"I'd like to sit down with you when it's convenient and discuss what we can offer you. Dinner tonight, perhaps?"

There was something in the way he looked at her that made her wonder if his invitation was just about business. Or did he use his good looks to his professional advantage? That thought did not sit well with her. And with good reason.

"I'm afraid I won't have time tonight." Or any night, she thought as she accepted his card. "But when I'm ready to make those kinds of decisions, I'll know how to reach you."

She thought for a moment he might press for the "hard sell" approach, but thankfully he just nodded.

"The dinner invitation is a standing one. I'm through this area quite often."

She simply nodded and offered a polite smile. No need to reveal that when she wasn't working on *Brazos Baker*–related business, she was doing her best to not suck at being a mom. She'd save that tidbit in reserve in case he attempted to get personal. Nothing like the responsibility of twins in diapers to scare off unwanted advances.

Evidently getting the message that he wasn't going to make any more progress today—professionally or otherwise—Tim gave a nod of his own and headed for the exit. Halfway there, he turned and took a few steps backward as he scanned what would become the dining room.

"Can't wait to see what you do with the place."

After he left, she was hit with just how much work she faced before decisions such as which food vendors to use made any sense. And none of that work was going to move to the "completed" column if she didn't get to it. She rolled up her sleeves and took another step toward her dream.

It was time for Adam Hartley to stop stewing over the potential customer he'd lost and forge ahead. His family had been understanding of the time and funds he'd put in to the branded-beef operation so far, but each day he wondered when that understanding would disappear. Everything his siblings did in addition to their regular ranch duties added to the Rocking Horse Ranch's bottom line. Sure, Sloane's camps for underprivileged kids cost money, but those funds were now coming from the product endorsements her new husband, Jason, had signed after winning the national title in steer wrestling the previous winter.

Adam kept reminding himself that big rewards required big risks. He just hoped his risks ended in the types of rewards he envisioned.

At the sound of the front door opening, followed by fast-approaching footsteps, he looked up from the list of possible customers throughout the Hill Country and into Austin.

"I have great news," Angel said as she darn near slid into the dining room like Tom Cruise in *Risky Business*.

"You sold some photos?" His sister was slowly gaining recognition for her beautiful photos of ranch and rodeo life.

"No, great news for you."

He leaned back in his chair. "I could use some of that."

"I just heard from Justine Ware that the Brazos Baker is opening a restaurant here in town."

"Who?"

"The Brazos Baker, Lauren Shayne." At what must be a confused look on his face, she continued, "She has a cooking show on TV. Mom watches it all the time. She has a magazine, too. Some cookbooks. And now she's planning to open a barbecue restaurant in what used to be Otto's."

No, anywhere but there.

Part of him was excited to have such a high-profile prospective customer, but he'd had his eye on that building for a while. His imagination had seen it as a mercantile filled with Rocking Horse Ranch–branded products—prime steaks from their herd, Ben's hand-tooled saddles and leatherwork, Angel's photographs, his mom's chocolate cake. He'd seen it all so clearly—except for the money to make it possible. The branded-beef operation was supposed to fund those big ideas, but he needed time for it to grow. Time he evidently no longer had.

He had to stop investing so much time and energy in the cart before he could even afford the horse. But maybe, despite the disappointment, this opportunity would help him take a leap forward toward the eventual goal. A goal that would now have to reside somewhere else, though at the moment he couldn't imagine where.

Still, the prospect of supplying not only a restaurant of that size, but also one operated by someone famous felt like Christmas presents for the next decade dropped into his lap.

Angel motioned for him to stand. "You need to go shower and put on clean clothes."

"Um, why?"

"Because when I came through town just now, I saw vehicles at the restaurant. She's probably there right now, just waiting to hear all about awesome locally grown beef."

A shot of adrenaline raced through him. When he started to gather the papers strewn across the table, Angel waved him away.

"I'll take care of this. Go on." As he headed toward the bathroom, Angel called out, "Oh, and tell her Mom loves her show. Maybe that will win you brownie points."

Adam raced through his shower and getting dressed. Before hurtling out the door, however, he decided he should learn a little bit more about this famous cook before showing up to meet her unprepared. He couldn't blow his only shot to make a positive first impression. He opened his laptop, which Angel had deposited in his room, and did a search for the Brazos Baker.

A quick web search brought up her page. He wasn't prepared for the beautiful, smiling face that greeted him. With that long, straight blond hair and those pretty blue eyes, she looked one part model and one part girl-next-door. He wasn't a viewer of cooking shows, but he had to admit the deep-dish apple pie in her hands made his mouth water.

He forced himself to navigate away from her photo

and read about how she got her start—learning from her grandmother, entering 4-H baking competitions, publishing her first cookbook when she was only twenty. Lauren Shayne appeared to be a lot more than just a pretty face.

Nowhere on her site was there any mention of plans for a restaurant, but perhaps that was under wraps. Well, it would be until the Blue Falls gossips got hold of the news, which they probably had ten seconds before she'd even rolled into town. The fact his sister had already found out and blown in like a storm to tell him was proof enough of that.

Not wanting to delay contacting her any longer, he shut down his computer and headed out the door. As he drove toward town, he couldn't keep his imagination from wondering what it would mean to have his family's beef used by a celebrity. Would she mention it on her national television program? The possibilities began to supplant some of the disappointment over her choice of building.

His mind skipped ahead to Rocking Horse Ranch beef appearing on the menus of fancy hotels and the catered events of the increasing number of actors and musicians calling the Austin area home. A flash of brown on the side of the road intruded on his daydream a moment before a deer jumped in front of his truck.

He hit the brakes and tensed less than a breath before the unavoidable *thunk* and jolt as he hit the deer dead-center. His heart was still racing when the hiss of steam rose from his radiator. There were times when Adam thought his family's motto should be One Step Forward, Two Steps Back. Why did that deer decide today was the day he couldn't handle the pressures of life anymore and taken a flying leap in front of a pickup truck? A truck Adam had bought used and finally managed to pay off exactly one week ago, just in time for its tenth birthday. And as a bonus, it appeared his air bags were not operational.

After turning on his hazard flashers, he stepped out onto the pavement to verify the deer that had gotten knocked into the ditch was indeed dead. One look was all the confirmation he needed. Same with the front grille of his truck. With a sigh, he pulled out his phone and dialed Greg Bozeman and his always-busy tow truck.

Half an hour later, instead of introducing himself to Lauren Shayne and singing the praises of his family's locally raised beef, he was at Greg's garage, waiting for the man to tell him how much the tow and repairs were going to cost him.

He considered buying a bag of chips from the wire rack to calm his growling stomach, but he figured that was a buck he should save.

Greg stepped through the doorway between the repair bays and the small office of the garage, which had been in his family for as long as Adam could remember.

"I think your family could keep me in business just replacing radiators and front grilles."

Adam knew Greg was referring to when Adam's brother Ben had accidentally run into Mandy Richardson's car the previous year thanks to a pigeon flying through his truck's window and hitting him in the side of the head. He'd had to repair Mandy's car, but it hadn't turned out so badly in the end. Ben and Mandy were now happily married with an adorable little girl. Adam was pretty sure his encounter wasn't going to turn out with that sort of happily-ever-after ending. The best he could hope for was the lowest possible repair bill Greg could manage.

"Yeah, seems the area wildlife has it in for us."

"At least the deer didn't hit you in the head."

After Greg gave Adam the estimated price and said he needed a couple of days to complete the repairs, he asked if Adam needed a ride anywhere.

"No, thanks. Got a couple things to take care of in town." He'd figure out how to get back to the ranch after that.

Greg waved as he picked up his ringing phone.

Adam started walking toward downtown Blue Falls, thankful the day was overcast so he wouldn't be sweating buckets by the time he reached his destination. Now he needed Lauren Shayne's business more than ever. He'd launched the branded-beef business with his family's blessing, hoping to contribute his part to the diversification that would allow the Rocking Horse Ranch to stay solvent and in the family, something that had been touch-and-go on more than one occasion. But if he didn't land some big accounts soon, he wasn't sure how much longer he could keep seeing money going out without enough coming back in.

Sure, the business was less than a year old, but there wasn't a day that went by when he wasn't conscious of the figures in the operation's balance sheet. None of his siblings, or his parents, had said anything about his shuttering the operation, but he was also aware that his attempt to carve out a distinctive place for himself in the family's business was costing more than Ben's saddle-making or Angel's photography supplies.

By the time he reached the restaurant, he'd managed to adjust his attitude from his earlier annoyance to being the friendly, approachable local businessman he needed to be to meet a potential customer. A small blue hatchback sat alone outside the building. He grinned at the big yellow smiley face sticker on the hatch. It was surrounded by several other stickers—a few flowers, one that said I Brake for Cake, one of a stick figure lying beneath a palm tree and another that read Don't Worry, Be Happy.

Lauren Shayne seemed to be a happy-with-life type of person. He supposed that was easier when your business was a roaring success. Although her car didn't look as if it was driven by one of the rich and famous.

Well, if nothing else, maybe some of her happy vibes would rub off on him and finish vanquishing his frustration and concern.

He took a deep breath, stood tall, fixed his pitch in his mind and walked through the large, wooden double doors. The first thing he saw when he stepped inside was Lauren Shayne standing on the top step of a ten-foot ladder, stretching to reach a banner hanging from one of the large posts supporting the ceiling. His instinct was to steady the ladder, but he was afraid any sudden movement would cause her to fall. Instead, he stood perfectly still until she gave up with a sound of frustration and settled into a safer position on the ladder.

"Would you like some help with that?"

She startled a bit, but not enough to send her careening off her perch, thank goodness.

"Can I help you?" she asked.

He couldn't help but smile. "I thought that's what I was offering." He pointed at the banner.

She stared at him for a moment before descending

the ladder. "That's not necessary. I'll get some help in here at some point."

"I don't mind," he said as he walked slowly toward the ladder, giving her ample time to move away. His mom had taught him and his brothers to never make a woman feel as if she was trapped or threatened. The fact that there was only one vehicle outside and no signs of other people in the building told him that Lauren was here alone. "You almost had it anyway. My just being a little taller should do the trick."

She didn't object again so he climbed the ladder and nabbed the cloth banner bearing some unknown German coat of arms and several years' worth of dust. When his feet hit the wooden floor again, he held up the banner.

"This thing has seen better days."

Lauren made a small sound of amusement. "That it has."

He shifted his gaze to her and momentarily forgot what planet he was on. The picture on Lauren's website didn't do her justice.

"I'd introduce myself, but I'm guessing you already know who I am." She didn't sound snotty or full of herself, more like...

"I suppose you've already had several visitors stop by."

"You suppose correctly."

"Small town. News travels fast."

"Oh, I know. I grew up in a town not much bigger than Blue Falls."

He found himself wanting to ask her about where she grew up, to compare experiences of small-town life, but his visit had a purpose. And that purpose wasn't to keep

Lauren talking so that he could continue to appreciate how pretty she was or how much he liked the sound of her voice, which for some reason reminded him of a field of sunflowers.

Wouldn't his brothers—heck, even his sisters—hurt themselves laughing over the thoughts traipsing through his head right now?

"So, the question remains, what brings you by?"

Right, back to business.

"I'm Adam Hartley, and I wanted to talk to you about locally sourced beef from the Rocking Horse Ranch."

"No mistaking this for anything but the heart of Texas. You're the second beef producer to come see me in the last hour."

Someone had beaten him here? He silently cursed that deer for making him later to arrive than he planned. A sick feeling settled in his stomach.

"May I ask who it was?"

Please don't say Carrington Beef. They'd claimed a number of contracts he'd been in the running for, and if he missed out on being first with this huge opportunity because of hitting a deer, he might have to go to the middle of the ranch so he could scream as loud as he was able.

"Carrington Beef."

Somehow Adam managed not to curse out loud, though the parade of words racing through his head was certainly colorful.

Lauren pulled a business card from her pocket. "A rep named Tim Wainwright."

It was as if Fate said, "You think I can't make your day any worse? Here, hold my beer."

Chapter 2

"Honestly, it's going to be a while before I'm ready for any sort of food products," Lauren said as she shoved the business card back in her pocket. She lifted her gaze to Adam Hartley's in time to see a flash of what looked like frustration on his face before he managed to hide it.

"I understand," he said, back to the friendly, engaging man he'd been since his arrival, as if the moment when he'd clenched his jaw and then finally let out a breath had been nothing more than a figment of her imagination. "I'd appreciate it if I could tell you about our products, however."

His approach was different enough from Tim Wainwright's that she wanted to give him a chance. It was possible that his good looks—dark wavy hair, lean build and a face that was far from difficult to look at—might be a factor in her decision, too. She wasn't interested in getting involved to any extent with anyone—might never be again after what Phil had put her through—but it didn't hurt anything to look.

And while Tim Wainwright had also been attractive, his personality was a little too slick and polished—a bit too much like Phil's, she now realized—for him to appeal to her in that way. Granted, it could all be an act he put on for work, but it didn't really matter. She was so not in the market for a man. The market wasn't even on the same continent.

"If you don't mind talking while I work, go for it."

"Okay," he replied, sounding a bit surprised by her response.

"I'm sorry. I don't mean to be rude. It's just that I have limited time to get a lot done, and I'm running behind." Which hadn't been helped by all the interruptions. Well-meaning ones, but interruptions nonetheless.

"No need to explain. I should have called ahead and made an appointment to meet with you."

"Hard to do when you don't know the number."

"True." He smiled, and wow, did he have a nice smile. He ought to be able to sell beef to half of Texas on that smile alone.

But she also knew better than to trust smiles alone. Phil had an attractive smile, too—until you realized it belonged to a snake.

"The Rocking Horse Ranch has been in my family nearly a century. Everyone who works there is family, and we have a history of producing high-quality beef products—steaks, ground, ribs."

As she listened to Adam's sales pitch, she grabbed one of the tables she aimed to get rid of and started dragging it toward the front wall.

"Here, let me help you with that." Adam lifted the opposite side of the table and together they carried it away from the middle of the large dining room.

Before she could voice an objection to his continuing to help her with manual labor, Adam launched back into his spiel.

"I'm sure you already know that diners are more and more interested in where their food comes from, and with our products you'd be able to tell them it's from a few miles down the road, raised by a family that's been part of Blue Falls for a hundred years."

She had to give him credit—he certainly was passionate about his family's business. Considering her own strong ties to family and the hard work to share her love of food with others, she admired that passion. Still, when it came down to the decision-making, it would have to be based on the price and quality of the beef. Adam Hartley could have all the charm and belief in his products the world had to offer, but it wouldn't matter if she didn't deem his ranch's beef good enough to associate with her own brand.

"Sounds as if you have a fine operation," she said. "If you'll leave your card, I'll call for a sample when I'm closer to making those types of decisions."

After a slight hesitation, he nodded and retrieved a card from his wallet, then handed it over. The ranch brand was like none she'd ever seen before, a little rocking horse like a child might use. She made a mental note to provide rocking horses for the girls when they were old enough.

"Interesting brand."

"With an interesting story behind it," he said as he helped her move another table.

"Well, don't keep me hanging."

"Shortly after my great-grandfather bought the first part of the ranch acreage, he found out my great-grandmother was pregnant with their first child, my grandfather. He used part of a tree he cleared where the house was to be built to make a rocking horse for the baby. And he made the first sign with the name of the ranch using what was left."

"That's sweet."

"Yeah, my mom gets teary every time she tells that story. Oh, by the way, I was informed by my sister to tell you that our mom is a big fan of your show."

"I appreciate that. Are you a fan?" For some reason, she couldn't resist the teasing question.

He placed one of the old chairs next to the growing collection of furniture she needed to get out of the way. "I'm just going to be honest here and say that before today I didn't even know who you were."

She caught the look of concern on his face, as if maybe he'd just shot a giant hole in his chances to land her business. Even seeing that, she couldn't help but laugh.

"I can't say that I'm surprised. I wouldn't peg you as the main demographic."

"If it helps, I do like baked goods. I don't think I've ever said no to pie, cake or cookies."

She pointed at him. "And that's what keeps me in business, the country's collective sweet tooth."

Without direction, Adam rolled an old salad bar toward the rest of the castoffs. "I hope you don't mind me asking, but if you're known for baking—"

"Why a barbecue restaurant?"

"Yeah."

"My grandfather has won more blue ribbons than I can count in barbecue competitions. I want to feature his recipe. He's actually the reason I'm here." She gestured toward their surroundings, glancing up at the high ceiling with the log beams that she imagined gleaming after a good cleaning and polish. "He grew up in Blue Falls."

"I wonder if my parents know him."

"Probably not. He left about fifty years ago."

"Has he moved back?"

She shook her head. Not unless you counted the fact he was camped out at their hotel babysitting while she worked.

"No, and yet he somehow convinced me that this was the place to launch the next phase of my business."

"Blue Falls is a good place to settle."

"I won't be living here, either," she said. "I'll just be here to get this place up and running, then I'll leave it in a manager's hands and go back home."

"Which is where?"

That felt a little too personal to reveal to a man she'd just met.

"Sorry, didn't mean to pry."

Settling for a compromise answer, she said, "North Texas."

Lauren realized when they picked up the next table to move it that it was the last one. "So, have you been helping me haul all this stuff in the hopes I'll award you a contract?"

"No, ma'am. Just being neighborly."

He seemed genuine with that answer, but she wasn't sure she totally bought it. Or maybe she was just extra cautious now, having been so recently burned in a very public way. She wondered if Adam Hartley knew about that. She found herself hoping not, and hated the idea that her recent troubles were what sprang to mind when people saw her now. Maybe if he hadn't known who she was before today, he didn't know all the ugly backstory, either. That would be refreshing.

"Okay, neighbor, I could use a suggestion of who to call to make all this stuff disappear." She pointed toward the pile of furniture they'd moved. It was still serviceable but not at all like what she had in mind for her restaurant.

"Actually, I know someone who would probably love to take if off your hands at no cost. She repurposes things other people don't want anymore."

"Sounds great."

He pulled out his phone and started scrolling through his contacts until he found what he was looking for, then extended the phone to her. She added Ella Bryant's name and number to her own phone before returning his to him.

"Well, I best get out of your hair," he said as he slid the phone back into his pocket.

"Are you kidding? You helped me make up for all the time I lost this morning."

"Glad to help, ma'am."

"Lauren, please."

"It was nice talking with you, Lauren. I look forward to hearing from you about that sample."

As he walked toward the front door, she thought that if she was any other single woman who'd had any other recent past than the one that she'd just experienced over the past eighteen months, she might want a sample all right. A sampling of Adam Hartley.

* * *

Adam hurried across the parking lot of what had until this morning been his dream purchase. Well, he supposed it was still technically a dream, but one that wasn't going to come true. But maybe he could still salvage something positive from the unexpected turn of events. Though he didn't have any sort of commitment of her business, he thought the meeting with Lauren had gone pretty well. He'd even managed not to allow his instant attraction to her show. At least he hoped it hadn't. Now he just needed to get out of sight of the restaurant before she noticed he'd arrived on foot. It wouldn't speak to his professionalism and the success of his company that he didn't even have a running vehicle to drive.

Thinking about his damaged truck brought to mind the fact that he'd almost beaten Tim Wainwright to the punch this time. It was as if the man had spies all over Central Texas, feeding him advance information about potential customers. Judging by the number of accounts Adam had lost to the man, he'd wager Wainwright's commission income was quite a tidy sum. Enough to make him cocky. The times they'd crossed paths, Wainwright acted friendly but it was in that way that said without words that he knew he was always going to win the day. He really hadn't changed that much since his days as quarterback at Jones-Bennett High, one of Blue Falls High's biggest rivals.

Adam's jaw tensed just thinking about the guy's smug look if Carrington Beef convinced Lauren to go with their products. That commission alone would probably send Wainwright on some Caribbean vacation. He likely didn't have a family ranch he was trying to take to the next level, to save for future generations. The idea of Lauren doing business with him stuck in Adam's craw.

Though their initial meeting had gone well, Adam felt as if he needed to do something more to bring Lauren over to his side. But he couldn't be pushy, wouldn't put on a practiced smile and say whatever necessary to garner her business. There had to be a happy medium. He just had to figure out what that was, and quickly.

His stomach let out a growl that would make a grizzly jealous. Thankfully the sound had held off until he was out of earshot of Lauren. Before he texted some member of his family for a ride home, he aimed to settle the ravenous beast. Lunch at the Primrose Café would be a perfect solution. Maybe while he downed the daily special, some tremendous idea for guaranteeing Lauren went with Rocking Horse Ranch beef would occur to him.

At the sound of an approaching vehicle, he moved farther onto the side of the road. When the car slowed and stopped next to him, he looked over and saw Lauren staring back at him. She looked confused, probably because she hadn't passed any disabled vehicles between her building and him.

"Need a ride?"

"I'm good, thanks."

As if to negate his words, a rumble of thunder picked that moment to accompany the overcast skies.

"I wouldn't be very neighborly if I let you get drenched, would I?"

With a sigh, he opened the passenger-side door and slipped inside the car just as the first raindrops fell.

"Thanks."

"No problem. Where to?" Thank goodness she didn't

ask him why he'd been hoofing it down the shoulder of the road.

"Primrose Café, downtown."

"They have good food?"

"Yeah."

"Great. I'll give it a try, too. Was headed out in search of lunch, just hadn't decided where. Though I look a fright."

"No, you don't." Far from it. "And besides, the Primrose isn't fancy. You'll see everyone from tourists to ranchers who have a load of cattle waiting outside."

When they reached the café, the parking lot was pretty full. With her small car, however, she was able to squeeze into a space that would hold only about half of his truck if he split it down the center. Thankfully, the spot was close to the door.

"One of the joys of having a small car," she said. "Along with great gas mileage."

They raced for the front door to the café, which he held open for her.

"Thanks." She offered a brief smile, but it was enough to make his insides feel wobbly. He looked away, trying to convince himself it was just his hunger reasserting itself.

Lauren got the attention of a waitress when they stepped inside. "Who do I see about placing a to-go order?"

"Any of us. But honestly, you'll probably get your food faster if you just eat here. We got a big group take-out order in about two minutes ago, so you'd be behind all those. Different cook working on dine-ins."

Adam looked around the crowded room, not unusual for this time of day, and spotted a two-top over by the wall. He caught Lauren's gaze and pointed toward the table. "You're welcome to join me if you think you can stand me a little longer."

He tried not to take it personally when she hesitated a little too long before nodding.

They'd barely sat down before a woman at the next table said, "Oh, my God. You're the Brazos Baker, aren't you?"

Lauren smiled, similar to the smile she showed on her website. It was different than the more natural ones she wore when not in what could be considered the public spotlight.

"Yes, ma'am."

"I don't believe it." The woman looked at her friends, who suddenly appeared just as excited. "We all love your show."

"I made your pineapple cream cake for my daughter's wedding," one of the other women said. "I had to hide the top tier for her and her husband or it would have been gobbled up, too."

"Well, I'm glad everyone enjoyed it."

The back-and-forth was interrupted by the same waitress who'd greeted them at the entrance. "What can I get for you?"

They hadn't even cracked the menus open, not that Adam ever had to. Other than the daily specials, the menu at the Primrose didn't really change. Still, Lauren hadn't been here before.

"She needs time to look at the menu," he said.

"No, I'm okay. You go ahead. I can decide quickly." She opened up her menu to give it a quick perusal.

"Burger and fries for me," he said, not feeling the daily special of turkey and dressing.

"That actually sounds good," Lauren said. "Give me that, too."

When the waitress hurried away, Lauren pulled out her buzzing phone. "Sorry, I have to respond to this."

"No need to apologize. You're a busy woman."

She flew through answering the text like a teenager who could text faster than she could speak. He took the opportunity to text Angel for a ride home after he ate. When he looked up, Lauren pointed at his phone.

"Looks as if I'm not the only one."

"Arranging the family version of Uber." At the curious expression on her face, he confessed, "I might have run over a deer and crunched the front of my truck on the way into town."

"Oh, no. My sister once completely destroyed her car when she hit, I swear, the biggest buck I've ever seen. He was like a ninety-eight-pointer or something."

He laughed at that mental image. "Bet he had a neck ache before his untimely demise."

One of those genuine smiles appeared on her face, and he swore he'd never seen anything so beautiful.

The waitress had been right. She appeared with their food just as the other staff members behind the counter started bagging up a large number of takeout containers. As their waitress moved on to her next customers, he noticed a couple of the women who'd been chatting with Lauren were now looking at him. They smiled then shifted their gazes away, but he felt odd, as if they'd been sizing him up.

He'd taken one bite of his burger when the group of women started making moves to leave. When they stood, the one who'd originally recognized Lauren drew her attention again.

"I'm so glad to see you doing well and moving on. The way that boy treated you was so wrong. I wanted to hit him upside the head with my purse, and it's not an unsubstantial weapon," she said, lifting what to Adam's eyes looked more like a piece of luggage.

"Uh, thank you." Lauren's answer sounded strangled, as if she suddenly wished she was anywhere but where she sat.

Thankfully, the women didn't stick around any longer, especially since one of the waitresses was already clearing their table so more customers could be seated. But Adam only saw that activity with his peripheral vision because his gaze was fixed on Lauren and how any hint of a smile, of happiness, had just evaporated right before his eyes.

Chapter 3

Lauren had read books where the characters were placed in situations so embarrassing that they wished for a hole to open up and swallow them, but she'd never experienced it herself. Not until now anyway. Even during the trial Phil had forced her into with claims she'd promised him half her business, she hadn't experienced the need to pull herself into a shell to hide like a turtle. Then she'd had her attorney beside her, and she'd been filled instead with righteous anger and a fierce determination to prove that Phil was full of crap and not entitled to one red cent of her money.

The determination had paid off. Only after it was all over did she realize the emotional toll it had taken on her. But as the woman had said, Lauren was moving forward—just not in the way the other woman had assumed. Before Lauren figured out some way to correct her while also not offending Adam, the woman and her friends were already headed for the exit.

Oh, how she wished she hadn't gotten a text from Papa Ed earlier that he and the girls had already eaten and were about to take a nap. She'd intended to order her lunch to go so she could head back to work. She wanted to get a good amount accomplished but also leave plenty of time to play with Bethany and Harper before their bedtime.

Movement across the table brought her back to the present. She couldn't meet Adam's gaze, didn't want to invite any questions about what the other woman had meant. Hoping by some miracle he'd missed it entirely, she latched on to the first nonrelated topic that came to mind.

"So, you said your company only employs family members. How many people is that?"

"We're up to eleven if you don't count the kids, although one's a toddler so she gets a free pass." She smiled at his joke, causing him to do the same. "Some have other jobs, too, but we all pitch in on the ranch whenever and wherever needed. You're welcome to come out and see the operation sometime, if that would help make your decision easier."

"I'll keep that in mind," she said, more out of gratitude that he'd not asked about the woman's comment than any real need to see the beef still on the hoof.

Thankfully, their conversation flowed into even safer territory with him telling her about the various businesses in town that brought in tourists, or that were popular with the locals—or both.

"You're going to have some competition from Keri

Teague. She owns Mehlerhaus Bakery and is considered the best baker in Blue Falls."

"I don't mind a little friendly competition. It's been my experience that there can never be too many desserts available. The number of people with a fondness for sweets is directly proportional to the number of sweets they can get their hands on."

Adam laughed. "You and Keri should get a cut of Dr. Brown's business. He's the local dentist."

She smiled. "That's not a half-bad idea."

Adam's smile lessened a fraction as he glanced beyond her. Before she could turn to investigate why, an older woman stepped up to the table and placed her hand on Adam's shoulder.

"I hear your family's about to get a little bigger again."

"You hear correctly."

Was Adam married? She didn't see a ring on his hand, but that didn't mean anything. She knew ranchers who didn't wear rings so they didn't get caught on machinery and rip off a finger. Of course, he could be a father without a wife. He had mentioned kids on the ranch earlier. Though she barely knew him, she really didn't want to believe he might be married and having a friendly, chatty lunch with her. She was well aware that men and women had business lunches all the time, but the fact that Adam didn't come across as a married man made her hope he wasn't. Not that she wanted to be with him. She just didn't want to be faced with another lying, self-serving man.

Adam made eye contact with Lauren. "My oldest brother, Neil, and his wife just announced they're having their first baby."

"Oh, good for them." She ignored the strange and unexpected feeling of relief that the child wasn't his. She tried finding a valid reason for her reaction. When she couldn't, she chose to ignore it.

"Yeah, it's so nice seeing all the joyful events your family has been having—weddings, babies." The woman shifted her attention toward Lauren. "I'm sorry. I must have left my manners in the car. I'm Verona Charles. I wanted to welcome you to Blue Falls. Everyone is so excited to have you here, and we can't wait to see what you do with your place."

"Thank you. I appreciate that." She wondered if there was a soul left in the county who didn't know what she was up to. She accepted Verona's hand for a shake. "It's nice to meet you."

"Verona used to be the head of the Blue Falls Tourist Bureau before she retired," Adam said.

"Yeah, but old habits die hard. I still have this urge to greet newcomers and visitors as soon as they cross the city limits."

Lauren caught a shift in Adam's expression—as if he was trying really hard not to smile or maybe even laugh. What was that about?

"Verona, your order's ready," one of the waitresses called out from behind the counter.

"Oh, I better get that. Taking lunch out to everyone at the nursery."

After Verona took her leave, Adam explained her final statement. "Her niece, Elissa, owns Paradise Garden Nursery, a big garden center a short distance outside of town. That's another tourist draw to the area, especially in the spring."

"Ah. So now explain what was so funny."

"You caught that, huh?"

She nodded as she swirled a fry through her pool of ketchup.

"I guess someone should warn you. Verona has appointed herself town matchmaker. If you spend any time here at all, she'll try to pair you up with someone."

A cold ball of dread formed in Lauren's middle. A matchmaker was the absolute last thing she needed in her life right now.

Adam considered himself lucky that his attempt to not laugh at Verona was all Lauren had noticed. If she'd guessed that he'd momentarily been okay with the idea of Verona trying to match up the two of them, that likely would have been the end of any chance he had of winning her business. He had all the evidence he needed in her reactions to what both the unknown woman and Verona had said. He wasn't Sherlock Holmes or anything, but even he was able to deduce she wasn't interested in a romantic relationship. He had to admit he was curious why, but he wasn't about to ask such a personal question of someone he'd met only a little more than an hour ago.

After they'd finished their meals, he asked Lauren if she wanted dessert.

"Better not. I'm so full now that I'm likely to want to take a nap when I get back instead of working."

"Speaking of, you'll want to be careful with that ladder, especially if you're alone. When I first came by earlier, I was afraid you were about to topple off it."

"I'll be careful. A full body cast isn't my idea of a good time."

"That's nobody's idea of a good time."

After they both paid for their meals, he once again

held the door open for her. The rain had passed, leaving behind a faint hint of sun trying to burn its way through the clouds.

"You need a ride somewhere else?"

He spotted Angel just pulling into the parking lot. "No, thank you. My ride just showed up."

She glanced across the parking lot. He could tell when she spotted Angel.

"One of the family members who works at Rocking Horse Ranch?"

He nodded. "My sister, Angel. She's mainly a photographer, a darn good one, but she's been known to string fence and muck out stalls."

"My little sister dabbles in photography, too. Nature stuff, mostly. Does Angel specialize?"

"Ranch life and rodeos. She's beginning to gain some recognition, has had some photos in a couple of national magazines."

"That's great. Well, I'll stop talking your ear off and let you get on with your day."

"No problem. Hope to hear from you soon."

She simply nodded and headed toward her car, and he hoped he hadn't come across as too pushy. He didn't think he had, but you never knew how far was too far for other people.

When he realized he'd been watching her a bit too long, he turned away and headed for Angel's vehicle.

"That was her, wasn't it?" Angel asked as soon as he opened the door to her car.

"Yeah."

"Looks as if things must have gone well if you two had lunch together."

"I think our meeting went okay, but lunch was just an accident."

Angel started the engine but didn't pull out of the lot. Instead, she watched as Lauren drove by and gave a quick wave to them.

"How does an accidental lunch happen exactly?"

With a sigh, he recounted the story of his morning, right up until Lauren had given him a ride to the Primrose.

"Well, that's a good sign."

"Not necessarily. She was just being a decent person, preventing me from getting soaked to the bone."

"I'd give you that except she agreed to have lunch with you, too."

"It wasn't her first choice." As Angel finally drove out of the lot onto Main Street, he told her how he and Lauren had come to share a table.

"She could have waited for takeout or gone somewhere else."

"Yeah, but she was hungry then."

"Whatever. I just think you must have made a good impression."

He hoped so, and he tried to tell himself it was only for professional reasons.

"I think she's already in Verona's crosshairs."

"I wonder who Verona has in mind for her," Angel said, not even trying to disguise her teasing tone.

"Well, judging by Lauren's reaction to the idea of a matchmaker, I'm guessing Verona is out of luck on this one."

"Oh, I suppose that does make sense."

"What does that mean?"

"Lauren went through a really ugly and public

breakup with her fiancé. And then the bastard took her to court, tried to sue her for a big chunk of her profits."

"Did he help her start her business or something?"

"No. From what I read, he claimed she'd promised him a half stake when they got married. When the engagement got called off, he sued, saying he was still entitled to what he was promised."

"He sounds like an ass." Adam supposed this ex could have been cheated somehow, but his gut told him Lauren wasn't the type of person who would treat someone that way. He based that on the look he'd seen on her face when the woman at the café had mentioned the guy doing Lauren wrong. She'd seemed very adamant in her support of Lauren. What was it with men who couldn't treat women decently?

"That's the general consensus," Angel said.

"Verona ought to know about that and lay off."

"Maybe she thinks the way to get past such a bad breakup is to find someone new and better."

"She might mean well, but she should mind her own business."

"I've wondered sometimes if Verona is lonely. She's never married, and I've never seen her out with anyone."

"Still doesn't give her the right to push people together."

"I think it's more like gentle nudges."

Adam snorted. "I'd hate to receive one of those nudges if I was anywhere near a cliff."

When they reached the ranch, he changed back into work clothes so he could help his brothers replace some rotting timbers on the side of the barn. As he rounded the corner of the barn, he spotted Neil first. His eldest brother was standing back and watching as Ben nailed a board in place.

"Playing supervisor again?" Adam asked.

Neil smiled. "Perk of being the oldest."

"Yeah, you're going to feel old soon when that baby gets here," Ben said. "I speak from experience. There were days in those early months after Cassie was born that I almost had to tape my eyes open to get any work done."

Suddenly, Adam felt more separate from his brothers than he ever had before. Their lives had moved into a different stage, which included marriage and children. They could share experiences, along with their sister, Sloane, to which he had nothing to add. Even Angel had a child, though no husband. In that moment, Adam felt more like an outsider than he had since arriving on this ranch as a child.

"How'd the meeting go?" Neil asked, drawing Adam's attention back to something they did have in common—the ranch and its long-term viability.

"Pretty good. Will be a while before anything can come from it, though."

"Just make sure you kick Wainwright's butt this time," Ben said.

Adam decided not to reveal that Wainwright had beaten him to Lauren's door. He had to believe that one of these days the Rocking Horse operation was going to triumph over Carrington. And he admitted to himself that there was another reason he hoped he would win the contract with Lauren. It would be no hardship to see her on a regular basis. Or would it? He was attracted to her, but he respected that the feeling wasn't mutual. It would have to be enough if they had a business relationship, maybe even became friends.

But as he helped Ben and Neil finish making the repairs to the barn, he couldn't manage to push Lauren from his thoughts. He considered how Neil, Ben and Sloane had all found their other halves when they were least expecting it. And tried not to think about how he sure hadn't expected his reaction to Lauren Shayne.

Lauren walked outside the restaurant with two cold bottles of water in hand to find Ella Bryant and her husband, Austin, loading the last of the tables onto a trailer hooked up to their pickup.

"You two look thirsty," Lauren said as she extended the bottles toward them.

"I feel as if I could drink the lake," Austin said as he hopped down from the trailer.

"Eww," Ella said.

Lauren laughed. "Pretty does not equal potable."

Austin did manage to drink half the contents of his bottle before coming up for air, however.

"I really appreciate all this," Ella said.

"Thank Adam Hartley. He's the one who suggested I call you."

"I'll do that. He's a good guy. All the Hartleys are good people."

"That's reassuring to hear about someone I might do business with in the future."

"I haven't had their beef," Austin said, "but that family is as honest as anyone you'd ever hope to meet."

Now that was more welcome to hear than they could possibly know. Honesty was pretty much at the top of her list of desirable traits these days.

Lauren pointed toward the load of discarded furniture. "I have to admit I'm curious to see what you do with all that."

"I have more ideas and materials now than I have time to implement. But I guess that's a good problem to have."

"It is indeed."

Ella nodded toward the building. "Do you know what style you're going to put in its place?"

"Honestly, it's going to be like picking the building— I'll know it when I see it. But I want it to be Texas-themed. Part of the building is going to be a store filled with items with that theme, as well."

"You should check out the antiques stores in Poppy. They've always got neat stuff, lots of big items that could be turned into unique tables, large metal Texas stars. And there are a lot of craftsmen and artists in the area who I'm sure would be interested in putting their items in your store if that's the way you want to go with it. We have a local arts-and-crafts trail, so you could surreptitiously check them out in advance if you wanted to."

Now that did sound promising. "Thanks for the tip. I'll do that whenever I get the chance."

"Well, we'll let you get back to work," Austin said. "We look forward to your opening."

"Thanks." She waved goodbye to them, then went back inside to tackle washing all the windows. She'd been putting it off for three days because she hated the task so much. It probably made sense to just wait until all the interior work was done, but she wanted a better idea of how the place would look at different points of the day through actual clean windows. How the sun hit would likely influence how she organized the dining room and the shop.

But the moment she stepped inside, the enormity of the job—not to mention the time she'd have to spend on the ladder Adam had warned her about—hit her, and she just couldn't face the task today. In truth, she didn't feel as if she could face much more than a hot shower, dinner and a face-plant into her bed at the Wildflower Inn.

But mommy duties awaited, and the thought of seeing her smiling babies gave her a boost of energy. At least two wonderful things had come from her relationship with Phil.

She promised herself she'd tackle the windows tomorrow, then grabbed her keys to lock up. As she drove the short distance to the inn, her thoughts wandered through the names and faces she'd met since her arrival in Blue Falls. Everyone seemed nice and she could see why Papa Ed had fond memories of the place. Though she'd been hesitant initially about placing her flagship restaurant here, now she could see that it would fit in perfectly with the community's other offerings.

Thankfully, no one else had mentioned Phil or the trial, so they either didn't know about it or had decided not to bring up the topic. She'd prefer the former but would take either. What she wanted more than anything was to forget Phil even existed and that she'd ever been so blind that she hadn't seen through to his real motive for wanting to marry her. She would never make that kind of mistake again.

For some reason, she wondered if Adam Hartley now knew all the details. After meeting him and Tim Wainwright, she'd done an internet search on both their companies. So it would stand to reason they'd done the same for her. She felt sick to her stomach thinking about Adam sitting in front of his computer reading about the trial. He seemed like a nice guy, but she detested the idea that someone learning about her past might see her as an easy mark.

She shook her head, not wanting to be so cynical. Instead, she'd rather think of Adam as a potential friend. She didn't want him to know about what Phil had done, because it might taint the possibility of a friendship without the accompanying pity she'd seen in the eyes of more than one person she knew. Their hearts were in the right place, but those reactions had only served to make her feel like an even bigger fool.

When she reached the inn, she didn't immediately get out of her car. Instead, she sat in the quiet, looking out across Blue Falls Lake, its surface painted gold by the slant of the setting sun. This area was pretty now, even with winter approaching. She'd bet it was gorgeous in the spring, when all the wildflowers were blooming and carpeting the roadsides throughout the Hill Country.

Hopefully, all the busloads of tourists who visited the area in search of the iconic bluebonnets would fill her restaurant to bursting and keep the cash registers busy. Maybe it was petty or needy of her, but she wanted her first venture since leaving Phil to be so successful he choked on the idea of all the money not going into his pockets. And it would provide undeniable proof that his claim she would be a failure without him was complete garbage.

Not wanting to think about her ex anymore, she made her way inside.

She heard the girls giggling before she even opened

the door to her room. When she stepped inside, she smiled at the sight that greeted her. Papa Ed was playing peekaboo with Bethany and Harper, much to their mutual delight.

He straightened from where he was sitting on the edge of the bed next to the girls' travel crib. "Look who's home," he said in that special voice he used with his great-granddaughters.

Lauren didn't point out that nice as it was, the Wildflower Inn wasn't home. Instead, she headed straight for her little blonde bundles of grins and baby claps. She lifted Bethany from the crib and booped her nose with the tip of her finger.

"Have you been good for Papa Ed today?"

"They were angels, of course," Papa Ed said as he picked up Harper and delivered her into Lauren's other arm.

"I think Papa Ed is fibbing, don't you?" she asked Harper, drawing a slobbery smile.

"Well, you can't fault them for being fussy when they're cutting teeth."

"Yeah, probably a good thing that's something none of us remember doing." Lauren sank onto the chair in the corner of the room so the girls could use her as a jungle gym. "So, what did you all do today?"

"Before the rain, we went for a stroll through the park and played in the sandbox they have down there," he said, referencing the public park at the bottom of the hill below the inn. "We had a picnic and watched ducks on the lake."

"That sounds like quite the exciting day." She dropped kisses on the top of both her babies' heads. "You must be worn out," she said to her grandfather.

"Not at all. We had a nice nap this afternoon. Plus, reinforcements are on the way. Your mom called and said she was coming down to see the new place."

Lauren laughed a little. "I think it's more likely she's coming to see these two."

"Can't say that I blame her. She's never been away from her grandbabies this long."

"My girls are going to be spoiled so rotten they'll stink all the way to Oklahoma."

"There is no such thing as too much spoiling."

Lauren outright snorted at that comment, making the girls startle then giggle at the strange sound Mommy made.

"I'm pretty sure that's a recent change in opinion. I don't recall it being in place when Violet and I were growing up."

"When someone becomes a great-grandpa, he's allowed to change his mind."

Lauren smiled and shook her head.

"How did your day go?" he asked.

She gave him the rundown as well as what she hoped to get accomplished tomorrow.

"I wish you had some help."

"I will eventually. I just need to be conscious of my expenses right now and do everything I can myself. Plus, Violet will be here soon. She's almost caught up with everything on the to-do list that needs to get done before she can work remotely."

"I'm so glad you two work so well together," Papa Ed said.

"I don't know what I'd do without her, especially over the past year and a half. But don't tell her that or she'll get a big head."

Papa Ed chuckled. "You're probably ready for a shower."

"That I am. And then some food."

He took Harper from her just as there was a knock on the door. Lauren carried Bethany with her as she went to open it. Her mother's face lit up as soon as she saw Bethany. She immediately held out her hands for her granddaughter.

"Gammy's here," her mom said, resulting in some excited bouncing by Bethany.

"Well, I see I've been usurped," Lauren said as she handed over her daughter.

"Someday you'll enjoy being the usurper when they have babies of their own."

"A long, long, long time from now." She was barely used to the idea of having two children of her own. There wasn't enough room in her mind to even contemplate grandchildren someday.

Once the girls were safely ensconced with her mom and grandfather, Lauren grabbed clean clothes and headed for the shower.

After washing away another day of dust and sweat, she was surprised by how much better she felt. She came out of the bathroom to find a note saying for her to join her family in the dining room. When she arrived, she found them talking with Skyler Bradshaw, the owner of the inn.

"Good evening," Skyler said. "I couldn't resist stopping to see these little cuties."

Harper held Skyler's finger as if she'd known her from the day of her birth.

Lauren gently caressed the pair of downy heads. "They do have the ability to stop people in their tracks."

"Is there anything I can do to make your stay more pleasant?"

"No, thank you. Everything has been wonderful."

"Glad to hear it."

After Skyler moved on to chat with other guests, Lauren slipped onto her seat and pulled two jars of baby food from the diaper bag decorated with baby animals.

"Do you want to see the building after dinner?" she asked her mom.

"No, tomorrow's soon enough. Tonight, I just want to spend time with my granddaughters."

Bethany let out an enthusiastic squeal as if to say that was the best idea ever, drawing chuckles from the older couple at the next table.

"Nice set of lungs on that one," the older guy said.

"Let me assure you they are twins in every way," Lauren said as she held a tiny spoon of green beans up to Harper's lips.

After they'd all had a delicious meal, Lauren accompanied her mom back to the room they would share while Papa Ed headed back to his own for a well-deserved rest and, if he could find one, probably a fishing show on TV.

Once back in her room, Lauren opened her computer to check if there were any pressing messages. She grinned at the sight of her mom tickling the girls' bellies, making them laugh.

"They adore you."

"The feeling is mutual." Her mom glanced toward Lauren. "Are we interrupting your work?"

Lauren shook her head. "I've had about enough work for the day. Just checking email and social media."

"If you want to go to sleep—"

"No. It's too early. If I went to sleep now, I'd wake up at two in the morning."

Despite having worked all day, an odd restlessness took hold of her.

"You should go out and do something fun."

"I've already left the girls with Papa Ed all day. I can't just pass them off to you now."

"Why not? You never take time for yourself."

"There's a bit too much on my plate for spur-of-the-moment girls' nights. Besides, I barely know anyone here."

Despite her protestations that she shouldn't just up and leave the girls again after being gone all day, Lauren couldn't concentrate on anything. Maybe it was that she felt confined in such a small space.

Or maybe her mom was right. Since her breakup with Phil and the discovery not long after that she was pregnant with not just one baby, but two, Lauren hadn't taken any real "me" time. She told herself she couldn't afford it, or it wasn't right to leave the girls or expect her family to take care of them while she went off to do something that wasn't work-related. And now she'd added opening a restaurant to the mix, as if she had an unending reserve of both time and energy.

"Why don't you at least go take a walk?" her mom said. "It's supposed to be a lovely, clear night, not too cold yet."

This time Lauren didn't argue against the idea. "I won't be gone long."

"No need to hurry back. These little stinkers and I will be right here discussing all the yummy things their mommy will bake for them when they have more teeth."

The mention of teeth caused Lauren to remember

Adam Hartley's comment about her getting a share of the local dentist's profits. A ball of warmth formed in her chest at the memory of how easy it had been to talk with him, even after the awkward moment with the other woman at the café.

"Lauren?"

"Huh?"

"You had this faraway smile on your face." The unspoken question in her mom's tone sent a jolt through Lauren.

"Just imagining how I'm going to convince the daughters of a baker that they can't have dessert for the main course of every meal."

After a couple minutes of loving on her babies, Lauren left the room for an evening stroll to clear her head and stretch her legs.

Though there was a slight chill in the air, she decided on a walk through town. She felt like meandering along Main Street, since it was quieter and less crowded than during the middle of the day.

As she checked out the window displays of the downtown shops, she made a mental note to do some Christmas shopping soon. It'd be much easier to keep her purchases secret if she shopped when her family was otherwise occupied, especially Violet. Her sister had a habit of trying to find and figure out what her presents were well before Christmas morning. The habit was so annoying that their mother had threatened to stop buying her presents on more than one occasion. Violet would swear she'd reform, but that only lasted about a day at most. Lauren thought Violet perhaps did it mostly to see everyone's reaction.

She promised herself she'd check out the cute outfit

displayed in the window at Yesterwear Boutique, see if A Good Yarn had the lavender-scented candles her mom liked and browse the shelves at the little bookstore. At some point, she'd introduce herself to Keri Teague, the resident baker of Blue Falls, and hope Keri didn't see her as an adversary. But though the bakery still appeared to be open, Lauren didn't feel up to it tonight.

As she eyed a lovely western-themed living room set in the window of a furniture store, the sound of music drew her attention. She followed it to what turned out to be the Blue Falls Music Hall. A man in cowboy attire opened the door for a woman, allowing the sound of a band playing to rush out into the early evening. She found herself walking toward the entrance. After all, if she was going to be a local business owner, she should support the other businesses in town. Maybe it would help pave the way into the fabric of the town, toward acceptance, considering she was an outsider.

She knew how small towns worked. While she had a recognizable name that could bring in additional tourists, some locals might see her as unfair competition. Her goal was to assure everyone she wanted to create a mutually beneficial relationship with the lifelong residents of Blue Falls. She'd only stay a few minutes then return to the inn.

The moment she stepped into the building, Blue Falls didn't seem so small. That or the entire population of the town had crammed inside to drink, dance and listen to music. Picturing all these people streaming into her restaurant brought a smile to her face as she made her way toward the bar. Before she reached it, however, someone asked, "Is that smile for me?" before spinning her onto the dance floor.

Chapter 4

For one horrifying moment, Lauren thought it was Phil who'd grabbed her. Even when she looked up into the face of Tim Wainwright, it still took several moments for her heart to start its descent back to its proper place in her chest from her throat.

"Glad to see you came out to enjoy the nightlife," Tim said.

"Can't say I expected to be accosted as a result."

Tim's eyebrows lifted. "Accosted? I merely meant to claim the first dance before a line formed."

She rolled her eyes. "No need to butter me up. I'm not closer to making a decision about vendors than I was a few days ago."

"Did I say anything about beef?"

She hesitated a moment as he spun her expertly between two couples to avoid a collision that could result in a pile of cowboy hats and boots. Even Tim was dressed in jeans, boots and Stetson tonight. If she wasn't a born-and-bred Texan, she might actually buy that he was a real cowboy.

"No," she finally said.

"I'm off the clock and just wanted to dance with a pretty woman."

She doubted he was ever really off the clock, but what could one dance hurt? It wasn't as if it was a date, or would lead to one.

"Just a bit of friendly advice—perhaps ask for the dance next time rather than assume." Sure, she wanted to make friends here, but his action had rubbed her the wrong way.

He nodded. "Duly noted. I'm sorry."

She simply offered a polite smile in return, not the "It's okay" he possibly expected. Once upon a time she might have uttered it without thinking, but that was before the events of the past year and a half.

"So, how are you liking Blue Falls so far?" he asked.

Thankful to have a neutral topic to discuss, she said, "I really like it. The people are nice, and it has a great feel to the business district. Not to mention it's pretty."

"Glad to hear it."

Lauren began to relax and even allowed Tim to lead her around the dance floor for a second song. Occasionally, she spotted someone she'd met over the course of the past few days. Thank goodness Verona Charles didn't seem to be in attendance. She didn't need the woman getting any ideas about her and Tim. If Tim or Verona headed down that path, Lauren was going to break out her stockpile of stories about poopy diapers and buying teething gel in bulk.

Her breath caught unexpectedly when she spotted Adam Hartley sitting at the bar. Tim spun her around so quickly that she wasn't sure, but she thought Adam had been watching them. And while her gaze had met his only for the briefest of moments, it was long enough for her to get the impression he wasn't pleased.

Most likely it was because he'd seen her dancing with his competitor and feared he'd lost the contract with her. Was he just another guy who'd been nice to her for his own gain? For some reason, the idea of that trait applying to Adam bothered her more than if that was what Tim was doing. Maybe it was because she expected it from Tim from the moment she met him. But she should know better than anybody that it was the ones you didn't expect that posed the biggest threat.

Still, she really hadn't gotten that vibe from Adam, even though she'd been looking for it. That she might have been gravely mistaken again caused her mood to dampen, enough that after the song was finished she excused herself from the dance floor.

"Maybe we can do this again sometime," Tim said as she stepped away.

"It's a small town, so I'm sure we'll see each other here at some point." She saw her noncommittal answer register with him a moment before she turned away and headed for the bar.

She told herself it was to purchase a drink, not to orchestrate a meeting with Adam. But she wasn't very good at lying to herself. The truth was she liked him, and had she not been so recently burned she might be interested in him for reasons beyond friendship. He certainly was attractive, and he'd gotten a seal of approval from the Bryants. But at this stage in her life, she needed to focus on her family, her business and healing herself. Her soul still felt bruised and battered by Phil's betrayal. And she couldn't even think about being with anyone else until that wasn't the case anymore.

Truthfully, with her daughters to consider now, she didn't know if it was possible to trust anyone enough to risk not only her own heart, but also those of her precious babies. They were too young now to realize their father wanted nothing to do with them, so Lauren tried her best to shower them with the love of two parents.

By the time she reached the bar area, she no longer saw Adam. She glanced around but couldn't find him in the crowd, which seemed to have gotten bigger during the time she'd been on the dance floor. Had he left? Maybe that was for the best. No, it was *definitely* for the best. She attributed the unexpected pull toward him as a side effect of being in a new place where she didn't really know anyone, being away from the familiarity and comfort of home, and the frustrating human desire to feel wanted for the right reasons.

A moment after she claimed one of the bar stools, the bartender stepped up in front of her. "What can I get for you?"

She glanced at the menu board above the shelves of liquor bottles. "Just a lemonade."

"Coming right up."

"So, I hear you're going to be my new competition."

Lauren turned to see a pretty woman not more than a few years older than her and quickly deduced her identity.

"Keri Teague, right?"

The sense of apprehension tightening Lauren's muscles eased the moment Keri smiled. "In the flesh."

"I hear you are known far and wide as quite the baker."

"Not as far as you, but I do all right."

"Well, as I told someone earlier this week, I don't think there can ever be too many baked goods within close proximity."

Keri laughed. "We're going to get along just fine."

"You don't know how glad I am to hear that."

"Don't tell me that you thought I'd be an ogre. Okay, who's been telling stories about me?"

"Nothing bad," Lauren said. "Adam Hartley just said I might have some friendly competition."

"That's a fair assessment. Good, I won't have to have him arrested."

Lauren felt her eyebrows shoot upward. "Arrested?"

Keri laughed. "Sorry, guess no one told you I'm married to the sheriff and that I get a kick out of teasing people about having him arrest them."

"Uh, no. But I'll be sure to be on my best behavior."

The bartender delivered Lauren's lemonade in a big frosty glass.

"So how do you know Adam?" Keri asked.

"He came by to pitch his family's beef products."

"You going with them?"

"Haven't decided yet. That's a ways down the road."

Keri nodded as if she totally understood, which she probably did since she also ran a food-related business and likely got unsolicited visits from vendors all the time, as well.

"Adam's good people."

"So I keep hearing."

Keri gave her a questioning look, but Lauren pretended not to notice. She didn't know how many of the locals Verona Charles had in league with her on the whole matchmaking thing.

"I saw him a little while ago. Not sure where he got off to." Keri scanned the crowd, and again Lauren pretended not to notice. "Oh, he's out on the dance floor."

He was? Though she was curious as to the identity of his dance partner, Lauren had the presence of mind not to look. Instead, she steered the conversation with Keri in a different direction, asking how long she'd owned the bakery.

For the next few minutes, they shared stories about everything from baking disasters and successes to the inside scoop on various locals. To be honest, with a single conversation and a lot of laughs, Lauren felt more a part of the community. But when she glanced at her phone, she was surprised by how much time had passed.

"I better get going," she said.

"So soon. You barely made use of the dance floor."

"Been a long day. Going to be another one tomorrow."

Keri nodded in understanding. "Well, come by the bakery sometime soon and I'll give you a little treat on the house."

As she thanked Keri and stood to leave, she deliberately didn't check the dance floor or any of the surrounding tables for Adam. One would think after what she'd gone through with Phil, the part of her brain wired to notice attractive men would have been out of order. Evidently not. Thank goodness she had enough sense not to indulge it too far.

As she made her way through the crowd, she felt as if someone was watching her. Though she said she wouldn't, she directed her attention toward the dance floor. Adam was still out there, but he wasn't looking her way. She scanned the sea of faces and didn't see anything out of the ordinary. She shook her head, telling herself not to be so paranoid, and resumed her trek toward the exit.

The moment she stepped outside and the door closed behind her, it was as if someone had turned down a blaring radio to its lowest volume. She could still hear the music inside, but her ears thanked her for the comparative silence of the surrounding night.

It'd gotten chillier since she went inside, so she zipped up her jacket and quickly texted her mom that she was on her way back. She headed across the parking lot, glancing up at the blanket of stars above.

"Well, ain't you a pretty one?"

Her heart leaped immediately to her throat at the sound of the man's voice. Her brain supplied the extra bit of information that he'd had too much to drink and that he wasn't alone. From the look on the other man's face, he was equally inebriated. Neither of them was a small man. Rather, they looked as if they could wrestle a full-size bull to the ground.

Blue Falls seemed so friendly and safe that she hadn't once thought being out after dark by herself would be dangerous, but she supposed there were drunk jerks everywhere. Which was little consolation at the moment. With most of the downtown businesses closed and the noise level inside the music hall, she doubted anyone would even hear her scream.

Her babies' faces flashed through her mind. Thank goodness they were safe with her mother.

"What, you can't speak?" the second guy asked, taking a couple of steps toward her, prompting her to take three backward and hoping she didn't trip over her own feet.

At first she hesitated to take her eyes off the men. But she knew she couldn't get past them, so her only choice was to get back to the safety of the throng of people inside the building. She shot a quick glance toward the entrance, judging how quickly she could make it. *If* she could make it.

As if her thundering heart had willed it, the door to the hall opened...and out stepped none other than Adam Hartley.

Adam had danced to a few songs with Courtney Heard, a friend from high school, and her cousin, Shannon, who was visiting from El Paso, but as he left the music hall he found his mood hadn't improved to any great extent. He wasn't sure if the sour feeling in his middle was because Lauren had been dancing with someone else, or the fact that the someone else was Tim Wainwright. He'd found himself wondering if Lauren was really averse to dating someone new, or if smooth-talking Tim had already managed to change her mind.

He should have stayed home tonight, but the realization that he was the only adult member of the family who didn't have someone—significant other, child or both—had him itching to get out and do something. Blue Falls nightlife being what it was, he'd had two choices—the Frothy Stein bar or the music hall. Deciding the Stein was the more pathetic of the two, he'd headed for the music hall to see who was playing tonight. The band from Austin was pretty good, and the crowd had helped him shake off the "odd man out" feeling. At least until he'd seen Lauren in Tim's arms on the dance floor. When she'd smiled up at Tim, Adam felt as if a bit too much of his siblings' newfound affinity for happily ever after had rubbed off on him.

When finding his own dance partners hadn't helped, he'd said his good-nights and headed for the exit. But who did he see as soon as he stepped out into the crisp night air? One Lauren Shayne. His momentary "you've got to be kidding me" was immediately replaced by the realization that she was wild-eyed scared. The two hefty guys encroaching on her personal space was obviously the reason why.

Wasting no time, he ate up the distance between them. He'd take on both guys if he had to in order to protect her, even knowing he'd likely be the worse for it after everything was over.

"There you are," he said, swooping in next to Lauren and wrapping his arm around her waist. "Sorry. I got caught up inside."

She stiffened next to him, but must have realized what he was doing because she relaxed slightly the next moment.

"Get your own," one of the guys said, his breath evidence he'd fail a field sobriety test.

"Already did, and you're making her uncomfortable. Why don't you all go inside and ask the bartender for some coffee?" And give Adam time to get Lauren safely away from their meaty claws, not to mention make a call to the sheriff's office to keep these two off the roads tonight.

The two drunks glanced at each other, and it was as if Adam could read their minds.

"Don't even think about it."

Adam didn't know if his warning swayed them or

the fact that the door to the music hall opened, spilling out light as well as half a dozen patrons. Whatever the reason, they backed off but cursed as they headed toward the other end of the parking lot. But Adam didn't relinquish his hold on Lauren as he asked her where she was parked.

"I walked here from the Wildflower Inn."

"Then I guess it's my turn to give you a lift."

"Thanks. I'd appreciate that."

He noticed Lauren glance back over her shoulder as he escorted her toward his truck, as if she was afraid the guys would change their minds again and attack them from behind. Once they reached his truck, he opened the passenger door for her.

"Sorry to inconvenience you," she said once she was in the seat and pulling her seat belt across her body.

"It's not a problem. I drive right past the inn on the way home."

"Oh, good."

He hurried around to the driver's side and hit the door locks as soon as he shut his door, giving Lauren an extra layer of protection from her would-be attackers.

"If you don't mind, I'm going to call the sheriff's office first. Those two," he said, pointing toward the men, who now appeared to be arguing, "don't need to be on the road endangering people."

"Good idea."

A sheriff's department vehicle pulled up to the edge of the parking lot before he even got off the phone. Sheriff Simon Teague got out of his cruiser at the same time a department SUV also arrived.

"Is one of those the sheriff?" Lauren asked.

"Yeah, the one already out of his car."

"I met his wife tonight."

"Should we expect the bake-off at the O.K. Corral?"

As he'd hoped, she laughed. "No, Keri's very nice. And despite your teasing me about her competition, she had only nice things to say about you. So do the Bryants. Seems you're 'good people.'"

"Had I given the impression that I wasn't?"

"No. They were completely unsolicited comments."

"It's always good to hear people think well of you, I guess."

He started his truck's engine and left the music hall and the law enforcement activity behind.

"How did you like your first trip to the music hall? I assume it's your first visit anyway."

"It was. Had no intention of going, but I was out for a walk and got drawn in by the music. Nice place, but I think I was just too tired to be in the mood to dance the night away."

She'd seemed to be having a good time with Tim, but he reminded himself that she had practice putting on a friendly face. He'd seen it with the women in the café. At least she hadn't left with Tim. Although her leaving alone had nearly cost her dearly. He squeezed the steering wheel harder, almost wishing the guys had thrown a punch or two at him so he could give it right back. A cold chill went through him just thinking about what might have happened if he hadn't decided to head home when he had.

"I hope you don't let those guys sour your opinion of Blue Falls."

"No. Unfortunately, it doesn't matter how big or small a place is, there are going to be drunken brutes at some point or another."

She was making a valiant effort to not seem too concerned about what had just happened, but he noticed how she had her hands clasped tightly together in her lap. Before he could think better of it, he reached across and gave her arm a reassuring squeeze.

"You're safe now."

He removed his hand after only a moment, not wanting her to fear she'd traded one scary situation for another, and turned in to the inn's lot. He pulled up to the front entrance so she'd only have to walk a few steps to get inside.

"Thank you for the ride. And for helping me out with those guys. I was afraid they were going to jump you."

He grinned. "I'd have made them wish they hadn't."

"You might have gotten in some good licks, but there were two of them and they seemed like the type who'd tackle a *chupacabra* wearing a cactus coat just for the hell of it."

He laughed at that colorful description. "Can't say I've heard that one before."

"It's a Lauren Shayne original. Just now thought of it."

"Somebody ought to draw that and put it on T-shirts. They'd probably sell like beer on the Fourth of July."

"Seriously, though, thank you."

"You're welcome. I doubt you have any more trouble from them, but if you do let me know. We've got enough Hartleys to form a posse."

"I appreciate the offer, but I don't think we have to go full-on Old West." She had her door open in the next breath, then stepped out. "Good night, Adam."

"Good night, Lauren."

He didn't move until he was sure she was safely inside. It wasn't until he was halfway home that he realized he'd been replaying how his name sounded when she said it. And that he'd been imagining her standing much closer to him, looking up into his eyes with the type of interest that had nothing to do with business contracts.

Yep, he was up crazy creek without a paddle.

Chapter 5

As Lauren stepped into the lobby of the inn, she was startled to come face-to-face with Papa Ed. He nodded toward the door, and quite possibly where Adam still was to make sure she got inside safely.

"Who was that?"

"One of the vendors I met earlier in the week. I took a walk through the downtown area, and he gave me a lift back up here."

"That was nice of him." There was no mistaking the tone of her grandfather's voice. It was much more a question than a statement of fact. But she wasn't about to tell him what had happened to precipitate the front-door drop-off.

"Yeah. You were right. People are nice here." With the exception of the two guys who were now hopefully either spending the night in the drunk tank, or were at least in need of a ride of their own because the sheriff had taken their keys away.

Papa Ed gave her one of his looks that said he knew there was more to the story and if he just watched her long enough she'd reveal all. She pretended she didn't notice and instead nodded at the package of little chocolate doughnuts in his hand.

"Munchies?"

He lifted the package and looked at it, then lowered it again as if disappointed in himself. "I know it's not fine eating, but they're a guilty pleasure."

"Plus you already ate all the snacks I brought along."

"It's your fault. If they weren't so good, there'd be plenty left."

She smiled and laughed a little. "And I wouldn't have the career I do."

"True. But at least those little girls give me plenty of ways to stay active and keep the weight at bay."

"Speaking of, I better go relieve Mom. I was gone longer than I anticipated."

"Any particular reason why?"

She'd opened herself back up to the questioning she'd managed to divert him from, dang it. Might as well tell the truth—at least the nonscary part of it.

"I wanted to walk along Main Street when there weren't a lot of people around, and I ended up stopping by the music hall. Thought it was a good idea to start meeting other local business owners. I did meet the owner of the local bakery, Keri Teague, and we talked longer than I planned to be gone."

No need to mention the dancing with Tim or how she'd headed to the bar in order to say hello to Adam, or how the night could have come to a very different end were it not for his fortuitous timing. She barely controlled a shiver down her spine at that train of thought.

"So, your chauffeur back—he the one you said was a little too full of himself, or the one who helped you move the furniture?"

Evidently Violet had spilled the details Lauren had shared with her during one of their phone calls.

"Furniture."

"Hmm, he *is* a nice guy."

Thankfully, Lauren yawned then, and she hadn't even resorted to faking it. Her long day was catching up with her.

"I need to hit the hay. I have an early meeting with an electrician in the morning."

Papa Ed and his processed snack accompanied her down the hall. She gave him a quick peck on the cheek before opening the door to her room. By the quiet that greeted her, she knew the girls were already asleep. Her mom was sitting in bed wearing her pajamas and reading the latest mystery in a series she liked about a baker who solved crimes. Lauren always found it odd that a baker happened upon so many dead bodies.

Lauren eased her way over to the crib and her heart filled at the sight that greeted her. Harper and Bethany were sound asleep with their little hands touching. She couldn't imagine it being possible to love another human more than she loved her babies. She longed to kiss them both, but she didn't want to risk waking them—especially in a hotel room where the other occupants might not be thrilled with the sound of crying infants.

When she turned away from the temptation of snuggling the girls, she said, "Sorry I was gone so long."

"It's no problem, hon. See anything interesting?"

Adam Hartley.

In another life, maybe.

"Some nice shops downtown I'll explore when I have some time." She almost laughed at the idea of having free time before giving her mom the same version of events at the music hall that she'd given Papa Ed.

"Sounds as if Dad might be trying to edge you back into the dating game."

Surprised by her mom's assessment, Lauren looked over at her. "Why would he do that? He knows men aren't high on my favorites list right now."

"He believes people shouldn't go through life alone. He did the same thing to me a couple of years after your father died. It took Dad a long time to realize I wasn't interested in dating again. I had my girls, my teaching career, a life that was satisfying if, admittedly, sometimes a little lonely."

Lauren's heart squeezed. Her mom hadn't ever admitted to that loneliness before.

"But what happened to me wasn't the same thing. Dad didn't choose to leave you." It had been an accident on an icy road, not anyone's fault unless you chose to blame Mother Nature or God.

"I think Dad felt guilty, or maybe just sad, that what your father and I had was cut short while he and Mom were happy all through their long marriage. He was happy and so he wanted everyone around him to be happy, too."

The pain Papa Ed must be going through without Nana Gloria hit Lauren anew. Still, she couldn't imagine her grandfather thinking she'd be the least bit interested in a new relationship, even a casual one. When would she even have time for such a thing?

And yet there was that little flicker of attraction that had led her to the bar in search of Adam Hartley. How did she explain that? Maybe it was possible to still feel physical attraction without wanting anything to come from it. If she was being honest, she didn't know how a woman couldn't be at least somewhat attracted to Adam. Based on her few interactions with him, he was a very pleasing blend of handsome, kind, helpful and dedicated to family and honest work. That was a difficult cocktail to not want to drink in one delicious gulp. Not that she had much opportunity for cocktails these days, either.

"Considering everything, I'm happier than people might expect. Who could complain when they have an awesome job, a great family and two beautiful, healthy baby girls?" And if she sometimes felt lonely while lying alone in her bed, it was a small price to pay for all the other positive things in her life.

"I might seem a hypocrite for saying this, but don't rule out having more when you're ready. Contrary to what Dad may think, I didn't. I just never met anyone else I could imagine spending my life with. I suppose I still could, but I stopped thinking that way quite some time ago. But you're still young."

"With two babies. Most guys aren't into instant family."

"Maybe not, but someone might surprise you."

That would be a surprise indeed. But then she thought about the look on Adam's face when he talked about his family, about his nieces and nephews. Maybe guys who didn't mind being around other people's kids did exist, but it would have to be a special man indeed to make her willing to take a chance again. He might have to be miraculous.

Instead of turning right out of the inn's parking lot, Adam drove back down into the main part of town. There was no sign of either of the guys who'd frightened Lauren in front of the music hall anymore—or law enforcement for that matter. So he headed toward the sheriff's office, intent on making sure those two didn't pose a threat to Lauren or anyone else. Though he'd wanted to teach them a lesson they wouldn't forget, he'd had enough sense to know he was outnumbered. If only his brothers had been with him. He wasn't by nature a violent person, but he'd seen bright red when he'd realized what was happening when he stepped outside the music hall. Thank God he'd left when he had. It didn't escape him that Lauren—or rather his reaction to seeing her with Tim—was what had made him decide to vacate the premises.

As he cruised up to the sheriff's office, he spotted Simon coming out of the building. When he pulled in next to the sheriff, he rolled down his window.

"Please tell me those idiots are sleeping it off in a cell tonight."

Simon crossed his arms. "I'll do you one better. They managed to get themselves arrested. The bigger fella decided it might be fun to take a swing at me. I disavowed him of that notion."

Adam smiled wide. "You just made my night."

"Any reason you're extra interested in them?"

"When I came out of the building, they were about to attack Lauren Shayne."

The look on Simon's face hardened. "I should talk to her."

Adam instinctually shook his head. "They never touched her, just scared the living daylights out of her. But it looked like it was about to go further when I intervened. Honestly, I was probably about to get my ass kicked, but some other people came out before anything happened."

"So I get the impression Miss Shayne doesn't want to be involved any further in this?"

"No." She hadn't actually said that out loud, but he'd somehow managed to read that in her body language. She'd only wanted to leave. "I just wanted to make sure they wouldn't be a problem anymore, for anyone."

It wasn't only about Lauren. His sisters sometimes had a night out at the music hall. Also female friends, tourists and barrel racers in town for the regular rodeos.

"I suspect when they sober up, they'll make bail and go back to Johnsonville and choose to party elsewhere next time around."

"Good."

"So, you already making a move on the pretty baker lady? Got to say from experience that being with a woman that good with desserts is not a bad bonus."

"No, I just happened to be in the right place at the right time to help her out."

"Her knight in shining armor, huh?"

Adam rolled his eyes. "Good night, Simon," he said, then drove away.

As he passed by the inn, he glanced over as if he might catch a glimpse of Lauren. But he doubted after her experience with the drunks that she'd step foot back outside until the sun was well above the horizon.

And when that time came, he needed to be hard at work doing anything but thinking about how he'd been wishing she was dancing with him instead of his biggest rival.

Lauren didn't think she'd ever been so happy to see a sunrise, despite the fact her night had been filled with some of the worst, most interrupted sleep ever. If she wasn't having nightmares about what could have happened outside the music hall if Adam hadn't shown up when he had, she was being awakened—likely along with everyone else in the hotel—by not one but both of the girls crying. It seemed her precious girls were similar in more ways than one, including when they were upset by hunger, wet diapers or the pains of teething. The challenge was trying to get them to stop crying at the same time. Neither seemed to want to be first in that regard. At home it was one thing, but knowing their upset was bothering other people trying to get a good night's sleep frayed Lauren's nerves. Keeping a hotel full of people awake wasn't the best way to win friends and future customers.

When her mom came out of the bathroom, she looked as worn out as Lauren felt.

"Pardon me for saying this," Lauren said, keeping quiet since the girls were actually sleeping peacefully now, "but it doesn't look as if the shower helped much."

Her mom rubbed her hand over her face. "It's been a few years since I've had babies crying their lungs out, and I only had one at a time. You, my dear, are a saint."

She didn't feel like a saint. More like exhausted before the day even started.

"I hate to leave you here with them again today."

Her mom waved off her concern. "I'll let them sleep now, then we'll come down to visit later. Dad and I can lend a hand if you'll let us."

"Normally, I'd say I'm good, but today I may take you up on it." Though it might be nice just to have the quiet and solitude for a few hours. She loved her girls more than life itself, but she'd bet every cent she had that there wasn't a mother alive who didn't want to run away from her children for a little bit every now and then.

Though when she arrived at the restaurant building a few minutes later, she didn't immediately get out of her car. Instead, she fought an uncharacteristic wave of anxiety. What if those guys were inside waiting on her to finish what they'd started? She thought about Adam's business card in her wallet and considered texting him to see if he knew what had happened to the men after they left. But why would he? He'd been going home after he dropped her off, and it wasn't as if the drunks had actually attacked either of them. Thus, no need to have further contact with the sheriff's department.

Taking a deep breath, she told herself that the faster she got in that building and to work, the sooner she and her family could go home. And the thought of letting any other man halt her forward progress sent enough anger through her that it propelled her out of the car and into the blessedly empty building.

She did lock the door behind her this time, but keeping out anyone who could just wander in made sense. Despite her lack of sleep, she managed to get some of the windows cleaned before the electrician arrived. By the time he finished his inspection, however, she was back to wondering what she'd gotten herself into. It was going to take more work to bring things up to code than she'd hoped. The news knocked what little energy she'd mustered right out of her. After the electrician left, she sank onto an old metal bench outside the front door and dropped her head into her hands.

She didn't look up until she heard footsteps approaching. The shot of fear was quickly replaced when she noticed her visitor was Adam. Again, he'd arrived on foot.

"Don't tell me you hit another deer," she said.

"No." He motioned diagonally across the street to the Shop Mart. "Coming back from Austin. I had to stop and get a couple of things for my dad."

She recognized his truck at the edge of the other lot.

"Are you okay?" he asked as he sank onto the identical bench on the opposite side of the front walkway from her. "Excuse me for saying so, but you look as if you didn't sleep last night."

"That's because I didn't, not much anyway."

"Maybe you should take a day off."

She shook her head. "Don't have the time."

"Then how about some help? What do you need?"

"Adam, you've already helped me more than anybody in town." She hadn't consciously realized just how much until she said it out loud. "I'm sure you have your own work to do."

"Not so much that I can't spare a few hours."

"I wouldn't feel right—"

He held up a hand. "You're not going to win this argument, so you might as well put me to work."

She lifted an eyebrow. "And here everyone has been telling me you're a nice guy, but you've got a bossy streak."

He smiled, and she tried to pretend she hadn't felt a flutter in her middle.

Lauren gave up. And if she admitted the truth, she liked having him around. Though he caused her to have unexpected reactions, he was also easy to be around. With each interaction, she was beginning to believe more and more that everyone who said he was a genuinely nice guy was telling the truth. He'd given her no reason to believe otherwise. As long as she didn't allow herself to admire him too much, she'd be okay.

"So, do you do windows?" she asked.

Lauren couldn't believe how much quicker her work progressed with just one extra set of hands. And though she'd still had the same pitiful amount of sleep, having Adam there to talk to made her feel more awake. Granted, that could be the bit of adrenaline still zinging its way through her body after they'd nearly bumped into each other and he'd instinctively placed his hand on her bare arm to steady her. It had been nothing more than a brief touch, and yet she'd swear in a court of law she could still feel his strong, warm fingers against her flesh.

She glanced up to where he stood on the ladder, washing the windows up high. Well, he was supposed to be washing them. It appeared that he was instead writing in the accumulated dust with his finger.

"What are you doing?"

Instead of answering, he shot her a mischievous grin. She pictured a little-boy version of him smiling that same way after some naughty misadventure.

Lauren took a few steps back in order to read what he'd written. *I should get free meals for life for doing this. Including dessert.*

"I don't know. That would depend on how long you're planning on living. What's the longevity like in your family?"

His smile dimmed, and she felt like kicking herself. Life and death wasn't something to joke about, especially when there was the possibility of loss associated with the subject. She ought to know that from experience.

"I'm sorry." She wasn't even sure how to articulate the rest of what she was thinking.

"It's okay. I'm adopted so my parents' genetics don't have any bearing on mine."

"Oh." But what about his birth parents? His grandparents? If he was adopted, did that mean they weren't around anymore? And hadn't been since he was a kid?

Adam proceeded to wash away the humorous words from the window, and it made her inexplicably sad. It was as if the moment a bit of humor strolled into her life, she found a way to erase it.

When he was finished washing the high-up windows, Adam descended the ladder and came over to the front counter, where she was standing sketching out ideas for the placement of customer seating and the gift-shop area. The thoughts that had been eating at her the past few minutes found their way out of her mouth.

"I really am sorry if I brought up bad memories. I should have thought before I spoke."

"It's really okay. It happened a long time ago."

She started to ask what but managed to stop herself. It wasn't any of her business.

"You don't have to be so careful around me," he said. "I won't break."

She looked up at him and realized again just how

much she liked him already. If she hadn't been through what she had with Phil, she wouldn't even question her assessment of Adam. She hated that she now always looked for hidden meaning behind words, selfish intent behind actions.

"My birth parents died in a bridge collapse when I was six. I went to live with my grandmother after that for a year, but then she had a stroke and had to be moved to a care facility."

Without any conscious thought, she placed her hand atop his on the counter. "I'm so sorry." That was a lot of loss to deal with. "I lost my dad when I was five, but I can't imagine losing both parents at once."

"I won't lie and say it wasn't hard, but I got lucky in the end. My parents now are great, and I ended up with brothers and sisters instead of being an only child. They're all adopted, too, so I wasn't alone in that experience, either."

"How many of you are there?"

"Five. Neil, Ben and Sloane are older, and Angel is younger."

"That's amazing that your parents adopted so many kids."

"We tease them that they like to collect strays."

Lauren smiled at that and wondered what life was like when all the Hartleys got together. Just then the door opened, revealing Papa Ed and her mother pushing the double stroller. Lauren realized her hand was still lying atop the masculine warmth of Adam's and she pulled it away, so quickly that it made her appear as if she'd been doing something wrong.

"Hey," she said to the new arrivals, probably sounding way brighter and cheerier than she should.

She didn't miss the curious glances both her mother and Papa Ed leveled at Adam. Before their imaginations ran wild, she gestured toward Adam.

"You're just in time to see what a great job Adam did on washing the windows."

"You hired someone?" her mother asked.

Lauren shook her head. "No, Adam was kind enough to help with the stuff up high."

"This the young man who drove you back last night?" Papa Ed asked.

"Yes. Adam Hartley, this is my grandfather, Ed, and my mom, Jeanie." And now for the part of the introductions that would likely have her seeing the backside of Adam as he suddenly had to be somewhere else. She reminded herself that was okay. "And these two sleeping beauties are my daughters, Harper and Bethany."

Instead of causing a blur as he ran for the exit, Adam crossed the few feet that separated him from the stroller. Lauren held her breath for some reason. When he smiled as he crouched down in front of them, she inexplicably felt like crying happy tears.

"They sure do look as if they don't have a care in the world, don't they?"

Lauren couldn't help the sudden laugh. "Don't let their cherubic faces fool you. They both have an incredible lung capacity, which they put to good use last night."

Adam looked up at her. "That explains why you're so tired."

"You don't know the half of it." There was so much, so very much, behind that simple statement. And to her great surprise, Adam didn't run away. In fact, if she didn't know better she'd swear he'd be perfectly willing to listen to every gory detail. And a bigger surprise than anything was that down deep, a part of her wanted to tell him.

Not trusting herself or the part of her brain that had evidently forgotten the past eighteen months, she shifted her attention to her mom. "Let me show you around."

She forced herself not to look back at Adam again as she led her mom toward the area of the building where the gift shop would eventually be located.

"It certainly has a lovely view," her mom said as she looked out the now-clean windows a couple of minutes later.

"Yeah, that was a big selling point."

Her mom glanced back toward the front of the building, where Lauren could hear Adam talking to Papa Ed but couldn't tell what they were saying. She realized she hadn't warned Adam not to say anything about the two guys outside the music hall. Hopefully, he wouldn't divulge that bit of information she purposely hadn't shared with her family.

"Can't say the view of the other direction is bad, either."

"Mom!" Lauren miraculously kept her voice low enough that she didn't attract the attention of the men.

"What? Am I lying?"

Well, no. Not by a long shot. "He's just being friendly, nothing more."

Her mom gave her one of those "mom" looks that said she was highly suspicious there was something Lauren wasn't telling her.

"Did I say otherwise?"

Damn it. Lauren realized she'd just revealed more than she wanted to admit to herself. She was really attracted to Adam, and not just because he was pleasing to the eye. The part of her that still ached from Phil's betrayal was looking for a balm, and it seemed to want that balm to be named Adam Hartley.

"You don't have to completely turn off your feelings, hon," her mom said. "Use caution, yes, but don't allow yourself to live the rest of your life afraid."

"I barely know him."

"I'm not saying he's the one or if there even is a 'one,' just that I don't want you to let Phil burrow too deeply into your mind. He's not worth it."

She was right about that, but that didn't mean she had any idea how to not let the experience with him color how she responded to people going forward.

Not wanting Adam to realize they were talking about him and perhaps get the wrong idea, she walked back across the building. As they drew close, Harper woke up and her gaze fixed on the tall, handsome man in front of her.

"Well, hello there, cutie," Adam said.

Lauren smiled at the genuine tenderness in his voice. At least it sounded genuine. Surely he wouldn't use fake affection for her children as another way to influence her to do business with him.

Harper smiled and wiggled her feet at the same time she thrust out her arms toward him. Lauren couldn't have been more surprised if her daughter had unhooked herself from the stroller and proceeded to walk across to the windows for a view of the lake.

"Well, will you look at that?" Papa Ed said.

Adam looked confused.

"She's never done anything like that with someone who isn't family," Lauren said. "Neither of them has."

"Do you mind if I hold her? I'll be careful."

"Uh, sure."

Lauren reached down to release the lap belt, but Adam already had it freed and was lifting Harper into his arms. Lauren resisted the urge to stand close in case he dropped his happy bundle. He must have seen the worry on her face because he smiled.

"Don't worry. I have lots of practice. I'm an uncle, remember?"

She had to admit he looked as if he knew what he was doing. He tapped the pad of his finger against the tip of Harper's nose and said, "Boop." Evidently, Harper found that hilarious because she let out a belly laugh before planting her little palm against Adam's nose.

Lauren was pretty sure her ovaries struck up a lively tune and started tap dancing. Not good. Not good at all.

"I think she likes you," Papa Ed said.

As if she didn't like being left out, Bethany woke up and started fussing. Knowing her ovaries couldn't handle seeing both of her babies in Adam's arms, Lauren picked up Bethany and proceeded to do a little dance with her. It had the desired effect of replacing the eminent tears with a precious baby grin.

Adam reached over and booped Bethany's nose the same as he had Harper's and got a similar result.

"Okay, stop trying to become their favorite human," Lauren said. "That's my title."

"Can't help it. They must smell the spoiling uncle on me."

Lauren had the craziest thought that she didn't want him to be their uncle. But she couldn't allow herself to even think he'd be anything more than just a funny guy who made them laugh. There were so many reasons to demand her ovaries knock off the dancing.

But, seriously, how was she supposed to ignore how sexy the man looked holding her daughter and making the babies laugh? That was impossible. Even women who didn't want children would darn near melt at the sight. Women with eyes and any shred of maternal instinct didn't stand a chance.

Adam wasn't quite sure how to interpret the look on Lauren's face. It was almost as if she couldn't believe what she was seeing. Did she think he'd hurt her babies somehow? Was she surprised he actually liked kids? He guessed he should have expected that kind of reaction. After all, he'd witnessed how protective his sisters and sisters-in-law were of their children. And he knew enough guys who didn't want anything to do with kids, especially if they weren't their own.

It hit him that the twins' father must be the ex-fiancé who'd dragged Lauren into court. Did she have to continue to deal with him for their daughters' sake? He couldn't imagine being forced to speak to someone he couldn't stand for the next couple of decades.

"How many nieces and nephews do you have?" Lauren's mother asked.

"Two nieces and one nephew for now, but there's another on the way."

"Big family?"

"Yeah. One big, cobbled-together family."

At Jeanie's look of confusion, Lauren explained, "Adam and his four siblings are all adopted."

"From different families," he added, realizing he hadn't revealed that detail before.

"Well, bless your parents," Jeanie said.

He smiled. "I'm sure there were times when they wondered what they'd gotten themselves into."

"I think all parents wonder that from time to time."

Lauren made an expression of mock affront. "I don't know what you're talking about, Mom. Granted, Violet was a pill, but I was perfect."

Her mom actually snorted at that. "Just like you thought these two were without fault about four this morning."

Adam jostled Harper, causing her to grin and reveal the hint of a tiny tooth about to make its appearance.

"I don't know what these people are talking about," he said to the little girl. "You seem pretty perfect to me."

This time, all three of the other adults were looking at him as if he was a unicorn.

Almost as if they all realized what they were doing at the same time, their expressions changed as they redirected their attention.

"Well, I should probably be heading out," Adam said as he handed over Harper to her grandmother.

"Don't run on our account," Jeanie said. "At least let us treat you to lunch."

"No need, but thank you." Even though he needed to get back to the ranch, he found himself not wanting to leave. Maybe that was why he found himself extending an invitation. "Why don't you all come out to the ranch for dinner while you're here?"

"We wouldn't want to intrude," Lauren replied quickly.

Had he overstepped somehow? Or was she just being polite? One way to find out.

"No imposition. My mom loves having people over. Like I said, she loves your show, so I might even win some 'favorite son' points if I bring you all over for dinner."

Lauren hesitated. It was her grandfather who answered for all of them.

"Well, in that case, we'd be happy to accept." Both Lauren and her mother looked at Ed with surprise, but Lauren was quick to refocus her attention on Adam.

"Thank you. We appreciate it. Hopefully you'll have the same calming effect on Harper and Bethany then." Even though she was nice, he got the feeling she was worried. If she thought a couple of crying babies would bother his family, she was mistaken.

"If I don't, someone will be able to."

As he finally headed for the door a couple of minutes later, he still had the feeling Lauren was on edge. He was honestly surprised she accompanied him outside.

"Thanks again for your help today," she said.

"It was nothing." Despite not being a great fan of washing windows, he'd enjoyed spending time with her. "Listen, I'm sorry if inviting you and your family to dinner made you uncomfortable."

She shook her head. "No, it's okay. That's just a lot of people to invite without asking your mother first."

He laughed. "I could bring home an entire tour bus full of flower peepers and she'd be in hog heaven. We've joked that when we all eventually move out, she's probably going to turn the house into a bed-and-breakfast."

"At least let me bring something. I can bake a cake."

"Where?" He pointed toward the building. "You don't have an operational kitchen yet. Plus, Mom isn't a slouch when it comes to dessert, so no worries there."

Finally, Lauren looked marginally more comfortable with the idea of eating with a family of strangers.

"I promise we don't bite," he said.

She smiled at that, and he found himself wanting to do more to make her smile. "I can't say the same for the girls. Teething makes them want to chew on whatever is handy."

"Then we'll make sure the dog's chew toys aren't within their reach."

He became aware of her mother and grandfather inside, watching them while trying to seem as if they weren't. "Well, see you tomorrow night."

"Okay. And—"

"Don't you dare thank me again."

She made a show of pressing her lips together but he could still see the gratitude in her eyes. Though he didn't need her thanks, it was nicer to see than suspicion.

As he walked across the street to his truck, he tried not to think about other emotions he wouldn't mind seeing in Lauren's eyes.

Chapter 6

Adam walked into the dining room where his mom was busy wrapping Christmas presents. Rolls of colorful paper, tape, tags and scissors were scattered across the surface of the table.

"Any of that for me?"

"No, this is all for the kids. I have to sneak my wrapping in when they aren't here."

He wondered if Lauren was the type of mom to spoil her kids at Christmas, especially their first one.

"I hope you don't mind but I invited some people over for dinner tomorrow night."

"These people have names?"

"Lauren Shayne, her mother, grandfather and twin daughters."

His mom dropped the box containing a toy ranch set, no doubt for Brent. The stunned expression on her face surprised him.

"Lauren is coming here for dinner?"

"Yeah. I thought it would be okay. If not—"

She waved off what he'd been about to say. "No, it's fine. I just…well, she's famous for her cooking."

"So are you."

"No, I'm not."

"You have no idea how many people we've all told about your chocolate cake. I'm surprised Texas hasn't been invaded by surrounding states yet for a taste."

She made a *pffftt* sound of disbelief. "Nobody would give me a TV show."

"I disagree wholeheartedly with that assumption."

"Be that as it may, I need to figure out what I'm going to cook."

"Mom, seriously, anything will be fine. They're nice, down-to-earth people."

"That right?" There was more to that question than it appeared on the surface. "Did you meet them in town just now?"

"Yes." Better to tell the truth than have her find out some other way. "I was helping Lauren wash some windows she couldn't reach when they came by."

"You seem to be helping Lauren a lot."

"I'm trying to get her business, remember?"

"And yet I've never seen you do manual labor for any other potential customers."

Damn it, she had him there. He'd never felt an attraction toward any of them, and he suspected his mom knew it.

"None of them could give us this kind of exposure."

His mom started cleaning up her wrapping station. "You go ahead and keep telling yourself it's only business."

"What's that supposed to mean?" He knew full well how her mind worked, especially since her children had started falling in love and getting married. She only had two left unattached, and since they seemed to be going in order of age he was up to the plate.

"You like that girl."

"She's nice." And his heart rate had a habit of speeding up whenever he looked at her, but he wasn't about to say that out loud. Especially since Lauren had already made it known that she wasn't relocating to Blue Falls. And after what she'd gone through with her ex, he suspected she wasn't too hot on dating anyway. Not that it kept him from wondering what it would be like.

"Uh-huh," his mom said, fully aware in that freaky way she had that he was not being totally forthcoming.

He leaned back against the table next to her. "Listen, I'm going to level with you. Yes, I like her. Yes, I think she's pretty and interesting. But you're aware of what her ex-fiancé put her through, right?"

The layer of teasing disappeared from his mom's face. "Yeah, very unfortunate."

"Then don't you think that dating is probably the last thing on her mind right now, especially since she has two babies?"

"I don't know."

He cocked an eyebrow at her. "Yes, you do. I know you're on this kick to see us all married off, and I'm not against the idea with the right person at the right time. But this isn't it."

And that fact made him feel way more disappointed than his and Lauren's short acquaintance should have.

"You never know."

"Mom, please. Just approach this as a new friendship, maybe eventually a working relationship, nothing more. Okay?"

She sighed. "Fine. I wish it was different, but I see your point."

He smiled. "I still think you should make your chocolate cake, though."

She shot him a look that said she knew good and well that he was asking for the cake for his own benefit more than anything else.

"Get out of here or I'll be serving you tapioca pudding."

He made a gagging noise. He hated tapioca. As he turned to leave, she swatted him on the behind with a roll of wrapping paper covered in cartoon reindeer, causing him to laugh.

As he headed outside to haul some hay out to the far side of the pasture, he caught himself whistling a happy tune. And he didn't think it had anything to do with the knowledge that come tomorrow night, he'd be able to dig into his mom's chocolate cake.

Lauren pulled into the ranch's driveway and asked herself for what must have been the thousandth time why she'd agreed to this dinner with the Hartley family. Not only were her feelings toward Adam oddly disconcerting, but she'd also sworn an oath to herself that she'd never mix business and personal relationships again. Not that a business relationship existed yet, and she would classify the personal side of things as budding friendship, nothing more.

Yeah, right. One did not fantasize about the sexy physical attributes of mere friends.

She once again played the refrain in her mind that

just because she found him attractive didn't mean she had to act on it. Granted, being around him would be easier without the attraction, but her brain flatly refused to purge the knowledge that Adam Hartley was very pleasing to the eye. Which was only strengthened by the fact that he was friendly, helpful and got along famously with her daughters.

And yet it remained that she'd been on the verge of marrying a man, spending her life with him, only to find out that everything she'd believed about him had been a lie. There was too much at stake now for her to ever allow herself to make that kind of grievous error in judgment again.

Her mom reached across and squeezed Lauren's hand. "You're thinking too much."

Lauren glanced across the car. "How could you possibly know that?"

"I've been your mother for twenty-eight years. This is not a great mystery."

"Annoying."

Her mom laughed. "I'll remind you that you said that in a few years when your daughters are annoyed at you for reading them correctly."

"Seems I know someone else who was irritated by her mother knowing when she was hiding something, too," Papa Ed said from the back seat.

"Oh, hush, Dad," her mom said.

Lauren laughed, thankful for the break in the tension that had been knotted up in her middle. She was overthinking this whole evening anyway. There were just nice people in the world who wanted to be friendly and welcoming. Evidently the Hartleys were among them. There was nothing wrong with being friends with people with whom she might eventually have a business relationship. But that was as far as it could go. It was beyond surprising she was even having to tell herself that.

When they came within sight of the house, she had an immediate sense of welcome. The house was fronted by a long porch, where she could imagine watching the sunset across the pasture that rolled off to the west. On a chilly night like the one ahead promised to be, sitting out here wrapped in a quilt and drinking hot chocolate sounded heavenly. Though it looked completely different, she got the same sense of peace that she did at her own home overlooking the Brazos.

"This place is lovely," her mom said.

Harper piped up with what sounded like a sound of agreement from her car seat in the back.

"The stone and wood does fit in nicely with the surrounding landscape," Lauren said.

After parking, she went to remove Harper from her seat while her mom retrieved Bethany and Papa Ed unfurled himself from the back seat. He stretched and Lauren looked over at him when she heard some of his bones crack.

"Just wait," he said. "One day you'll sound like a bowl of Rice Krispies, too."

A beautiful Australian shepherd came around the back of her car, startling Lauren. She lifted Harper quickly out of reach, not knowing whether the dog would bite.

"She's harmless."

Lauren looked toward the sound of Adam's deep voice. Was it her imagination or did it sound richer, sexier, today? The sight of him in a checked shirt, jeans and a cowboy hat robbed her of speech. It was as if he got better-looking every time she saw him. More likely, her brain was malfunctioning.

Thankfully, Papa Ed bending down to pet the dog diverted her attention.

"What's her name?" Papa Ed asked.

"Maggie," Adam said, though he continued to look at Lauren for a moment longer before shifting his attention to her grandfather. "She's the official welcoming committee around here. I'm just her assistant."

Harper waved her little chubby arm in Adam's direction, as if she remembered him from their one interaction.

"Hey there, gorgeous," he said to Harper as he waved at her.

Lauren forced herself not to react to the sound of those words on Adam's lips, that for a heart-jolting second she'd imagined him saying them to her.

"Come on in," Adam said, motioning them toward the house.

As they moved that way, Lauren let her mom and grandfather go ahead, and Adam fell into step beside her. His proximity did nothing to help the jittery feeling coursing through her, making her wonder if good sense was a thing of the past.

"Mom is so excited to meet you it's been amusing to watch."

Despite her success, it still seemed so odd to Lauren that people viewed her as a celebrity.

"That's sweet, but I'm just an average person who got lucky."

"From what I hear, you're not giving yourself enough credit."

"Oh, I can cook and I work hard, but the same can be said for a lot of other people."

Adam leaned closer to her. "Maybe just let Mom have her 'meeting a celebrity' moment. The closest she's gotten before is my brother-in-law, Jason, who won the national title in steer wrestling."

She wasn't sure why that struck her as funny, but Lauren laughed. The resulting smile on Adam's face threatened to melt her resolve to not think of him in any sort of romantic light.

As they entered the house to find it filled to the gills with people, Lauren didn't know whether to be over-whelmed or thankful she had more of a buffer between her and Adam.

"Hello, hello," a woman who appeared close to her mother's age said as she crossed the room. "I'm so happy you all could make it."

"Lauren, this is my mom, Diane," Adam said, suddenly at Lauren's side again.

Whether it was because of her buzzing awareness of Adam standing near her or the sheer number of people present, she only retained about a third of the names she heard as he introduced her to his siblings, their spouses, and his nieces, nephew and parents.

"I can't get over how adorable these two are," Diane said as she allowed Harper and Bethany to each grab hold of one of her fingers.

"Thank you. I'm pretty partial to them myself."

Adam's sister Sloane wrapped her arm around her mom's shoulders. "Watch her. She hasn't met a kid she didn't try to spoil absolutely rotten."

Lauren smiled and nodded toward her mom. "She'd have some hefty competition."

"They just don't understand that it's the duty of a grandmother to spoil her grandbabies," Lauren's mom said.

"I know, right?" Diane replied.

"Can I hold the babies?" a pretty young girl asked as she looked up at Diane.

"I don't think so, honey. Go wash your hands. We're about to eat."

The girl—Julia, Angel's daughter, if Lauren was remembering correctly—looked disappointed but did as she was told.

"She was the only child around here for several years," Diane said. "Now that she has cousins and another on the way, she's beside herself."

"I think she's going to take after Mom," Sloane said, "and want to keep them all."

If they hadn't been talking about a child, Lauren would have been tempted to take the twins and run. Maybe all mothers were like that, or maybe her fierce protectiveness of them was at least in part due to what she'd gone through, and that she never wanted them to be hurt in any way. Her rational brain knew they couldn't go through their entire lives without suffering somehow, but it didn't erase her need to prevent it whenever she could.

"Well, dinner is ready, so everyone find a seat," Diane said, directing everyone to the dining room.

Lauren stopped short when she entered the room to find two high chairs set up next to the table.

"I still had the chair I used for Julia, and Mandy brought over Cassie's since she's sitting in a booster now," Angel said.

"That's very thoughtful," Lauren said. "Thank you."

The Hartleys had brought in an extra fold-up table and an odd assortment of chairs to seat everyone, but not a single soul seemed to mind. Lauren got the impression this wasn't the first time this arrangement had occurred here.

"I'm not a professional like you," Diane said as she was the last to take her seat, "but I hope you enjoy everything."

Lauren looked along the length of the table at the wide variety and sheer amount of food filling bowls and covering platters.

"It looks and smells delicious." The same could be said for the man sitting across from her, though she wasn't about to reveal that fact to everyone.

Instead, she focused on alternating between filling her plate from the dishes being passed around and opening up jars of baby food.

When she attempted to get Bethany to eat some carrots, a new food for her, Bethany let her displeasure show by spitting the orange mess back out and screwing up her face.

"I don't blame you," Adam's brother Ben said to Bethany. "Carrots are gross."

As the conversation and laughter flowed throughout the meal, Lauren gradually relaxed. Even the twins seemed to be having a good time, but that was likely because they had a seemingly endless supply of people to tell them how cute they were and with whom they could play peekaboo.

"There is no better sound than a baby laughing," Diane said.

"I agree," Lauren said as she cleaned the mushy green beans from Harper's chin.

"So when do you think you'll open the restaurant?" Andrew, Adam's dad, asked.

"Unsure. I'd like to be open as early in the New Year as possible so we can work out any kinks before the spring wildflower season starts bringing in tourists."

Of course, it would help if little roadblocks didn't keep popping up. She'd anticipated certain undertakings when it came to cleaning the place and ensuring it was up to code. With Adam's help, some of those smaller tasks during her first few days in Blue Falls had gone quite smoothly. But there'd been other obstacles she hadn't predicted. Like the softball-sized hole she'd found yesterday in one of the restaurant's windows overlooking the lake. Again, her first thought had been of Phil. It felt like a petty type of action she could imagine him taking. But then she'd heard a couple of other businesses in town had experienced the same problem during the overnight hours.

Andrew nodded. "Sounds like a solid plan. If you need any help, you let one of us know." He gestured toward the assembled Hartley clan with his butter knife.

"Thank you. It's kind of you to offer."

Was this family for real? Were they all this nice and helpful, or was she in the midst of a group effort to ensure she chose Rocking Horse Ranch beef for her restaurant? She really hoped it was the former, because she hated to think this many seemingly nice people could deceive her at once.

She listened as Ben told Papa Ed about his saddle-making business, then as Jason detailed the life he'd led on the rodeo circuit before retiring in favor of marriage, fatherhood and training budding steer wrestlers.

It seemed a large percentage of the Hartleys had other careers besides working on the ranch.

"How did you all get into the branded-beef business?" she asked.

Adam glanced up from his plate. "Seemed like a good fit for a cattle operation."

Angel bumped her brother's shoulder with her own. "He's being too modest. Adam is our big idea guy."

"Angel," Adam said, obviously wanting her to be quiet, which of course caused Lauren's suspicion antennae to vibrate.

"What, I'm not allowed to brag about my big brother?" Angel shifted her attention to Lauren. "He's always thinking twelve steps ahead of everyone around him. Since we all have such disparate talents, he wants to brand not only the beef, but everything all of us do under the Rocking Horse Ranch name."

Lauren had seen that done successfully by another ranch in Texas, so it made sense on a business level.

"We might have eventually set up shop in the building you bought, but you beat us to the punch," Angel said.

Lauren noticed the tense look on Adam's face, as if he wished he could rewind time to stop his sister from revealing that nugget of information. She searched for some ulterior motive for him getting close to her that was somehow tied to the building he wanted, but wouldn't he want to see her fail instead of doing business with her?

When he met her gaze across the table, she saw a man searching for the right thing to say.

"It was just a thought. It wasn't anywhere near becoming reality."

He was clearly uncomfortable with the subject, which caused her mind to spin with possible reasons why. A quick glance at Angel revealed that she'd shifted her attention to her daughter. No one else seemed to be concerned about the turn of the conversation, which made Lauren wonder if she was once again looking for self-serving purpose where there wasn't any.

Some days she felt as if she needed to start seeing a therapist to work through her erosion of trust—of others and of herself. Because even though she was experiencing it and felt there were valid reasons for its existence, she also was aware enough to know it wasn't healthy or productive.

"Well, who's up for cake?" Diane asked.

Like a classroom filled with eager students who'd just been asked if they wanted an ice-cream party, hands shot up all around the table. Lauren laughed in response.

"Either this family really loves dessert or this is one tremendous cake," she said.

"Both," Adam said, appearing to have shrugged off his discomfort with the earlier topic of conversation.

"It's not Brazos Baker-level baking, but I've never had a complaint," Diane said.

The moment Lauren took her first bite of the rich chocolate cake, she realized just how much Diane had undervalued her baking skills.

"This is delicious," Lauren said. "And I promise you I'm not just saying that to be polite."

Diane beamed. "Oh, my, you've made my day."

"Mom, we've told you a million times that your cake is awesome," Sloane said.

"I know, but—"

Lauren held up a hand. "Please, don't think my opinion matters any more than anyone else's. Like I told Adam, I'm just someone who got lucky."

"And worked hard," her mother said.

"Luck is what happens when preparation meets opportunity."

Lauren couldn't believe her ears. She turned her gaze to Adam, who'd voiced the famous words by the Roman philosopher Seneca. Though she'd never once thought him stupid, the combination of Roman philosophy with hot Texas rancher wasn't something she'd ever imagined witnessing.

"That's literally my favorite quote," she said. "I have it hanging in my office at home."

He smiled a little. "Great minds, I guess."

It felt more as if the universe was attempting to tell her something, but she suspected that was just the traitorous part of her brain trying to find any and all reasons to convince her that it was safe to like this man, to trust him. The problem was she didn't trust that part of her brain.

When the meal was over, Diane flatly refused any help clearing the table or loading the dishwasher. Instead, Lauren and her family were ushered along with the rest of the gathering into the living area. There weren't enough seats for everyone, so the kids and several of the adults plopped down on the floor.

This was the perfect moment for Lauren to say they should be leaving. But before she could form the words, Adam stepped up beside her.

"You can't really see the cattle now, but would you like to see a little bit of the ranch?"

"I don't want to take the girls outside. I'm sure it's gotten chillier now that night's fallen."

"Oh, don't worry," her mom said. "Plenty of hands here to take care of them."

Lauren gave her mom a hard look, but it didn't seem to faze her. Instead, she just took Bethany from Lauren's arms. Harper was busy patting Maggie the shepherd on the head while sitting on Papa Ed's knee.

"Looks as if the babies are in good hands," Adam said.

If she protested now, she risked everyone asking why. And if the thoughts she was having about this man wouldn't go away, they at least needed to stay firmly in her own mind. She couldn't have anyone getting ideas she wasn't willing to act on.

"Okay." Not the most enthusiastic or elegant response, but it seemed to be all she could manage.

She sure hoped no one could tell how fast her heart was beating as Adam opened the door for her. She felt as if she must look like one of those old cartoon characters with her heart visibly beating out of her chest.

Thankfully, the temperature outside had dropped to the point where it cooled her warm cheeks.

"So how did work go today?" he asked as they walked toward the barn.

"Fine right up until the exterminator found evidence of termites." Which had just been the icing on the cake after the rock through the window.

"Bad?"

"Thankfully no, but it's one more thing—along with having to redo some of the wiring—that I wasn't expecting."

"Starting a business seems to be like that. Just when you think you're going along fine, some obstacle pops up in your path, one you can't just go around."

What obstacles had he faced? Did he count her not making a commitment to buy beef from his ranch one of them?

When they reached the fence next to the barn, he pointed out across the dark rise and fall of the pasture. "Ranching is full of those kinds of things. Storms, drought, whatever Mother Nature decides to throw at you."

"Have you all had a lot of those kinds of problems?" Her suspicious side wondered if this conversation was aimed at generating sympathy.

He shrugged. "No more than pretty much every other rancher. It's just the nature of the business."

She glanced at his profile in the dim light. Even without full illumination, he was a handsome man.

"Is that why you came up with the branding plan Angel was talking about?"

He leaned his forearms against the top of the fence and stared out into the darkness. "I wish she hadn't mentioned that."

"Why?"

"Because they're just ideas at this point, might be all they ever are."

"Now that doesn't sound like you." How odd that she knew that about him after so brief an acquaintance.

He looked over at her. "What makes you say that?"

"You just seem like you're driven. I mean, you were willing to move furniture just so I'd listen to your sales pitch."

"That's not all it was."

An electric buzzing launched along her nerves. What did he mean by that?

A sudden gust of wind seemed to drop the temperature by several degrees, causing her to shiver.

"Here," Adam said as he pulled off his jacket and wrapped it around her shoulders before she could voice a protest.

The instant warmth that was a product of his body hit her in the same moment as his scent—earthy but clean, as if his shower could never fully wash away the pleasant smell of the outdoors. Without considering how close he still stood, she looked up to thank him. And promptly forgot what she was going to say. Forgot what words even were.

Chapter 7

He couldn't kiss her. No matter how much the need to do exactly that thrummed within him. He knew he should look away, remove his hands from where they held the lapels of the jacket he'd just draped around her shoulders. But he felt frozen in the moment, unwilling to let it thaw quite yet.

"You didn't have to do that," she said, her voice not sounding quite normal.

"I'm fine." When he wondered how she might react if he lowered his lips to hers, it somehow gave him the push he needed to step away. "It'll be warmer inside the barn."

He watched as she glanced toward the house before giving him a quick nod. When he looked away from her toward the barn door, his breath came rushing back into his lungs. It took some effort to remind himself that he shouldn't jeopardize a possible lucrative business relationship by kissing a woman who most likely didn't want to be kissed. If he'd been betrayed like she had been, he doubted he'd want anything to do with a woman for a good long time.

He flicked on the lights as soon as he stepped inside then closed the door behind Lauren to keep out the wind. She started to shrug out of his jacket, so he lightly touched her arm.

"You keep it. I'm really okay."

"I didn't think to bring one. I suppose I should pay more attention to the forecast." No doubt she hadn't had room in her brain for thoughts of the weather because too much had been occupied with nervous anticipation about seeing Adam again.

"Yeah, the weather can be moody this time of year."

Needing some distance between them, she walked over to a dappled gray horse and let him sniff her fingers. She desperately needed something to keep her mind off the words Adam had spoken before he'd wrapped her in his jacket.

That's not all it was.

What had he meant by that? Was she reading too much into a statement that only meant he'd been trying to be nice? Neighborly? She had to find a way to not think everyone had ulterior motives or life was going to be miserable.

Forcing down any hint of the attraction she felt toward him, she turned to face Adam. "So tell me about the plans Angel mentioned."

He leaned against the stall across from her. "Why do you want to know?"

She shrugged. "Curious. You know how they call

people who love politics policy wonks? Well, I'm a bit of a business wonk. I've always been interested in how people find creative ways to make money, especially doing stuff they love. Some kids had lemonade stands. I made little decorated cupcakes when I was a kid and sold them on the playground, on the school bus."

He smiled. "I can just imagine."

"Were you always the same?"

He shook his head and averted his eyes, looking down the length of the barn. "I was a pretty normal kid, both before and after my parents died. But when your livelihood depends on so many factors out of your control, there can be lean years. I saw that not long after Mom and Dad adopted me. One stroke of bad luck you can weather, even if it's hard, but two years in a row brings you to the breaking point. It affected all of us kids, and now we're all determined to make sure we're never that close to losing the ranch again."

His story struck a familiar chord in Lauren's heart, in her memory, and she was thankful he wasn't looking at her or he might see the tears that she quickly blinked away.

"Thing is I don't have a talent like Angel does with photography or Ben does with leather-working. Neil is so much like Dad and following in his footsteps that you'd never know they weren't related by blood. Even Sloane has found a way to increase the ranch's name recognition through philanthropy."

"So the beef operation and the idea for the branded merchandise is your contribution."

He returned his gaze to her. "That's the idea." He pointed toward his temple. "What goes through my head over and over is that it could ensure the ranch not only survives as a family-owned operation, but thrives. There's a new generation now, and I want the ranch to be safe for them as they grow up."

Did he envision that new generation including children of his own? He certainly didn't sound like a guy who would abandon his own children.

But that was totally different to being willing to be a father to children who weren't his. She mentally smacked herself. Could she really imagine him thinking that way when he and his siblings were raised by parents that they'd not been born to?

And why was she even thinking those kinds of thoughts anyway?

"It sounds like a good idea to me," she said.

"Thanks. I just have to be more patient. I get these ideas and wish I could make them a reality overnight."

She laughed a little. "Not how it works." She wandered over to a stack of hay bales and sat down. "People sometimes look at me and think I'm an overnight success, but that couldn't be further from the truth. It's taken years, countless hours of worry and hard work and sleep deprivation to get to this point. And if I'm being honest, I still think I'll make a mistake and lose it all."

Adam crossed to where she was sitting—slowly, as if giving her time to move if she felt crowded—and sat beside her.

"Is that what you're thinking about the restaurant now? If you don't mind me saying, you seem a bit tense and distracted."

Oh, if he only knew what the main reason for that was at this moment.

"Yeah. It's a big investment, and having it so far from

where I live… I guess I'll question the decision until the place is a success."

"It will be."

She glanced over at him, wishing that for a few minutes she was free of any and all concerns about giving in to her attraction. "What makes you so certain?"

"Your determination and the fact you've been a success at every other aspect of your business. That can't just be by chance." He smiled and her heart thumped a bit harder. "I bet even your elementary-school cupcake business was a success."

There was something about Adam that made her want to be open and honest with him, and that scared her. And yet she found herself speaking a truth she didn't share with many people.

"It helped." At his curious expression, she continued. "You said your family went through tough times. Mine did, too, after my dad died. Mom had just been a volunteer aide at my school, but after Dad's accident she went to work full-time at a convenience store. At the same time, she got her teaching degree. My sister and I spent a lot of time at Papa Ed and Nana Gloria's. Nana was the one who taught me how to bake."

"She's gone now?" The tone of Adam's voice was kind, understanding, and she realized there must have been something in the way she said Nana Gloria's name that had revealed the truth.

Lauren nodded. "She passed about a year ago."

"I'm sorry."

"It's honestly why I agreed to visit Blue Falls in the first place. I wanted to do something fun with Papa Ed, and he suggested a trip back to his boyhood home. I had no idea he had something up his sleeve until we were at an empty restaurant building and a real estate agent showed up. I'll admit I was a little worried he was losing it when he suggested I buy the building here."

"But you obviously came around to the idea."

"Nobody was more surprised than I was when I walked inside and it was perfect." She noticed how Adam looked down at the ground between his boots. "I'm sorry it was the place you had your eye on."

"No need to apologize. I mean, it's been sitting there empty for a while."

"Still."

"My mom always says that things turn out how they're supposed to."

"I really like your mom," Lauren said.

"Your family is nice, too. And they obviously think your girls hung the moon."

"You have no idea. If I'm not careful between them and, admittedly, myself, the twins are going to be spoiled rotten to the core." She realized she was probably overcompensating for the fact they were going to grow up without a father in their lives.

"I think it's natural to want to give kids a better life than we had at their age."

She didn't just glance at Adam this time. She openly stared.

"What?" he asked when he noticed.

"You're very perceptive."

"My sisters would disagree with you."

"No, really." She paused, unable to look away from him. It might be dangerous, might be foolish, but she trusted him. "The reason I made those cupcakes and sold them when I was a kid was because I wanted to help my mom pay the bills. I was young but I still saw the worry on her face. I don't want my girls to ever have to experience that. I don't want any of my family to ever have to be concerned about money ever again."

"Sounds as if we're in the same boat."

She had an image of floating along the lake's surface with him in a little boat, much like Rapunzel and Flynn in *Tangled*. She had the same butterfly-wings feeling in her chest now as she'd imagined those two characters felt during that scene.

Logically she knew it was only mere moments, but the time that passed as they stared at each other seemed much longer. When Adam's gaze dropped momentarily to her lips, part of Lauren urged her to lean in and give him permission. But a memory of the last time she'd kissed a man shoved its way to the front of her brain, causing her to look away so quickly it bordered on rude.

"I should be going. Won't be long before I need to get the girls to bed. Hopefully they'll sleep better tonight." She stood and took a few steps away from him.

"If you want a place with more privacy, where you don't have to worry about the girls' crying waking other guests, you should check out the cabins at the Vista Hills Guest Ranch."

"Maybe I will. Thanks."

When he stood, she started to slip out of his jacket again.

"Wait until we get back to the house."

"I won't freeze between here and there."

He smiled. "Neither will I."

As they left the barn, she had to admit she was thankful for the extra layer of protection his jacket provided. The only sounds she heard as they crossed the darker area between the barn and house were the crunch of the gravel under their feet and the call of some night bird she couldn't identify. When they neared the porch, Adam slowed, causing her to do the same, and then she stopped when he did.

He appeared on the verge of asking her something, and her breath caught in her throat—half in anticipation, half in fear. But she saw him change what he'd been about to say as surely as if she'd seen him change hats.

"I hope you all had a nice time tonight."

"Uh, we did. Thank you for inviting us."

"The offer stands to come out and tour the operation when you can actually see something."

She realized it was the first time since her arrival at the ranch that he'd directly addressed their potential working relationship.

"When I get a chance."

He nodded. Again, she thought he had something else to say, but instead he simply escorted her up the front steps.

She was so occupied with wondering what he'd been going to say that she forgot to remove his jacket until she'd already stepped through the front door. Though she was likely imagining things, it felt as if every set of eyes in the room noticed and immediately started assigning deeper meaning to Adam's kind gesture.

Sure, she wasn't entirely sure there wasn't some unspoken meaning, but no one else needed to know that. So she deliberately made eye contact with Adam as she slipped out of the jacket and handed it back to him.

"Thanks." Then before he could respond, she turned toward her mom. "It's gotten quite chilly out there. We need to make sure to wrap up the girls really well."

With so many people present, it was impossible to

make a quick exit. But the flurry of goodbyes did give her time to calm herself a bit before she found herself on the porch with Adam for the final farewell of the night.

"Thanks again for dinner. It was nice to meet everyone and have such a good meal."

"Well, you made my mom's night. Possibly her year."

She imagined him leaning down to kiss her goodnight, found herself wanting that even if it was a peck on the cheek. Which was her cue to leave.

As she drove back toward Blue Falls a few minutes later, she couldn't stop thinking about that moment in the yard when she'd swear he'd been about to say something entirely different to her. She had a feeling that question was much more likely to keep her awake tonight than cranky babies.

Adam was thankful for the late-night storm that had blown through. It gave him an excuse to go ride around the ranch the next day to check on the fencing and the cattle. He needed the time away from his mom's curious gaze. She hadn't questioned him or even made any comments alluding to the time he'd spent outside with Lauren the night before, or the fact Lauren had come back to the house wearing his jacket, but that didn't mean he couldn't see the curiosity, and probably hope, in his mom's eyes.

Despite his determination not to jeopardize the possible contract with her restaurant, he'd almost asked her out. With one question, he could have torpedoed the deal. Maybe even his business if word got out he'd been denied by the famous Brazos Baker in favor of another supplier.

But what if he could land another large account?

Would that give him the freedom to ask her out to dinner?

He shook his head as he rode over a rise in the land that gave one of the prettiest panoramic views on the ranch. He reined his horse to a stop and soaked in the sight before him. This was what he was working to protect, ensuring that it stayed in the Hartley family no matter what Mother Nature or the temperamental economy threw at them.

Adam inhaled deeply of the fresh, rain-scented air, always good for clearing his mind. Though Lauren had shared personal details with him the night before, that didn't mean she was interested in him the way he was in her. He reminded himself she had good reason.

And yet there'd been that moment when she'd looked up at him as he'd wrapped his jacket around her shoulders. Had he read it so wrong? Because he would have sworn he saw interest on her part, as well.

Maybe she'd just been startled by his action. But she'd been willing to sit beside him inside the barn and talk about the tough years they'd both experienced as kids. That, however, was something friends would do, not necessarily more than friends.

He rubbed his hand over his face and rode on. But try as he might to think about other things, his thoughts kept coming back to Lauren. What was it about her that drew him so much? Yes, she was beautiful, but she wasn't the only beautiful woman in the world. Not even the only one in Blue Falls. There was more to it, something that pulled at him on a deeper level, though for the life of him he couldn't identify what.

When he saw her again, he had to remember, however, that it wasn't just the potential business deal that should keep him from voicing his feelings. She'd been through a lot, and maybe memories of the past were what caused the nervousness he sometimes sensed she felt around him. Maybe the best thing now was to keep his distance, only occasionally check in with a professional call.

His phone dinged with a text, pulling him from his mental meandering. He slipped the phone from his jacket pocket and a jolt of excitement went through him at the sight of Lauren's name on the display. So much for shoving her from his mind.

He tapped the screen to read the message.

Got any recommendations for a roofer?

Okay, so that wasn't exactly the kind of message he imagined getting from her, but at least it wasn't radio silence. He hadn't scared her off completely.

He texted back a couple of suggestions, then like some sort of lovesick teenager, he stared at his phone until she texted back a simple Thanks. He blew out a breath and headed on toward the southern property boundary.

It was a good thing mind reading wasn't actually a thing because he still hadn't been able to stop thinking about Lauren when he returned to the house late in the afternoon. His brain refused to stop running possible scenarios in which he could preserve the chance to do business with her while also exploring his attraction.

As he left the barn and headed toward the house, he met Arden, Neil's wife, leaving. He remembered then that she'd had a prenatal checkup that morning.

"Hey, how are things going with the little peanut?"

She smiled and placed her hand against her still-flat stomach. "Good. Though I thought your brother was going to pass out he was so nervous. I can't imagine what he'll be like when I actually go in to have the baby."

Adam laughed. "You are the best sister-in-law ever for telling me that. Just don't tell Mandy I said so."

They started to go their separate ways again.

"Adam?"

He turned back toward Arden. "Yeah?"

"Can I ask you something?"

"Sure."

"Is it my imagination or are you interested in Lauren?"

Ah, hell. "She's nice, and I'm hoping we can land her restaurant as a customer."

Arden crossed her arms and gave him an incredulous look he imagined she'd used to great effect with tough interviewees during her years as an international reporter.

"You know that's not what I mean."

He sighed. There was no use lying to someone who'd literally gone to war-torn areas of the globe and gotten the truth out of people who didn't like telling the truth.

"Yes, but I can't do anything about it."

"Why not?"

He retraced his steps and leaned against the side of Arden's car. "Do you know anything about what she's been through?"

"A bit."

He filled in the gaps, and when he was finished, his brother's wife leaned back against the car beside him.

"So you're afraid that she's gun-shy."

He nodded.

She was quiet for a few seconds before speaking again. "It's kind of you to put her feelings first, but she hasn't actually told you she's not interested, has she?"

"No, but I haven't asked, either."

"Then maybe you should."

"I don't want to jeopardize the potential business deal. We need a big win."

"I understand. But I don't want you to miss something that could be way more important."

"How can I tell if she's interested or if I should keep my distance because of what she's been through?"

"Don't come on too strong. One little step at a time. And honestly, she might not be receptive at first. The hurt might be too fresh in her memory. But take it from me, sometimes people don't know what they need until someone shows them."

He knew she was talking about how Neil had initially offered her friendship after she'd come home from being a captive of human traffickers in Africa, and how that friendship had slowly built into something more that neither of them had expected. And now Adam couldn't imagine two people more in love.

He didn't know if anything even remotely similar was in store for him and Lauren. Him and anyone, for that matter. But Arden was right. He wasn't going to find out if he avoided Lauren, if he let his fear of failure keep him from figuring out if their new friendship might eventually grow into something more.

Chapter 8

A cold wind blew off the lake into downtown Blue Falls, making it feel like the perfect weather to do some Christmas shopping. Add in the fact that the restaurant was unbearably noisy at the moment with the roofers doing the needed repairs, and Lauren decided to use the time wisely. Her mom had returned home and to her classroom, but Papa Ed was still on babysitting duty.

Lauren had been so busy lately that she hadn't given the holiday season much thought. But as she strolled down the sidewalk and saw the storefront windows filled with Christmas displays, and as she hummed along with the familiar carols playing on outdoor speakers the length of the Main Street shopping district, she felt the holiday spirit bubble up within her.

At each shop she entered, she was greeted with warmth and enthusiasm. Inevitably people wanted to know when she'd be opening for business, and she would always say the same thing—that she hoped to be open by spring. She still thought she could make that goal if unexpected repairs didn't keep popping up, along with their accompanying price tags. Despite the setbacks, she wasn't about to skimp on Christmas. After everything her family had been through the past couple of years, they all deserved a big, beautiful, happy holiday season.

By the time she reached A Good Yarn, she was toting several bags filled with gifts. The moment she stepped inside the store, she felt as if her first breath inhaled Christmas itself. The delicious scents of cinnamon, clove and nutmeg with a hint of pine filled the air and "Let it Snow" by Dean Martin reminded her of her family's tradition of spending Christmas Eve watching old black-and-white Christmas movies. Everything from classics like *Miracle on 34th Street* to lesser-known films such as *The Shop Around the Corner*, which many people didn't realize was the inspiration for *You've Got Mail*.

"Can I help you?" a pretty woman with curly waves of red hair asked as she emerged from the center aisle.

"It feels so much like Christmas in here I feel as if it might start snowing."

The woman laughed. "Well, that would certainly get the shop on the front page of the paper."

"Lauren, I thought that sounded like you." Mandy Hartley appeared from the back of the store, causing Lauren to remember one of the family facts she'd learned during her dinner with the Hartley family. Mandy was part owner of this store.

Mandy came forward and pulled Lauren into a hug

as if they'd known each other for ages, then turned toward the other woman.

"This is Lauren Shayne."

"Oh, the baker I've heard so much about. Nice to meet you."

"You, too."

"Sorry," Mandy said. "This is Devon Davis, my best friend and the person who started all this." She gestured toward their surroundings.

"Can I stow your shopping bags for you while you look around?" Devon asked.

"Thanks. That would be great. I may have gone a little overboard."

Devon smiled as she accepted the bags. "Feel free to continue to do so."

Lauren smiled, already able to tell she liked Mandy's business partner.

As Devon walked behind the front counter, Mandy asked, "Is there something I can help you find?"

"Do you have lavender-scented candles? My mom loves them."

"Yes, we do." Mandy motioned for Lauren to follow her.

On a large wooden shelving unit along one wall of the store was a display of seemingly every size and scent of candle anyone could ever want.

"Wow."

Mandy smiled. "Yeah, we feature candles from a few different area artisans. Same with a lot of the other products we have."

"I have the oddest desire to take up knitting while enjoying the scent of vanilla candles."

"Well, we can hook you up."

"Hey, I'm going to run to the bakery," Devon called from the front of the store. "Either of you want anything?"

"A hot chocolate sounds nice." Mandy looked at Lauren. "Want one?"

"I don't want to be any trouble."

Mandy waved off Lauren's concern while making a dismissive sound. "Make that two."

"That's taking customer service to a new level," Lauren said as she picked up a large jar containing a lavender candle.

"Small town. And this time of year puts us in a good mood."

"I've got to admit that Blue Falls feels a bit like one of those quintessential small towns in a holiday movie. Everyone is so friendly."

"It has a few stinkers like anywhere else, but overall it's a great place to live and work."

The front door opened, though it was too soon for Devon to be back.

"Look around and if I can help you with anything else, just let me know." Mandy headed toward the front of the store to greet the new arrivals.

The store was so cozy and appealing that Lauren took her time browsing, partly because she didn't want to miss anything and partly because she had a feeling she'd get some good ideas for creating atmosphere for her own gift shop. By the time she wandered back up to the front of the building, she'd put not only the candles for her mom in a basket, but also two large vanilla ones to burn at the restaurant while she was working, some goat milk soaps that smelled heavenly and two little knitted hats for the twins. She also carried a striking painting of a field of wildflowers that she could already envision gracing the entrance to her restaurant.

Even more customers had entered the store, claiming Mandy's attention. It must be just as busy at the bakery because Devon hadn't yet returned. But for once, Lauren wasn't in a hurry. She didn't often allow herself time to just be alone to do whatever she wanted, but the incessant hammering of roofers gave her the perfect excuse. That and the fact Christmas was likely to sneak up on her front steps and pound on the door, demanding to be let in, before she was ready.

Though she didn't knit, she let her gaze drift across the skeins of brightly colored yarn stacked in wooden cubbies along the wall opposite the wall of candles. The woolen rainbow could be seen from outside, which she was certain was by design, aiming to lure inside anyone who'd ever even had a passing thought about knitting.

She glanced past the lovely Christmas display in the window and spotted Adam across the street. He was talking to a man she didn't recognize. Since he was unaware of her gaze upon him, she didn't immediately look away. Instead, she took her first opportunity to simply look at him. Though he wore a tan cowboy hat, she could see the ends of his dark hair curling at the bottom edges. For that unobserved moment, she imagined what it might be like to run her fingers through it. Was the texture soft or coarse? Would he respond in kind, threading his fingers through the length of her hair, as well?

"Like the view?"

Lauren jumped and let loose a little yelp of surprise. So much for being unobserved.

"Was just watching for the hot-chocolate delivery."

"So this has nothing to do with the fact that my brother-in-law is standing across the street?"

"Who?" Seriously, did she just try to pretend she hadn't seen Adam even though she'd been caught staring straight at him. "Oh, Adam. Who is that he's talking to?"

"Adrian Stone, local attorney."

An attorney? A chill ran down her back. Why would he have reason to talk with an attorney? Did this have something to do with the ranch? His plans to open a mercantile?

Or maybe it's a small town and people just know each other.

When she dared a glance at Mandy, Lauren could tell the other woman had picked up on her interest in Adam. But that didn't mean Lauren was going to verify it in any shape or form. And whether Mandy read something on her face or she knew about what had gone down with Phil and decided not to press the point, Mandy didn't pursue the topic of her brother-in-law any further. Instead, she pointed at the basket Lauren held.

"Looks as if you took Devon's advice and found plenty of things to buy."

"It was amazingly easy."

"That's what we like to hear."

Just then Devon returned with a cup carrier and white bag in tow.

"Wow, the bakery is full today," Devon said as she placed her purchases atop the round table surrounded by comfy chairs in the corner opposite the checkout counter. "Seems word has gotten out that Keri is giving away a free cookie—a new flavor—with every beverage purchase."

"Please tell me that's what is in the bag," Mandy said.

"Of course. Do you think I'd refuse free cookies?" Devon pulled out three cookies in paper sleeves and handed one to Mandy and one to Lauren. "Salted caramel sugar cookies."

Lauren's mouth watered and when she took a bite she shut her eyes as the flavors danced across her tongue. At the sounds of appreciation from the other women, she opened her eyes.

"I think I might have chosen to go into business in the wrong community."

"Nonsense," Mandy said. "We need a good barbecue place. I think it's actually against the law for a town in Texas not to have one."

Lauren waited for Mandy to say something about the Rocking Horse Ranch providing the necessary beef for said barbecue, but she didn't. Maybe she was just too busy enjoying what Lauren had to admit was an excellent cookie.

"Tell you what might be interesting, though," Mandy said. "There's a Christmas carnival coming up soon at the elementary school, and one of the booths is going to be a cakewalk. Keri always donates at least one cake. Maybe you could make one, too? We could bill it as 'Battle of the Bakers' and draw a nice crowd."

"I don't think antagonizing the long-established local baker is a good business move."

Mandy and Devon snickered.

"Are you kidding?" Devon said. "Keri will eat it up with a spoon. The people who donate cakes regularly help run the booth, and there is good-natured heckling of each other."

"Plus the money is a big fund-raiser for the local

schools," Mandy added. "This year the funds are going to buy new science textbooks and drums for the band."

"Well, I can't really say no to that, can I?"

"Awesome." Mandy sure did look as if she was happy about Lauren taking part in the carnival.

Lauren was afraid it had less to do with the good of the school and more to do with Adam. If Blue Falls was like most small towns, activities at the schools drew at least half the population.

As Lauren left with her purchases a few minutes later, she had a hard time not fantasizing about Adam winning her cake in the musical-chairs style game and proclaiming it the best thing he'd ever eaten. Thank goodness he no longer stood across the street or she was certain he'd see the truth written on her face.

Lauren had been right about half the town showing up for the Christmas carnival. The gym was so filled with people browsing the craft booths, waiting in line for hot dogs and giant soft pretzels, and playing a wide array of games for prizes that it was a challenge to weave her way through the crowd without dropping or having someone knock the seven-layer spice cake with cream-cheese icing from her hands. Though if it did topple, maybe she could salvage enough to eat herself. Her mouth had watered when she'd pulled it out of the oven that morning.

Baking back in the familiar warmth of her own kitchen had been wonderful, but she'd also found herself anxious to return to Blue Falls at the same time. She knew that had a good bit to do with the fact that she expected to see Adam tonight. It didn't seem to matter how often she told herself the attraction she felt toward him could go no further than daydreams, she continued to think of him way too often.

Evidently she mentioned him too often as well because her sister had picked up on it and felt it necessary to point it out.

"Is there anyone else who lives in Blue Falls?" Violet had asked as they'd cleaned up after the Thanksgiving meal at their mom's house a few days ago.

"What?"

Violet grinned in that playfully wicked way she had. "I should have started a tally chart to see how many times you mentioned Adam Hartley's name."

"You're exaggerating."

"Am I?"

"He's just helped me out a bit. And he has a vested interest."

"Do you really think he's doing all these things to help just so you'll do business with him?"

Her instinct told her no, but how could she be certain? She also suspected if she said no, Violet was going to read way more into his actions than was there.

"It wouldn't be the first time a man has fooled me, would it?"

Violet's gaze darkened. "I can't tell you how many times I've wanted to go find Phil and slap him right off the continent."

"Line forms behind me." Not surprisingly, Phil's child-support payment was missing in action. Of course, so was he.

Thankfully she was in a position to provide whatever her daughters needed. She felt angry on behalf of all the women who weren't as financially stable as she was and still had to deal with deadbeat dads.

Two little boys, each with a handful of game tickets, barreled past Lauren, bringing her back to the present in time to lift her cake up to a safe height. Behind her, Violet squealed and nearly dropped the raspberry strudel she'd made. Her sister had the ability to bake some tasty treats herself when she put her mind to it.

"I feel as if I'm on one of those obstacle-course shows," Violet said.

"Almost there." Ahead she spied the rather elaborately decorated cakewalk area crowned with, no joke, a curved sign that said Battle of the Bakers over the entrance to the cordoned-off, numbered-spaces area for the walkers. She also spotted Mandy, India Parrish, who owned the Yesterwear Boutique, and Keri Teague chatting next to the table already filling up with cakes.

"Hey!" Mandy said and waved when she spotted Lauren. "Glad you made it. I've had probably three dozen people ask me if your cake was here yet." She glanced at Keri. "Inquiries have been neck and neck for you two."

"I'm sure it has nothing to do with the 'Battle of the Bakers' sign," Lauren said.

Mandy smiled. "Remember, it's a good cause."

"Well, here's my contribution to the cause, then." Lauren extended her cake.

"Great, what kind is it?"

"Seven-layer spice with cream-cheese icing."

"Mmm, sounds delicious. Going to be a hard call between this and Keri's gorgeous red velvet cake." Mandy nodded toward what was, indeed, a cake so pretty you wouldn't want to make the first cut.

"Well, I'm only famous adjacent, but here's a raspberry strudel."

"This is my sister, Violet," Lauren said.

Mandy accepted the strudel and extended her hand. "Very nice to meet you."

Lauren made all the introductions as more cakes arrived and attendees made inquiries about when the cakewalk was going to begin.

"In about five minutes," Mandy said. "We have the cakes divided into different rounds."

When the people inquiring left, Mandy turned back toward Lauren and the rest of their little group. "We decided to put your cakes in the last round to build up the suspense." She smiled. "Feel free to take your time showing the twins around the carnival until then."

"Where are those beautiful babies of yours?" Keri asked.

"Our grandfather has them in the stroller out in the lobby. Hard to make it quickly across a crowd this size when everyone wants to admire not one but two babies."

True to her word, Mandy started the cakewalk five minutes later. Lauren got drawn into talking to fans of her show and signing autographs. Even though her cake wasn't up for a prize in the earlier rounds, she convinced several people to go ahead and take part because there were a lot of yummy-looking cakes available. And it was true. Not one of the cakes spread out along the tables looked unappetizing. Even the two store-bought cakes looked good. Granted, she was hungry, but they did look moist and very, very chocolatey, a good combination in her opinion.

It was a good fifteen to twenty minutes before Papa Ed made it to the cakewalk area. Bethany was batting at a yellow helium balloon while Harper examined her little pink terry-cloth bunny as if she'd never seen it before. Some kids had security blankets. Harper had a security bunny.

"There are my girls," Lauren said as she crouched in front of them and played with their little sock-clad toes.

"They've sure been a hit," Papa Ed said, obviously proud to have been able to show them off.

"So has their mom," Violet said. "We may have a cake riot before the night is out."

"Don't be ridiculous." Lauren shook her head. Sure, the people she'd met seemed enthusiastic and she never minded talking to fans, but there was still a part of her that was uncomfortable with being put on any kind of pedestal, even imaginary. She probably always would be. She had to admit that part of her was jealous of Keri, who enjoyed the accolades for her baking and owned a successful business, but who wasn't so exposed. Her relationships and betrayals weren't played out before the public eye.

Though no one had mentioned anything about Phil tonight, had they? Another point in the favor of the residents of Blue Falls.

The music for the cakewalk ended and Mandy called out the winning number. The woman who'd won went immediately to Violet's strudel, which made Violet smile and do a little dance. Lauren couldn't help but laugh at her sister's antics.

"Watch out, sis," Violet called out. "I'm hot on your heels."

As the evening progressed, Lauren saw several more members of the Hartley family. All except the one she hoped to see. Maybe his absence was a sign from the universe, one she should have the good sense to heed. One she shouldn't need in the first place.

Then why did she feel so disheartened?

It was just the season. Christmas was always a tough time of year when you didn't have, or had lost, a significant other. She'd already been through one such holiday season since her breakup with Phil. How quickly she forgot.

"So I hear this is where the action is."

Lauren's pulse jumped at the sound of Adam's voice. It was thrilling and scary at the same time that she could recognize his voice without seeing him. She'd swear it vibrated something within her that she'd feared had been torched to nonexistence by how Phil had treated her.

"It is indeed," Lauren said as she turned to face him.

Mandy called out that the final grouping of cakes was now up for grabs. Several people who'd been lingering around waiting for this moment surged forward onto the numbered spaces.

"Looks as if I'm just in time," Adam said as he held up one red ticket.

"Yes, Keri's red velvet cake looks delicious."

Adam smiled as he stepped onto the last available space. "It's not her cake I intend to win."

There was something new in Adam's eyes tonight, some mixture of determination and… She didn't dare name what else she thought she might see, afraid if she did she'd want it more than she should.

They broke eye contact when the music started.

"I see now why you talk about him so much," Violet

said as she came to stand next to Lauren and bumped her shoulder with her own. "He's capital *H-O-T*."

Yes, he was. And she was afraid she wanted him to win her cake more than she had wanted anything in a very long time.

Chapter 9

Adam still wasn't sure his decision to make known his interest in Lauren the person, and not just Lauren the business owner, was the right one. He was making a big gamble, in more ways than one. But his conversation with Arden had stuck with him, making him look at the situation from a different angle. He still wasn't going to push Lauren or give her any reason to doubt him, but he couldn't ignore that he thought about her way more than a passing acquaintance would warrant.

And he trusted Arden. She'd been through a type of hell he'd never wish on anyone, and she'd come back to Blue Falls a broken version of herself. But Neil's friendship and support, based partly on his own experience with trauma, had helped her regain her strength—both physically and mentally—and their friendship had grown into love.

He didn't know if that's what lay ahead for him and Lauren, but he wanted to find out. Arden had suggested he go slowly but to be honest at the same time.

And so he was here feeling admittedly a little silly trying to win her cake. He had to land on the winning number because there was no doubt in his mind that whoever did was going to choose the cake by the famous Brazos Baker.

He glanced over to where she stood with another woman, who looked a good deal like her. Must be her sister, Violet.

The music stopped so suddenly that he nearly bumped into the woman in front of him.

"Number eleven is the lucky winner," Mandy called out.

He looked down and saw that he stood on number seven. Damn. Maybe he should have bribed his sister-in-law to allow him to win.

The kid standing on the winning spot hurried to the table and chose a tray of cupcakes decorated with superheroes. Unbelievably Adam had another chance. But his excitement dimmed when none other than Tim Wainwright stepped onto the spot vacated by the winner.

Adam's jaw clenched. Tim couldn't win Lauren's cake. The man already had enough going for him, and the memory of seeing him dancing with Lauren raked across Adam's nerves like coarse sandpaper.

"Good luck, everyone," Mandy called out as she started the music again. She looked at Adam, and he could see in her eyes that she was pulling for him. Especially considering one part of his competition.

He made eye contact with Lauren as he walked the circle. She offered a small smile, and he liked to think that maybe she was rooting for him, as well. Of course, it wouldn't matter if the entire gym full of people were on his side, it would all come down to the luck of the draw.

The music seemed to go on forever. When it finally stopped and Mandy identified five as the winner, Adam pressed his lips together to keep from cursing. Wainwright stood on the winning number. And he went right to Lauren's cake.

Feeling like a fool, Adam started to step out of the circle. But before he could, Violet stepped up next to him.

"Give me one of your tickets," she said.

"What?"

"Hurry, before the music starts again."

He did as requested then watched as Violet strode back to where Tim was talking to Lauren, probably trying to convince her that his winning her cake was some sort of sign she should have dinner with him. Adam damn near growled like a bear about to charge. Violet wrapped her arm around her sister's, said something brief and led Lauren toward the circle. Lauren looked startled by her sister's actions, but the disappointed look on Tim's face made Adam's day.

As soon as Lauren stepped onto her spot, Mandy started the music. This time, the round seemed to go quickly, but then Adam spent the entire time watching Lauren up ahead of him while trying to appear as if he wasn't.

When the music stopped yet again and Mandy announced the winning number, Adam glanced down to find he'd finally landed on the right spot. Maybe this was still salvageable. He crossed to the table and spotted Keri's red velvet cake. Though Lauren might be the more famous baker, Keri's talent was a known quantity. He couldn't go wrong with anything she'd made.

"Excellent choice," Keri said from the opposite side of the table as she extended a plastic knife and two forks.

He hadn't seen anyone else offered utensils.

"Which one did you choose?" Violet asked as she once again ushered her older sister where Violet evidently wanted her to go.

He lifted his prize. "Keri's red velvet."

"It looks delicious," Lauren said and smiled at Keri.

"I'm sure Adam can't eat the entire thing," Keri said. "Why don't you help him out?"

Adam suddenly felt as if he'd been sucked into one of Verona Charles's master matchmaking plans. And for once in his life he didn't mind.

"She's right," he said. "But if I take this home, I'll likely not get more than a single slice."

Lauren looked uncertain. "I need to tend to the girls."

"Two little babies don't need three people to take care of them," Violet said. "Papa Ed and I will be fine. We'll check out what else this lovely carnival has to offer."

Adam didn't miss the "you're going to pay for this later" look that Lauren shot her sister. But when she turned toward him, Lauren offered a smile.

"Looks like I get to enjoy some dessert. Been eyeing that cake all night."

Adam nodded toward the bleachers on the top level of the gym. "We can watch all the action from up there."

"Sounds good."

He led the way up the stairs, all the way to the top, where they could lean against the wall. Once they were seated, he handed her a fork then sliced two generous helpings. The moment Lauren took her first bite she closed her eyes and made an "mmm" of appreciation. Adam had to focus his attention on his own slice to keep from thinking about how that sound affected him.

"It's a good thing I'm opening a barbecue restaurant instead of a bakery here," Lauren said. "The two things I've had that Keri made have been to die for."

"I'm sure your cake was delicious, too." As soon as the words left his mouth, he was fully aware of how annoyed he sounded.

"You don't like Tim, do you?"

He shrugged. "Friendly rivalry is all."

Lauren laughed in that way that said she didn't believe him. "I'm not sure friendly is how I'd describe it."

"Would you believe not openly hostile?"

"Yeah, barely."

"I hope that doesn't make you think worse of me."

"No, I understand. He's a bit full of himself. He tried to convince me that since he'd won dessert, we should go out to dinner first."

"I knew it." Adam shoved another bite of cake in his mouth.

"I wasn't going to go. He's not my type."

He looked over at her and decided not to hold in the question that surged to the front of his mind. "What is your type?"

"Honestly, I'm not sure. I thought I knew once, but that didn't turn out so well."

"Sorry. I didn't mean to bring up bad memories."

"No, it's okay. I can't let what happened rule the rest of my life." As soon as she said the words, she looked surprised. As if she hadn't meant to say them out loud or perhaps that she hadn't had the realization before that moment.

It was the closest thing to an opening as he was likely to get.

"If I was to ask you out, would you think I'm no better than Wainwright?"

"I know you're not the same as him, but I don't know if I'm ready for that."

"No pressure but we seem to get along well, and the truth is I really like you. Would it be easier if we started with a coffee?"

Lauren didn't answer. Instead, she cut off another bite of cake with her fork. As she ate it, she looked out over all the activity down on the gym floor. He followed her gaze and spotted her sister pushing the double stroller toward the ladies room.

"Poop happens," Lauren said.

"What?"

She pointed toward the bathroom. "Chances are either they've both gone doody in their diapers or one has and the other one will about the time Violet starts out of the bathroom."

"Oh. For a minute there I thought you were equating a date with me with poop."

"No, of course not."

He took encouragement from how strong her response was, how she seemed horrified he'd thought such a thing.

"Is that a yes, then?"

He noticed the death grip she had on her fork and wondered if she was imagining it was her ex's throat.

"Coffee and Danish at the bakery?" She sounded hesitant, as if she wasn't sure she was doing the right thing.

342   *Twins for the Rancher*

"Sounds great."

They settled on meeting the next morning before Lauren said she needed to get back to the hotel room and her family.

"I've been up since the crack of dawn, so I'm hitting the wall."

He covered the remainder of the cake and accompanied Lauren back down to the floor.

"Thanks for the cake," she said.

"You're welcome. Still curious what yours tastes like."

"Maybe you'll get the chance to find out sometime." The tentative smile that accompanied her words gave him hope that maybe their coffee date was just the beginning.

Had she just agreed to go on a date with Adam, a man she truly didn't know all that well? By the smile he wore, she'd guess the answer was yes. She knew she should be more concerned, but oddly she wasn't. Like he said, no pressure. Just coffee and a Danish. It wasn't the same level of date seriousness as dinner, and since they were meeting at the bakery she could leave anytime she wanted.

Though would she really want to?

"See you tomorrow morning." Adam looked as if he wanted to hug her goodbye, maybe even plant a kiss on her cheek, but she wasn't ready for that—especially not in the midst of such a large crowd.

A crowd that included her sister, who'd taken one look at Adam and proceeded to push Lauren toward him. It was as if Violet had taken leave of her senses, developed sudden-onset amnesia regarding the past year and a half.

And yet Lauren had enjoyed sharing Adam's cake with him high above the carnival activity.

After Adam disappeared into the crowd that was beginning to thin a little, Lauren couldn't look away like she should have. Adam Hartley looked almost as good walking away as he did facing her.

"See anything interesting?" Violet's voice was full of the kind of teasing that had filled their teenage years.

Instead of answering her sister's question, Lauren turned toward Violet. "What was that?"

"What?" Violet did her best impersonation of innocence.

"You know what. You also know how I feel about getting involved with anyone else."

Then why did you agree to the breakfast date?

"Phil was the king of the asses, but he was only one guy. The best way to stick it to him is to be happy."

"I am happy."

"To a point. But you're young, beautiful and have a lot of love inside you to give."

"I give it every day to my daughters, you, Mom, Papa Ed."

"Not that kind of love. The kind that makes you feel whole and excited to wake up next to someone every morning."

"I had that and look where it got me."

"You didn't really have it, sis, because it didn't go both ways."

"And you think some near stranger with a red velvet cake is the one to change that?"

"Maybe. You two seemed to be having a nice time up there." Violet pointed toward the top level of the bleacher seating.

Lauren was tired of resisting a truth that she would never have expected to blossom at this point in her life—she really liked Adam, and not in a budding-friendship kind of way.

"Fine, you win."

"What did you win?" Papa Ed asked as he walked up with two tired babies in tow. The bright-eyed twins that had gloried in all the attention paid to them earlier now sported droopy eyelids.

Violet smiled, obviously satisfied with herself. "Lauren just admitted she likes Adam."

"He's a nice young man," Papa Ed said.

"Yeah, he is," Lauren said.

"You don't sound thrilled by that fact."

"It just complicates everything."

"Maybe you just think it does," he said. "No denying you were burned, and badly, but it makes my heart happy to think of you finally moving past it enough to even consider seeing someone else."

Lauren sighed. "It really doesn't make sense though. Even if it could be something, I'm not going to be here in Blue Falls forever. And I don't have it in me to do a long-distance relationship."

"Stop thinking about all the obstacles there could be in the future," Violet said. "Just enjoy the moment. Maybe it doesn't have to be anything other than a bit of fun, which you deserve."

Lauren looked down at her daughters. Harper was already asleep, and Bethany wasn't far behind.

"Don't even think about using these babies as an excuse why you can't go out. Plenty of single moms date."

"I'm aware."

"Now, how do you feel about asking him out?"

"No need."

"Lauren—"

"He already asked me to have coffee in the morning."

For a moment, Violet didn't seem to comprehend. But then her face lit up a moment before she squealed in obvious delight. The noise startled Bethany so much her eyes went wide.

"Sorry," Violet said as she soothed Bethany. "Go to sleep, sweetie."

That was all it took for Bethany's eyes to close. "How do you do that?" Lauren asked her baby-whisperer sister.

"They already know that I'm the cool aunt who will let them get away with all manner of mischief when they're older."

"If your sister doesn't disown you first."

"Aren't they just so precious?"

Lauren looked over to see Verona Charles eyeing the twins.

"Thank you. I think so."

Verona touched Lauren's shoulder in a gesture that said, "Of course you do, and rightly so."

"Verona Charles, I'd like you to meet my sister, Violet, and my grandfather—"

"Ed."

The sound of her grandfather's name spoken by Verona in such utter disbelief caused Lauren to look at the older woman. She appeared as if she might faint.

"Verona, are you okay?" Lauren reached toward the other woman in case she was having a stroke or a heart attack.

Instead of answering Lauren's question, Verona continued to stare at Papa Ed. And when Lauren shifted her gaze to her grandfather, he wore such an expression

of sorrow that it was like seeing him the day of Nana
Gloria's funeral all over again.

Before Lauren could ask what was going on, Verona
took a sudden step back.

"Excuse me."

As she hurried away through the crowd, Lauren
shifted her gaze to her grandfather again. "You know
Verona?"

He didn't answer immediately, just continued to
watch Verona until she disappeared out the door into
the gym lobby. "A long time ago."

The look on his face said in no uncertain terms that
there was way more to the story, but Lauren feared
asking for specifics. Not while Papa Ed wore such a
mournful look on his face.

Violet didn't have any such qualms, evidently. "Were
you involved?"

Papa Ed finally pulled his gaze away from the door.
"Not here. Not now."

Lauren realized he meant he didn't want to talk about
it now. She had so many questions, but honestly, she
wasn't sure she wanted to know the answers.

As he started walking toward the exit, Lauren and
Violet stared after him and then at each other.

"I feel as if I just got dropped into another universe,
where Papa Ed has secrets," Violet said.

That summed things up perfectly. Now that she
thought about it, maybe an alternate reality also explained why she'd agreed to a date with Adam when
Phil's betrayal still burned like a scorpion's sting.

Chapter 10

"You looked like you were having fun last night," Angel said to Adam as he walked into the kitchen the next morning.

"I was." No sense in denying it, even though the cautious voice in his head still worried that he was making a mistake that would torpedo his business.

"So, when you going to ask her out?"

"Already did."

The surprise on his sister's face almost made him laugh.

"When? Where are you taking her? I need details."

"Now. The bakery."

Angel just stared at him as if he was lying. "You're taking a famous baker to a bakery for your first date?"

"Taking it slow."

Angel seemed to think about that for a moment. "You

know, I think you're smarter than I give you credit for. Wise move."

"Well, now that I have my little sister's seal of approval…" he said with no small amount of sarcasm before heading toward the door.

As he drove toward town, a sudden wave of nervousness hit him. Normally, he wasn't prone to being nervous, especially not when going on a date. The fact that he was now told him that this—whatever it was with Lauren—was different. How different, he couldn't say.

When he arrived at the bakery, there was a line nearly out the door. He hadn't thought about all the pairs of eyes belonging to people he knew bearing witness to his date. People who would have questions and who would spread the sighting far and wide.

Oh, who was he kidding? The fact they'd sat in the gym away from everyone else while eating cake the night before likely was already setting the local grapevine on fire. It was just a fact of life in a small town.

Though the place was busy, most of the people were ordering to go. After stopping to talk to three different people in line, Adam finally made it to one of the small tables. He glanced at the time on his phone to find it was ten minutes past when he and Lauren were to meet. Had she heard enough local gossip to make her change her mind? She didn't seem like the type of person to stand him up without at least a text message. Just as he had that thought, she stepped through the front door. He considered it a good sign that she smiled as she approached the table, but as she drew closer he noticed how tired she looked. So much so that he was on the verge of asking if she'd had a bad night with the twins before thinking about how pointing out she looked tired probably wasn't the best way to start their date or get her to agree to a second one.

Instead, he stood to greet her. "Good morning."

"Good morning. Sorry I'm late."

Before he could respond, Karen Harrington, the head of the PTA at the school, came up to them.

"I just wanted to thank you for taking part in the cakewalk last night," she said to Lauren. "We made more on that event than in the twenty-year history of the carnival."

"I'm glad to hear it." Lauren was no doubt sincere, but Adam heard the distraction in her voice.

After Karen headed toward the door, Adam asked, "Would you like to postpone this?" Part of him screamed inside his skull, asking him why he was giving her a chance to walk away and never say yes to a date with him again.

"No." Her answer wasn't particularly convincing, and she seemed to realize it. "Sorry. There's just something going on, family stuff."

"You won't hurt my feelings if you want to reschedule."

She shook her head. "No, it's definitely a 'maple-glazed doughnut' kind of morning."

"One maple-glazed doughnut coming right up. Coffee?"

"Yes, black and strong enough to walk by itself."

When Adam approached the front counter, Keri gave him a knowing grin. As he exchanged money for the order, she glanced to where Lauren sat at a small round table against the wall.

"You two are cute together."

He glanced toward his date, hoping Lauren thought so, too.

When he slipped not one but three maple-glazed doughnuts and a large coffee in front of her, Lauren looked up at him with the least amount of distraction in her expression since she'd arrived.

"You might be my new favorite person."

He smiled, liking the sound of that. "The power of sugar."

"Amen."

Adam sat opposite her and took a bite of his cruller. He watched as Lauren indulged in a huge bite of her first doughnut and dove into her coffee as if it was a life-saving device.

"Want to talk about it?" Adam asked.

Lauren looked up from her coffee. "What?"

"Whatever is bothering you."

She placed her coffee cup back on the table slowly. "That obvious, huh?"

He held up his hand with the tips of his thumb and forefinger close to each other. "A little."

"I'm not entirely sure what it is."

He gave her a curious expression, so she leaned her forearms on the table. "What do you know about Verona Charles?"

Judging by the look on his face, her question wasn't even in the ballpark of what he might have expected.

"She's retired from the tourist bureau. Her niece owns the garden center outside town. And she's the self-appointed matchmaker of Blue Falls." All of which he'd told her before.

"Single?"

"Uh, yeah. Don't think she ever married. Honestly, I've never even seen her out with anyone. Why?"

"We ran into her at the carnival right after you left, and it was obvious she and Papa Ed knew each other. They both looked like they'd received a shock from those paddles they use to restart people's hearts."

"Has he ever mentioned her before?"

"No. In fact, he's always said that he's been gone from Blue Falls so long that he doesn't know anyone from here anymore."

"Did you ask him about it?"

"Yes, not that it did us any good. I've never known him to be so silent on a subject."

"And that has you worried."

"Not really." She sounded as if she wasn't sure of her answer. "Maybe some. It's just so atypical I don't know what to think."

"Gossip being what it is, I'm sure someone knows something if you ask around."

"Don't think I haven't thought about it, but I owe it to Papa Ed to wait until he's ready to share." No matter how hard that might prove to be.

She watched as Adam took a drink of his coffee, as he swallowed. Though he wasn't dressed up, there was no mistaking how handsome he was. Or the fact he was perceptive enough to know something was bothering her. Had Phil ever been that attentive to her moods and feelings? Why had she overlooked the fact he most likely hadn't? Love really did make you blind.

And that made love dangerous.

But there was no reason to worry about that in the current situation. Right? She worried when the answer didn't easily present itself.

"I'm sorry to go on about personal stuff," she said.

"I thought that's what dates were for—to share at least some personal details with each other. Granted, I'm a little rusty."

"At what?" Surely he didn't mean dating, but he hadn't mentioned anything else.

"Honestly, it's been a while since I've been out with anyone."

"I find that hard to believe."

"So either you think I'm a liar or so irresistible that I have dates lined up for miles."

Lauren opened her mouth to respond before she realized she didn't know how. After a moment, Adam laughed.

"It's neither," he said.

"So why haven't you been on a date recently?" Better to talk about his reasons than hers.

He shrugged. "Busy, I guess. Ranches don't run themselves, and I've been putting a lot of time into trying to build the branded-beef business."

She parsed his words, trying to determine if he was aiming to get her to commit to working with him. When she didn't find any pressure directed at her, she was thankful. Because if she decided to go out with him again, there would be no business deal between them. Never again was she mixing business with pleasure.

And pleasure was what she was increasingly thinking of when she was around Adam. Even when she wasn't and simply thought about him. She wondered if his interest in her would disappear if she told him the loss of a contract was the price of going out with her.

Lauren yanked back on her thoughts. She was getting ahead of herself. There was no guarantee that they would see each other again after they shared this one breakfast. Did she even want to?

Yes.

The answer came to her with a speed and certainty that scared her. She really liked him, enjoyed spending time with him. She just hoped she wasn't making another mistake. How was she supposed to know for sure?

"I used to think that all work and no play wasn't the way to live one's life, but I'm not sure anymore."

"Because of your ex-fiancé?"

"Yeah. It's hard to trust after someone betrays you."

"True." He sounded as if he was speaking from experience, and the thought that someone had betrayed him as well caused her anger to heat a few degrees.

"Did someone hurt you?"

He shook his head. "No, but I've seen the effect on some of my brothers and sisters."

Her thoughts went immediately to Angel and the fact that Julia's father didn't seem to be in the picture. But even though she felt herself getting gradually closer to Adam, it wasn't close enough to ask about his sister's situation. Angel's story wasn't her brother's to tell.

"You ever think there are way too many crappy people in the world?"

"More times than I can count. And if you don't mind me saying so, your ex is near the top of that list. He's an idiot for hurting you and his daughters."

The sincerity in Adam's words touched her so deeply that tears sprang to her eyes. "Thank you."

Adam reached across the table and took her hand in his. He gave it a reassuring squeeze. Even though it was gentle, she felt a silent offer of his strength if she needed it. When she met his gaze, she saw the same and it caused a warm, tingly feeling to travel across her skin before sinking down deep into her heart.

The fear she had of trusting a man again made a valiant effort to assert itself, but her growing affection for Adam beat it back.

"You don't have to talk about it, but if you ever want to, I'll listen. I don't know if I can offer anything of value in response, but sometimes it just helps to get it out."

"More experience with your brothers and sisters?"

He nodded. "Really, I think it applies to everyone, even someone who hasn't had it as bad as other people."

Was he saying that compared to his siblings, he'd had an easy past? If so, she couldn't imagine what they'd been through because losing one's entire family at a young age wasn't exactly a "rainbows and puppies" type of childhood.

This time she squeezed his hand. "Don't give your own pain less weight just because others might have more or different traumas to deal with."

His eyes reflected surprise, and then they softened in a way that made her want very much to be taken into his arms. When Adam moved his hand so that he laced his fingers with hers, she wondered if he could read her thoughts.

"I know it's probably hard to trust someone after what your ex did to you, but I like you, Lauren. A lot. And I'd like to take you out on a proper date if you'll let me."

Her heart screamed *Yes!* But her mind, which tended to search constantly for threats to her and her family, for flaws in her own judgment, told her to proceed with caution.

"That sounds nice, but I don't know. I already leave the girls with my sister and grandfather too often."

"We can take the twins with us."

She stared at him, suddenly wondering if he had some sort of angle. "You want to take two teething babies on a date with us?"

"Sure, why not?"

"Um, because they're teething babies, and they tend to cry." Which didn't seem like the most romantic image in her mind.

Though his willingness to include Harper and Bethany certainly was.

"We could go to the Christmas parade and then the ice-sculpture exhibit in Austin. Angel took Julia a couple of times and she loved it."

He was actually serious. She searched for any indication his offer was a joke or some plot to gain something for himself, particularly anything that would benefit his bottom line. But either she was still as blind as she'd been with Phil, or it wasn't there. She didn't think she could adequately express how much she hoped it was the latter.

"Okay." She'd go in with her eyes open this time, but there was no denying that she wanted to spend more time with Adam.

The wide smile that spread across his face filled her heart with something it hadn't felt in a while—hope.

Lauren finished bundling Bethany in her little red outfit that sported dancing reindeer across the front and then gave her a gentle tap on the end of her nose, making her daughter laugh. Spurred by her sister's giggles,

Harper—wearing a similar green outfit with dancing candy canes—joined in.

"They sound as if they're ready for a night on the town," Violet said.

"If only their mom could be as carefree." Lauren placed a hand against her unsettled stomach. "Am I making a mistake dating so soon?"

"It's not that soon."

"Still."

"Has Adam said or done anything suspicious? Remotely Phil-like?"

"No."

"Then why would it be a mistake?"

"Lots of reasons, not the least of which is the fact that my plate is already full. Beyond full."

"You, of all people, should know there's always room for dessert."

Lauren's cheeks heated at the thought of tasting Adam like a decadent dessert.

"I'd bet every dime I have in the bank that you're having naughty thoughts right now," Violet said with mischief in her voice.

"Oh, shut up." Lauren looked around the hotel room as if she might miraculously find an ally. Not even Papa Ed was around. The day after the winter carnival and the awkward interaction with Verona, he'd borrowed Violet's car, claiming he had to go home to take care of some things.

Neither she nor Violet had bought the explanation for his hasty departure, but the look on his face had been enough to keep them from probing for a more believable reason.

And even though she'd spotted Verona across the

street when she'd left the Mehlerhaus Bakery with Adam after their breakfast date, the town's self-professed matchmaker had made herself scarce. Lauren might have chalked it up to the other woman being busy, but Adam had said Verona was never too busy to miss an opportunity to push two people toward each other, especially if they were already pointed in the right direction.

"Have you heard from Papa Ed?"

Violet's expression changed to one of concern. "No. But don't think about that now. Tonight you are to have fun with your babies and that sexy rancher."

"And what exactly are you going to do with your evening?"

"My job. And if I happen to need something to drink and that need takes me to the music hall, where I might find a sexy cowboy of my own, well, who am I to argue with Fate?"

Lauren snorted at her sister then remembered what had happened to her when she'd gone to the music hall alone. She still hadn't told anyone about that incident, but she had to break that silence now.

"Be careful if you go out," she said, then told Violet about her run-in with the two drunk men and how Adam had come to her aid.

"I suddenly like Adam a whole lot more," Violet said when Lauren finished telling her about that night.

"Don't tell Mom or Papa Ed about what happened. I don't want them to worry." Or to read too much into her relationship with Adam before she even knew how serious it might become. She still wasn't sure agreeing to go out with him was wise, but she was finding it more and more difficult to deny what she wanted.

Lauren was so lost in her thoughts that she jumped

when someone knocked on the door. Before she could answer it, Violet gripped Lauren's shoulders and all hint of teasing was gone from her expression.

"Try to have a good time. You deserve to be happy, and from what I've seen, spending time with Adam makes you happy."

"I'm just so scared to hope for too much."

"Maybe Adam is your reward for having to go through what you did with Phil."

Lauren liked that idea, and when she opened the door and saw Adam standing there in all his tall, dark-haired, heartwarming-smile glory, she admitted to herself that it would be really easy to fall for him despite how badly she'd been burned before. She hoped with all her heart that Violet was right and Adam Hartley was the universe's way of balancing the scales of Lauren's life, giving her someone who was as good as Phil was bad.

Chapter 11

Adam's heart sped up at the sight of Lauren when she opened the door to her hotel room. It wasn't as if she was dressed appropriately for four-star dining. It had nothing to do with her casual attire, fit for a night out with her babies as companions, but rather there was something new in her eyes. She looked glad to see him instead of afraid he was one step away from betraying her trust. He'd never wanted to prove himself to someone so much in his life, not even his parents when they'd adopted him.

"You look beautiful." He didn't know he'd been about to say those words until they tumbled out of his mouth, but he'd never uttered anything truer.

Lauren's eyes widened a fraction, and she looked flustered by his compliment.

"Uh, thanks." She looked down at the red sweater she

wore as if it had magically transformed into a designer gown, like the kind actresses wore to big award shows.

"You ready to head out?"

She looked up at him and the flustered expression had been replaced by a smile that warmed him all over.

"Your chaperones are ready to blow this joint," Violet said as she rolled the double stroller toward the door. She crouched next to the babies. "I'm trusting you to watch those two and make sure they have tons of fun."

Adam laughed at the sight of Lauren rolling her eyes at her younger sister.

It took a few minutes to get the kids loaded into the car seats they put in the back seat of his mom's SUV. As Lauren secured Bethany, he did the same for Harper and checked to make sure he'd done it right three times. He wasn't going to put Lauren or her twins in any unnecessary danger.

When he and Lauren belted themselves into their seats, Lauren reached across and placed her hand atop his.

"Thank you," she said.

"For what?"

"Taking such care with Harper, for being willing to bring them with us."

"Are you kidding? I get three lovely dates instead of one."

She smiled at that, which caused that warm, tingly feeling all over his body again. The fact he'd never felt anything like it before told him he was falling for her. He didn't know if or how things would work out for them, considering it wasn't a path without obstacles, but he'd take each day and each interaction one at a time in the hope that she would be willing to walk that path with him.

"Plus," he said as he started the engine, "having kids with me gives me a legitimate reason to go down a slide made of ice."

"Oh, well, as long as you don't have an ulterior motive," Lauren said with a laugh.

By the time they reached Austin, the parade route was already filling up with spectators. Adam lucked into a decent parking space and helped Lauren bundle up the girls against the chill.

"It'll probably be easier in this crowd to just carry them," he said as Lauren moved to the back of the SUV to retrieve the stroller.

"They might be small but they get heavy pretty quickly."

"You know what's heavier? Bales of hay." He gave an exaggerated flex of his biceps.

Lauren laughed at his antics. "Remember I warned you."

Making Lauren laugh gave him the best feeling, one he wouldn't mind being a constant companion.

As they searched for a good spot to watch the parade, he carried Harper while Lauren held Bethany. He stepped onto a section of curb vacated by a mom and a wailing youngster who'd obviously gotten in trouble and thus given up his right to watch the parade. Just as Adam ushered Lauren in beside him, a siren announced the beginning of the parade.

"Good timing," Lauren said.

As the siren drew closer, Harper jumped in his arms and let out a cry.

"Now, now," he said as he distracted her by making funny faces.

When Bethany expressed her displeasure at the loud noise, Lauren covered the child's ears.

"Maybe this wasn't such a good idea," Lauren said.

Adam couldn't let her doubts cause her to back out now. Because despite the fact that the noise was indeed bothering the twins, he had no doubt that Lauren's fear of getting involved with someone again was at the root of her sudden hint that they leave. He protected Harper's little ears with his chest and free hand as the police cruiser come closer.

"The siren will be past in a minute." Adam wasn't giving up on this date—or Lauren—that easily. He had the feeling she needed this as much as he wanted it.

Lauren and the girls seemed to relax as the police car gave way to decorated floats, troops of uniformed scouts and bands playing Christmas carols. When he glanced over and saw Lauren smiling as she pointed out to Bethany a person dressed as that snowman from *Frozen*, his heart felt abnormally full. In this moment, he felt as if they were a family and he liked the feeling more than he'd ever expected.

He suspected Lauren's arms were getting tired when she shifted Bethany from one to the other.

"Give her here," he said.

"You already have your arms full."

"This little bit?" He jostled Harper playfully, making her laugh. What was it about baby laughter that made all seem right with the world? He remembered having the same feeling when Julia was a baby, and how his niece's peals of laughter had helped Angel get through those early days of single motherhood with her heart and sanity intact. Did Lauren feel the same?

He scooped Bethany out of Lauren's arms, and the twins seemed to be delighted to be in close proximity again. Lauren stepped closer to him, her arm brushing his, to allow a couple to pass from the street to the sidewalk behind him. When Lauren didn't move away after the man and woman had made their way by, he tried not to grin like the luckiest man in the world. It was early in his and Lauren's relationship, with no guarantee it would progress, but in this moment he felt as if this was one of those big turning points in his life he'd look back on with fondness when he was an old man surrounded by grandchildren. He couldn't help but wonder if Bethany and Harper would be the ones to give him those grandchildren.

With his heart speeding up, he looked over at Lauren and envisioned having even more children with her, of making and growing a family together that would fill in some more empty spaces on the Rocking Horse Ranch.

And in their hearts.

Lauren held on tightly to Bethany as they sped down a slide made of ice descending from an ice castle. Bethany's infectious giggles filled Lauren's heart nearly to bursting. When it came right down to it, the thing she wanted most in the world was to make sure her daughters had a safe and happy childhood. Tonight, Adam was helping her fulfill that wish. Not once had she seen any indication that bringing the twins along on their date annoyed Adam in any way. He really did appear to be having fun with them. When she started to think about how sad it was that their own father wasn't the one giving them these experiences and making them laugh, she forcefully shoved away thoughts of Phil. She didn't want him intruding on this outing.

At the bottom of the slide, she stood and held Bethany close as they watched Adam approach the top of the slide with Harper. The fact she wasn't nervous about Harper's safety told her that Adam had earned her trust—a realization that stunned her.

But it was more than trust she was feeling for Adam, wasn't it?

She doubted all her concerns about trusting too easily had disappeared for good, but tonight they seemed to have at least taken a vacation. And the truth was it felt good to not be so guarded. It felt as if she'd been walking around with all of her muscles tensed, as if prepared for an attack, and now they'd finally relaxed, allowing her to rest and enjoy living in the moment without dwelling on the past or worrying about the future.

"He's really good with your babies."

Lauren looked over to a worker dressed as one of Santa's elves. The woman seemed to have assumed that they were a couple, that Adam was the twins' father.

She found she didn't want to correct the woman's erroneous assumption. For one night she wanted to just pretend she was part of a happy, whole family. And that she was with a man who was honest, kind and loved her daughters—and maybe could love her as well.

Realizing the elf woman was staring at her, Lauren smiled. "Yes, he is," she said, before the other woman smiled and walked away.

With a "whee!" that would be more at home coming from a child, Adam pushed off from the top of the slide with Harper. The wave of laughter coming from

Harper brought tears of happiness to Lauren's eyes. They must have still been there when Adam stood and made eye contact with her.

The joy faded from his face. "Are you okay?"

She nodded.

"But you look like you're about to cry." The concern in his voice just added to the rising well of feeling in her chest.

"Just really happy. Thank you for all this."

Adam took a slow step toward her. Were it not for the fact they each held a baby, she thought he might kiss her. And she might let him.

More than might.

When he lifted his hand to cup her jaw and run a thumb across her cheek that was warm despite their frozen surroundings, she wondered if he was going to kiss her anyway.

"You're welcome." It was a simple response, one she might expect, but the way he was looking at her said so much more.

If she didn't look away, the heat building in her body was going to melt the ice palace and turn this wintry attraction into an indoor whitewater river instead.

After what seemed like hours of staring into Adam's eyes, Lauren became aware that they were standing in the way of other people waiting to descend the slide. Adam's hand dropped away from her face but resettled at the small of her back as they moved on to the next exhibit—a small carousel made of colored ice.

"It's amazing...everything they have in here," Lauren said.

"Yeah, it is."

Something about the tone of Adam's voice drew her

attention back to him. Instead of admiring the crafts-
manship of the ice carvers, he instead was looking at
her as if she was some sort of masterpiece.

Had Phil ever looked at her that way? She knew the
answer before the question fully formed. Looking back
now, she could see how blind she'd been. Granted, Phil
had been good at acting his role as devoted and loving
fiancé, but in the wake of his betrayal it was as if a veil
hiding his true intent had been lifted from her eyes—
one that hid the fact Phil had only cared for himself.

Try as she might, she detected no veil with Adam.
She sent up a silent prayer that she wasn't wrong.

He'd just finished taking some photos of her holding
the girls in a scene of the North Pole made of ice when
another worker dressed as an elf walked up to Adam.

"I can take a picture of all of you together if you'd
like."

When Lauren saw Adam about to decline, she said,
"Thanks. That's nice of you."

Adam's quick look of surprise gave way to a smile
as he handed over her phone and moved to join her and
the girls. He didn't say anything as he took Harper from
her then wrapped his arm around Lauren's shoulders
and pulled her close as if he'd done it a thousand times
before. A lump formed in her throat at the thought that
she wanted this picture-perfect family scene to be real.

"Give me some big smiles," the elf lady said.

Complying wasn't difficult. In fact, Lauren found it
easier to smile in that moment than she had in a long
time.

By the time they left the ice palace and grabbed a
quick dinner at a gourmet burger place, the girls were
tired and getting fussy.

"Sorry," Lauren said as Bethany let out a wail that turned the head of everyone on the sidewalk for a solid block as Lauren and Adam walked back toward his mom's SUV.

"No need to apologize. It's not the first time I've been around a cranky baby. Nothing's going to beat when Julia had colic. I thought her cries might bring down the roof of the house on top of all of us."

Lauren tried to imagine Phil being so understanding and couldn't picture it. Of course, he'd purposely raised doubts about whether the twins were his, even though she'd given him no reason to question her faithfulness.

Neither she nor Adam spoke again until they were on the road heading out the western edge of Austin and the girls had fallen asleep in their car seats. Lauren gazed out her window at the occasional brightly colored Christmas tree in someone's window, or a yard filled with inflatable representations of holiday cheer. She relished the peace and quiet. And thought about how this moment never would have happened with Phil. She couldn't imagine him acting like a child as he headed down a slide made of ice. If she was being honest with herself, she couldn't even picture him holding his daughters. Especially not with undisguised affection the way Adam did.

"You're thinking about him again, aren't you?"

She turned her head to look at Adam. He glanced at her and there was still enough light from their surroundings that she saw the unsure expression on his face. Somehow she knew it wasn't his question he was unsure of, but whether he should have asked it. Oddly, a part of her was glad he had. It showed he paid attention, was concerned about her.

"How could you tell?"

"You get a different look in your eyes—as if your mind has traveled somewhere else—and you go quiet."

"I'm sorry."

Adam took her hand and squeezed. "You keep apologizing for things you don't need to."

"It's just that crying babies and my wandering thoughts probably aren't your idea of a good date."

"Have you heard me complain?"

"Well, no, but—"

"No *buts*. If I minded you bringing the girls, I wouldn't have suggested it. I do, however, wish you could enjoy yourself without thoughts of your ex invading."

"I'm—" She caught herself mid-apology. "It's hard not to see the world through a different lens now."

"I understand."

Maybe he thought he did, but how could he when he didn't know the whole story?

"Did I do something that reminded you of him?"

"No," she said, but then realized that was actually a lie. "I mean, yes, but in a good way."

He glanced at her briefly before returning his attention to the highway. "That's going to require more explanation."

"I was just thinking I couldn't imagine Phil actually having fun at the ice palace."

"Not even for his daughters?"

"Considering he has barely acknowledged their existence and even tried to claim in court they weren't his, no."

"He thought you'd been with someone else?"

The way Adam sounded as he posed the question—as if he couldn't fathom her cheating in a million years—caused a strange fluttering sensation in her chest.

"More like he was looking for any way he could to punish me."

"For what?"

"For ruining his grand plan to use me as his gravy train."

The look of confusion visible even by viewing only Adam's profile told her he hadn't dug too deeply into the details of the trial.

For the first time, she found herself wanting to share what had happened. When she'd had to reveal everything before, it hadn't been of her choosing. She'd been in a courtroom, forced to stick only to facts with little explanation allowed. Even though she'd won the case, thinking about the ordeal still made her feel raw and exposed.

"You don't have to explain," he said.

But there was something about riding along in the dark and not actually facing him that made it easier for the words to start tumbling out.

"Phil and I were together almost two years. I thought I knew him or I would have never agreed to marry him. But it turned out I didn't really know him at all."

When Adam didn't ask any questions, and instead gave her the freedom to reveal as much or little as she wanted, Lauren took a deep breath and dove into the telling of the most exhausting time of her life.

"I've been trying not to feel like a fool ever since I found out Phil wasn't the person I thought. Some days are harder than others." Like when the fear she'd make the same mistake again reared its head. "I found out he was making promises of business deals for my company without my knowledge. He was signing contracts and taking money when he had no legal right to do so. I didn't want to believe it and couldn't bring myself to confront him—at least not until I was certain. Violet convinced me to hire a private investigator. I still get sick at my stomach thinking about it. I was so afraid of what he'd find or if there was no evidence of wrongdoing Phil would feel betrayed and leave."

"But he did find something," Adam said after a few seconds, making her realize she'd lapsed into silence.

"Yeah. The PI posed as someone wanting to do business with Brazos Baker, and Phil went through with signing a fake contract, claiming he spoke for the company. One, he wasn't an employee. And we weren't married, so even that tie wasn't there. He had his own job as a salesman for a company that sells commercial kitchen supplies. That's how we met—at a trade show for chefs."

She'd once thought if she could go back in time, she'd skip that trade show and thus avoid Phil being a part of her life completely. But then she wouldn't have Bethany and Harper, and despite how frazzled and tired she often felt, she couldn't imagine her life without them now.

"I confronted Phil about it and he tried to wave it off as a misunderstanding. That was until I slapped the evidence from the PI down in front of him. Then he got angry, said I was just trying to find an excuse to get out of the marriage and giving him what he was owed. He was talking nonsense and continued to do so with his attorney. I think the guy actually believed Phil's lies."

"Did he claim he acted on your authority?"

"Yes, and when he couldn't provide proof of that, he claimed that I'd promised him half the company as a wedding present. I'd done no such thing, and he actually shot himself in the foot with that claim because an attorney came forward with evidence that Phil had him draw up a prenuptial agreement." Lauren swallowed the bile rising in her throat. "He intended to get me to agree to it and rob me of half of what I'd worked so hard to build."

Adam reached over and took her hand in his. She latched on to his support before getting to the worst part of the story.

"I sense there's more," he said.

"When I found out I was pregnant, I still felt I should tell him he was going to be a father. A part of me thought it would make him back down, that it would change his entire outlook on things. Instead, he had his attorney blindside me in court, claiming the girls weren't his. He knew they were, and a DNA test proved it. He just wanted to embarrass me, make my viewers question the entire wholesome, family-centered tone of my business. If he couldn't have what he wanted, he didn't intend for me to have it, either."

"Please tell me he's rotting in a prison cell for fraud."

How many times had Lauren fantasized about that very thing?

"No."

"I thought he lost the case."

"He did. It was my choice. It took some convincing of the people he'd conned, the judge, even my own attorney, but everyone finally agreed that it was better he remain free so he could make reparations and do a boatload of community service."

"Why did you let him off so easy?"

"Because his going to jail would have just made bigger headlines, and I wanted all the negative attention to go away so I could move on and do damage control." She paused, took a shaky breath. "And because I didn't want the girls to grow up with the stigma of having a father in prison."

Adam was quiet for a long moment, one during which Lauren wondered if he now thought she was the fool she feared.

"You're a good mother. A great one."

"Thank you," she said, her throat full of rising emotion she couldn't name.

Or was too scared to.

Chapter 12

Adam didn't typically have violent tendencies, even less so than his normally pretty chill brothers. But the more Lauren told him about what Phil had done, the more he wanted to punch the guy into another galaxy. The thought of the jerk walking around free—even if he had lost his job and now had to do court-ordered community service, no doubt working as part of a sanitation crew—just didn't seem right. The fact that Lauren had set aside her own hurt, and probably desire for revenge, in order to protect her daughters said a lot about the kind of person she was—the kind he liked more with each passing minute.

When he pulled in to the parking lot of the Wildflower Inn, he wished the drive back had been longer. He didn't want the night to end, but with two babies to get to bed, there was no chance of it extending further than the next few minutes.

He expected Lauren to get out of the SUV as soon as he parked. Instead, she sat staring out the windshield toward the dark surface of Blue Falls Lake.

"Other than family and attorneys, you're the only person I've told any of that," she said.

Though he wished she hadn't been put through such hell, he felt honored she trusted him enough to share the details with him—especially when he knew trust was a huge obstacle for her.

"For what it's worth, you're one of the strongest women I've ever met. Not a lot of people could have gone through what you did without coming out the other side bitter and angry."

"Oh, trust me there's been plenty of that."

"But it doesn't rule you. It's not what people see when they meet you."

She looked at him and he'd swear he'd never seen anyone so beautiful; she didn't even have to be in full light for it to show.

"What do they see?"

He stared at her, wanting to pull her into his arms and kiss her until they both were forced to surface for oxygen.

"*They* or me?"

Lauren didn't respond at first, instead licking her lips. "You."

He cupped her jaw, loving the feel of her soft skin against his rougher palm. "A woman who is strong, caring, hardworking and so beautiful I sometimes forget how to form words."

She placed her palm against the hand he held to her cheek and swallowed visibly. "Thank you. I haven't heard anything like that in a long time—and then only from someone who probably didn't mean it."

"Which in itself is a crime."

Lauren lowered her gaze, appearing as if she had no idea how to respond.

Adam started to lean toward her, but one of the girls made a sound in the back, dispersing any romantic thoughts Lauren might have been entertaining.

"I better get them inside. I don't want them getting too cold."

The interior of the SUV might have been cooling now that the engine and thus the heater weren't running, but Adam hadn't noticed. His blood had heated at Lauren's nearness, at the fact she hadn't pulled away, even more so when he'd thought they might finally share a kiss.

The speed with which she opened her door and slipped out caused him to wonder if it had less to do with getting the babies inside and a lot more with the fact he'd spooked her. What he'd said about her being strong was true, but he had to wonder if Phil's actions had done more damage than Lauren realized.

With a sigh, he got out as well, aiming to retrieve Harper from her seat behind his. When they reached Lauren's room with the babies still half-asleep a few minutes later, he handed Harper off to Violet. He noticed Lauren's sister glancing between them, no doubt curious how the date went. He'd likely encounter similar curiosity when he arrived home. The thought made him halfway want to get a room here at the inn tonight.

Of course, that thought made him think of how he might use that room.

When Lauren turned to say good-night, he wondered

if she could see his thoughts. Especially when he considered she wore a smile that was shyer than he knew her to be.

"Thanks for tonight," she said. "I had a nice time. And though they can't say it yet, the girls did, too."

He nodded. "Me, too." The moment grew awkward. "Well, good night."

"Good night."

During his walk back to the parking lot, an odd emptiness accompanied him. A feeling of being incomplete. He walked a few feet past his mom's SUV to the grassy crest of the hill that led down to the lakeside park. He shivered against a sudden brisk wind off the lake that eliminated what little of his earlier warmth still lingered.

"Adam?"

At first he thought he'd imagined Lauren's voice, but then he heard footsteps behind him. He turned to find her standing a short distance away.

"Is everything okay?" he asked.

She appeared to be about to say something, but in the next moment she erased the few feet between them, placed her hands on his shoulders and lifted onto her toes. As her lips touched his, Adam wrapped his arms around her and pulled her even closer.

And the incomplete feeling went completely away.

Lauren let go of the last bit of resistance holding her back and fell completely into the kiss. When Adam's arms came around her, pulling her closer, she didn't think she'd ever loved the feel of anything more.

Though the air around them was cold enough she'd seen her breath on the walk out here, she was fairly certain flames were licking at her body. Were it not for her sister and daughters inside, she would lead Adam back to the room and see where things went. It'd been so long since she'd been held by a man, since she'd felt any passion.

Truth was she'd never felt a hunger like what was gnawing at her now. She wanted Adam, all of him, more than she could adequately describe. That should scare her, would have only minutes ago, but in this moment it didn't. Because crossing this line had been her move. He'd given her that. And now he was showing her just how much he had been holding back. Because there was no way the hunger she felt from him had just been born when she captured his lips with hers.

She had no idea how much time had elapsed when their lips finally left each other. Were it not for Adam's hands against her back, Lauren would have been pretty certain she would have stumbled and perhaps toppled right over. The feeling in her head was similar to the dizzy feeling she got when on a boat.

"I'm sorry," Adam said, sounding breathless. "Too much?"

Not enough. Not nearly enough.

"Don't apologize. I seem to remember I started that."

A slow, sexy grin transformed Adam from apologist to a man she was having an extraordinarily hard time not shoving into the back seat of his mom's SUV and steaming up the windows so much that someone was bound to call the cops.

That mental image caused her to laugh, which wiped the grin from Adam's face.

"My turn to apologize," she said as she motioned toward her head. "Inappropriate thoughts."

The grin raced back to his mouth. "That right?"

"And no, I'm not sharing them."

Adam tugged her closer, and there was no mistaking just what kind of effect their hot make-out session had on him. Honestly, she was surprised there wasn't visible steam coming off her own body.

Lauren thought about how she'd run out on Violet without an explanation, not that she didn't think her sister had already come up with something juicy. "I should get back inside."

"Can't say I like that idea."

She smiled up at Adam and hoped with all her might that he was the good guy he seemed. "I should be scared out of my mind right now, but I'm not."

Adam ran the tips of his fingers softly along the edge of her face. "Does that mean you'll go out with me again?"

"Yes. And maybe I can arrange a babysitter next time." She hated to keep depending on her family to look after the girls so much, but if she didn't get some alone time with Adam she was afraid she might combust. Maybe she could hire a babysitter and give them all a free night.

"As cute as the girls are, I like the sound of that."

Though she didn't want to, she made herself take a step backward and then another. "I'll let you know, okay?"

Another step and the only part of them that was still touching was their hands, but then Adam pulled her quickly back into his arms and kissed her again—a deep, thorough kiss that left her wondering if she had enough energy left to walk back to the room.

"I better let you go before I act on some of my own

inappropriate thoughts," he said, but then gave her another mind-spinning kiss before breaking all contact and stepping toward the SUV. "I'll wait until you get inside."

Inside the SUV? Yes, please.

But no, he meant the inn. Somehow she remembered how walking worked, so she turned and headed for the light of the lobby. She didn't allow herself to look back at Adam or she might walk right back to him. Possibly run. Her entire body was shaking as she entered the light and warmth of the lobby. A quick glance toward the check-in desk revealed that the young woman there appeared to be hiding a smile. Had she seen Lauren and Adam getting hot and heavy in the parking lot?

Good grief, she had to be careful. Everyone had a cell phone, and the last thing she needed was a video of her and Adam all over each other in a dark parking lot hitting the internet. It would shoot all her work to put the coverage of the trial and questions about her morality firmly behind her and out of the minds of her viewers.

She walked on legs that felt like overcooked noodles down the hallway toward her room. When she reached it, she didn't immediately enter. Instead, she leaned against the wall and tried to get her breathing under control. To slow her heart rate. To formulate some sort of response to the questions she knew waited for her on the other side of the door.

She caught movement out of the corner of her eye, and her heart jumped into her throat. When she turned toward the end of the corridor, she fully expected to see Phil staring at her. She'd swear she saw him. Anger propelled her down the hallway. When she reached him, she was going to fire at him with both barrels with everything she'd imagined saying to him that she hadn't been able to in that courtroom. Punish him for intruding on this moment when she was basking in the glow of having kissed Adam.

But when she reached the end of the hallway and looked in both directions, there was no one in sight. And there was nowhere he could have hidden that quickly. She'd imagined him. Was this the universe's way of warning her she was making a mistake again?

No, Adam was a good guy. He'd proven that over and over, hadn't he?

With a sigh, she turned and walked back to her room. She took a deep breath and pulled the key card out of her pocket. But before she could slip it into the slot, the exit door at the end of the hall opened and she jerked toward the sound. But it still wasn't Phil. Instead, Papa Ed stepped inside. Had he arrived back while she was gone to Austin? If so, why had he just been outside? Surely he hadn't driven back this late.

What worried her more than his driving several hours alone after dark was how he appeared to be carrying a heavy but invisible burden on his shoulders.

"Papa Ed?"

He looked up as he neared her, seeming startled to find her out in the corridor.

"Did you just get back?"

He gave a quick nod, looking as if he wanted nothing more than to slip inside his room and fall asleep. But he halted midway to reaching for his door and turned toward her.

"Is Violet awake?"

"Yeah."

"I'd like to talk to you both."

Something cold and foreboding settled in the pit of her stomach. "Is Mom okay?"

"She's fine, honey. And before you ask, I'm okay, too. I just have something I need to talk to you about."

Despite what he said, it had to be something serious if he wasn't willing to wait until morning. Before she allowed her mind to jump to all kinds of horrible conclusions, she slipped her key in the door and eased inside so as not to wake up the girls.

Violet jumped up from where she sat at the small desk working on the computer with an excited look on her face, all those questions Lauren had imagined shining in her sister's eyes—until she saw Papa Ed behind her.

"What's wrong?"

Lauren gave a little shake of her head as she checked the girls and saw they were fast asleep. She also noticed that Violet had gotten a miniature lighted Christmas tree from somewhere and placed it on top of the small fridge. It'd be enough to make Lauren smile if she wasn't so concerned about Papa Ed. She had the awful feeling that after the most wonderful night she'd had in ages, a bomb was about to be dropped on her life yet again.

Suddenly exhausted, she sank onto the side of her bed. She watched as Papa Ed walked over to where his great-granddaughters were sleeping. He smiled as he looked down at them.

"They really are the most beautiful little girls," he said.

"Papa Ed, tell us what's going on. You're freaking me out," Violet said.

Lauren couldn't have more perfectly voiced her feelings as her grandfather sat on Violet's bed. She noticed him fidgeting with the fabric of his pants, as if nervous. It wasn't a state in which she'd very often seen him. Just as she was about to ask him again what was wrong, he took a deep breath and began to speak.

"I know you have been curious about that incident with Verona Charles at the carnival," he said. "The simple answer is that we used to know each other a long time ago."

"And the 'not simple' answer?" Lauren prompted. "Was she an old girlfriend?" It was hard to imagine him with anyone other than Nana Gloria, but she knew they'd had lives before they'd gotten married.

He nodded. "We were pretty serious." He paused, as if the weight of the past was crushing him. "I loved her."

Lauren glanced at Violet, whose eyes had widened at that revelation, before she returned her attention to Papa Ed. "What happened?"

"I had dated your grandmother before Verona and I got together, and...well, your mother was the result."

It was as if Lauren's brain encountered a thick bank of fog, preventing it from processing her grandfather's meaning. But then Violet gasped, jerking Lauren out of the fog as if she'd been lassoed and yanked out by a speeding horse.

"Explain." It was the only word she could get past her lips, though she was beginning to form a picture in her mind.

"It was a different time then, so I did the right thing and married your grandmother."

"You didn't love Nana?" Violet said, sounding one part sad and one part angry.

"Of course I did," Papa Ed responded with so much

feeling that Lauren believed him. Plus, there was no way he could have feigned the obvious love for Nana Gloria all those years. "I cared for her before, but we had a fight about something stupid and inconsequential, and broke up. I started dating Verona and fell hard for her, but there was no way I was going to leave Gloria to raise our child alone. So we got married and moved away from Blue Falls."

"To get away from Verona?" Lauren asked.

"And to protect Gloria's reputation."

"But you still loved Verona?" Violet asked as she got up to pace the room.

Lauren didn't know how her sister found the energy to stand. She sure didn't have enough herself.

"Yes, but I never talked to her again." He hesitated, looking as if his mind had been transported to another time. "I didn't have the courage to face her, so I just left her a note telling her I had to go." He shook his head. "I handled it so wrong, but I was a scared kid who'd just found out he was going to be a father."

He sighed and shook his head slowly.

"Distance and time changed things," he said. "Gloria and I grew closer, and I would not trade all the years I had with her for anything. I loved her with all my heart." His voice broke on the last word.

Lauren reached over and took his hand in hers. "We know you did. That much was obvious."

"Is Verona the reason you wanted Lauren to come here, to open her restaurant in Blue Falls?" Violet was still pacing, in danger of wearing a visible path in the carpet.

Papa Ed shook his head. "No. I had no idea she was still here, or that she'd even recognize me if we did happen to cross paths. I just… I guess a part of me was homesick for my boyhood home after Gloria passed. I wanted to see it one more time. But when I happened across the empty restaurant for sale, it felt like some sort of sign. I can't really explain other than to say I thought…" He stopped and didn't appear as if he was going to go on.

It hit Lauren what he'd been about to say.

"You felt as if Nana was telling you something."

He nodded. "I know that sounds crazy, that I was just looking for a connection to her that wasn't there."

"I don't think it's crazy," Lauren said.

"You don't?" Violet looked at her sister as if she thought everyone in the room was off their rocker except for her and the sleeping babies.

"I think there are lots of things that none of us will ever fully understand. Whether Nana wanted us to come to Blue Falls, I have no idea. But I think the fact that Papa Ed ran into someone he used to love, someone who never got married, isn't pure coincidence."

"She never got married?" Papa Ed sounded shocked and as if maybe the news had broken his heart all over again.

"That's what I heard." She had to say something to banish the sadness she saw in his eyes. "But from all accounts she had a successful career and is now known far and wide as the town's unofficial matchmaker."

Lauren wondered if Verona spent so much time arranging happily-ever-afters for other people because she'd never gotten her own. The thought was incredibly sad, and there was just too damn much sadness in the world. Especially for good people.

"Maybe Nana wants you to have a second chance."

Papa Ed's forehead crinkled in confusion.

"With Verona," Lauren said to clarify.

He shook his head. "Oh, no, I can't do that to her."

"Who? Nana or Verona?"

"I loved your grandmother."

Lauren squeezed his hand. "We know that. But you don't have to live the rest of your life alone to prove that to anyone, not even yourself."

"You're talking silliness," he said. "Besides, you saw how she reacted when she saw me. I doubt she ever wants to clap eyes on me again."

"You won't know until you ask."

"Lauren—"

It had been a long time since she'd shushed her little sister, but Lauren did it now. Violet looked shocked but thankfully kept quiet.

"I don't know." Papa Ed looked down at where Lauren's hand sat atop his.

"Listen, if nothing else maybe you can reconnect and set things right."

"It seems a little late for that."

"I'm speaking not as your granddaughter now, but as a woman. I saw the look on Verona's face. I don't really know her, but that look told me that she hasn't forgotten." Probably hadn't forgiven. "I think you have to try. If it doesn't work, then at least you tried. If you can be friends, even better. And if you can rekindle a spark, well, I want to see you happy. I've always worried about Mom being alone since Dad died, and I know you've been sad since Nana passed." Not to mention how she'd felt since the truth about Phil had come to light, though it wasn't the same thing. "It feels like time for our family to have something positive happen in the romantic realm, you know?"

"My money's on you," Papa Ed said as he looked up at her.

Lauren glanced at Violet, who shrugged. "I might have mentioned to Mom you were out on a date tonight."

"He seems like a fine young man, and the fact he took the girls with you speaks highly of him."

Papa Ed was likely using the turn in the conversation to avoid talking about Verona anymore, but Lauren had said her piece and any further action was up to him.

Time for her own honesty.

"He is. At least he seems to be."

Papa Ed sandwiched her hand between his. "We can never be one-hundred-percent certain about a person. We just have to go on our best judgment and faith."

"My belief in both of those is pretty shaky right now."

"But not shaky enough to prevent you from going back outside to grab a good-night kiss?" Violet asked, her natural teasing seeming to edge out her upset over Papa Ed's revelation.

"Did you leave the girls alone to spy on me?"

Violet smiled. "No, but you just confirmed my suspicion."

"We're not talking about me."

"Yeah, we are."

Lauren started to object before realizing she was just too tired.

Papa Ed stood. "I'll go and let you all get some rest. I feel as if I could sleep twelve hours myself."

Lauren accompanied him to the door. "Will you at least think about what I said?"

He placed his hand on her shoulder. "If you promise to give that young man a real chance. You deserve to be happy the same as the rest of us."

She nodded because she didn't know how else to respond. And the truth was those minutes in the parking lot had her thinking that she'd allowed herself to feel more for Adam than she'd even realized. If she was alone, she might very well close her eyes, touch her lips and relive every delicious moment of his kisses, the heart-pumping feel of his hands running over her. How much better would it feel if there was nothing between them?

Before her face lit up like a bright red railroad-crossing sign, she opened the door and kissed Papa Ed on the cheek. When she closed the door behind him, she halfway dreaded turning to face her sister. But the rest of her wanted to hop on her bed and tell Violet everything, to squeal like a teenage girl who'd just gone on a date with her dream guy.

Could Adam be that—a dream come true? Because the last man in her life had turned out to be a nightmare.

When she retraced her steps into the room, she found Violet sitting against the headboard of her bed.

"I honestly don't know what to even feel right now," Violet said.

"Papa Ed's not getting any younger. If there's the possibility that he could find love again, wouldn't you want him to?"

Violet shrugged. "I guess. But what if Verona hurts him instead? I don't want to have to go off on an old lady."

"I think Papa Ed can handle things himself." Not that she wouldn't be there for him if he needed it, but something was telling her that everything would be okay with him. Maybe Nana Gloria was speaking to her, too. She smiled at that thought.

"So, that smile have to do with what happened in the parking lot? Speaking of, tell me exactly what did happen in the parking lot."

Lauren sat on the edge of her bed and flopped backward to stare at the ceiling. "Tell me I'm not being a fool."

"Well, I can't do that until you tell me what happened."

"I walked straight up to Adam and kissed him. Really kissed him."

"And did he kiss you back?"

"Yes."

"Peck? Smooch? French? I need details, woman."

Lauren lifted her feet. "Are there still soles on my shoes? Because it felt as if they might have melted off."

Violet squealed, causing one of the twins to make a startled sound in her sleep.

Lauren sat up straight and pointed at her sister. "If you wake them up, I'm going to leave you here with them and go sleep at the restaurant."

An evil grin spread across Violet's face. "Are you sure that's where you'd go? Or maybe you wouldn't be alone there."

Lauren's cheeks heated at the thought, at the way her skin tingled as if she could already feel Adam's hands there.

"My initial question remains."

"Are you a fool?" Violet scooted to the edge of her bed to face Lauren. "No. You'd be a fool if you let what happened with Phil keep you from finding happiness with someone else."

"But there are—"

Violet held up her hand. "I'm going to stop you right there. I understand why you do it—I probably would as well in your situation—but you need to stop overthinking everything. There is no way to know with total certainty that someone will never hurt you."

Lauren let out her breath and dropped her face into her hands for a few seconds before facing her sister again. "I really like him, but I'm scared. And it's not just me I have to consider now."

"The man just took your babies on a date with you."

"True."

"Go slowly if you want to, but just go."

Lauren bit her bottom lip and realized she could still taste Adam there. "Okay."

It took an amazing amount of willpower not to go immediately. Go toward what she hoped was the beginning of something great.

Chapter 13

Adam smiled as he looked at the photo Lauren had just texted him. She was in the midst of cleaning out the flowerbeds around the restaurant building, thus hot, sweaty and dirty, with her hair escaping from the edges of the bandanna on her head.

Sure you still want to go out with this?

He typed a response.

More than ever.

She responded with several laughing emojis, but he was telling the truth. Since the night she'd walked out of the inn to kiss him two weeks before, they'd seen each other every day. And never missed an opportunity to kiss. Just the night before, she and her sister had come out to the ranch for dinner with the twins. He'd stolen Lauren away for a few minutes and taken her to the barn, where they had some time alone. Their kisses had gotten so hot and heavy that he'd had to force himself to step away. He wanted more, but he didn't know if she was ready to make herself that vulnerable, especially when he still saw doubt in her eyes sometimes. He counted himself lucky she'd gone as far as she had considering all he knew about Phil and how wrong he'd treated her. He hoped Phil was gone from her life for good, but he worried. The more he learned about the guy, the more he wondered if he'd really accept his humiliation without some sort of attempt at payback.

Phil had better not do anything that even approached hurting Lauren again. Or the twins. Adam had grown to love those little girls. It was impossible not to. And to say his mom had fallen for them too was the biggest of understatements. He knew without her saying a word that she was already envisioning them being her grandchildren someday.

Of course, that was putting the romantic cart way, way before the horse.

"That has to be the goofiest grin I've ever seen on your face, and that's saying something," Angel said as she plopped down on the opposite side of the dining room table, where he was sitting with his computer and a pile of paperwork he'd been working on before Lauren's text came in.

He placed his phone display down on the table. "Anyone ever tell you that you're a pest?"

"Repeatedly. It's the curse of being the baby of the family."

He scrolled down on his screen, making a notation about a new appointment he'd made a few minutes earlier to meet with a hotel owner in San Antonio. In order to increase the likelihood of making the branded-beef business profitable, he was expanding his area of exploration. He still hoped to be able to be Lauren's supplier, but lately business was the furthest thing from his mind when he was with her.

"So it seems things are going well with Lauren," Angel said.

"So far, so good."

Angel laughed.

He looked up from the computer screen. "What?"

"You've fallen for her."

He didn't deny it. He doubted there was any use.

"Have you told her?"

Adam shook his head. "I don't want to scare her away."

"You don't think she feels the same?"

He sat back in his chair with his hands laced behind his head. "I think she cares, but I could just be a rebound relationship."

He hated the very thought of that being true because he fell for Lauren more each time they were together. Maybe he'd been falling since the first moment he'd met her and feared she'd topple off that rickety ladder.

"Not a chance."

Adam focused on his sister. "What makes you say that?"

"I'm a woman. I can tell when another woman more than just cares for a man. There's a difference between just wanting to get, shall we say, carnal with a guy and loving him."

"Okay, this conversation just got weird." Though the possibility that Lauren might be falling for him, too, sent a thrill through him he'd never experienced before.

Angel smiled. "I'm happy for you."

"Don't jinx it."

The fact that he worried something was going to make Lauren change her mind kept dogging him over the next few days. When he was out meeting with clients, ironing out details with the meat packager, even when he was with Lauren. It didn't matter if they were sharing pizza at Gia's, helping his parents set up their enormous Christmas tree, or enjoying lingering kisses before they went their separate ways for the night, he couldn't shake the feeling that their time together was ticking down.

He told himself he was being paranoid, that he was just thinking that way because he wasn't sure how invested Lauren was in their relationship. Sure, she seemed to enjoy their time together. Really enjoy it when they were in each other's arms. But she hadn't even hinted she wanted more, and he was concerned if he pushed for it he'd lose her altogether. And she'd come to mean too much to him for her to not be in his life anymore.

He was getting ready to meet her for dinner at the Wildflower Inn when she texted that she'd moved to a cabin at the Vista Hills Guest Ranch and to meet her there and they'd figure out what to do for the evening.

She and Violet had talked about making the move as the twins got crankier with their teething, so maybe Lauren had finally decided to exchange the convenience of being in town for the privacy of being in a cabin, where the girls crying in the middle of the night wouldn't bother any other guests.

He waved at Ryan Teague as he passed him on the drive into the Teagues' guest ranch half an hour later. The family had done what he and his siblings hoped to—diversified their ranch's income to ensure its future survival.

When he reached the cabin Lauren had indicated, he noticed that only her car was parked next to it. Violet's and Ed's weren't anywhere in sight. The idea of actually being alone with Lauren sent a rush of heat through him.

As he walked up to the front door, he noticed the miniature Christmas tree that had been in their hotel room now sat on a table in the front window. He supposed he should start thinking about a Christmas present for Lauren. And something for the twins.

He raised his hand to knock on the door, but Lauren opened it before he could. She greeted him with a smile he had the sudden need to see every day for the rest of his life. Best not to say that out loud and risk freaking her out.

"You look beautiful," he said instead as he glanced at the bright blue dress that made her eyes look even bluer.

"Thanks." She ran her hand down the side of the dress, looking as if she was nervous.

That's when he noticed the candles and place settings on the dining table. *Two* place settings. His heart rate sped up. Then the delicious smells coming from the kitchen hit him and his stomach growled in response.

Lauren chuckled. "I hope that means you're hungry."

"You cooked?" Maybe that was why she'd moved to the cabin, so she'd have a kitchen again. Perhaps she had to do some cooking for her magazine pieces, or she was trying out new recipes for the restaurant.

"Yeah, I hope you don't mind that instead of going out."

Or maybe this was exactly what it looked like, a romantic dinner for two.

"Based on the smell, I doubt any place could beat it." Adam stepped inside and shut the door against the December chill. He took Lauren's hand and gently pulled her close. "But I'd be happy eating gas-station food if it was with you."

He lowered his mouth to hers and indulged in a kiss that stoked the flames that had been smoldering within him since that night in the Wildflower Inn parking lot.

A ding from the kitchen caused Lauren to startle, thus ending the kiss.

"Sorry, I have to get that," she said before hurrying off toward the small kitchen area.

He watched as she bent to pull what looked and smelled like barbecued chicken from the oven.

"I know it's not beef, but this is one of my favorite dishes."

"I live on a cattle ranch. I can have beef anytime I want it."

A flash of something that almost looked like a wince crossed her face before she turned back to moving the casserole dish from the oven to the spot reserved for it on the table.

"Everything okay?"

"Yeah, fine."

But as they ate and talked about other things, he could tell something was still weighing on her mind.

"Out with it," he said as he took her hand in his and ran his thumb across her knuckles.

"Nothing, just more annoyances at the restaurant this week. A variety of little things, but combined with the new roof and the unexpected wiring issues, I just sometimes wonder if I bit off more than I can chew."

"Nope. You're going to make this a big success, no doubt about it."

She stared at him as if looking for something more, then glanced down at where their hands were joined. "I need to tell you something."

Her tone concerned him, but the fact she'd made this delicious dinner just for the two of them indicated she wasn't going to toss him out of her life, right?

"Okay."

She looked up and it seemed she had a conflicting mix of determination and sorrow in her expression.

"I know you've been hoping to get a deal with the restaurant for your ranch's beef, but I promised myself that I would never again mix business with personal relationships. The last time I let the two coexist, it nearly destroyed my life."

Maybe he was wrong and she was about to dump him.

"I've loved all this time we've been spending together," she said. "I care about you, a lot, but if we continue to see each other, you have to know that I won't be able to use the Rocking Horse's beef."

He didn't realize until that moment how much he'd grown convinced that the deal was as good as signed, and a shot of anger went through him, as if he'd been strung along. But when he took a breath and considered everything she'd shared with him about what Phil had done, he had to admit he understood where she was coming from. A wave of concern about the viability of the branded-beef operation hit him, but he did his best to hide it. He'd figure out some way to make it profitable. He had to have faith something would present itself. The business had taken hits before and he always found some way to scrape by. But in that moment, the woman sitting across the table meant so much more to him than selling beef. He was pretty damn sure he loved her.

"If you think I'd walk away from you because of losing business, you're wrong." He lifted her hand and planted a soft kiss on her fingers without breaking eye contact.

She blinked eyes that looked brighter on the heels of his words. "How would you feel about skipping dessert?"

It took a moment for it to register what she meant. When it did, his entire body seemed to vibrate in anticipation. Instead of answering, he stood without releasing her hand and urged her to her feet. He pulled her close and caressed her cheek.

"Are you sure?"

"I won't lie and say I'm not nervous, but I've been fantasizing about this for a while."

He grinned. "That right?"

She ran her hand slowly up his chest. "Yes."

He glanced toward the clock on the mantel above the fireplace. "How long do we have?"

"All night."

Those flames within him exploded into a wildfire as he wrapped his arms around Lauren and captured her mouth with his.

* * *

Lauren's nervousness about taking the next, huge step with Adam got shoved way into the background as he kissed her as if he was a hero in some great love story. She'd swear she heard a swell of romantic music wrap around them as she gave in to her desire. She kissed Adam back with the full force of all the feelings she'd been holding back for fear he'd crush her even more than Phil had.

Adam's hands on her bare arms made her want to rid them both of anything standing between more skin-on-skin contact. When had she ever felt so much potent desire? Ever?

She had loved Phil once, but she was certain the very idea of sex with him had never felt like what was consuming her now.

Not willing to wait any longer, she clasped Adam's hand and led him toward the bedroom. Once they were standing next to the bed, she slowly started to unbutton his shirt. He let her. His watching her without saying a word or making a move was the sexiest thing she'd ever experienced.

When she shoved his shirt from his arms and he simply let it drop to the floor, she had difficulty catching her breath. Unable to stop herself, she let her fingertips travel lightly over his exposed chest. His sharp intake of breath sent a thrill of power and excitement through her.

In the next moment he lowered his lips to hers again, and it seemed his hands were everywhere. So many places it was hard to focus. All her senses jumped from the taste of his lips and the feel of his tongue dueling with hers to the length of his body pressed against her to the slide of the zipper along the back of her dress.

Lauren wasn't a novice in the bedroom, but she'd never experienced anything like being undressed by Adam. He took his time even though she suspected there was a part of him that just wanted to rip off every stitch of their clothing and get to business. Or maybe that was just her.

Instead, he paused and ran his fingertips across the swell of her breasts, kissed the curve of her shoulder, let his breath linger next to her ear, making her tingle from her scalp to the tips of her toes.

Needing to feel more of him, she ran her hands up his arms then pressed her lips against his chest. Feeling more daring than she ever had before, she ran her tongue along his warm flesh as her fingers began the work of freeing him from his jeans. The sharp intake of his breath was like a fresh supply of fuel to her desire.

Adam stepped out of his jeans and grabbed her at the back of her thighs, lifting her so that her legs were on either side of his hips as he crossed the rest of the distance to the bed. The strength it took for him to lower her slowly to the bed caused her pulse to accelerate.

"You're so beautiful," he said as he ran his fingertips along the edge of her face. The way he said those simple words made it apparent he believed what he said but that her physical attributes were not the only things that attracted him.

She wanted to tell him how handsome she thought he was, how being near him made her feel more alive than she ever had, but before she could speak he lowered his mouth to hers and she was lost.

What little was left of their clothing was tossed aside, leaving absolutely nothing between them. When Adam took care of the protection without her even having to ask, she fell for him even more. Not that she hated the idea of more children, especially with the right man, but at this stage she had all she could handle without losing her mind.

All of which she could tackle later. Now she wanted to focus on nothing but the man in her arms. And the feeling seemed to be mutual, judging by the way Adam was making every inch of her come alive beneath his touch.

The moment she'd been literally dreaming about arrived and she answered the question in his eyes with a smile. Everything else in her life disappeared as they made love. It wasn't just sex. And he wasn't only making love to her. It was the most beautiful give-and-take, like a ride on the world's most sensual roller coaster. When she felt herself approaching climax, she dug her fingers into Adam's strong shoulders, deriving even more pleasure from the feel of his muscles moving beneath his warm, taut skin.

She closed her eyes and pressed her head back into her pillow as she climaxed, followed in the next breath by Adam.

Her mind was still spinning when Adam curled around her body and pulled a quilt over them.

"Well, I don't need anything else for Christmas," he said.

She playfully swatted against his shoulder, causing him to laugh. Although she could safely echo his words and mean every one. So many things were flying through her mind, but she found herself drifting. Wasn't it the man who usually fell asleep approximately five seconds after finishing? Of course, between the various aspects of work and caring for two teething babies, sleep was a rare commodity. So feeling more relaxed than she had in ages, she snuggled close to Adam's warmth, smiling as he wrapped his wonderful arms around her, and allowed herself to drift toward blissful sleep.

In the days following his night with Lauren, Adam alternated between whistling and grinning like a fool. At least that's how he felt. He'd never had a more wonderful night in his life, and the days since hadn't been half-bad either. He'd helped Lauren at the restaurant, and they were making decent progress despite minor annoyances continuing to crop up or how many times they got distracted by kissing and, well, other things.

Even business for the branded-beef operation was looking up. He'd signed a deal with a small restaurant in Fredericksburg, agreed to provide the steaks for a large society wedding in Austin, and was moments away from inking another contract to provide a variety of beef products for a newer winery bed-and-breakfast about an hour away from Blue Falls.

Jamie Barrett looked up before signing her portion of the agreement. "I know our customers are going to love your products."

"I appreciate your business."

"It's so exciting to think we'll have the same supplier as the Brazos Baker's new restaurant."

What? Where had she heard that?

"Maybe you can convince her to come out and do a demonstration for our guests sometime. And I'd love for her shop to carry some of our wine." The way she said it implied she knew that he and Lauren were dating and that he'd use his influence to give his customers special access.

Before he could correct her assumption, she signed her name on the contract with an excited flourish. Damn it. He'd have to tell Lauren about this and hope she didn't assume he'd used her the same way Phil had.

He could tell Jamie she was mistaken, but would that do more harm than good now? Though he'd not even mentioned Lauren, would Jamie feel misled into a business deal that wouldn't provide all the benefits she'd hoped? What if she decided to sue? Of course, she didn't have a case, but neither had Phil when he'd taken Lauren to court. Lauren had won but her business had taken a hit—the kind of hit his wouldn't survive. He'd just explain the situation to Lauren and ask her how she'd prefer he handle it. Maybe she'd even like the idea of working with the winery, despite how the connection had come about.

When he left a few minutes later, he sat in his truck staring at his phone. He didn't want to have this conversation with Lauren over the phone. He needed her to see his eyes when he told her, hear his voice in person. But that wouldn't be able to happen until later that night at the earliest. He had three more appointments, one of them all the way in Seguin, east of San Antonio. He'd been happy that his widening the area he was canvassing had yielded some results, but now he wondered if somehow word had gotten out that if someone did business with him they'd have an in with the famous Brazos Baker.

A sick pit formed in his stomach, not only at the potential mistake on everyone else's part, but also that his recent successes might have nothing to do with his hard work, or the quality of the Rocking Horse's beef.

Movement outside drew his attention and he looked up from where he'd been staring at his phone. Jamie gave him a big smile and a wave before she got into her car. Realizing he was going to be late to his next appointment if he didn't leave, he started the truck's engine and pulled out onto the road. But the sick, tight ball in his stomach didn't ease, not even when no one mentioned Lauren at his next meeting. Instead, it grew larger, and he remembered the feeling he'd had that something was going to derail his relationship with her.

Telling himself that he was simply blowing a misunderstanding out of proportion and promising himself he'd address it with Lauren as soon as he got back to Blue Falls, he drove toward his last appointment in Seguin even though he wanted nothing more than to race back home to Lauren. But he needed to keep building his business, to succeed on his own so that no one, not even Lauren, could say he'd only succeeded because of his association with her. To prove to her that he didn't need or want part of her company. He only wanted her.

Chapter 14

Lauren paused outside of the Blue Falls Tourist Bureau and Chamber of Commerce's combined office when she got a text. She smiled when she saw it was from Adam. Just the thought of him made her happier than she'd ever been. The time they spent together was the most awesome reward for her allowing herself to believe she might find love again, and with someone who wouldn't betray her.

Can I see you when I get back to town later?

Of course the answer was yes, no matter how tired she was at the end of a long day. She typed her response.

Yes. What time will you be back?

In two or three hours. Last meeting got delayed.

Okay, heading into the business holiday mixer.

Have a good time.

She'd have a better time with him, but she needed to push those sexy thoughts aside so that no one could read them on her face like a headline in two-hundred-point bold type. When she stepped inside, she spotted her sister. Papa Ed was on babysitting duty tonight along with Verona, who had finally warmed up to him after they'd had several long talks about the past and the intervening years over coffee and pastries.

"From the grin on your face, you must have just talked to a certain hunky cowboy," Violet said.

"Possibly."

Lauren glanced around the room filled with people who owned businesses in Blue Falls and the surrounding Hill Country. This was a social event for the holidays, but she was hoping to make more connections now that the time to actually start planning for the restaurant's opening was near. Earlier that day, she'd met with some food vendors, and a couple of days before, she and Adam had driven the arts-and-crafts trail so she could meet local artisans. She came away with plans to carry some of their items in her gift shop.

Though he didn't say anything, she suspected that Adam wished there was a way for them to be together and still have the Rocking Horse's beef served in her restaurant. Honestly, she'd been thinking about caving. After all, Adam was nothing like Phil. And what were the odds that two men in a row would use her success to advance their own? Could she mix business with pleasure again?

She and Violet began to mingle as they snacked on a variety of yummy hors d'oeuvres. It wasn't until Lauren bit into a crab-stuffed mushroom that she realized how hungry she was, that she'd barely eaten all day with how packed her schedule had been. Between meeting with vendors and overseeing the polishing of the floor, not to mention doing some editing on her next cookbook, lunch had come and gone with her only managing to down a leftover mini pork slider from the night before.

A pretty redhead wearing a wide smile approached Lauren just as she swallowed the last bite of mushroom. The other woman extended her hand.

"Lauren Shayne, it's so nice to meet you," she said. "Jamie Barrett. I own a winery and bed-and-breakfast about a half hour on the other side of Poppy."

Lauren shook the other woman's hand. "Nice to meet you, too."

"I'm sure you hear this a lot, but I'm a big fan. I was just telling Adam that this afternoon when we finalized our deal to serve Rocking Horse beef. I figure if it's good enough for the Brazos Baker, it's a 'can't lose' business decision on my part."

The appetizers she'd eaten threatened to come back up. Surely this woman wasn't saying what it sounded like, that Adam was telling potential customers that she'd agreed to serve Rocking Horse Ranch beef in her restaurant. That couldn't be right. He'd chosen her over business. Hadn't he? She had to know the truth, but the moment she opened her mouth to ask for clarification, Violet was suddenly at her elbow.

"I'm sorry to interrupt, but do you mind if I borrow my sister for a minute?" Violet asked Jamie.

"Not at all. The night's young. Maybe we can chat

about your gift shop carrying a selection of our wine later."

Violet made a noncommittal sound and practically dragged Lauren out to the building's lobby.

"I know what you're thinking, and I don't want you to jump to conclusions," Violet said before Lauren could object to her sister's behavior.

"What else could it mean?" Her stomach started to churn. "Oh, my God, I've been a complete fool yet again."

"No, you haven't."

"You don't know that." Lauren pointed toward the gathering in the other part of the building. "Because it sounded a whole lot like Adam told that woman that we would be serving Rocking Horse beef at the restaurant when we're not."

"It could just be a misunderstanding."

"How? How could there be a misunderstanding if the topic doesn't even come up? And if it did, why didn't he correct her?"

"I don't know, but perhaps that's something you should ask him."

Lauren forced herself to take a deep breath, to try not to jump to the most-dreaded conclusion. After all, she'd even given Phil the benefit of the doubt until she'd had irrevocable proof that he'd betrayed her, used her. The mere thought that Adam might have done the same, knowing how much it had hurt her the last time, made her heart ache terribly.

"Adam isn't like Phil," Violet said.

"You don't know that for sure."

"I'd bet every cent I have that I'm right. You're letting your old fears shove aside how great these past weeks have been for you. I haven't seen you this happy in a very long time." Violet made a dismissive motion with her hand. "No, I take that back. I've never seen you this happy. Adam is a good guy, and he's good for you. He deserves a chance to explain, if he's even aware of what's going on."

Lauren wanted to believe her sister, to believe in Adam's faithfulness, but she couldn't silence the doubts barraging her mind. If he had betrayed her, she was done with men. She would follow in her mother's footsteps and raise her daughters alone, live the rest of her life surrounded only by the family she already had and be content with that.

But as she thought about life without Adam in it, tears welled in her eyes.

"Let's go back inside and mingle some more," Violet said. "I was just talking to Ryan Teague and I love the idea of carrying his carved wooden angels in the shop."

Lauren shook her head. "I can't. You go ahead, but I'm going back to the restaurant."

"You've already put in, what, twelve hours today?"

"I aim to talk to Adam about this tonight, and I'd rather do it somewhere other than the cabin." If this ended up being the end of her and Adam, she didn't want to have the rest of her family witness the demise of yet another of her relationships.

Violet grabbed Lauren's hands. "Please just give him a chance to explain, and try to listen without having already judged him guilty."

Lauren nodded. "I will."

Because she would love nothing more than for Jamie Barrett to have made the entire thing up, though that didn't seem likely, either.

"Want me to go with you? I can stay until he gets there."

"No. I'd rather have some time to think and calm down by myself."

"Okay, but I'm only a call or text away. The beauty of small towns—I can be there in a handful of minutes."

Lauren bit her lip as she accepted a hug from Violet before heading out to her car and driving back to the restaurant. Every conversation, every interaction she'd ever had with Adam, replayed in her head. She hoped the fact that she couldn't think of anything that made him look guilty was a good sign, but she remembered she hadn't suspected Phil, either.

Unbidden, reasons why Adam might betray her in the same way bubbled up from the darkest part of her mind. He wanted to increase his own business, which he'd admitted had been hard, by association with someone more successful. He was upset that she had refused to do business with him. Did he think that if it got out that she would be serving Rocking Horse beef, she'd have to reverse her decision? Heck, even the building she'd bought had once been part of his big plan for the Rocking Horse's future.

But he'd told her he understood why she couldn't buy his products and have a romantic relationship with him at the same time. And she'd believed him. Had he done so knowing he could benefit from their relationship in another way?

She pulled into the parking lot outside the restaurant but didn't immediately get out of her car. She felt as if any strength or energy she'd once possessed had been siphoned out of her the moment Jamie Barrett had introduced herself. But sitting here in the dark wasn't going to accomplish anything. If she was going to stay here and wait for Adam's return, she could at least get some more work done. There were dishes to order and menus to plan and a sign to design. Violet had worked on a lot of those things earlier, but it was still Lauren's job to finalize every aspect of her business.

She drew a shaky breath, almost as if her lungs had forgotten how to work in concert, and headed inside. Suddenly, she got the feeling someone was watching her—the same as that night at the inn. A chill ran down her spine as she remembered the two drunk guys outside the music hall. Did they blame her for their arrest? Had they come back and found her even more alone this time? She hurried toward the building since it was closer than her car.

As soon as she stepped through the door and her foot made a splashing sound, the creeped-out feeling gave way to a hard thud of her heart against her chest.

Oh, no. No, no, no!

She flicked on the overhead lights to reveal the awful truth. As far as she could see in each direction, the floor stood under what looked like an indoor lake.

When Adam returned to Blue Falls and texted Lauren, she didn't respond with where he could find her. He noticed several people standing around talking outside the tourist bureau office, so he parked and went in search of her. Maybe she'd gotten to chatting with other business owners and hadn't heard her phone.

"Hey, Adam," Keri Teague said when she spotted him. "You missed the festivities."

"I'm looking for Lauren. She said she was here earlier."

A concerned expression erased Keri's smile. "She left pretty early in the evening. Then Violet left soon thereafter, rather quickly."

There was no way they could have found out about the misunderstanding with Jamie Barrett, was there? Did Lauren just have a sixth sense for betrayal now and had somehow detected it without him saying a word?

A couple of the other people standing outside moved to leave, and what he saw made his heart stop. Jamie Barrett stood talking with India Parrish, owner of Yesterwear Boutique. Without saying goodbye to Keri, he strode straight toward the other woman.

"Excuse me," he said, butting in to the conversation between Jamie and India, then staring straight at Jamie. "Can I speak with you?"

He knew he sounded abrupt, but this was partly— no, there was no *partly* about it. This was *entirely* his fault, but he had to know if what he was assuming was indeed true.

India, likely detecting his mood, moved away after saying it was nice to chat with Jamie.

"Is something wrong?" Jamie looked so genuinely concerned that he did his best to calm down.

"Did you talk to Lauren here tonight?"

Jamie smiled. "Oh, yes. Such a lovely person. I might have gushed a bit about being a fan."

He bit his bottom lip before asking his next question. "Did you mention our business deal?"

Now she appeared confused. "Yes. Why?"

He took a fortifying breath, knowing what he was about to say might lead to the invalidation of his contract with her and quite possibly send a ripple of bad publicity out about Rocking Horse Ranch. Might even sound the death knell for the branded-beef business. He'd deal with that if the time came. Making things right with Lauren was more important.

"I allowed you to believe that Lauren's restaurant would be serving our beef products, but it won't be. We decided to keep our personal and professional relationships separate. I'm sorry about the misunderstanding, and I'll understand if you want to cancel our contract."

"Oh, my God," Jamie said with a gasp. "Please tell me I didn't mess up things between you."

Adam hadn't expected that reaction and it took him a few seconds to form an appropriate reply. "I don't know. I'm sure it'll be okay."

He sure hoped so.

"I'm so sorry."

"It's not your fault. It's mine. If you'll excuse me…"

He had to find Lauren. Before driving all the way out to the Vista Hills Guest Ranch, he headed toward the restaurant. Chances were better than average that she was there, considering how much time she spent working toward her goal of being open before the spring wildflowers started blooming.

When he pulled into the parking lot, he noticed not only Lauren's vehicle, but also Violet's. And the front door was standing wide open. He'd much rather talk to Lauren by herself, but he couldn't put off the conversation even if Violet was within earshot.

He heard the slosh of water as he approached the entrance before it registered why. He stopped at the threshold and just stared at the water covering every inch of the floor. Lauren looked up at him from where she stood in the middle of it with her sister.

"What happened?"

"I need to know you didn't do this," Lauren said, looking as if she were on the verge of breaking down. "And don't lie."

Shocked by the question and the heat of the anger toward him, he just stared at her for a long moment. "Of course not. Why would I do this?"

"Revenge."

A wave of his own anger rose up so fast that it nearly choked Adam. Yes, he'd made a mistake not correcting Jamie's assumption immediately, but how could Lauren think he'd do this kind of damage to her restaurant? It made no sense, and he didn't deserve her anger—at least not for that. Especially when he'd been nothing but supportive despite the fact she refused to do business with his family's ranch.

Before he could vent his anger, Violet stepped forward. "She's upset. Someone came in and deliberately flooded the place by turning on every faucet, the water heater and just about every water valve in the building, not to mention stopping up the sinks and toilets."

"Phil," he growled. Who else would have this much obvious hate for Lauren?

"That's my thought." Violet looked over her shoulder toward Lauren. "But she's upset and doubting—"

"Because of Jamie Barrett."

Violet looked startled for a moment before nodding. "I'll wait outside while you two talk."

Despite how frustrated and mad he was, Adam wanted to hug Violet. She seemed to believe in him despite everything that potentially put him in the same horrible light as Lauren's ex-fiancé. She gave his upper arm a quick squeeze of support before heading outside.

He cringed at the sound his feet made moving

through the water, and he shivered. December was far from the best month for something like this to happen, if there was such a thing. Thank goodness they weren't somewhere like Montana.

"You should get out of the water before you catch a chill." He might be upset by her attack, but he still cared about her.

"I doubt I could get any colder."

He didn't think she was talking entirely about the water and the winter air.

"I stopped by the tourist bureau and I saw Jamie Barrett—"

"Did you use me, Adam?"

"No." The answer came out fast and sharp, with the same kind of edge as her accusatory questions. "I didn't even know she had any idea we knew each other until she mentioned it right as she was signing the contract." He stepped toward her and brought his hands up to touch her, but she moved away as if she never wanted to touch him again. "I swear to you on my life that I would never treat you the way Phil did."

He told her every single detail of the meeting, including how he'd been so surprised by the turn in the conversation that he'd made the mistake of not immediately correcting Jamie's erroneous assumption. She listened but the way she held herself stiff, arms wrapped around herself, made him wonder if his words were getting through.

"It's what I wanted to talk to you about when I texted you earlier, but I wanted to tell you in person."

He couldn't tell if she believed him, and he grudgingly admitted that from her point of view it could be seen as a convenient explanation.

"It doesn't matter now," she said.

"What do you mean?"

She gestured toward the standing water. "It's the final straw, a sign that this wasn't meant to be."

Adam feared she was talking about more than the restaurant.

"You're insured, right?"

"Yes, but I'm just tired." And she sounded it. Below the anger and perceived betrayal, she sounded completely spent. "I put so much into this place even though it was crazy to start a business so far from where I live. There were all the unexpected expenses. I need to just stick to what I know and chalk this up to another of my huge life mistakes."

He got the feeling she was lumping her relationship with him into that mistake. Still, he wanted to pull her close, make her believe that she could get through this and have success on the other side. But instinct told him that she wouldn't be receptive to any of that. And a part of him was ticked off that she was pushing him away, using this setback as an excuse to put her walls back up. But he clamped down on that part that wanted to scream at her to stop feeling sorry for herself and see the truth.

"You need a hot shower and a good night's sleep. Tomorrow is soon enough to deal with this."

"I can't leave yet. I'm waiting for the sheriff."

His heart thumped, but then he realized why Simon Teague would be called. If it was obvious someone had sabotaged the restaurant, this was a crime scene.

The arrival of another vehicle outside, followed by a second, proved to be Simon and one of his deputies, Conner Murphy, who'd just gotten free of another call on the far side of the county. Over the next hour, the two questioned Lauren, Violet and Adam. He'd had to account for his whereabouts from the time Lauren left the restaurant until she'd returned to find the flooding. Even though Adam hadn't had anything to do with the damage, he found himself squirming and forcing himself to keep a lid on his frustration when Lauren wouldn't even look at him.

By the time all statements were taken and what felt like thousands of photos snapped of the damage and the identified sources, it was getting late and Lauren looked as if she might fall over from exhaustion. To be honest, he was beginning to feel the same. He wanted nothing more than for Lauren to realize she'd been wrong to suspect him so he could curl up with her, comfort her and sleep until noon the next day. But the fact that she couldn't meet his eyes told him she wouldn't welcome the company. He just needed to give her time to rest and come to grips with the shock of what had happened. Hopefully, then she'd be able to forgive him for his mistake and believe he'd never deliberately betray her.

As they all walked outside, Lauren paused next to her car as if feeling she needed to say something, but either didn't know what or didn't have the energy.

"You look completely exhausted," he said. "I don't think you should drive right now."

"She won't," Violet said as she approached them.

Violet may very well believe he was innocent in the vandalism, but she was wearing enough protective-sister vibes that he took a step away from Lauren.

"I'll call you tomorrow," he said to Lauren.

After Violet got into the driver's seat and started the car, Lauren turned halfway toward him but still didn't look him in the eye.

"Please don't." She took a shaky breath. "I can't do this."

His heart sank. "Do what?"

"I can't be with someone I can't trust."

"I didn't do this. You know that."

She motioned between the two of them. "This was a mistake."

Damn it, he was getting angry again. "You're using your past as an excuse to run away. That's not fair, to either of us."

"Life's not fair."

Her complete belief in her words, that life had once again put someone in her path who'd betrayed her, hollowed him out as he watched her get into the car and close the door. As he watched the Shayne sisters drive away into the night, the night seemed to cry out that it was for the last time.

Chapter 15

Adam listened to the laughter of his family in the living room as they opened up a round of Christmas gag gifts. He'd somehow made it through the big holiday meal and the opening of his gifts before he vacated the room. There were few times in his life he'd felt less like celebrating.

He sat on the side of his bed turning the small, gift-wrapped box in his hands over and over. He'd looked forward to giving the silver charm bracelet to Lauren, imagined her smiling as she examined the tiny spatula, mixing bowl, whisk and cookbook. He should have returned it for a refund by now because it was obvious they were over. He didn't know it was possible for a person to feel this empty.

She'd been gone for a week without a word. Even his anger couldn't cover up his heartache anymore.

Someone knocked on his bedroom door and he shoved the box into a drawer in his dresser.

"Yeah."

Angel opened the door then came to sit beside him on the bed. "Missing Lauren, huh?"

He nodded. No sense in pretending otherwise.

"Have you talked to her?"

"No." Some of his anger tried to reassert itself when he thought about how his voice mails and texts had been met with telling silence.

"You're not giving up, are you?"

"She doesn't want anything to do with me, and I don't want to be with someone who looks at me and only sees the ways I might betray her."

"Maybe she just needs time to get over the shock of what happened."

He shook his head. "She's not coming back to Blue Falls."

"Then you need to make sure she has a reason to come back."

He sighed. "Such as?"

"Well, you could start by telling her you love her, for one."

He didn't even bother asking Angel how she knew that when he'd just admitted the truth to himself in the days since Lauren had left town.

"Pretty sure she wouldn't believe me." And did he even want to admit the truth to a woman who'd so easily dumped him?

"Won't know until you try. And remember what we told Ben when he was trying to win Mandy—women love big, romantic gestures."

He was lying in bed later that night thinking about

what his sister had said. A big, romantic gesture. Was he willing to try one more time to save what he and Lauren had? Could he think of something that would fit that "big, romantic gesture" description? He fell asleep still turning the idea over and over in his head, but it wasn't until he woke up the next morning that the perfect plan came to him. At least he hoped it was perfect. But he couldn't do it alone.

"Where are you headed?" Angel asked when he was walking out the front door with his truck keys a while later.

"Operation Big, Romantic Gesture."

Angel pumped her fist. "Yes!"

Adam laughed for the first time in more than a week.

Lauren tested the lemon cake she'd just baked and found it lacking. She shoved it across the counter in frustration.

"What's wrong?" Violet asked as she entered their kitchen.

"I've lost my ability to bake anything remotely edible."

Violet came over and took a bite. "Are you kidding? This is delicious."

"You're just saying that." Her entire family had been noticeably careful around her since their return home.

"When have I ever given you false praise?"

Admittedly that wasn't her sister's style.

"Okay, enough," Violet said. "You're finding fault with your baking because you're not willing to admit you screwed up with Adam."

Lauren wanted to defend herself but it was difficult to find the words. Maybe because she knew Violet was right. Even before she'd found out that Phil was behind the flooding, the rock through the window and even the creepy feelings of being watched, she'd realized she'd been wrong to doubt Adam.

Lauren stared out the window at the Brazos River. "I've let too much time pass. He'll never be able to forgive me."

"Think maybe you're underestimating him again?"

Was she? "How do I fix this?"

"I suggest groveling. And, oh, I don't know, telling him the truth."

Violet's suggestions were a good start, but she needed something more, something bigger.

It wasn't until she was walking beside the river later and spotted her neighbor's cattle that the answer came to her. She smiled then hurried back to the house.

Violet and the twins startled when Lauren came rushing back in.

"What in the world is chasing you?"

"A plan to win back Adam."

"Which is?"

"Cows."

Violet looked at the girls. "Your mom has gone crazy."

Yeah, crazy in love.

Lauren watched the world flash by outside the passenger-side window of Violet's car. It'd been almost three weeks since she'd been in Blue Falls, and her stomach was in knots as they got closer. What if she'd totally ruined her chances with Adam? What if the fact she was asking for his forgiveness only after the investigation cleared him made him believe she'd never trust him? She'd been missing Adam terribly. But after she'd run away from him after basically accusing him of being just like Phil and then not communicating with him, she couldn't imagine that he'd welcome the sight of her. She had to change his mind.

At least Papa Ed's romantic prospects were looking up. He and Verona were taking it slowly, but they talked every day and had discovered the spark that had once burned between them was still there. Older, wiser, but still there.

Violet pulled over at a gas station at the edge of Blue Falls. "Gotta pee."

"We're literally a mile from the restaurant." Where her grand plan had to be put into motion.

"When you've got to go, you've got to go."

Violet thankfully didn't take long. When they reached the restaurant, Lauren felt a wave of exhaustion similar to the night she'd left here. The thought of all the work she faced could overwhelm her if she let it. But right now that took a back seat to winning back the man she loved.

"Ready to go in?" Violet asked.

She nodded.

"We should probably see how things look before we take that in." Violet pointed over her shoulder toward Lauren's gift to Adam.

"Agreed." She didn't want to lug it inside only to find the water removal and mold remediation hadn't worked.

Violet walked in ahead of Lauren then quickly stepped to the side.

"Surprise!"

Lauren jumped at the sound of so many voices calling out at once. At first her mind couldn't comprehend what she was seeing, but then she started to recognize individual faces. Her mother and Papa Ed holding the twins. Verona smiling as she gripped Papa Ed's arm. Several of the town's other business owners. Even Jamie Barrett. And the entirety of the Hartley family stood smiling at Lauren.

Her heart leaped when she spotted Adam standing right in the middle.

They all stood on a brand-new floor. The tables and chairs she'd ordered were set up, ready for diners. Art hung on the walls. The corner devoted to the gift shop was prepped to receive merchandise.

"I don't understand," she said, her words having to push their way past the lump in her throat.

"Adam organized the community to fix what Phil tried to destroy," Violet said.

Lauren couldn't hold back the tears anymore. "I can't believe what you all did here."

"We weren't going to let your dream die," Papa Ed said. "Adam is one determined young man."

"Thank you." The words felt so weak, so unable to convey the depth of her gratitude. Nowhere near powerful enough to let this man know how much he meant to her. She hoped the work he'd put into resurrecting her restaurant meant he could forgive her, that this wasn't just a grand apology for the misunderstanding with Jamie Barrett.

The crowd moved then, some coming forward to greet her and say how excited they were about the restaurant's future opening and others moving toward a wide assortment of food. She eventually made her way through all the well-wishers to Adam. She faced him with her heart threatening to beat so fast she couldn't distinguish between one beat and the next.

"I can't believe you did this," she said.

"I had a lot of help."

"It looks beautiful. I don't know how I'll ever be able to thank you."

"If you'll give us another chance, that's enough."

She bit her lip to keep it from trembling before responding. "I was thinking on the way here how you'd never be able to forgive me. I'm sorry for how I doubted you, how I ran away and broke off all contact."

Adam stepped forward and placed his palms gently against her shoulders. "Part of me understood."

"But part didn't."

"It hurt that you could believe I'd do anything to harm you, but I've let that go."

"Why?" He had every right to be upset.

"Because I'm hopelessly in love with you."

Her lip trembled. "I love you, too."

Adam's eyes widened as if he hadn't expected his feelings to be reciprocated. "Can I kiss you?"

"I wish you would."

His lips had barely touched hers when she heard applause. Adam's mouth curved into a smile for just a moment before he pulled her close and sealed his declaration with a kiss that erased any last vestiges of doubt that might have been hanging around in her mind, waiting to pounce.

Over the next hour or so, she enjoyed spending time with the people that she now knew were the very best kind of friends. When everyone finally left, leaving her and Adam alone, he escorted her out to the stone patio that would be used for outdoor dining come spring.

"I have something I want to give you," he said as he produced a small box wrapped in red foil.

"You've already given me the best gift possible." And she didn't just mean the repairs to the restaurant.

"This was your Christmas present I wasn't able to give you."

She accepted the box and opened it. When she saw the silver charm bracelet, she ran her fingertip over the adorable charms. "It's perfect."

"I'm glad you like it."

"I have a present for you, too."

"Another kiss, I hope."

She didn't argue with that assumption and kissed him, trying to make up for the time they'd been apart.

"While very enjoyable," she said when they finally parted, "that wasn't what I was going to say. You weren't the only one who had plans of trying to get back together today."

"Well, now I'm really curious."

She nodded toward the gift she'd had Violet and her mom hide out here.

"What is it?"

"Uncover it and find out."

He lifted the blanket to reveal a sign she'd had made—Brazos Baker Gift Shop, Featuring the Rocking Horse Ranch Collection.

"And when Brazos Baker Barbecue opens in the spring, we're going to be serving Rocking Horse Ranch beef."

He stared down at her as if he didn't trust what he'd seen or heard. "What happened to not mixing business with personal relationships?"

"I thought I needed that policy in place to protect me

from making another stupid mistake." She lifted her hand to his face and smiled. "I don't need it anymore because letting myself love you was the best decision I've ever made."

"You're not scared?"

"Not one bit." She waited for the inner fear she'd carried around for so long to make a liar of her, but it didn't appear. She was pretty sure it no longer existed.

"Does this mean you might move to Blue Falls?"

She let her hands slide down the front of his shirt. "You might be able to convince me."

Adam pulled her close to his delicious, strong warmth and set about convincing. She'd already made her decision that Blue Falls would be her new home, but maybe she'd let him think she needed convincing for a little bit longer.

"You've already decided, haven't you?" he asked.

"Yes. But that doesn't mean we have to stop this."

He grinned. "You're right, it doesn't."

And his lips returned to hers.

* * * * *